A
Treasu

the Sword of Light

CAROLINE LOGAN

gob stopper

First published in 2021 by Gob Stopper

Gob Stopper is an imprint of Cranachan Publishing Limited

ISBN: 978-1-911279-87-7

eISBN: 978-1-911279-88-4

Unicorn Illustration © Shutterstock.com / Elle Arden Images

Foliage & Frame © Maria Letta

Map Illustration © Caroline Logan

www.cranachanpublishing.co.uk

@cranachanbooks

cranachan

To Vince

"If the stars burn
out and no longer
shine, I'll still search
for heaven right in
your eyes."

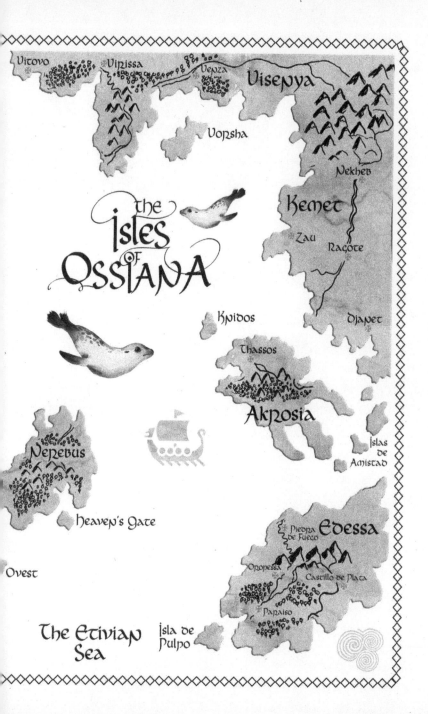

Chapter 1

Ailsa MacAra, princess of nowhere and heir to nothing, stood on the roof of the castle and held lightning in her veins.

You're becoming addicted, whispered a voice in her mind.

"Yes," Ailsa said, out loud. "But this is what you wanted."

What I wanted was for you to smite any who stand in your way.

Ailsa huffed a laugh. "When there is someone in my way, I'll decide whether to smite them or not. For now, I want a distraction."

Oh, don't worry, said the voice. *I won't try to dissuade you. The more you get used to using your power, the easier you'll find it when you need to use it.*

Ailsa rolled her eyes. "Can you go somewhere else for a bit? I've got enough to worry about without a murderous spirit guide muttering in my ear."

Is that because of the selkie? Ishbel asked slyly.

"Leave me alone," Ailsa growled, as thunder cracked overhead.

There was no answer from the voice.

Ailsa wiped her hand over her face and looked down to the courtyard below. When she had first climbed up on the roof, it had been a flurry of activity as servants scurried around in their preparations. Now, most had run inside, away from the impending storm. But behind closed doors, she could still hear them getting ready for the king of Eilanmòr's ceilidh. His last for a while.

The foreign dignitaries that had come from afar for King Duncan's coronation had overstayed their welcome. It had been more than a month and they were still roaming the halls of Dunrigh Castle and eating their food. So Duncan had proclaimed there would be a farewell ceilidh, in honour of his guests. His brother, Angus, had called it the 'piss-off-ceilidh'.

"When I saw it was raining, I knew you'd be up here," came the voice of the prince in question. Angus sank onto the roof tiles beside her.

"Not every storm is one of mine," Ailsa told him, keeping her eyes on the stones below. "It happens to rain quite a lot in Eilanmòr, even without me."

"So you're not in a foul mood?"

Ailsa scowled. "That's beside the point."

"Do you want to talk about it? Or can I guess? Does it have anything to do with a selkie who you're avoiding? Or someone else?"

"Right now, it's because a certain prince is poking his nose in my business."

"It's my business, too, when my two best friends can't even be in the same room together," Angus grumbled. "You're going to have to talk to him, eventually."

Ailsa hung her head. *I know.* "I don't know how."

"How about," Angus cleared his throat, his voice rising several octaves, "*Hello Harris, if it's all the same to you, I don't really fancy kissing you anymore.*"

"I don't sound like that," Ailsa said, gritting her teeth.

Angus grinned before continuing in an even squeakier

voice. *"I reckon we should go back to being friends so we can stop giving Angus a headache, and you'll be free to kiss whoever you like and I can go winch some big, scary demon in the woods."* He snickered, his voice returning to normal. "How does that sound?"

Ailsa ducked her head as her cheeks grew hotter. "You're an eejit."

"Maybe so," Angus laughed. "But I am an observant one. Now, come on, we have to get ready for the party."

"May I remind you, prince, that I am a mere commoner. There are some downsides to that status, but one big plus is I don't have to do anything. You, on the other hand, have to go to as many parties as your brother wishes. But you get to live in a life of luxury as payment."

"And may I remind you, that you are my friend and I really want you there?"

"See, that's not fair. What's my payment?"

"My love and adoration?"

"You're a charmer. No wonder my brother fell for you."

Angus gave a weak smile. "Yeah, well, that was a long time ago."

Gods, Ailsa thought as she watched him stand and head back to the window. *That's another mess to sort out.*

Angus hadn't been avoiding her brother Cameron like she'd been avoiding Harris. Quite the opposite, actually.

The prince had been by her brother's bedside in the weeks he'd spent recovering from being Nicnevan's prisoner. The only problem was, Angus had hardly said a word to him in all that time.

As soon as Cameron was awake, Angus would turn into a mumbling mess. So instead of talking, the prince would do

3

anything to keep himself busy. Fetching food, fixing curtains, stoking the fire. All done while Cameron watched on in puzzlement. Ailsa was pretty sure she'd noticed her brother pretending to sleep, if only to avoid the awkward silences.

Now Cameron was healed, Angus had taken to following him like some sort of bodyguard. A silent bodyguard. The prince would only ever speak when there was someone else in the room. Ailsa had played mediator more than once and it was getting annoying.

I need to get away from civilization for a while.

You could go back to The Forest of Frith? The voice of her spirit guide whispered in her ear. *You know he's waiting for you.*

But what if he doesn't really want me to come back? Ailsa thought back to the last words the demon had spoken to her. *I want you to go,* he'd said.

You know he didn't mean it, Ishbel admonished.

I hope not. Ailsa sighed. *Soon. Soon I'll go back. I need to sort things out here first.*

Harris's grinning face flashed through her mind. It was quickly replaced by Angus's. Then Cameron's.

Finally, she allowed another face into her mind's eye. He looked as he had when she'd left him: tear tracks running down dark cheeks, curling golden antlers poking out of messy hair. And eyes that were fully pitch black. Ailsa's stomach twisted, thinking of the demon who was once an angel, committed to saving lives, trying to make up for the ones he had taken.

"I'll be there soon, Maalik," Ailsa said into the storm. "Whether you want me there or not."

Chapter 2

Ailsa looked in the mirror trying to resist the urge to stare at her left cheek. Her gaze went to her body instead. She was shorter than average, but her body had filled out in the weeks lounging around the castle and eating whenever she wanted. She'd developed some curves underneath her muscle.

Ailsa smoothed down the fabric of her gown. "That'll do." She'd selected the darkest dress she found inside the bulging wardrobe: a midnight blue gown embroidered with silver stars.

"You look pretty," Cameron supplied from where he lay sprawled on the couch.

"I don't want to look pretty," Ailsa said with a frown. "I want to look threatening."

"Well, dear sister," Cameron chuckled, "You've always looked like that, even when we were young."

A servant hesitated nearby, holding a comb in one hand and grimacing.

Ailsa caught the servant watching and waved her away with a sigh. "No, thank you."

Before Ailsa could blink, the girl was gone from the dressing room.

"See? Very threatening." Cameron laughed, and the gesture stretched the scars across his face. His tanned skin was covered in nicks and cuts, some years old, and some only now healing.

Ailsa examined the table in front of her. It was covered in beautiful jewellery, much more than anyone could wear. "And you look bright," she told her brother.

Cameron grinned. "Found some hair dye. What do you think of the pink?"

"It suits you," Ailsa said, and meant it. She brushed back her own hair with her fingers, revealing her pale face, save for the dark red birthmark. It was a mark she'd had to hide her entire life, in case anyone thought her a changeling. It was the reason they had separated her and Cameron. And all that time she'd believed it to be mere superstition. Now she knew better. "Are you going to get changed soon?"

"I'd rather sit in your rooms and eat all the cake they've brought you." He waved to the coffee table, groaning with the spread of pastries and tarts. "Seriously, who do I have to sweet-talk to get this sort of setup in my room?"

Ailsa pursed her lips. "You know who."

Cameron grabbed a muffin and stuffed it in his mouth. "Yeah, well," he mumbled as he ate. "I would if he ever actually spoke to me. I don't think he's even uttered a sentence to me since we've been back."

"He's shy," Ailsa said. *Give me strength… these men!* She selected two silver and leather cuffs from the pile of jewellery and a matching headband. It was studded with little spikes, and when she slid it onto her head, it framed her face like a crown.

"He was never shy before."

"I imagine he was more worried about all the torture you were enduring as baby soldiers." Cameron and Angus had met when the prince had run off to training camp. Angus had told Ailsa stories of his time there, and of the boy he'd fallen in love with, until his father caught up to him. She'd had no idea that the boy was her own brother until they'd rescued Cameron from the faerie court and they'd seen each other.

The world is full of surprises.

"Yeah," Cameron said. "I'm glad that time in my life is over. I just wish I'd been able to stay with you."

"You don't wish that," she mumbled. "It wasn't exactly a nice few years for me either." Immediately, Ailsa wished she hadn't mentioned it. The guilt on her brother's face was plain to see. No matter how many times she told him it hadn't been his fault, he never seemed to believe her. He'd been a victim of her town's closed mindedness, as much as she had. As soon as their mother had died, their grandmother had whisked him away, leaving Ailsa to fend for herself. Knowing the old bat, her house couldn't have been an easy place to finish growing up.

Before she could mutter an apology, Cameron let out a groan, rubbing the side of his head.

"Are you okay?"

His face scrunched up. "I keep getting headaches. Nothing to worry about," he said with a wince.

Ailsa arched an eyebrow. "It doesn't seem like nothing."

"It's… weird. Whenever I feel a shooting pain, I get a flash of something. Not quite light. Like I'm glimpsing a scene through a window for a second."

She leaned against the dressing table, crossing her arms. That didn't sound good. "What did you see this time?"

"It's going to sound really weird." He bit his lip, staring off into nothing. "I saw movement. Like the shadows cast on the floor when lots of people are moving around."

"Maybe your eyes need checked."

"Maybe," Cameron agreed, though it took him a moment to lose that far-off look.

"What are you going to wear?" Ailsa asked, intending to distract herself as much as him.

It seemed to work. Cameron crossed his long legs out in front of him on the couch and said, "I think they've given me some trews. They might even be in the MacAra tartan."

"Well, you'd better get on with changing. Iona should be here soon." She was late, actually. Ailsa sank back down into the chair, fiddling with her hair again, in fear that if it wasn't decent, the selkie would call another servant in to fix it.

In the mirror, she watched as Cameron stuffed one last cake slice in his mouth before rising and sauntering from the couch to stand behind Ailsa at the dressing table. His movement was casual, but she still noted the slight limp. *Not completely healed yet.* Perhaps that was why he was having headaches. He just needed more time.

"I still can't believe I get to see you every day," he said, wrapping his arms about her shoulders.

Ailsa watched their reflection, noting the family resemblance. All a lie, of course. They had changed her to look like him. Her true face was lost until the day she gazed upon her birth mother. Which, since she had no idea who that was, could mean it was gone forever. "I didn't think we'd ever find each other again," she murmured with a half smile.

"Well," Cameron said, dropping a kiss onto her head and stepping back. "We'll have to make up for lost time. See you at the ceilidh?"

"I'll be down whenever Iona is ready," Ailsa replied.

As soon as the door closed behind Cameron, Ailsa slumped down in her chair. It wasn't that she didn't enjoy spending time with Cameron. In fact, once the shock had worn off, she had been ecstatic to see him again. But she'd gone years on her little beach, alone, with only the waves for company. Sometimes it was nice to be on her own.

The silence was short-lived, however. Not five minutes after Cameron had left, Iona strolled through the door, wearing a robe and a towel wrapped around her hair.

"Where have you been?" Ailsa asked. Iona's room connected to her own, and they shared a bathing room.

"Swimming," she answered briskly.

"I was beginning to think you weren't going to the ceilidh. There's still time to ditch it? I could come with you." *Please, please, please.*

Iona sniffed. "You know there's nothing I love more than a bit of dancing. I wouldn't miss it for the world. I just wanted a dip. Sometimes being in this skin can get itchy. You look nice, by the way."

Ailsa blushed at the compliment. "Do you think Duncan's plan will work?" she asked to change the subject. "Are we going to be rid of all the foreign dignitaries at last?"

Iona snorted and headed for the wardrobe. "Need I remind you *I* am a foreign dignitary?"

"You know what I mean." Ailsa moved from the dressing table to free it up. She sank down into the couch cushions, doing her best to appear as unladylike as possible. "I swear I keep finding Mirandellis hiding in dark corners all over the castle, like vampires hiding from the sun."

"Well, if they don't leave, garlic will protect you." The selkie opened the wardrobe doors, sorting through the colourful dresses decisively.

"Does garlic repel vampires?"

Iona grinned. "Not particularly, but it'll probably keep most people away if you wear enough of it. Now, I need a dress that's going to match up to how beautiful yours is." She pulled down a tumble of teal and red fabric. "I'm afraid I don't suit dark colours, but which one of these do you prefer?"

Ailsa bit her lip. "The red one?"

"Excellent choice." With a flourish, Iona pulled the towel out of her hair and allowed the robe to fall off her body to the ground.

Ailsa quickly averted her eyes to the pastries in front of her. She listened to the sounds of shuffling coming from Iona's direction, trying to gauge when it was safe to look again. Finally, Ailsa cautiously raised her gaze back to the selkie.

The dress was covered in sequins, the weight of which pulled the fabric down and close to the redhead's body. The one shoulder strap split in half to reveal the skin across the chest and upper stomach. If Ailsa had tried to wear such a gown, she would have risked indecency. But Iona looked elegant as the material skimmed against her skin.

She stepped in front of the mirror, admiring herself unashamedly. "And no shoes, I think. I want to dance all night." Iona shook out her still damp hair and spun around. "Do you think I'll find any tall, dark, handsome partners?"

Ailsa smiled. "No doubt you'll find partners, but I can't guarantee tall, dark, handsome ones."

"And what about you? I can think of at least one person who'd love to spin you around the ballroom."

Ailsa ducked her head. "No dancing for me tonight, I'm afraid. I've not done nearly enough brooding in the shadows lately."

Iona tutted. "That's all you've done."

"Well, can't let people down by acting differently, now can I?"

The selkie frowned and there was an uncomfortable squirming in Ailsa's gut. She knew that her own words had been too close to the truth. She had been letting someone down by avoiding them, and it couldn't go on any longer.

"I think I'll head down before the crowds become too overwhelming," she muttered, rising from the couch.

Iona turned back to the mirror. "I'm sure *everyone* is looking forward to seeing you," she said pointedly.

Ailsa gave a non-committal grunt and slunk out of the room, down to the party below stairs.

Chapter 3

Luckily, there were plenty of dark corners and hidden alcoves surrounding Dunrigh's grand ballroom to sneak into. Ailsa did a single sweep of the room before making her way to one, grabbing a glass of an unknown liquid from a servant's tray as she passed. The corner she'd selected had a few low couches, perfect for lounging and watching the dancers go by while she drank in the half-dark. There was no way she'd be joining them, no matter how many times Iona nagged her. She sank down and took a sip from the glass, almost choking as she realised it was very strong whisky. She took another, more cautious sip. *Still disgusting.*

Ailsa watched the ceilidh swing into life, mesmerised by the swirling dancers. A month ago, it had been easier to tell who belonged to which country. The Mirandellis of the south would wear huge ball gowns or pressed suits, with traditional painted masks on their faces. Visenyans of the north often styled their long black hair in elaborate braids, which would whip about as they spun in their mirrored tunics. The Edessans could be seen in bright fabrics, complimenting their tanned skin. Their neighbours, the Akrosii, favoured instead white linens wound over their bodies and pinned in place. But slowly, over the last few weeks, the lines had blurred. Foreigners were donning kilts, kicking their shoes off to better dance to the upbeat music. Perhaps many had fallen in love with Eilanmòr. A tenuous peace had been established.

Will they remember that when they all go home? Ailsa wondered.

When her glass was empty, she sat, digging it into her knee with one hand as she watched for people she knew. Cameron came down first, grabbing himself more food from the buffet. Then Iona walked in, arm in arm with an older Visenyan woman she seemed to know. Eventually, she caught sight Harris's red hair on the dance floor. She hadn't seen him come in, but he was unmissable now, spinning his partner around to the music, his kilt whipping behind him. Ailsa sank deeper into the couch cushions and wondered if she should get herself another drink.

"I thought I'd find you here."

Ailsa jumped at the voice, but it was Angus that lowered himself down beside her and she let out a huff. "I wanted to be alone for a bit before—"

"What?" Angus laughed. "Before dancing? Or before running back up to your room?"

Ailsa groaned. "I definitely need more whisky."

Angus didn't answer. He didn't even chuckle. Ailsa turned her head to look at him, but he wasn't paying attention to her anymore. Instead, he was staring wistfully off across the ballroom.

Ailsa followed his line of sight, knowing full well who she'd find at the end. Cameron was leaning against the stone wall beside the door, his head tossed back and his hands in the pockets of his trousers. One foot tapped along to the music, as if the only thing he cared about at that moment was the beat of the song.

"Ask him to dance," Ailsa told Angus.

The prince's face coloured. "Who? I mean… the song is nearly over."

"But there will be another song afterwards. You haven't really spoken to him since we've been back."

Angus adjusted the collar of his shirt. "He hasn't spoken to me either. Sorry, he's your brother; I must be putting you in a difficult situation."

"Yeah, well, our little circle seems to be very interconnected currently. Do you still like him?"

"I don't know, it's been years—"

"I didn't ask you if you were in love with him," Ailsa clarified. "I asked if you like him. As a person?"

"Of course—"

"Well, start there. Be his friend first."

Angus looked like she'd suggested he wrestle a lion. "Okay."

"And if you want to dance, you could ask him." She said it slowly, attempting a soothing tone, but it came off more like she was explaining something to a moronic toddler. "Or you could ask someone else. It wouldn't be the first time you've danced with a friend. Not even the first time you've danced with a male friend."

Angus squared his shoulders. "Right. Wish me luck." Then he was out of his chair and across the room.

Ailsa watched as the prince approached, walking as fast as possible, probably so he wouldn't lose his nerve before he made it to Cameron. Her lips twitched, but she fought down the snigger. It really wasn't nice to laugh, but she'd never seen Angus so flustered. She couldn't see his face when he got to her brother, but Cameron's eyes grew wide for a moment. Then, something Angus said made him smile, and they were making their way to the dancefloor. She let out a whoop on the inside and turned her attention away, giving them some privacy.

You can't resist sticking your nose in other people's business, can you? Ishbel asked.

"You're one to talk," Ailsa muttered with a scowl.

Should you really be encouraging them? A prince of the realm and a soldier?

"I'm not encouraging anything. I just need them to talk to each other."

Perhaps you should take your own advice, Ishbel said with a cackle as a head of curling red hair walked across the room towards the bar. *Go on, your turn.* And then she was gone.

Ailsa gritted her teeth. It really was rich of Ishbel to accuse her of meddling. But, deep down, she knew the spirit guide was right. She had been avoiding a particular conversation. *If Angus can face his fears, so can I.* Stealing her nerves, she rose from the couches and made her way to the bar.

Harris was leaning over the counter, laughing at something the barman had said, when she caught up with him. His grin had produced dimples on his cheeks and a lock of hair hung over his freckled forehead. Ailsa's hands itched to push it away, and she had a flash of anger. *Stupid hair.*

Ailsa was almost right beside him before he noticed she was there. He gave a snort when he locked eyes with her. "Have I ever told you, you look beautiful when you glower?"

"No," Ailsa said, sucking on a tooth. "I haven't heard that one yet."

Harris gestured to the tankard of ale in front of him. "Want a drink?"

"I've already had a whisky and I'm feeling it a bit in my legs." Indeed, there was a fuzziness beginning in her toes, making her wobbly. Perhaps not the best time to get drunk.

"I feel like I haven't spoken to you much since we returned." Harris rapped on the side of his glass. "If I was paranoid, I'd have thought you've been avoiding me. Though, I suppose you've had a lot to catch up on with your brother."

Ailsa shifted her weight from one foot to the other. "Yeah, we've been filling each other in on the last few years."

Tell him. Tell him now.

"Harris," she said, her voice wobbling. "There's something I need to say."

"Is this where you're going to tell me you're in love with me?"

"No."

"No," he said softly. "I didn't think so."

"You knew about me being half-fae."

"Yes."

Gods, her eyes were prickling. "Why didn't you tell me?"

Harris bit his lip. "I didn't think you were ready to hear it."

"That would have been for me to decide."

"I'm sorry, Ailsa." He swiped a hand through his hair, messing it up further. "I didn't mean to keep that from you. Sometimes I think I'm being really clever, but I'm really just being an eejit."

"You have to learn not to toy with people's feelings."

They were silent for a moment. Ailsa desperately reached for her next words, but Harris beat her to it.

"I take it that the things we said to each other in the inn are void."

The inn, the things they'd said, the kisses they'd shared - it was like a lifetime ago. "I care about you, Harris. I think I proved that when I trekked across Eilanmòr to rescue you, even though I knew you'd lied to me." Ailsa shook her head, trying to find a way to explain. "You're like a raindrop that people keep trying to catch with their hands, but you keep slipping through. One day, someone will hold out a glass and you'll stop falling."

He snorted. "That sounds like being trapped."

"Maybe that's a poor analogy. You won't feel trapped when it's the right person."

His face hardened ever so slightly. "It sounds like you're speaking from experience? Perhaps a demon has filled his glass with you."

Ailsa's cheeks heated. "How much has Iona said?"

His barked laugh was too loud. "Oh, my sister isn't the gossip. You can blame Angus for that."

"Nothing happened. I would never—"

"-See, that's why you're a better person than me, Ailsa. If a handsome, brooding man had saved me, I'm afraid I wouldn't have hesitated from drinking my fill."

"You're incorrigible."

He sighed, turning serious. "I care about you and I want you to be happy. Can we still be friends?"

"Of course." Ailsa let her shoulders relax. That had gone better than expected.

"But please be careful." He added, staring up at the rows of bottles. "Demons don't exactly have the friendliest reputations."

If only he knew.

"Maalik isn't like the rest."

He made a non-committal noise. "Have a drink with me? You've got the hard part out of the way, might as well celebrate."

17

"Sure, that would be nice. I think I'm going to go to the bathing room first though," she said. She needed to get some fresh air. "Will you get me what you're having?"

The smile he hoisted onto his face now was wide, genuine. "That's a lot of power you've given me, MacAra."

"I trust you," Ailsa said. *Just not with my heart.*

Chapter 4

Ailsa dabbed water on her neck and wrists, trying to cool herself down. The blood was still pumping through her veins at high speed. At least, now that was over, she could stop avoiding Harris.

And you can go and find Maalik, Ishbel teased.

Ailsa rolled her eyes and left the bathroom. Only a few candles lit the way back to the ballroom through the darkened hall. Even from the toilets, though, she could hear the band were playing a slower tune. *Will Angus and Cameron be dancing to this one?* she wondered. Her lips curved into a smile until she realised someone was watching her.

A man leaned up against the wall, his hands in his pockets. He wore the heavy woollen dress suit of the Mirandelli army, and his hair had been shaved at the sides. At odds with the military uniform was a tattoo of a heart below his right eye. Ailsa quickly flicked her gaze away, fixing them instead on the end of the corridor. His stare followed her, however, as she moved to walk past. Just as she was beyond him and with her back turned, he let out a whistle.

Say nothing, she told herself.

And why not? Ishbel grumbled. *He is asking for your wrath.*

She was about to ignore the spirit guide, but then the stranger chuckled.

"Hello, beautiful," he said.

Ailsa saw red. She rounded on the man and pinned him with barely contained rage in her eyes. "Do you have a problem?" she gritted out.

"I was admiring the view," he answered with a shrug, not understanding the danger he was in. "Isn't that what you wanted when you put on that dress?"

"What I wanted was to enjoy a party without committing murder, but we don't always get what we want, do we?" she said.

The man blinked, stunned for a moment, before a sneer twisted his face. "You women are all the same. You want to be admired, but when someone compliments you, you take it as an insult. Can't any of you ever just be grateful?"

"Oh my," Ailsa said, as though she was mulling over her next move. "I don't even think it can be called murder at this point. Surely I was provoked?"

"I'd like to see you try." The man spat on the ground beside him, right on the carpet. "You have no idea who you're talking to."

"Well, you'd better tell me so I can make sure they get the name right on your headstone."

"I am Lieutenant DiAngelo of the Miradelli army and you're just some changeling bitch who would never be allowed near a royal party if we were in my country."

The words landed like blows, freezing Ailsa's tongue. Her body did not want to talk, it wanted to throw out her magic and hit him with everything she had. But they were in Dunrigh Castle and this man was a guest. She couldn't just toast him where he stood, could she?

"But we're not in your country," said a sultry voice from the shadows, stopping Ailsa's train of thought. "And you clearly do not know who you are talking to."

Ailsa raised her eyes to meet those of the speaker. Up, up, up. The woman who stepped out of the shadows was at least a head taller than the soldier in front of her. She was dressed in bright, billowing trousers and her hair hung down her back in braids dyed turquoise, blue and purple.

Large golden rings glinted at her ears, and a smaller hoop poked out below her upper lip, hanging over her white teeth. They gleamed against her dark skin as she smiled menacingly at the soldier. At her side, she carried a curved cutlass, one of her hands resting on the hilt.

"That is Ailsa MacAra, bodyguard to the prince and slayer of the Faerie Queen," said the woman in her deep voice. She tilted her head, like a predator assessing its prey. "And I calculate you have about two minutes before she electrifies your insides, unless you leave."

"One minute," Ailsa clarified.

Lieutenant DiAngelo looked between them, his lip curling. Finally, he spat on the ground beside his own boot and pushed off the wall. "I can't wait to report this back to my captain." He stalked off, leaving Ailsa alone with the tall woman.

"Thank you," Ailsa said, allowing her hands to unclench. "I worried killing him would be frowned upon at a party."

"It would have made it a lot more interesting." The woman swaggered forward, extending a hand. "Miss MacAra, it is my pleasure to meet you."

Ailsa took the proffered palm. It was warm and strong as it enveloped her own. "Well, I'm glad I met you too, Lady—?"

The woman let go, placing the hand on her hip. "Capitana Del Asturio, of the Ninfa del Mar. From Edessa. I have been hoping to speak to you since you returned from Ephraim, but there was never an opportune moment and unfortunately it seems us foreigners have overstayed our welcome. Can I get you a drink?"

"A friend of mine has already got me one," she said, thinking of Harris waiting for her back at the bar. "You can join us if you want, though?"

The woman grinned. "Lead on."

Ailsa wound her way through the crowds in the ballroom, with the tall woman following close behind. "How do you know me?" Ailsa asked, nervous for the answer.

She had been used to a level of infamy in her village and those surrounding it. Everyone knew who the changeling girl was and how to avoid her.

"I've heard a lot about you," the captain said. "In particular, I know it was you who found the Stone of Destiny."

"Yes, though I don't have it anymore." They found an empty spot at the bar, leaning against the stools rather than sitting on them. Harris had disappeared, but Ailsa was sure he was still nearby.

"That's a shame." The woman tapped her fingers against the granite surface. "Who has it now?"

"I'm sure King Duncan has it. We delivered it to him before his coronation."

"And does he keep it on his person, or is there a treasury for such trinkets?" Her mouth quirked, as if holding in a laugh, though it didn't reach her eyes.

What's funny? Ailsa wondered. Her shoulders tensed. There was something this stranger wasn't telling her.

Yet. Perhaps she's working up to it. "I wouldn't know, sorry."

"But you probably know more about how it works than the average person?"

"We only had the stone for a day before we brought it here."

"Did you use its magic?" the woman pressed.

Ailsa bristled. The persistence seemed wrong. This was more than a passing interest.

Harris's booming laughter cut through the moment and then he was at her elbow, his face still stretched into a grin from whatever joke he'd been having. "Oh, Ailsa, there you are." His gaze flicked to the stranger, widening in surprise. "And who is this?"

"Capitana del Asturio," the woman said coolly. "Harris of Struanmuir, yes?"

"We just met. The captain was asking me about the Stone of Destiny." Ailsa tried to inject her misgivings into her words. *I do not know this person well, be careful.*

"Ah yes, Ailsa and I retrieved the stone a couple of months ago," Harris ploughed on, totally oblivious. "Along with Prince Angus. Pretty useful object, did you know it can transport you wherever you like? Made getting back to Dunrigh easy, didn't it Ailsa?" Harris took a sip of his ale, eyes watching the captain over his tankard.

The captain's eyes sparkled. "But it's not the only treasure Eilanmòr contains."

Something in Ailsa's memory sparked at that. *Other treasures?* Hadn't she heard someone else talking about treasure recently?

Harris set his glass back on the bar and leaned forward. "I've heard Edessa is also full of treasures."

Ailsa fought the urge to push him away by the face. Instead, she said, "What do you know about that?"

"Just that you have many myths about magical objects here in Eilanmòr. I've been reading about them and I found something very interesting indeed. Have you ever heard of the Four Treasures?"

Ailsa cast her mind back. She was sure she'd heard that name before... "Perhaps? Is the Stone of Destiny one of them?"

Harris stopped his fawning for a moment, looking confused. "Now I'm lost. There's other treasure?"

The captain's jaw worked for a moment, like she was assessing them. Then she wet her lips and began. "The Four Treasures—"

But before she could continue, a noise sounded across the ballroom. Someone was shouting and whatever they were saying was spreading whispers amongst the crowd.

"What?" Harris said, standing on the lower bar of the seat behind him to get a better look.

People were running from the source of the shouting, but whoever it was seemed to be coming their way. The captain put her hand on the sword at her hip and Ailsa suddenly wished she'd brought her axe too.

You don't need an axe, Ishbel told her. *The very air is your weapon.*

"Stay here," Harris told them, but the crowd parted and Cameron came charging through, Angus behind him.

"Stop!" he bellowed, and Ailsa realised he'd been the one shouting earlier. "Everybody stop dancing and run. This whole place is going to blow up."

Someone nearby screamed and, like a ripple, it surged through the room. Still, only a few had the presence of mind to flee for the doors.

Ailsa was off, sprinting to her wide-eyed brother as fast as her dress would allow. "Cameron? What's going on?" He looked like he'd seen a ghost. His face had paled like spilt milk, and his eyes darted back and forth between her and the still busy ballroom. Ailsa didn't think she'd ever seen her usually calm and collected brother so terrified.

Cameron gripped onto her shoulders so hard it felt like she would bruise. "I saw it, Ailsa. There's going to be an explosion. We need to get everyone out."

Has he gone mad? How could there be an explosion in the castle? Ailsa wasn't sure what to believe.

The captain, though, called to the onlooking crowd. "Well? You heard him! Get out."

Ailsa didn't raise her head to see if they'd complied. "Cameron, I don't understand. How did you see it?"

"He collapsed," Angus said, his voice sounding close to tears. "Then he started convulsing. When he stopped, he said he'd had a vision."

Cameron grabbed Ailsa's hand and pulled her towards the exit. "There's no time to explain. Move!"

Ailsa looked back to see Angus, Harris and the captain following closely behind. She stared open-mouthed at her friends, tripping over her own feet as she was dragged along. What was happening?

The next seconds ticked by in slow motion.

Harris turned to look over his shoulder.

With wide eyes, he bellowed something that was swallowed up in the panic.

A deep rumble shook the floor under Ailsa's feet.

Someone nearby screamed. "Get down!"

Ailsa was thrown to the ground. The world tilted, careening out of control as she fell. Then, as her head hit the floor with a sickening crack, the ball room erupted into fire and pain.

Chapter 5

Ailsa's ears were ringing as she blinked her eyes open. *How did I end up on the floor?* There had been a sound like thunder and a flash. Had she accidentally pulled a storm inside the ballroom?

What have I done?

She groaned and sat up, jagged bits of rock sticking into her hands as she pushed off the ground. As soon as she looked around, it was clear a storm hadn't done this.

Ailsa's mouth hung open in shock as she realised half of the stone wall that joined the greenhouse to the castle had been blown away.

Distantly, screams filled the air as others stirred in the blast's aftermath.

She remained there for a moment, feeling her body out. Nothing seemed broken except the headband she'd been wearing. She pulled it out of her hair, leaving it on the floor in front of her. Where was everyone else?

"Cameron?" Ailsa tried to shout, her voice coming out as a croak.

"I'm here," he groaned from beside her. The blast had wrenched his hand from hers, but he hadn't gone too far.

"Are you hurt?" Ailsa asked, crawling closer to her brother.

"Just dazed," he said, sitting up. There were a few fresh cuts on his face against the background of older scars. "Angus?

Harris?" he called out.

"Yeah," Angus said, from somewhere to the side. Ailsa turned to see him lying on his back, staring up at the ceiling as if the wind had been knocked out of him. Cameron half crawled, half ran over to him. He moved his hands deftly over the prince's body, checking for injuries, while Angus gaped up at him in wonder.

"Harris?" Ailsa called again. She couldn't see his red hair anywhere.

A groan pulled her attention to a pile of bodies behind them. The selkie was sprawled underneath another figure. They were both covered in dust, coating their skin, their hair, their clothes. Ailsa looked down at herself, realising she too was caked in it, though not as bad as Harris. He must have caught more of the blast than she had, being that little bit closer to the explosion.

Still, not close enough to have sustained too much injury. If they'd been back at the bar, however… Ailsa shivered.

"Oh gods, Harris. Are you okay?"

The person on top of him rolled away from his body with a choked-out growl, patting the fine powder off their clothes. Captain del Asturio.

Harris coughed, sitting up. "I'm okay, thanks to her."

"*Mis dioses,*" muttered the captain in a husky voice. She pushed up from the floor with a nimble grace and held out a hand to Harris. "Come on, it's not safe to lie there, we need to get out of the ballroom." Indeed, other party-goers had come to the same conclusion. Those in the crowd who were able stumbled out, pushing and shoving, to get away from the scene. The few who were too hurt moaned from where they lay.

There would have been many more if it hadn't been for Cameron.

Harris stared up at his rescuer and allowed the captain to yank him to his feet. He looked dazed, and a little stupefied, like he'd had a knock to his brain.

Or an arrow to the heart.

Since Harris didn't seem ready to say anything further, Ailsa rolled her eyes and turned back to her brother.

Cameron had apparently finished his examination. He put an arm under Angus's to help him sit up.

"How did you know that was going to happen?" Ailsa asked him.

Cameron shook his head. "I'll explain as soon as we're behind closed doors. For now, we need to get out of here." Then he was dragging Angus up the stairs and out of the ballroom.

"You need to find the king," Captain del Asturio muttered. "The entire council, even. I'll meet you, once I've found the source of the blast, and tell you all I know." The Edessan put her hands on her hips and Harris's eyes followed the motion.

Ailsa shook her head. *And here I was, worrying about how to let him down gently. All it took was for another woman to come along and distract him.* "Are you saying you know how the explosion happened?"

"I have a feeling in my gut," the woman replied, watching the fleeing crowd. "That blast was no accident. Come on, let's go." And with that she turned, going in the opposite direction from the horde.

"Wait, I'll come with you," Harris murmured and then he was off after the woman without a backwards glance at Ailsa.

Ailsa bit her lip, wondering whether she should follow the Edessan too. She hadn't been sure if she trusted the captain, but the world had turned upside down in the last few minutes.

You have more important things to worry about right now.

Without really deciding, her legs were carrying her further into the greenhouse. Her ripped skirts whispered across the rubble, so at odds with what had been moments before. The scene was unnervingly quiet; now only a handful of moaning casualties remained.

She bent down to the first person she came to, shoving the rock and debris off their body. The woman cried out as Ailsa freed her. "How hurt are you?" Ailsa asked, out of her depth. *You spent weeks learning how to care for people*, she reminded herself. Those times seemed very far away.

The woman screwed up her face. "I'm okay. I'm okay," she said, gritting her teeth against whatever pain she was in.

Ailsa didn't stick about to confirm. *She can talk. She says she's fine. Move on.*

The next person was on their back, covered in dust. "Come on," Ailsa told them. "Let's get you out of here." She removed the rubble as carefully as she could. "You'll be okay," she told him. The figure turned over with a wince, and Ailsa gasped. The man was tanned, with dark hair and from the chin down was soaked in blood. Heavy eyebrows winged above tired eyes that could easily have been pitch black under his lids. It wasn't until he blinked them open that the spell was broken.

Not him, Ailsa told herself. *He wouldn't be here.*

Just as the man wailed in pain, Ailsa heard a shout behind her. *At last, some help.* Servants and guards flooded into the ballroom, spreading out like a fan. They shouted instructions at each other, but Ailsa only vaguely heard them. She was still staring at the man lying in front of her.

"Are you hurt?" someone asked beside her. Ailsa blinked

and turned to find a woman crouched down, looking at her with concern. She wore a cloth wound around her upper arm and marked with a large M.

"No, but he is," Ailsa croaked out. Suddenly her skin was itching. She raised trembling fingers to her arm, scratching at the dirt.

"I'll take it from here," said the woman.

Ailsa nodded woodenly and rose from her spot beside the man. He gave a groan as though to ask where she was going, but she couldn't look at him again.

This was a mistake. I need to get out of here.

She stumbled back towards the grand staircase in a daze, vaguely appalled at the devastation that one explosion could bring. One blast had been enough to turn the ballroom, Dunrigh Castle's very heart, into a battlefield. Had Captain del Asturio been right? Had it been on purpose?

"Ailsa!" There was a shout of relief and hands were reaching out and grabbing her shoulders. Iona still wore her party dress. The sequins scratched against Ailsa's skin as she was pulled into a warm embrace. But she didn't care. Someone was here who wasn't covered in dust and grime—proof that outside this place, the world wasn't burning.

Iona pulled back, her sea-green eyes searching her face, her body for injuries. Ailsa stared at the selkie's freckled nose, so she wouldn't be tempted to look back out at the rubble.

"Are you alright?" Iona asked her.

"I'm okay. I'm okay," she replied, echoing the woman's words from earlier.

Iona stroked her arms, soothing her, but her tone was harsh as she said, "You need to come with me. The king wants to see us."

Duncan? "Why—"

"The explosion was a distraction." Iona gave her a little shake, trying to will the words into her. "The Stone of Destiny is gone."

Chapter 6

Ailsa leaned against the back wall of the library, feeling completely and utterly useless.

The Stone of Destiny was gone. Someone had set off a bomb inside the castle. And what had she been doing? Mooning around, worrying about her love life, of all things.

At least one MacAra had proved helpful. Her brother had somehow foreseen the explosion, giving the guests time to run. Now he was lying on a chaise longue beside the fire, looking pale as death, but alive.

Alive. We're all alive, thanks to him.

Angus hovered at his feet, fussing. He'd already sent some servants off for a glass of water, while he tucked a blanket about Cameron's legs. Despite her foul mood, Ailsa smiled at that.

She wasn't the only one in a rage. King Duncan was pacing over the worn ornate carpet. He'd been the one to assemble them all here in the library. The council room was too near the glass greenhouse, too near the damage, so they'd plan what to do amongst ancient books and maps instead.

She looked to Harris and Iona, both leaning against the reading table, visibly shaken. Harris had one arm wrapped around his sister in comfort.

Ailsa drummed her fingers on her arm. Duncan had called for them, but he'd also called for his commanders and advisors. And they were taking their sweet time.

"Another five minutes," General Fraser simpered. The grey-haired man didn't look like a soldier. Not anymore. He'd allowed his body to become soft, enjoying the comforts of court too much. But he'd served King Duncan's father, so he stayed. For now.

Sometimes Ailsa forgot how young Duncan was. Younger than her by a few months at least. What must it be like to shoulder the burden of an entire nation, before the age of twenty? With a new wife and son?

And war on the horizon.

"Two minutes, and we're starting." Duncan stopped his pacing, looking out of the night-black window instead.

"With all due respect," General Fraser said, scratching at his moustache. "Shouldn't this meeting be for your inner circle only? We don't know who we can trust."

Duncan bared his teeth. "Do you need me to spell out for you exactly why everyone is here? Who exactly do you not trust? My brother, your prince? Lady Iona or Lord Harris, who have been friends of this court since my grandfather was king? Ailsa who—"

"—is a changeling," the general supplied, turning his beady eyes on her. "Or her brother, who just happened to know when the explosion would happen?"

"Cameron was nowhere near the explosion," Angus growled. "He was with me."

"He could have planted it before the party."

"How did you know, Cameron?" Iona asked quietly.

Ailsa's brother stiffened before passing a trembling hand over his face. "I saw it happen before it actually did. One minute I was dreaming and the next the dream was reality."

Harris leaned forward. "What, like in a vision?"

He closed his eyes. "Yes."

Ailsa didn't like this, everyone questioning him when he looked so ill. But they had to know how this had happened. "You said earlier that you've been having odd flashes ever since you got back from Ephraim."

"It was like that, but much clearer this time," said Cameron. "I saw the blast, the building crumbling. People running."

General Fraser threw his hands up in the air. "Why should we believe him? Like I said, his sister is a changeling. Perhaps he's one too."

Ailsa raised her chin, itching to send a spark of lightning at the general's rump. That would only prove his point. "Leave my brother alone. He didn't do this."

"Without Cameron's warning, many more people could have died," said Harris.

But the soldier would not be swayed. "They probably have the Stone of Destiny on one of them right now. I can have them searched by the guards—"

"Neither Ailsa nor her brother were anywhere near me when it happened, so they can't have stolen the stone," Duncan cut across him. "But you were, General Fraser."

The general spluttered, but the king held up a hand for silence. "Need I remind you, Ailsa rescued the stone in the first place. And Cameron is one of our own soldiers."

"They could be working with someone—"

Ailsa was about to spit out a comeback when the doors slammed open.

Illuminated in the torchlight, Captain del Asturio was even more intimidating than she'd been in the dark hallway. There was a confidence to her steps as she sauntered into the room. "I apologise for showing up without an invitation, but we didn't want to miss the after party."

Three people trailed behind her, each wearing the same bright, loose trousers as the captain, and each with a hand on the rapiers at their sides. The tallest was a man who looked hewn from granite. His muscles rippled under his vest as if waiting to strike at any moment. The other man was shorter, smaller even than Ailsa herself. He was also the one who looked most like a pirate, with golden earrings dangling from one ear and a colourful scarf wrapped around his head, covering his right eye.

Next to them, Ailsa almost didn't notice the woman. Her clothing was black and unadorned, her skin almost the same shade. She'd shorn one side of her hair, but the other hung over her shoulder, braided with wooden beads. At her hips she wore two curious, metal instruments. *Pistols,* Ailsa realised. She watched the others, her gaze darting back and forth between them and the strangers in the room. Assessing.

The captain caught Ailsa looking at her companions and gave a lazy smile. "These are my crew. You can trust them. Agustin is my quartermaster," she gestured to the shorter man. "That tank is Orenzo, my gunner, and the wraith in the back is Nadya, my sailing master."

General Fraser's lip curled. "We did not invite you."

"I have information which I think you'll find very useful," the captain purred. "I know they took something from you."

"Sorry," Angus piped up from beside the fire. "Who are you?"

The brute named Orenzo snarled, "That, young man, is Princess Irené, the future Queen of Edessa."

Princess. Not merely a captain. Ailsa wracked her brain,

trying to remember if she'd ever heard anything about the Edessan royal family. But the only Edessan she'd ever known was Gris. Not once in the months he'd trained her had he ever talked about his home country.

A stab of grief pierced her heart. It had been a mere month since he'd died, killed by Nicnevan. She'd spent so much of her life fearing the monster who stalked her steps, when really he had been watching out for her. The Faerie Queen had cursed him, turned him into a huge, grey beast and he'd wasted his once in a decade chance at being human again to look after Ailsa, before disappearing back into the forest. They'd only just reconnected when he'd been murdered. What would he say to all of this?

He'd probably grunt and slink off somewhere.

"I didn't know Edessa had a princess," Harris said, pulling her out of her memories.

"Princess Irené is the only child of King Elias," the large man said. Ailsa didn't miss the flex of his arm as he clutched his sword tighter. The rest of the crew shifted almost imperceptibly, ready for a fight.

Why? Was there some sort of succession issue?

"I thought a man was the heir to the Edessan throne?" Harris frowned. "Wasn't his name Prince—"

"They made a mistake," the princess cut him off with a cool stare, even as her crew bared their teeth. "My name is Princess Irené del Asturio, future Queen of Edessa." She signalled behind her without looking and immediately the crew members relaxed.

Ailsa wasn't sure she'd understood what had just happened, but from the look on Harris's face, he had. He was blushing almost as red as his hair.

Whatever it is, I'm not surprised. He's always putting his foot in his mouth. "I thought you said you were a captain?" Ailsa cut across the tense atmosphere.

The princess relaxed her shoulders. "I am that. My crew and I sail The Etivian Sea on my ship, *The Nymph*."

"Are you pirates?" *I've always wanted to meet a pirate.*

Princess Irené smirked. "Privateers. We're commissioned by the Edessan royal family. Easy to arrange when you're one of them."

"Whether you are pirates or nobility, this is an Eilanmòrian matter," General Fraser huffed. "I suggest you wait with the other foreign dignitaries in the dining hall."

"This isn't merely an Eilanmòrian matter; this concerns us all." Irené crossed her arms in front of her, revealing a tattoo on each of her forearms: one of a shark and the other of an octopus. "I think I know who took the Stone of Destiny."

Duncan narrowed his eyes. "How do you know it was stolen?"

"Because I came here to steal it from you too."

Chapter 7

General Fraser was up in an instant, pulling his sword from his scabbard. "This is outrageous. We should lock them up for—"

"Enough, general." Duncan held up his hand, never taking his eyes off the captain. "I would like to hear what Princess Irené has to say. I assume she has a good reason for plotting to steal the stone, otherwise she would not freely admit she was after it." He rubbed his fingers against the fireplace mantle, weighing his next words. "But just in case, please go rally any soldiers that can be spared and set them up outside this room."

Irené shrugged, taking the seat the general had abandoned and setting her feet up on the table.

General Fraser watched her, spluttering at the arrogance, before storming out of the library doors.

Ailsa fought a smirk. *Good riddance.*

"Thank you, your Majesty, for hearing us out." Irené signalled to her crew, who also came to sit at the desk. The big man, Orenzo, seemed as relaxed as his captain, slumping over the wooden surface. Her quartermaster took out a pen and paper and looked expectantly at Irené. But it was the sailing master that caught Ailsa's attention. She took the seat closest to the door, hands flat on the table, but didn't relax her shoulders. A glint of metal shone at her leg, which she wouldn't stop jiggling. *A knife.*

Ailsa drifted closer, taking care to look like she merely wanted to hear better. From her new position against a bookshelf, she was right between the Edessan sailors and Duncan.

Irené swept her gaze between everyone in the room, and Ailsa mentally sized up their own party. Aside from herself, they had a king, a prince, a soldier and two selkies. Each had their own strengths in a fight, but did the captain know that?

"What I have to say is highly sensitive," Irené finally said. "I have cause to believe you have a traitor in your midst, your Majesty. Do you trust the people in this room?"

Duncan gave her a hard look. "I trust my brother. These are his companions. If he has faith in them, so do I."

Angus's companions. It occurred to Ailsa that Duncan was more alone in the world than she was. Did he even have any friends?

Irené sniffed. "We had planned to steal the Stone of Destiny, not to keep it, but to prevent it from falling into the wrong hands. We would have returned it when the threat was gone."

"What threat?" asked Iona.

"There is a group of immortals—of gods. They appear in all the history books—the ancient tomes of Edessa, Mirandelle, Akrossii and Eilanmòr mention them—albeit under different names. '*Destructores de almas*' we call them in Edessa. They're '*itheadair anam*' in your books. But it's the Mirandelli words that seem to have stuck: '*Edax anime*'—The Soul-Eaters. Also known as the *Edaxi* for short."

Gods. Ailsa knew there were many hundreds of them all over the world, some with limitless power, and others no more than incredibly old fae. Each country had their own deities to worship, though some they shared. "What do they want?"

"To destroy. To devour, until there's nothing left. Thousands of years ago, they were banished to the island of Nerebus," the captain gave a half smile, "by an ancient Eilanmòrian queen. There are wards here, preventing them from stepping foot on your land."

Ailsa's stomach dropped. But could they be summoned? "What are their names? What do they look like?"

"Again, they have many. But most commonly, they are: Chao, God of Chaos, with madness in his eyes; Timor, Goddess of Fear, who appears as a child; Dolor, Goddess of—"

"Pain," Ailsa said, a shiver of ice running down her back. "The Goddess of Pain. We've met."

Everyone in the room turned to stare at her but she pressed her lips together. *This isn't the time.*

"There is one more," Irené continued. "Desper, God of Despair. He is the most wicked of all, so say the texts."

Ailsa sucked in a shaky breath, just so she could feel the air filling her lungs. "I can't imagine anyone being more wicked than Dolor."

"You never mentioned you met a god," said Angus.

"It's something I'd rather forget." When Angus, Iona, and Gris had found her at Maalik's cabin, she'd been too concerned with travelling to Ephraim to tell them about the encounter.

"It seems you have your own stories to tell," Irené said, looking her up and down.

Ailsa drew her eyebrows together. "A friend of mine knows Dolor. She tried to recruit him. She said she needed a being of fire?"

"To wield one of the Four Treasures," the captain murmured. "So, it is true."

Duncan looked between the two women, clearly growing impatient. Ailsa agreed with the sentiment. Half the ballroom was gone, the stone was missing. She wanted to be doing something.

"Tell us everything you know," he said, clenching his fists.

"I too had a 'run in,'" said Irené. "We were off the coast of Nerebus when we were attacked."

"By an army?" asked Angus.

Irené shook her head. "By our worst nightmares. Terrifying things came crawling out of the water that day. Giant spiders, birds with enormous claws, even copies of ourselves, came to torment us. We tried to fight them, but they were just visions. The creatures weren't there."

"It petrified our crew," added the quartermaster. "Some even tried to jump overboard to get away from them, drowning in the raging sea. It was only thanks to the quick thinking of our captain that we survived."

"How did you stop them?" asked Iona.

"We didn't," said Orenzo. "The captain told us to tie ourselves to the rigging and close our eyes. We had to wait them out."

"If they weren't real, they couldn't hurt you," Harris said with a frown.

"We could still feel them, though." The big man shivered. "Every slither of a snake across our skin, every icy touch of a ghostly figure, brushing against us. But no, they couldn't harm us. So we waited and eventually they disappeared."

What would I see? What would be my greatest fear? It used to be a creature in the woods. But now... Ailsa had seen so many horrors in these few short weeks. Which of them would have emerged out of the water to torment her if she'd been on the ship?

"Our father was in Nerebus when he got sick," said Angus quietly at Cameron's feet.

Ailsa remembered the late king's gaunt face, his rotting skin. Had whatever conjured those visions done that to him?

"We've heard reports of similar occurrences all over Ossiana," Irené continued. "It seems the Edaxi have spread themselves out. They are looking for the Four Treasures. Four objects, that, when united, are so powerful they can guarantee a victory in battle."

Ailsa bit her lip. "A friend of mine mentioned them. There was the Stone of Destiny and the Cauldron of Life, but he didn't find the names of the others."

"There is also the Sword of Light and the Spear of Truth." The quartermaster handed the princess a book, which she placed on the table in front of her.

She turned the pages until she found what she was looking for. On it was a picture of a stone, a cauldron, a blade, and a spear. "Each of the treasures is tied to an element. They can only be used to their full power by fae with that elemental magic. This is by far the most I've found in relation to the Four Treasures, but it's hard to make out the meanings of the words. Perhaps you could shed a little light on it?" the captain said hopefully.

Ailsa folded her arms. "I can't read."

"I'll have a go," said Angus, moving to the table. He held the book out in front of him and read in a solemn voice.

"Treasure o' yird, the Destiny Stone,
Transports the bearer tae whaur it is known,

Treasure o' water, Cauldron o' Life,
Reverses conditions o' magik an strife,
Treasure o' fire, the Sword o' Licht,
Cleaves through rivals, bringer o' micht,
Treasure o' air, the Spear o' Truth,
Niver misses, bites lik a tooth,
Handlit apart, fierce i' the hour,
Held close tae hand, maisterfull power,
Exack magik these weapons require,
Else wieldit by man, life they desire.
A warnyn, mortals handle thaim not,
'Cept Sovereign's bluid, whose talent forgot."

The captain sighed. "See, there are a few words I don't quite understand. Yird?"

"Earth," Angus clarified. "It's talking about the Stone of Destiny. It's the treasure of earth."

"*The Cauldron of Life, reverses conditions of magic an strife.*" Iona opened her fist to reveal the cauldron sitting in the middle of her palm. "Well, we saw that. It can absorb spells and curses. But it can also place that curse on someone else—if the same water is used. That's how we trapped Nicnevan."

Angus nodded. "There are the other two treasures. '*Licht*' means 'light'. *Cleaves through rivals.*"

"Is it just really sharp?" Harris asked.

"It says '*exack magik*' which I think refers to who can use them." Irené licked her lips. "Not only do we need to find the Four Treasures, we also need fae with elemental magic. You are selkies, are you not? You have water magic."

"So we need a fae with earth magic, one with fire and one with air," said Ailsa.

"Well, we've got air covered." Harris jerked his chin in her direction. "Ailsa has power over storms and winds."

Iona clicked her tongue as she thought. "For earth, we'll need something like an elf or a faerie. Does it matter how powerful they are?"

"I'd imagine the more powerful they are, the better," said the captain with a shrug. "And fire?"

"That's going to be the most difficult," said Iona. "Fire fae are usually the most dangerous. We'd need a phoenix or a dragon or—"

"What about a demon?" Ailsa asked.

Irené barked out a laugh. "Yes, but how are you going to convince a demon to work with us? They would be more likely to side with the gods."

"I know one." That didn't guarantee he would help them, though.

"What does the rest of it mean?" asked Harris.

Angus read the last three lines out again. "*Else wieldit by man, life they desire. A warnyn, mortals handle thaim not.*"

"If you're human, don't touch them, got it," Cameron said. "The important part is that we find the Four Treasures and the fae to use them."

Duncan shifted from his place at the fire, done with listening. "Where do I need to send my people?"

"The Edaxi are rallying fae soldiers with magic to weaponise the treasures; they plan to seize power over all of Ossiana," the quartermaster said. "The only way to stop them is to gather the treasures and our own fae to fight against them. We need to recruit an earth fae and a fire fae. Miss MacAra, you said you knew a demon?"

Ailsa jumped. She hadn't realised Irené's companions

knew her name, too. "Yes. I'll find him and bring him back."

"And we need an earth fae," said Irené. "It was my plan to travel to Ephraim to find one. Since you have all been, would any of you care to act as my guide?"

"I will," Harris said with a grin, cutting a sideways glance at Ailsa.

She pursed her lips together. *Does he want to go because he likes the captain or because he's trying to get at me?*

Irené looked dubious. "Lastly, we need to find the other Four Treasures. You have the Cauldron. The Stone is missing, probably in the hands of the gods. I've been hearing rumours of where the other two may be. The Sword may be in Ephraim, but we've heard it could also be in a village south-east of here—a place called Kilvaig?"

"Laire and I can go there," Angus said, raising his hand like he was in the schoolroom volunteering for a job.

"I'll go with you," Iona said.

Smart choice, Ailsa thought. There was no way she'd be going back to Ephraim in a hurry.

"And the spear?" asked Harris.

The sailing master spoke up for the first time, her voice heavily accented. "My sources tell me the spear is on the island of Monadh."

You should be the one to go there, a voice whispered in Ailsa's ear. *The Spear of Truth is yours.*

Ailsa scowled. *I need to find Maalik.*

Take him with you, said Ishbel.

Ailsa began to argue, but the spirit guide cut across her, more insistent that Ailsa had ever heard her before.

Do what I say, girl.

Well, that was that.

"I'll go," Ailsa said, before she could question Ishbel's motivations. "I'll go further north after I find the demon. Any idea where the spear is? Monadh looks pretty big."

"Atop the highest mountain on the island, there is a palace made of ice and light," the woman said. "Its name is Findias. Few have seen it; it's protected with powerful magic. We've tried to send men up there, but none can get close enough."

"Who built the palace?" asked Ailsa.

The sailing master shivered. "Witches."

Witches.

The rest of the crew made a sign across their bodies at that, clearly meant to ward off evil.

Irené swung her legs off the table and stood. "I'll give you all passage on my boat, it'll be quicker that way. I can drop you off around the coast."

"There is much to plan, still," Duncan said. "How are we going to protect Eilanmòr, should these gods find all the treasures? I don't want anyone outside this room knowing what you hunt. That goes for you too, princess."

Irené gave a small bow. "I wouldn't dream of telling anyone, except my crew."

Duncan's mouth twisted. "Fair enough, but the fewer people know, the better. When can you leave?"

"Tomorrow."

"Good. For now, we all need to rest. I expect you all to be ready to go in the morning." The king's eyes swept the room and, with a bob of his head, he strode out, leaving them with the Edessan pirates and the tatters of a plan.

Chapter 8

Ailsa scrubbed her hands over her face and sank onto the edge of her bed. To say it had been a long day was an understatement.

The road ahead stretched in front of her. Travel to the Forest of Frith. Find Maalik and convince him to come with her. Go north and find…

"Witches," Ailsa said with disbelief. As if selkies and faeries and demons weren't enough. Now there were witches.

Are you scared? Ishbel whispered, almost gleefully.

"Should I be?" Ailsa asked.

Her spirit guide paused, seeming to mull this over. *The journey will be tough, but you should not fear the witches.*

"What do you know about them?"

I know many things, but whether I choose to tell them to you is another story.

Ailsa scowled. "Sometimes I do wonder whose side you're on."

I am on my side. It so happens that I cannot live on without you, so I am invested in your wellbeing.

"You realise that makes you sound like a parasite?"

Have I ever harmed you?

Ailsa thought back to the first time she felt a supernatural force was controlling her. She had been on an Avalognian ship and Ishbel had wrestled her powers from her in a bid to sink them. Ailsa played the memory through, including the horror when she'd realised she couldn't stop the destruction. She knew Ishbel was witnessing the scene, too.

You survived, didn't you? Came a tart reply. Then Ailsa sensed the spirit withdraw, going back to wherever she was when not inside Ailsa's head.

"Ailsa?" Cameron's voice called from the other room.

She sighed and pushed herself up, ripping off the rest of her jewellery before joining him.

Cam was leaning on the side of the couch, chewing one nail. Iona sat poised on her side while Harris was pacing back and forth. Angus was nowhere to be seen.

"I don't like this," Iona said. "The idea of us all splitting up."

Ailsa sighed. "We have to—there's too much ground to cover to find the Treasures. At least we'll be together aboard the captain's ship before she drops us where we need to be."

Harris kicked his boots off and threw himself onto the couch with a swish of his kilt. "So, Angus and Iona are going to Kilvaig. I'm going to Ephraim with Irené and Ailsa is heading into the Forest of Frith and on to Monadh?"

"I don't suppose you could do with someone tagging along with you?" Cameron asked, raising his eyes to Ailsa's.

Ailsa's insides clenched. "Actually, I think it's best if I go north by myself. You should go with Iona and Angus. I'm sure they would appreciate a navigator since you'll be travelling the furthest by land." Seeing Cameron's face fall, she almost took it back. *No, there's no way I can bring him.* She was not going to risk her brother's life when she'd just found him again.

"Of course," Iona said quickly. "We'd love to have you with us."

Ailsa caught the selkie's eye, sending her a silent thank you.

"That settles it," said Harris. "We'll all go with the captain, dropping you three off at Inshmore. Ailsa and I will split up when we get to the east coast."

"And we'll all meet back in Dunrigh with the Four Treasures," Iona said brightly.

Ailsa bit her lip. "Ready to save the world?"

"How hard could it be?" Harris asked with a grin.

Ailsa did not share their enthusiasm. The last time they'd been at the faerie court, one of their own had died. And the last time she'd wandered into the Forest of Frith, a horde of superstitious villagers had captured her and sacrificed her to a demon. Of the three options, Kilvaig seemed the safest. *I hope so*, she thought, flicking her gaze to Cameron.

"A lot harder than if we had the Stone of Destiny," she said.

Harris shrugged. "At least we have the Cauldron of Life."

"I was thinking about that," said Iona with a frown. "You're heading to Ephraim, right?"

"Yes..." Harris said slowly.

"Where the most powerful earth fae in the world is currently trapped?"

Cameron's head snapped up, as his face drained of colour, but it was Harris that spluttered out, "Are you saying we should try to recruit Nicnevan to fight for us? You know that'll never happen. She's evil, Iona. We don't want to give Nicnevan a magical weapon."

Iona flicked a piece of lint off her dress. "I'm not saying that. I was only wondering if she'd be able to answer some questions, point us in the right direction. If the Sword of Light was in Ephraim, she'd know about it."

Harris shook his head. "She's too dangerous."

"A few drops of cauldron water won't set her free

completely, but it would be enough to remove the curse so she can speak. I can bottle some for you."

"I don't like that idea," said Cameron.

"Me neither," Iona sighed. "But we don't have the luxury of time. From what the princess said, these Soul-Eaters are much worse than the Faerie Queen ever was."

Ailsa shivered. If that was true, they were in big trouble. Still, there were other things to worry about first. "Would you be able to make up another bottle for me?"

Iona turned to Ailsa. A muscle ticked in her jaw, as though she was deciding whether to ask what it was for. She seemed to decide against it. "Of course," she finally said.

Harris flopped his head back into the cushions as if he'd fall asleep right there on the couch now that the conversation was over. "Okay, so we're all agreed."

Sleep tugged at Ailsa's edges, too.

Just as she was about to excuse herself, the doors swung open and Angus trudged into the room, carrying a bundle of fabric. He set it down on the coffee table with a huff. "I swear, Duncan needs to fire all his advisors. They're too old and too set in their ways. As soon as my brother left, they were all over him for information."

"How are things downstairs?" Ailsa asked. *How many casualties?*

"A few serious injuries, but most easily healed. The explosion was meant to distract us, not cause lots of deaths." He scratched his head, ruffling the hair into even more of a mess. "Anyway, Duncan is doing his best to get things ready for tomorrow."

"What are those?" asked Cameron, pointing to the bundle.

Angus only managed a small blush. "Travelling clothes;

courtesy of the crown." He rustled through the fabric, separating them into piles. "Seems my brother wants us to travel in a bit more style than last time."

Ailsa accepted a pile from the prince, marvelling at the efficiency. The jacket was made of a thick, navy velvet, embroidered with flowers, but underneath Ailsa could feel strong boiled leather, cut into strips so that she could move easily. Along with the jacket, there was a woollen cloak, a couple of pairs of trousers and tan knee-high boots.

"I believe your brother thinks we're going to a ball," Ailsa said, holding up a white linen shirt.

"You don't appreciate fine clothing." Iona separated out her own bundle of garments, revealing a very similar outfit to Ailsa's, but with shades of teal that complemented her hair. "It makes sense to dress finely. It opens a lot of doors."

"And makes us incredibly easy to pick out," Ailsa said, sucking on a tooth. At least the cloak was dark and subtle. She'd be able to hide the frippery underneath it. "And he had this lying around?"

"He had planned to kit us out before this. Wear them or don't." Angus shrugged. "Now, I'm off to bed before I get intercepted by another snotty official." And then he was gone, looking half asleep already, as he shouldered his way through the doors.

"I'm glad I'm not royalty," Ailsa said, scooping up her clothing. "I'm going to sleep too." She stopped by Cameron, who had gone pale again. "Are you going to be okay?"

"Fine," he said, straightening. "It'll be good to be out on the road, doing something useful." But he didn't look at her as he tossed a *'night'* over his shoulder and slunk off to his room.

He's annoyed you didn't want him to come, whispered

Ishbel.

Well, that can't be helped.

Harris and Iona were bickering on the couch when Ailsa left them to it. There were things she still had to do, still had to plan, before leaving the next day. And she wasn't going to tell anyone what they were because there was no way they'd let her go if they knew.

Chapter 9

Iona crept along the corridor, knowing full well she should be in bed. But if she was going to be leaving Dunrigh for the foreseeable future, she couldn't resist sneaking down to the darkened hall, to stare up at a younger version of herself.

The painting was small and unassuming. Most people would walk past it without a second glance. After all, there were far grander portraits of King Duncan's grandfather. King Alasdair had been a renowned leader and warrior. He had won many battles and brokered many more peace treaties. But that wasn't the man in the picture. Not really.

The Alasdair that gazed upon Iona in the painting was young and carefree. He hadn't had to think of diplomacy or what was best for his kingdom. He had been a mere prince then, and a second son at that. The chances of him becoming king were so slim, most of his family paid him no mind. He had been free to do whatever he wanted, to go wherever he wanted.

Iona remembered the summer the picture portrayed. She had met Alasdair at a ceilidh. He'd been hard to miss, with his shirt rumpled from dancing and his infectious smile. It was only when they'd been close enough that she'd noticed his eyes, one blue and one brown. She found she couldn't stop staring at them as they twirled through the ballroom. A few dances in and he was whisking her off to the gardens to talk under the stars. She'd whispered in his ear about how beautiful the sky was away from the capital. It had seemed like nothing to pack up and run off to the coast together. Until Alasdair's brother had died and he'd been made king.

Iona reached out a finger to trace the brush strokes. Alasdair had written to her every month, even after his arranged marriage. And she had never replied. Instead, she floated around Struanmuir, heartbroken, as news reached her of his wedding, then the birth of his daughter and his son. She had almost crumbled when she'd heard of the death of the Queen. Finally, she had received a letter, not from Alasdair, but from his son, informing her of his father's death. Murdered in his tent one night in the middle of a war.

She scrunched her hands into fists and tore her gaze away from the print. *Why do you keep doing this to yourself?* It had been over twenty years since Alasdair had died. It didn't help to dwell on it. Inhaling deeply, she turned away.

There were other portraits hanging on the walls, and she glanced at them as she passed. Pictures of Alasdair's children and grandchildren, as well as landscapes of Eilanmòr, were thrown up haphazardly.

She searched every face of the McFeidhs in the portraits, and still she couldn't see it. None resembled Alasdair. The noses were too pointed, their hair too dark. And none had inherited his mismatched eyes. Somehow, they'd got their looks from their mothers.

Before leaving the hall, Iona had one last thought, one she hardly ever allowed herself to entertain.

What would our children have looked like?

Then she shut that thought back deep inside her mind and went up to bed.

Chapter 10

Cameron MacAra rarely dreamed, but when he did, it was always the same.

He was in his mother's cottage, on the outskirts of town. The house smelled of pine from all the furniture that adorned the space; it was simple, made from the trees surrounding the property. The sun shone through the one window, lighting up dust motes like fireflies. He lay in the bed they shared, rubbing the scratchy wool throw against his face as he watched his mother pace from the hearth to the couch and back again. In her arms was a baby.

He would have been about three years old, perhaps too young to actually remember this. Yet, the scene was burned into his brain. His mother had been up for days with the baby, trying her best to soothe her as she cried.

Cameron remembered resenting the squawking thing in his mama's arms. His mother hadn't hugged him for days. She barely did anything but rock the baby. Cameron's grandmother had turned up a day into the crying, offering to take him away for a while. But his mother had refused. Cameron was secretly glad. His granny's home smelled like spoiled milk, and she was quick to anger.

Now he sat huddled in the bed, as the baby's cries grew steadily weaker and weaker. And he knew. Knew that his little sister would stop screaming soon. And when that happened, it meant something terrible.

"Cam," his mother said, her voice hoarse. "Why don't you go outside to play?"

He blinked once, taking in his mama's tired face. Her hair, which had escaped her plait to become a halo of golden brown around her head. Her eyes, which were red and sunken. He almost told her no. That he wanted to stay in bed. But you should do what adults tell you, shouldn't you?

"Okay, mama," he said, climbing out of his nest. He didn't have many toys, but that didn't matter. He'd find a stick or something outside and hit things. Not the beehives, though, never those.

As he passed his mother, she ran a hand over his hair. He looked up at her and smiled. Maybe she was going to leave the baby and play with him? But her eyes were still on the bundle in her arms.

His sister was small, despite being just over a year old. He'd seen other babies in the village: plump, little goblins which cooed and grabbed. His sister did none of those things. When she wasn't crying, she lay mute in her crib.

"Go on," his mother said.

And so he ran out the door into the small garden. Immediately, he felt better. His sister's cries had been smothered. There was no longer the oppressive wrongness pushing down on him.

First, he chased the chickens about their garden, picking up the feathers they dropped and rubbing them against his cheek. He found a stick under the big tree and walked around, hitting it against the fence posts. He was about to drop it to go searching for earthworms in the dirt, when he noticed something move outside the garden.

Beyond the fence was a thin stretch of heather-land, before the forest started. Cameron liked the woods. They smelled good and his mother liked to take him there on walks. He would pretend he was a bear or a squirrel, looking for a home for the winter.

It was in the forest that he saw the movement. He let go of his stick and peered through the fence, trying to glimpse whatever it was. Sometimes he saw deer in the woods. Was it one of those? Eventually, after straining his eyes for a moment, he saw it. It looked like a man. A very hairy man. The figure had been hard to spot because the hair which covered his entire body was dark, blending into the shadows between the trees. It was only when the man turned his bright red eyes on Cameron that he saw him.

"Hello," Cameron called out. It was always polite to say this first. "Who are you?"

The hairy man stumbled forward until he was at the forest edge. In a gruff voice, he said, "Hello, nice to meet you."

Cameron thought this was a good start, even if the man hadn't answered his question.

"Where is your mother?" asked the stranger. He had an odd accent. It didn't sound like anyone else in the village.

"She's inside with the baby," Cameron told him. "She's sick."

"Who is? Your mother?" The man seemed upset at this.

"No," Cameron said, shaking his head. "My sister. She's sick."

From inside the house, the sound of wailing punctured the air, as the baby confirmed Cameron's point.

"How sick is she?" the man asked. He held a bundle in his arms, and Cameron thought he saw it move.

"Very sick," Cameron said.

"I see. And how is your mother?"

"She's sad."

The man frowned and looked Cameron up and down. "When was the last time you ate?"

Cameron thought about this. He wasn't really sure. He'd been eating at odd hours since the baby had become sicker.

"Are you hungry?" asked the stranger.

He was always hungry.

"I have some food here, if you want it. But you'll have to come here and get it, I can't leave the forest."

"I'm not supposed to leave the garden," Cameron told the man. But he was so hungry.

"That's a good rule," the hairy stranger said. "And after this you should always follow it. You also shouldn't talk to strangers. But I promise you, I will not harm you. I only want to look after you while your mother is watching the baby."

This seemed sensible. Cameron walked round to the gate and lifted the latch. Then, quickly, before the chickens could follow, he slipped through and closed it behind him. The sounds of crying nipped at his heels, pushing him away from the cottage. It was only a quick scramble through the heather before he reached the forest edge, and the creature who waited for him.

Now that he was up close, the man's red eyes glowed eerily in the shadows. But Cameron soon forgot to be scared when the man produced a bag filled to the brim with food.

"I was going to have a picnic," the stranger explained. "Would you like to join us?"

"Us?" Cameron asked, tilting his head.

The man sat down against a boulder and carefully laid the bundle in his arms across his knees. Cameron crept closer, hoping that it was an animal, perhaps a puppy. Instead, the cloth folded back, revealing another baby.

This one was not screaming. Instead, it blinked its big blue eyes, ringed with dark lashes, up at him. It was a lot bigger than his sister, sitting up on its own and everything. Its rounded cheeks had a rosy glow, but on one of them there was a weird mark.

"What's that?" Cameron asked, pointing to the baby's face.

"A birthmark," the man said. He smiled down at the little bundle. "She's good and healthy though." He picked out a jar and a spoon from the bag of food and the baby kicked her feet inside her blankets. "Go on," the man said, gesturing to the bag. "Take anything you want." He began to feed the baby big spoonfuls of something brown and squishy.

Cameron picked out some bread and sat munching on it as he watched the infant. The food seemed to be getting everywhere except her mouth. She had bits of it on her nose, on her chin and even down the clothes she was in. The hairy man scooped the extra bits back into the spoon, feeding her bit by bit. And all while she ate, she blinked those enormous eyes around her, looking from the forest, to Cameron, to the big, grey man. Now and then she let out a squeal. But it wasn't an unpleasant sound. It was almost like laughter.

"Is it your baby?" Cameron asked as he ate. Babies usually belonged to mothers, after all.

"No," said the man. "I'm looking after her for a bit."

"Does she like to play?" Cameron had always wanted to play with his own sister, but she'd been too sick.

"I'm sure she does. Though she can't walk yet."

Cameron nodded, casting his mind around for a toy. As far as he knew, babies didn't like sticks. He rose from his spot, running back down to the garden to collect some things.

When he made it back, he spread everything out on the blanket in front of the baby. She had unwrapped herself and sat propped up against the hairy man's leg.

"Look," Cameron said, holding up a flower he'd plucked from the side of the house. The baby grabbed at it, squishing the petals in her hands, and cackled.

Undeterred, he lifted a feather from his pile and grabbed her pudgy hand, stroking it over her skin. She stopped laughing, and watched what he was doing, enraptured.

"I think she likes it," said the man.

Over the course of the next hour, Cameron stuffed himself full of food while he entertained the infant, hiding behind trees and tickling her toes. All the while she laughed, her little gurgles almost drowning out the cries from his house.

Finally, he sat beside the hairy man, with the baby lying down on her blanket between them.

"Do you like her?" asked the stranger.

"Yes, she's fun," Cameron answered.

The man sighed. "She needs a home."

"Can't she stay with you?"

"I wish I could keep her. But babies need to live in houses. I don't have one."

Cameron bit his lip and thought for a moment before deciding. "She could live in our house?"

"Would you mind?" asked the stranger. His teeth were sharp, but his smile was friendly.

"No, I can play with her all the time."

"Maybe," the man said, looking through the trees at Cameron's cottage. "For now, we'll let her sleep. And you can eat some more food."

Cameron grinned, rooting about in the bag once again. He hadn't realised that the crying had stopped.

Chapter 11

Angus did not sleep well that night. Every time he closed his eyes, another explosion would flash in his mind. He tossed and turned until finally the sun was up and he gave up his fight.

The castle was still at dawn. No one was milling around, not even the servants. *Probably on Duncan's orders,* he thought. If he had been in charge, he would have confined everyone to their rooms for safety.

He avoided the ballroom, not wishing to see the carnage dealt to the castle. This was his home, and if he was going to leave it for weeks on end, he'd rather remember the good parts. Instead, he made his way outside to his favourite place.

Angus had always loved the smell of the horse stables. Others often thought the hay and animal fur were unpleasant but there was something comforting—nostalgic—in the musky odour. He'd grown up riding a fat little pony called Puddle, and moved up to towering and powerful Akrosii horses, imported and expensive.

But the horse which now stood in the stables was another beast altogether. Her huge chestnut body gleamed in the morning sunlight. She was muscled and heavy, a creature designed more for strength than speed. Yet, she'd gone faster than any horse he'd ridden when he'd tested her in the castle grounds. Her head almost touched the ceiling when she looked up at his entrance. A single band of white fur led from her sniffing nose, past intelligent eyes, up to the horn atop her brow. The unicorn watched him intently as he approached, hardly moving except for the muscle ticking in her neck.

"I have a feeling you're not here for a visit." Though her mouth didn't move, Angus heard her voice inside his head. It was confident, amused.

"I take it you heard what happened last night?" he asked, dropping the bucket of food he'd been carrying. The contents sloshed about inside, catching Laire's attention.

She nudged her door open, tramping forward on legs that ended in hooves the size of dinner plates. Angus had carefully instructed the stable keeps not to lock Laire's door when they'd first arrived. She was not a tame pet. She could come and go as she pleased. "Is that for me?" she asked.

Angus waved to the bucket, and she dug in. Immediately, the blaze on her snout turned red with the blood flicking up from her meal. Someone had tried to feed the unicorn carrots and had almost had their hand chomped off. In fact, that had been a common occurrence in the first few days of Laire's stay. She barely tolerated anyone but Angus, so he'd had to take over her care himself. Not that he minded, of course. She was better company than any of the other horses.

"I heard a blast and the ground shook," she said around a mouthful of meat.

"There was an explosion. Someone stole the Stone of Destiny."

Laire raised her head up from the bucket. "So you plan to get it back?"

"That and some other weapons." He leaned against the stall. "I was wondering if you'd come with me?"

"I am in your debt," Laire said, tossing her head.

Once Laire had finished her food, she raised her head towards him and waited. Angus smiled, dipping a sponge into the water trough. With great care, he dabbed at the blood on her muzzle until the sponge was pink with it. "You've become soft," he teased. "I think you're getting used to being a prince's pet."

Laire snapped at the air in front of her, pretending to bite, but he could hear her chuckle in his head. "You do spoil me so. Perhaps I won't go back to being a wild unicorn."

"You can stay with me as long as you like."

"Who else is coming along?" she asked.

"Ailsa, Iona, Harris, Cameron—"

"Ooh?"

He frowned. "Don't say a word."

"Did you work up the nerve to speak to him yet?"

Angus pursed his lips. "We danced at the ceilidh—"

"That's—"

"Iit didn't go well. He almost fainted." Even now, Angus couldn't fight the cringe that shivered down his spine.

Laire let out a snicker. "I'd say that did go well, if he fainted in your arms."

Angus sighed. "He almost fainted because he had a vision of the explosion—before it occurred. Something happened to him in Ephraim…"

"You'll work it out. In the meantime, if he has to ride me on our journey, I suppose I'll let him."

Angus smirked. "Very generous of you."

One of her huge hooves stamped on the ground, sending hay and dust into the air. "It is indeed an honour to ride a unicorn. Don't you forget it."

"Come on, we'd better get ready. We'll be leaving soon." He reached up to the saddle rack, groaning under the weight of the only one which fit Laire.

"You'd better not be expecting me to wear that."

"It's easier to ride if you do."

Laire watched him come closer, pawing at the ground with her front foot. A thrill of fear shot through Angus. She really was a gigantic animal.

As soon as he was in touching distance, her body gave a tremendous shudder and she sank to the ground. "You are extremely fortunate that I like you, prince."

Angus didn't doubt that luck for a moment. He only worried when it would run out.

Chapter 12

Ailsa stared up at the ribbon tied to the tall tree in the courtyard as she waited for her companions to join her. When she'd first arrived in Dunrigh, she'd been told the colours of the fabric meant something. Blue for health. Green for prosperity. Or something like that. Most of them were white, probably tied up there after the late king had died. But near the bottom were older ones, their silks bleached of their colour, their ends frayed. Had the people who had tied them there got their wishes? Or had they at least felt better for the action? Thinking about their journeys, she briefly considered asking Angus what colour of ribbon to tie there for luck. But luck wasn't something a tree could give you. It was something you made yourself.

You'd think you'd be a little superstitious by now, Ishbel whispered into her ear.

Ailsa swatted the air beside her, trying to waft the spirit guide away. But they both knew that was impossible.

"How do you feel about being stuck with me?" Ailsa asked Ishbel, suddenly curious. When Maalik had explained she had a spirit guide, he hadn't ever really explained how she'd come by one.

Ishbel paused for a moment before answering. *I used to have a body once,* the spirit said. *And now I'm inside your head. I'd rather be a voice in your ear than not exist at all.*

"But why me?" Ailsa asked.

She could practically see Ishbel smirk when she answered. *You'll see.*

Ailsa gritted her teeth together. "You'd think you'd want to tell me these things. You are my guide after all."

But I'm not your mother. Never forget that, girl. I want to protect you, to keep you alive, but that doesn't mean I can't have a bit of fun while I'm doing it.

Ailsa gripped the axe at her hip. "Why did you want me to go to Monadh?" she asked, knowing already that the spirit wouldn't answer directly.

You'll see, Ishbel said again. Ailsa sensed her withdraw, sneaking away to wherever.

A noise broke Ailsa from her thoughts. Iona was walking across the courtyard, carrying her pack. "Were you talking to someone?" she asked.

Ailsa sighed. "Just myself."

"I do that all the time," Iona laughed. "As usual, we're waiting on all the boys. And my brother says I'm high maintenance."

Ailsa pressed her lips into a thin line. "I think your brother is a little distracted," she said, remembering the way Harris had stared after the Edessan princess the night before.

Iona understood what she meant. "And what do you think about that?" she asked.

"I mean, it makes things easier for me," Ailsa said with a shrug. "Honestly? I'm finding his behaviour quite grating. I only just talked to him about... feelings."

Iona placed a hand on Ailsa's elbow. "I know. Though, you did have an entire month," she said softly. "And I think he knew what you're going to say already."

"You're right," Ailsa said. "It's all so messy."

Iona looked back towards the castle. "What do you think of the captain?"

"First impressions? I want to like her, but I'm not certain she's telling the truth. She backed me up when a Mirandelli was trying it on. Though I'm not sure why she's so intent on helping us."

Iona considered this. "She said herself that this is a threat to the whole of Ossiana. I think she's seeing the bigger picture."

As though their discussion had summoned them, the captain and her crew ambled out of the castle doors and across the courtyard. Now that Irené wasn't at a party, she looked every inch a pirate queen.

Privateer, Ailsa corrected in her head. Though she didn't really see the difference. The rapier at Irené's side was as sharp as any she'd seen. The captain wore a long brown coat over her travelling clothes, and a tricorn hat atop her braids. Next to her vibrantly coloured hair, her clothing was almost drab. But it was perfect for spending weeks at sea. The rest of the Edessans were similarly dressed, though none wore any hats, as if that honour was only reserved for the captain.

Irené said something to the large man from the night before and raised her fingers to her lips letting out a piercing whistle. She seemed to wait, looking up to the sky until something came soaring down from the castle parapets and landed on her outstretched arm.

"An eagle?" Iona guessed as the Edessans approached.

The bird the captain carried was massive. Its belly and neck were gleaming white, but the feathers on its wings were a rich bronze. Irené reached out a single finger to stroke its neck. "Duende is an osprey," she clarified.

"I don't think I've ever seen someone with a tame osprey," Iona said, in awe.

The captain shrugged. "He's not very tame, but he does come when he's called. Most of the time."

The bird tilted its head, watching them through it's golden eyes.

"He's beautiful," Ailsa told her truthfully. She'd never seen a bird of prey so close before. Back at her beach, there had only ever been puffins with their waddling little bodies. Next to them, Duende was magnificent.

"You'll give him a big head, and he won't be able to fly," Irené laughed. "Are you both ready to go?"

"Yeah, we were waiting for Angus, Harris and Cameron." Ailsa looked to the doors, expecting them to come walking through, but they were taking their sweet time.

"Well, while we wait, we'll see if we can have the wagons brought round." Irené waved to her gunner, who peeled off toward the stables.

"Wagons?" asked Ailsa.

Irené put the hand that wasn't holding Duende on her hip. "You didn't think I would make you walk, did you?"

By the time three covered carts, pulled by horses, turned up in the courtyard, Cameron and Harris had arrived. Ailsa watched them approach, their arms bumping against each other as they walked, laughing and looking like they had been friends for years. Cameron was half an inch taller than Harris, his body slightly more muscular, despite being a captive for much longer. They both wore similar travelling clothes. Ailsa wondered for a moment if they looked more like soldiers in uniform or a band of minstrels with matching costumes.

"Good morning," Harris said, smiling widely.

Irené arched her brow. "Now it isn't," she grumbled so that only Ailsa could hear.

Oh, the captain did not like Harris! Whatever impression he'd made last night, it had been a bad one.

Ailsa couldn't help but smirk.

"Nice to see someone is excited for an adventure," Harris chirped.

"I don't know," Cameron said. "Ailsa has been grinning like that since she was little, and it's never ended well for me." He reached out to hook his arm about her, giving her a squeeze.

Ailsa fought the urge to pull away. It was still strange to have her brother hold her like that—like no time had passed. But she relaxed into his side. *You already let him down once in the last day.*

"Have you seen Angus?" Iona asked, looking behind them.

Before they could answer, the prince appeared from the direction of the stables, a massive horse walking by his side. Ailsa had only seen Laire a handful of times since they'd arrived back in Dunrigh, and she was even bigger than she'd remembered. She wore a saddle on her back but no bridle, as if that had been one step too far. Angus spoke in a low voice to the unicorn, reassuring her, no doubt. Irené's crew watched in silent awe as the creature approached. Even the captain seemed speechless.

"Morning," Angus greeted them. "Sorry we're late."

"Is that—" Irené began, her gaze sweeping over the unicorn's silken fur.

"This is Laire." Angus reached up to place a hand at Laire's neck. The unicorn leaned into his touch.

"And I thought Duende here was impressive," Irené said. "How did you come by a unicorn as a pet?"

Angus smiled. "Laire isn't my pet, I'm hers."

The next hour was spent checking the supplies, the wagons, and the horses. Ailsa sat under the gigantic tree, allowing it to shade her from the intermittent sunshine. She knew she could easily pull clouds over the sky, but that seemed selfish. Everyone else was probably enjoying the heat. Instead, she allowed the weather to do its own thing as she watched everyone ready for the journey.

Angus, Iona and Cameron were clustered around Laire as she sat on the cobblestones, her chestnut hair gleaming in the sun. Only Angus touched the unicorn, leaning against her great body while Cam and Iona looked at the map between them, planning their journey.

Harris had removed his jacket and pushed his sleeves up, revealing his freckled arms as he helped Irené's crew tie things into the three wooden wagons. All the while, he kept one eye on the captain. Irené appeared to be doing everything in her power to avoid him.

More of Irené's crew milled about the courtyard than Ailsa had seen the night before. There had to be at least thirty people, all dressed in similar loose clothing to the captain. Most were Edessan, like Irené, though Ailsa was sure she had heard snatches of Visenyan and Akrossi accents. It made Ailsa wonder how big the ship was. Surely larger than the tiny sailing boats she'd always spotted near her beach? Would she be able to find a spot to be alone or would they be packed in?

Cameron plopped down beside her, kicking his legs out in front of him. "What are you thinking?" he asked by way of greeting.

About how to escape everyone, she almost blurted out. *No, don't say that.*

"What do you think the ship will be like?" she asked instead.

Cam shrugged. "I don't know: sails, masts, lots of wood?"

"Have you been on many?" The last one she'd been on had been the Avalognian ship she'd sunk. *Perhaps I'm bad luck.*

"Sure," Cameron said. "I've been to almost every country. Had to get there somehow."

Ailsa felt a stab of jealousy. She'd never left Eilanmòr. That had been Cam's life once he'd escaped their grandmother. "Which country was your favourite?"

He looked up at the swaying branches, the flapping ribbons. "Would you believe me if I said Eilanmòr?"

Ailsa snorted. "You're just saying that to make your country bumpkin sister feel better."

"I'm not! I think we can sometimes forget how beautiful our home country is. One day I'll take you to the islands. Lahinish has the cleanest beaches you'll ever see. Jay has stunning mountains—"

"I used to see them from my beach," Ailsa cut in, remembering the views from her coastal home. "To think, you could have been there when I was looking out over the ocean."

Cameron smiled, but it didn't reach his eyes. "There are so many regrets I have in life, Ailsa, but my biggest is that I didn't find you before now." He placed a hand over his mouth, staring off into the distance. "If I had, I could have protected you."

"That would have been nice, but I learned to protect myself. I'm pretty good with an axe now," she said, attempting to pull him away from his melancholy.

It almost worked. "You were always pretty scrappy, even

when we were kids." He nudged his knee into hers, pressing his lips into an attempt at a grin. "I'm glad you're my sister."

Ailsa could have imagined it, but she thought there had been a slight emphasis on the '*you're*'. I'm glad *you're* my sister. As in, *I'm glad it's you and not someone else.*

And that, Ailsa thought as they climbed into the wagons, ready to depart Dunrigh, was something she'd always hoped to hear.

Chapter 13

Harris watched field after field roll by, the breeze ruffling his hair as the wagon procession trundled on. They'd been going for a few hours now and the landscape had changed little. This side of Dunrigh was all farmland with cultivated pockets of trees, used for logging. Corridors had been cut into the evergreens to limit fires spreading. Harris imagined himself up on the hills, running through them as the pines towered above. The ground would be a wonderful, scented carpet, covered in tree needles, bleached of their green by the beating sun. Perhaps he'd run past animals there too: scrabbling squirrels the same copper colour as his hair; wood pigeons cooing indignantly; or even a deer carving up the bark with its antlers.

A knee nudged his own, breaking his daydream. Iona was bundled up beside him on the open top wagon. In the next one down, he knew Ailsa and Cameron were sitting in a similar position. It was only Angus who rode outside on his unicorn. Lucky sod. Though, it was probably for the best. If the unicorn had let Harris ride her, he'd be off like a shot, and wouldn't come back.

"How are you doing?" asked Iona, always the mother hen.

Harris glanced at his sister. Despite the late night and the worry, she looked well. Maybe it was the fresh air which had brought a rosy glow to her pale skin, or maybe it was being out of Dunrigh. There were too many ghosts in Eilanmòr's capital for her.

"Just as well as I was the last time you asked me."

Iona pursed her lips. "Do you want to talk about—"

"-Stop your stirring. I'm fine." He cast around to change the subject from the changeling in the wagon behind them. "Besides, I've set my sights on someone else."

Iona snorted. "You can't possibly mean the captain?"

"Why not?"

"I don't think she likes you very much."

"I'll admit I put my foot in it last night, but she hardly knows me." *But I'm going to change that.* Irené had captured his attention the moment he'd laid eyes on her. It wasn't merely her beauty or the graceful way she moved, it was like something else hid under her skin, something that called to him. She practically glowed with it. Did everyone else see it too, or was he the only one?

"I don't want to see you hurt so soon after getting dumped," Iona said.

Harris resisted the urge to pinch his sister. "I wasn't dumped. We had a mutual agreement not to continue pursuing a relationship."

Iona rolled her eyes. "Whatever."

Well, that was a strangely brief bout of nagging. "Are you alright?"

She ran her fingers through her curls, playing with the ends as she watched the countryside go past. "I'm worried about... everything. About the explosion last night. Finding the Four Treasures and splitting up. And I miss home."

Home. Where there was nothing to do but drift or bask in the sun. Struanmuir was the home of the biggest selkie colony in Ossiana, located a stone's throw away from Eilanmòr's west coast. Iona and Harris had grown up there, raised by their two aunts since before Harris could remember.

Their Aunt Caitlyn and Aunt Isla were two of the most respected selkie leaders in recent times. It had been Isla who had hidden the Stone of Destiny before she'd passed away, leaving Harris as the only person who knew its whereabouts. The last time they'd been in Struanmuir, Aunt Caitlyn had sent them off to rescue the stone again. How long ago had that been now? Almost two months? Too long for a selkie to spend away from home.

"You could, if you wanted to, sit this one out," Harris told Iona. "All it would take would be an hour's swim."

His sister sighed. "I can't leave them to do this alone."

"Yeah, me neither. Guess we're stuck being heroes."

Iona nudged him again. "You love it really."

One last task, one last adventure, and then, Harris vowed, he'd go back to Struanmuir and float.

By the time they stopped to make camp, Harris's ass was numb. He'd tried every seating position he could think of, but the constant jolting of the wheels on the uneven road had made the latter half of the journey quite uncomfortable. Iona had somehow fallen asleep beside him and he envied her. She'd used her pack as a pillow and her cloak as a blanket, curling up at Harris's side for warmth. Despite the summer's day, the wind had picked up, icy cold as it swept in from the sea. Harris couldn't help but wonder what Ailsa was thinking about and if she was unknowingly manipulating the weather like she used to do before she knew about her magic. Or maybe it was just a chilly day.

Once the wagons had come to a stop, Harris shook his sister awake and climbed down onto the grassy plain, kicking his legs to get some sensation back. Many of the crew were already assembling tents and starting fires but he found Ailsa and Cameron at the edge of the field.

A fence separated them from a herd of dozy cows. The twilight sun shone on the creatures' red shaggy coats while they munched on the grass. One had lifted its great horned head so that Ailsa could pet its pink nose.

"I didn't realise you still had a thing for gingers," Harris said lightly as he came to stand beside them.

Ailsa scowled. "They're stupid beasts, but I suppose they're cute."

"Ouch. The cows and I will remember that next time you need saving." *Come on*, Harris wanted to say. *Tease me back. We're still friends, aren't we?*

But Ailsa only sniffed and said, "I can save myself."

"Do you two need me to leave?" asked Cameron.

"No," she said, too quickly.

Harris tried not to take it personally. At least she wasn't avoiding him now. That was progress, wasn't it?

In truth, he'd known during the journey back from Ephraim that something was wrong. Ailsa had built up her walls again, the ones that had been there when he'd first met her. *Give her space,* he'd told himself. He was just happy to be back. But then, Angus had told him about the demon. Harris didn't like to think of himself as jealous, but was that what he had felt? No, he was quite justified in his misgivings. Ailsa had been sacrificed to a demon, an evil fae, and had spent weeks with him. No matter what Angus had said about this Maalik being good, Harris couldn't quite bring himself to believe it.

I'll have that talk with her another time. For now, he'd let her have her space.

"Actually, I'm not staying," he said, clapping Cameron on the shoulder. "I'm starving after that wagon ride. I'll catch you both later." He strode off, not glancing back even when Ailsa and Cameron started their murmuring again.

Harris picked his way through the tents, towards the fire where the chef was spooning something onto tin camping plates. The scent of garlic and onions had Harris searching for the end of the queue. When he saw who stood there, he took a moment to run his fingers through his hair, to straighten his shirt. With deliberate casualness, he took the place behind the Princess of Edessa.

Irené was clutching an empty plate in her arms already, the huge osprey nowhere to be seen. She didn't notice Harris at first, allowing him to watch her for a moment. To assess. There was a slight droop to her shoulders as she stood there. They curved inward and Harris wondered if she'd been an awkward teenager, once upon a time. Well, they had that in common if it were true. He'd had an unfortunate case of acne in his early years that only disappeared when he was a seal. Even then, the soft pup fur had lingered a little too long.

Well, now Irené had nothing to be awkward about. Not only was she a princess, but a captain, too. If teenage Harris had met her as she was now, he didn't think he'd have been able to get one word out from nerves. But he wasn't that boy anymore. He'd charmed his way through all of Eilanmòr a few times over, trading dalliances with men, women and everyone in between.

Why was he so nervous now?

Speak to her, he told himself. But then he remembered the brief interaction they'd had. Could it be that Iona was right?

He mentally shook himself. *Don't be daft. Be friendly and—*

"Can I help you with something?" Irené said, glancing at him over her shoulder. "Or are you going to continue staring at me?"

"I was wondering if you had a map?" he spluttered.

"A map?" Irené said flatly.

"Because I got lost in your eyes." Even as the words came out, he cringed. So much for being charming.

She fixed him with a glare as sharp as knives. "My eyes were not what you were gawping at."

Harris shifted his feet and tried again. "You're so beautiful, I was working up the nerve to speak to you."

Irené didn't seem to believe him. "Is that a fact?"

"Yes, actually."

"I think you're full of crap."

This was not going well. "I'm trying to be friendly."

The captain turned to face him fully now, even as the line moved up without her. Harris tried not to shrink under the weight of her gaze.

"Oh, I know your type," she said, her accent thicker than before, turning her sentences up at the end. "You collect girls like trinkets, never meaning to be cruel, but breaking hearts nonetheless. You fancy yourself in love often, but when met with another pair of pretty eyes, you can easily be swayed in a different direction."

His heart was beating so hard he wondered if it was going to climb up his throat and out of his mouth. He'd probably offer it up to her, too. "You make me sound like a fiend," he said, pulling a lazy smile onto his lips.

"Aren't you?" she asked him.

"You don't know me, princess. I may be reckless and a flirt, but I'm loyal to my friends."

The captain raised a carefully manicured brow. "How many of their hearts have you broken?"

Harris squirmed and Irené smiled, vindicated. "Ah, see. Was it the prince? Or the girl?"

"Ailsa and I... I thought we had something," he said, sensing the conversation was getting away from him.

"But your eye went wandering?"

No, it seems hers did. Except, he knew that wasn't what happened, not really. If Ailsa hadn't met the demon, he knew, deep down, she still wouldn't want to be with him. He'd made too many mistakes, kept too many secrets. He snorted. "Why am I even trying to defend myself? You've clearly already made up your mind about me."

She shrugged. "My opinion of someone is based on action. If you don't act like the scoundrel I think you are, I'll change my mind. You can start by staying away from my crew." She turned back to the line, tossing the words over her shoulder.

"Oh, don't you trust your crew to look after themselves?"

Irené placed one hand on the sword at her hip. "They are my family. Many are young, impressionable. I will not take lightly to you trying to seduce any of them."

"Done and done. I just want to find the Stone of Destiny and get back to Eilanmòr." Deciding he wasn't hungry after all, he stalked away. *Maybe I'll come back when there are nicer people in line.*

"I'll be watching you, selkie-boy," the captain said to his retreating back.

And despite their argument, despite the things she'd accused him of, he couldn't help the thrill that shot through him at that.

Chapter 14

Angus spent that night under the stars, pressed up against Laire's warm body. The evening had been mild enough that the unicorn's body heat and his sleeping bag kept him comfortable. He watched the clouds swim across his vision, blocking the starlight for a few seconds at a time, and moving off again. He'd matched his breathing in time with Laire's until he'd fallen asleep.

His companions had been given tents close by, Iona and Ailsa in one and Harris and Cameron in another. He'd been surprised at that—he'd assumed they'd pair up as siblings—but Iona had grabbed Ailsa's arm, declaring they would have a sleepover. That had left Cameron and Harris to crawl into the next tent, leaving Angus with a sick churning in his stomach.

Jealous, he'd scolded himself. Harris and Cameron were friends. Still, he couldn't help watching them as they emerged the next day for signs beyond friendliness.

Harris had rolled out first, clipping the tent flap to the roof. His hair was mussed from sleep, and he squinted against the morning sun. He made his way over to Angus, who was still in the sleeping bag, savouring the last minutes of warmth before he had to get up.

"Your boyfriend snores," said the selkie, dropping onto the grass.

Angus snorted. "Are you sure you didn't wake yourself

up with your own snoring? I seem to remember it being deafening when we were off looking for the stone." Then he realised what Harris had said and spluttered out, "he's not my boyfriend."

"Sure," was all Harris said.

They watched the crew slowly dismantle the camp. The captain had said they weren't far from the coast. Indeed, Angus could almost smell the salt in the air.

"How are you feeling about going back to Ephraim?" he asked. If he had been captured and tortured, he didn't think he would have jumped at the chance like Harris had.

The selkie cupped his hands around his knees. "Honestly? I'm petrified."

"So why did you volunteer?" *Was it just because the captain had?*

"I don't want fear stopping me from doing anything," Harris said. "Did you know, once upon a time, before Nicnevan turned evil, the faerie court was home to all fae?"

"Even selkies?"

Harris nodded. "Though my kind spent most of their time out at sea, they'd always come back to Ephraim. It was a meeting place, for all the selkies and other fae." He sighed, closing his eyes. "Maybe one day it can be like that again."

"Not with Nicnevan as queen," said Angus. "Maybe you all need to pick new rulers."

"Rulers, eh?" Harris said, picking up on the plural. "If I didn't know better, I'd say you're advocating for a democracy, prince."

Angus squirmed. He knew his friend was only teasing, but the conversation was straying too close to treason for his liking. "It's something Duncan and I had discussed before he became king. A council of elected officials, deciding for the people. But now that he's in charge…" Angus shrugged. "Still, it could work for the fae?"

Harris flashed him a smile. "It's a good idea, but it's not that easy for us. The faerie crown is tied to its one true bearer by magic and blood. Only someone of Nicnevan's bloodline can wear it."

"So we'd have to find her daughter?"

"We don't need to find anyone," Harris sniffed. "I'm done with searching for a girl who doesn't want to be found. I'm sure Nicnevan has some sort of half cousin somewhere. Let someone else find them."

Angus bit the inside of his cheek. He and Duncan had many history lectures when they were boys with stories about the monarchy in other countries, tailored as lessons and warnings. Whenever the line of succession was called into question, war was inevitable. Would the same happen amongst the fae? If that was the case, he doubted it would only amount to a few skirmishes, easily squashed. No, this was a problem they'd have to face, eventually.

The tent shook as Cameron emerged, and suddenly Angus wasn't thinking about politics anymore. He rolled out, still in the process of dressing, unfolding himself in a fluid motion as he tugged his shirt on. Angus glimpsed bare skin as the fabric was pulled down and his cheeks grew hot.

Gods! He had to stop acting like a lovesick schoolboy. But it was hard to concentrate on whatever Harris was saying when the morning sunlight was illuminating the object of his affection like that. Cameron had changed so much since their time in the training camp. Where once he'd been a gangly youth, his muscles had filled out, his movements more self-assured. There were the piercings, the dyed hair, and the tattoo Angus had spyed on his shoulder. All decisions Cameron had made since he'd last seen him. All stories Angus wished he had been part of. Even the scars which covered every inch of his skin were testament to adventures he'd had while Angus had been stuck in Dunrigh.

Cameron caught sight of them and strolled over, pushing his sleeves up as he walked to reveal tanned forearms. Angus had to look away before he did something really embarrassing.

Harris was still talking, oblivious to how distracted Angus was. "...and then she said—Oh, morning Cam. Sleep well?"

Cameron sat on the grass near Laire's head. "You snore." He held out the back of his hand for the unicorn to sniff.

Angus had seen many people try to win favour with the unicorn. They often received a bite for their troubles. But Laire stared down at the proffered hand before slowly leaning her head down and giving it a nuzzle. Cameron didn't seem surprised.

"*He comes to visit me sometimes,*" Laire said, confirming his suspicions. Angus knew only he heard her voice, so he bit his tongue instead of teasing her. It seemed he wasn't the only one who had a crush.

As soon as they'd had some breakfast of sweetened porridge, they split up to help Irené's crew finish dismantling the camp. Before midday, they were off again, travelling down the road towards the coast. Cameron, Ailsa, Harris and Iona were nestled in the wagons behind him, leaving Angus to ride Laire. He mostly let her choose her path herself, so she alternated between following the procession and wandering off across the heathered hillocks.

The scrub had flowered, dusting the landscape with

purple blooms amongst the green stems. The colours of Clan McFeidh. His ancestors had chosen them because of this exact sight. The purple and green were woven into their kilts, painted on their flags and embroidered on their coat of arms, alongside the stag and the unicorn. It meant that, though the land was theirs, they too belonged to Eilanmòr.

Soon they were descending, drawing closer and closer towards the sea. A flock of gulls shrieked overhead and Laire broke into a canter, drawn by the sea-salt smell as he was. They crested over a hill, spotting the harbour down below. Angus scanned the horizon, looking for sails. There were none. Where was the ship?

"Perhaps it's round the headland?" he asked the unicorn. There was a sinking in his stomach. *Something is wrong.*

Angus whispered to Laire to hold back, letting the Edessan crew overtake them. Warily, he followed them down to the little port, keeping a close eye on the captain.

She had hopped off her own wagon, choosing to walk at the head of the party. The enormous bird of prey circled her before landing on her arm. Irené whispered something to the osprey, sending it flying off again, towards the water. The princess was smiling, eyes alight as she gazed after the bird. One of her crew, the short quartermaster with the headscarf covering his eye, said something and Irené threw her head back in laughter.

They seem relaxed. Still, Angus hung back until he was in line with the wagon carrying Ailsa and Cameron.

Finally, they were on the same level as the harbour. It was dotted with fishing boats, too small to fit such a large crew. But there was still no sign of their ship.

The group halted at the water's edge and his companions

hopped out of their wagons, coming to stand in a loose circle around the unicorn. Angus stayed on her back, his hand moving to his sword hilt as his mind whirred with possibilities. Had their ship been stolen? No, the crew were all smiling. *Have they led us here to kidnap us? Or kill us?*

The captain turned, grinning, to her guests and swept her hat from her head. "We're here."

Even Harris looked suspicious. "Where's your ship?"

But just as he spoke, there was a noise from the water. In the middle of the harbour, the sea bubbled and frothed as if a creature was thrashing under the surface. Laire took a step back, almost running into Iona. Angus's apology died on his lips, however, as something golden emerged from the deep.

Chapter 15

Ailsa couldn't believe her eyes as a strange machine emerged from the brine. "What is that?"

"My boat," Irené said with a smirk.

But it was like no boat that Ailsa had ever seen. There were no sails, no rigging. It looked more like a giant metal fish peeking out of the water. Ailsa looked closer and realised the bulbous eyes were actually windows.

"How are we supposed to sail on it?" asked Cameron. He'd turned so pale, Ailsa could no longer see his scars against his skin.

"You go inside," the quartermaster with the jangling earrings said. "There's a door."

Irené strode towards the dock, speaking to them over her shoulder as she walked. "The Nymph can sail faster than any other ship and can dive under the waves, making her completely undetectable. We call her a submarine."

Ailsa stumbled forward after the captain, her friends close on her heels. A couple of crew members were hauling some long pieces of wood from the side of the pier closest to the enormous contraption. *They're making a gangplank,* Ailsa realised. She and Cameron had often made each other walk on an imaginary one in their pirate games as children.

"That's some piece of engineering," Harris said, admiring the craft as it bobbed in the harbour.

Irené merely shrugged. "We're Edessans."

The petite sailing master gave a whistle and the metallic fish rose further out of the water until its front was close enough to the end of the pier for the crew to pull it in. Ailsa had to crane her head back to look up at the top, where the metal protruded like a fin. It was easily as tall as any ship's mast and half of it was still submerged. With a grinding noise, a hatch opened underneath the yellow windows like the mouth of the fish, allowing them all to peer inside. A cloud of steam hissed inside the gaping maw, and then it was gone, revealing sailors running around, cranking levers and hauling rope. When Ailsa had first seen the boat, she'd wondered how all the wagons would fit inside. Now, it was clear: the boat would have easily fit another ten in this first room alone.

"Please," Irené said, indicating the planks of wood which had now been placed across the gap from the pier to the hatch. "This way."

Ailsa felt her first flicker of fear. If they went inside, would the whole boat plunge under the water with them in it? How would the metal stop the thousands of gallons of water from pouring in and drowning them all?

She was not the only one to hesitate on the dock.

"I'm not sure Laire is going to like this," Angus said, stroking the unicorn's nose.

Laire whinnied and Angus looked at her intently, like he understood what she was trying to tell him.

"Are you sure?" he asked. "We could always ride there by ourselves."

The unicorn tossed her head, sending her black mane into an arc.

"What's she saying?" Cameron asked.

Angus sighed. "She says she'll be fine."

"And she will be." Cameron stroked the silky fur on the side of her neck. "We can always find somewhere stable to ride out the worst of the waves. Would you like that?"

Ailsa wasn't sure what the unicorn said in response, but Angus's eyes were like saucers. A small smile played about his lips as he gazed at Ailsa's brother.

"Maybe you and Laire should get a room," she said to Cameron. "I'm sure Angus wouldn't mind being there too…"

Angus blushed and led the unicorn across the gangway and in through the hatch, petting her shoulder as they entered.

Cameron gave Ailsa a shove. "Meddler," he muttered, before following the prince.

"Shall we?" Iona asked from beside her.

Ailsa eyed the vast structure dubiously. "Do I need to remind you I can't actually breathe underwater like some people? Are you sure this is safe?"

Iona grabbed her arm, tucking it around her own, and led Ailsa inside as if she was some skittish mule.

"Well, if it's not," Harris chuckled, hot on their heels, "At least you'll have had an adventure before you die."

Once they were all inside, Irené indicated a safe place for Laire, down in the hold, before leading them on a tour. The passageways were only wide enough to allow two people side by side and they seemed to be laid out without rhyme or reason, like a rabbit warren. The walls and floors were covered in hammered metal, held together by rivets, which Ailsa caught her arm on a few times in passing.

Irené pointed out rooms as she passed, some with doors and others with round hatches. "That's the mess hall and the kitchen through there. Julio, our cook, is getting set up for dinner. And that door is for the infirmary. Our surgeon, Egeria, is the woman with the green hair you might have spotted on our journey." She stopped in a long corridor lined with doors on either side. "These are the sleeping quarters. Choose any room that has a blank door. The others are owned by the crew." Ailsa noticed each door had been decorated. There was one with an Akrossi flag and another with flowers painted on the metal. Others had ribbons tied at the handles or torn out pages from books stuck there.

Irené led them up flights of stairs and along hallways until Ailsa was dizzy. Finally, when she thought they must be near the top of the boat, the captain paused before an ornate archway.

"This is the bridge," explained Irené. "If you're ever looking for me on our journey, I'll be in here." She led them into a much larger space than Ailsa was expecting after the narrow corridors. They came out onto a balcony of sorts that sat above the grand room below. A set of stairs curved down to the wooden floor, where a few desks were arranged in a circle. Each was covered in curious instruments. Some crew members were already down there, darting around, checking papers and peering at the objects. In the middle sat a giant golden globe, framed with rings of brass. And taking up most of the front wall were two immense windows.

This must be the fish's eyes I saw earlier, Ailsa realised.

The glass was yellow and thick, distorting the view outside, though she could make out the edge of the pier, the buildings of the port town in the background.

"Welcome, to the bridge of The Nymph," Irené said, sweeping her arms out. A half dozen of the crew behind them descended the stairs to join those already working, shouting orders at each other as they went.

"Is this where you steer from?" asked Harris. He ran a finger along the lacquered wooden railing on the balcony.

"Like I said, this is where I'll be." The captain smiled, ignoring Harris. She was clearly pleased to be back on her boat. "Don't worry. I'll get you safely to your destinations."

Ailsa didn't doubt it; Irené hadn't led them wrong yet. Still, she peered round the room, confused. "But there isn't a wheel." She knew little about ships, but there had to be a way to steer it.

Irené smirked and stalked down the stairs after her crew. Ailsa decided to see this as an invitation and followed, her friends close at her heels.

"This," Irené said, gesturing to the great globe, "is how I steer. It's how I control the whole boat." She reached out a hand and pulled at one of the gold rings circling the sphere. Immediately, the floor of the boat shook and Cameron had to grab onto Harris's shoulder to steady himself.

"Are we almost ready to set off?" Iona asked, examining a brass telescope on the desk in front of her.

The captain pulled on an instrument attached to the floor. It looked like a golden pipe, but ended in a glass disc. As soon as Irené flipped a switch on it, it extended up until she could look through it comfortably. "Looks like they're ready to close the hatch down there."

"You can see all the way down?" Angus asked in awe. The captain waved him forward, and he stared, open-mouthed, down the pipe. "How is that even possible?"

"Mirrors." Irené sank down into a winged leather chair in front of the globe and crossed one leg over the other. This seemed to be some sort of signal, as the other crew members who had been milling about positioned themselves behind the desks and in front of panels of blinking lights, waiting for their orders.

"Ready to launch, Commander Corso?" Irené asked one of the crew standing at the desk right at the front. Ailsa recognised the short man with the scarf across his eye from the library in Dunrigh. The quartermaster, Irené had called him.

The man cranked a lever beside him and smiled. "*Si, Capitana.*"

"Well then," Irené called. "Make haste."

The sailing master stepped silently up to the globe, pulling on one ring then another. There was a clanking sound, a whirring. Ailsa stepped back until her elbows hit the wall, using it to keep her balance as the boat began to shake. The light from the chandelier above dimmed, casting them in semi-darkness, until little blue bulbs popped on around the edges of the room one at a time.

With a shudder, the boat moved, backing away from the dock. Ailsa watched the rolling hills they'd descended from as they got smaller and smaller. The sailor in front of her, with swirling tattoos across his face, cranked a wheeled device and Ailsa felt the movements of the vessel change.

With her heart in her throat, she watched the water appear at the windows and move up over them as they sank under the waves. She couldn't help reaching out for Angus beside her, grabbing his hand and squeezing as she waited for the glass to crack and drown them all.

Please, please, please. Ailsa said a silent prayer to the gods. *Please let it hold.*

The sound of metal grinding filled the room, as if the golden fish itself was screaming from the cold sea. Finally, the water covered the whole window and the crew members erupted in a cheer.

"Were they worried it wouldn't work or something?" Harris asked, casting a glance towards his sister.

The captain shrugged. "It's tradition. Now, the exciting part is over. I recommend you find yourselves a room. Dinner will be in a few hours."

Ailsa inclined her head woodenly, unable to take her eyes off the water that had swallowed them. Vaguely, she felt Angus pull her back up the stairs, but even with her back turned she could still see it. The sea was like a dark wall, pressing in on the twin windows, ready at any moment to rush in and end their lives.

The sooner we're back on dry land, the better, Ailsa thought with a shiver as she was led back down into the belly of the submarine.

Chapter 16

Ailsa was still on edge for the next hour as they chose their rooms and settled in. But there was only so much time she could spend worrying. She couldn't exactly lie in her bunk for days, thinking about how many thousands of gallons of water were above them. So when Iona had produced a bottle of amber liquid and a tin of playing cards, she'd locked away her fear and nodded enthusiastically.

Ailsa didn't exactly enjoy organised fun, but when they were going to be stuck inside a metal fish for days on end, she'd take any form of entertainment, and distraction, she could.

The biggest room in the boat, aside from the bridge, was the mess hall, so Iona had told Ailsa to meet her there.

The room was sparse and practical, furnished with a dozen round tables. There had been a few crew members sitting and chatting when she'd arrived but their breaks had obviously ended, leaving her blessedly alone. Her stomach rumbled as the smell of frying fish emanated from a hatch in the wall that must have led to the kitchens.

"That smells good," Angus said by way of greeting as he joined her table. "I don't suppose dinner is far off?"

"I didn't want to ask." Ailsa eyed the hatch again, willing it to open. It seemed like half a day since they'd had their last meal. It didn't help that there was no natural light in the boat.

"Have you come to play Iona's game?" she asked, to keep her mind off her belly.

"I'd never pass up an opportunity to beat Harris at something."

Eventually, Iona appeared at the door with her brother and Cameron in tow. "That's everyone." Iona placed the bottle of whisky in the middle of the table with a flourish.

"Do you think we should have invited the captain?" Harris asked, looking at the door.

Ailsa fought the urge to roll her eyes.

"She's probably busy," Iona said. "Perhaps she'll join us later."

Cameron took a seat beside Ailsa and gave her shoulder a squeeze. "Well, you'd better deal out."

"I'll get some glasses," Angus said, scraping his chair back.

Cameron shrugged. "I wouldn't have minded sharing the bottle."

"Well, I do." Ailsa pointed to the sideboard that she'd seen crew members taking cups from while she'd waited.

Harris snorted. "Agreed. Who knows what nasty diseases you all have."

"Oh dear, sweet, little brother," Iona said with a laugh, shuffling the cards. "I think the person we'd have to worry about is you."

Harris pinched her forearm fondly as Angus came back with a handful of mugs. As he opened the bottle, Iona flicked her fingers and the liquid inside shot out, filling the cups by itself.

"You're in a good mood," Ailsa noted.

Iona smiled. "We haven't been able to sit together and just relax. Yes, we're on a mission to save the world, but it doesn't mean we can't enjoy the little downtime we have."

"Hear, hear," Harris said, snatching up his cards. "Now let's get riotously drunk like the big, damn heroes we are."

Ailsa studied the cards in her hands and tried not to frown. There were too many Moons and not nearly enough Stars, Mountains and Trees. Harris had explained the rules at the beginning, but, as she'd expected, they had been confusing and inconsistent. "Two," she said, eyeing up her fellow players.

Harris gave a whoop and jumped up from his seat. He spun once before throwing himself back down again, almost falling off in the process. Cameron did the same, though a little slower than Harris, who pointed at him as soon as they were both back in their chairs. "You lost. Hand it over."

"I can't follow all these rules," Cameron grumbled, but he handed over his card to Ailsa. She slotted it in between her one and three of Mountains.

"You'll catch on," Harris told him. He knocked on the table.

Immediately, Iona, Angus, and Ailsa scratched their noses. Harris looked between them all before finally pointing at Angus. "I don't believe you," he said.

Angus shook his head but tossed a card Harris's way. "You're making this up as you go along."

"This game has been passed down in our family since before your father was even born, I'll have you know. Isn't that right, Iona?"

"With some alterations, thanks to my brother." Iona grinned. "Anyone else for a top up?"

Ailsa sipped at her whisky and shook her head. "I'm still

trying to get through this cup." Despite scoffing down the fried squid and potatoes the cook had served, she was a little tipsy. Unfortunately, not everyone was pacing themselves. She was sure Harris and Iona had drunk half the bottle between them already, though Iona was wearing it better. Angus and Cameron weren't far behind.

Cameron raised his mug with a swaying hand. "I'll have some more. You get used to the burning taste when you're in the army."

Angus grinned goofily up at him. "Took you a while, though, didn't it? I distinctly remember you puking your guts up the first time we stole some." He stopped, like he'd realised he'd been bolder than usual.

"Yeah, well, you were right there with me," Cameron chuckled as the liquid magically made its way into his mug again. "Though, I am embarrassed now. At the time I assumed you were only a year younger than me, not three."

"Did you ever suspect?" Ailsa asked.

"No way. He had stubble and everything back then. Nothing like the beard he has now, but still impressive." Cameron's eyes swept over Angus's face.

Ailsa ducked her head, trying not to smile. "Your turn, Iona."

The selkie raised three fingers to her forehead. Everyone groaned.

Harris threw down his whole hand, picking up new cards from the stack in the middle of the table. "Seems like not being able to hold your drink is a family trait," he slurred, pointing at Cameron. "Has your sister told you about the last time I had to hold her hair back for her?"

"Oh?" asked Cameron, rounding on Ailsa. "Do tell."

Ailsa sniffed, studying her new cards. "I was trying to fit in with the locals after Angus and Harris abandoned me."

"We didn't abandon you," Harris argued.

"We kinda did." Angus scratched his nose again, taking a random card from Iona's hand. "I went to play the fiddle. You chased after some girls."

"Only because Ailsa didn't want to dance. It's fine. I convinced her eventually."

Ailsa bit her tongue. Harris had left her for hours alone with strangers, as he'd danced with nearly every girl in the room. Looking at the situation again, he'd only come back to her when he had been bored. But that was Harris. He'd kept his options open while pursuing her. It hurt. But it would hurt a lot more if he still had her heart. No, that belonged to another now. "I don't like dancing."

"Is that why you didn't like Angus when you first met him?"

"Harris!"

"It's fine. I kind of figured," Angus laughed. "The first few days after we left Dunrigh were... strained."

"But you got on fine after that?" Cameron asked.

"He won me over." Ailsa turned her attention back to her cards.

"Just as well. I'm pretty sure we all almost died on that journey," said Angus.

"You didn't go with them?" Cameron asked Iona.

She bit her lip. "I stayed in the capital, with the king."

Angus stopped smiling. His throat bobbed.

Cameron's forehead wrinkled. "I hadn't even heard he was sick."

"You wouldn't have. It was kept a secret," Iona said quietly.

"He came back from sailing near Nerebus, looking half dead. His skin was rotted, and his mind was broken. By the end, he could hardly remember his own name. He held on just long enough to hear Angus had found the Stone of Destiny."

"I'm sorry," said Cameron, reaching out to squeeze Angus's shoulder.

The prince gave him a half smile, then went back to focussing on his cards. "We saw more like him. In the village where Ailsa had been taken. They thought the fae had done it."

Ailsa leaned back in her chair, her enthusiasm for cards gone. "When I met Dolor, she was surrounded by people with the same sickness. But they looked like they'd already died, but they'd been kept standing and moving by magic. Maalik called them '*the Soulless*.'"

"If the Edaxi can't set foot upon Eilanmòrian soil, how did this Dolor get to the forest?" Iona asked.

How had she been there? Then Ailsa remembered something. "They had these crystals. A few of the Soulless stood in a circle and she just appeared."

"Yet she was able to hurt you?" said Iona.

Ailsa's fingers clenched on her cards. "She hurt both Maalik and me. When he destroyed the crystals, she disappeared again."

"He killed them?" Harris guessed.

"I think it was a mercy. Would you like to be a slave to an evil goddess? To be nothing more than a husk of a body? If that ever happens to me, I'd want you to end my suffering." Ailsa's stomach turned over at the thought.

"You can say that now," Harris said, an edge to his voice. "But those people weren't asked. They were sick."

Ailsa fixed him with a warning glare. "Maalik would never harm someone unless it was absolutely necessary."

"He's a demon," Harris snapped, as if that explained everything.

The room seemed to cool a few degrees. "He was an angel," Ailsa said quietly, puzzled at Harris's tone. Where was this even coming from? *He's drunk.* And she would have left it at that, if not for what he said next.

"He must have done something terrible if he fell." Harris's lip curled. "The gods only turn angels into demons if they truly deserve it. If they've done something monstrous."

Ailsa placed her cards down on the table and leaned forward. "You have no idea what you're talking about." Her tone was harsher than she'd intended, but then again, perhaps he deserved it. Deserved her rage. "Maalik sold his soul to save me." Up above, the electric lights flickered.

"What?" Iona's voice cut through the moment.

Ailsa gritted her teeth to avoid snapping at her, too. "Maalik and I were called into Hell to meet the demon council. Another demon tried to expose Maalik, to show them all that he'd been kind to me, that he'd been healing people. During our trial, I caused a distraction and a friend of his stole Maalik's soul from whenever they kept them down there. But you can't simply return a soul to your body, so he left it on his bookshelf until he could reunite himself with it."

Iona had paled beneath her freckles. "That's why you wanted the cauldron water."

Ailsa gritted her teeth. "Maalik had read about the Four Treasures and had realised he could use the Cauldron of Life to help himself." She stared at the table, reliving the events of that terrible day. "When I met Dolor, she didn't just hurt me, she broke me. My spine was shattered. I couldn't feel my legs. That's when Maalik destroyed the crystals, killed the Soulless." Her voice cracked. "He brought me back to his cabin and tried to heal me, but it didn't work. He called an angel, begged him to help me. But the angel wouldn't agree until Maalik gave up his soul again." She raised piercing eyes to Harris and snarled, "So don't sit there and judge him. He's twice the man you'll ever be."

"Ailsa, stop!" Cameron said, motioning to the table. "You need to calm down."

She wrestled her gaze from Harris's face and looked down at her own hands. Without realising, she'd been gripping the table. Between her fingers, sparks of electricity were snapping out onto the wood, burning it. Her powers had taken over, from reliving the pain or from her anger, she wasn't sure. The air crackled around her and she did her best to clamp down on it. When she looked back up, every single one of her friends was staring at her warily.

Ailsa scraped her chair back. "I'm done."

No one tried to stop her as she left them all, storming from the room.

That was dramatic, Ishbel said.

"Piss off."

Good for you, using that new backbone you grew.

"I said, piss off."

There were only so many places one could go in a metal fish-boat, dozens of leagues under the sea. Ailsa wandered the corridors blindly, not sure where she was going.

How dare he!

She couldn't stop picturing Harris's face drunkenly sneering as he'd voiced Maalik's own fears and regrets. The demon wasn't a monster, no matter what he'd done in the past. Just like she wasn't a monster for possessing a birthmark.

She came to the end of the corridor, to a hatch that, no matter how she pulled, wouldn't open. The fiery ache of tears welled up. Tears for her friend. Tears for her own childhood. Tears for what she'd just done. But she pushed them back, taking deep, gulping breaths. She had made herself a promise not to cry again, and she wasn't about to break it over a stupid drunken fight.

Sliding down the metal wall, she curled herself inward. There were still days and many miles before she reached her next destination and there was no use in weeping. Ailsa gulped the stale air into her lungs, pulled her broken pieces together and started to plan.

Chapter 17

harris wandered the metal corridors of the boat, a glass of whisky in hand. The fog of alcohol had lifted, and he was doing his very best to get it back again.

As soon as Ailsa had left the room, the party atmosphere had guttered and died. Everyone else had dragged themselves to bed an hour ago, but his mind was whirring too fast for sleep.

He had wanted to run after her, scream and shout that he couldn't have known any of that, that she had never told them. But he knew, deep down, that he'd been a right prick. Ailsa obviously liked this man. She thought they could trust him. That should have been enough.

Sold his soul. Well, that was one way to tell a girl you loved her.

Harris scrubbed his hand through his hair. He'd have to apologise tomorrow. If Ailsa was willing to hear him.

He turned a corner and saw light flickering on the wall, coming from an open door. Curious, he crept to the opening and peered inside.

The room was some sort of study, with books and maps lining the walls. In the centre was a desk of the richest mahogany. Like the command centre, it was covered in strange instruments. And amongst them all, the captain was slumped, poring over a piece of paper. A pair of glasses perched on her nose and her braids had been tied up in a purple scarf. She'd kicked off her boots and one foot was swinging idly.

Harris knew he should turn around and go to his quarters, but something about his fight with Ailsa made him reckless. If she wasn't going to stay and bicker with him, he knew who would.

"I didn't realise anyone would be awake." He leaned against the door and brought the glass to his lips, his throat bobbing as he drank the sweet liquid.

Irené fixed him with a withering stare over her spectacles. "I am this ship's captain; I'm always awake."

He took a few steps inside, still staying near the door but turning so he could admire the pictures hanging on the wall. Many of them were charts and maps, though dotted here and there were sketches. "You can't possibly be awake all the time. Humans can only survive a few days with no sleep." He trailed his fingers along the frame of one drawing, this one a portrait of the osprey. Duende, Iona had said its name was. *Where was it now?* he wondered. Probably somewhere high above, following the boat as it cut through the water. The sketch was good, almost like the bird really was here with them. Had Irené drawn it herself?

"Let me clarify: I am this ship's captain. I am always awake when I have foreign guests onboard," she said.

He gave her a crooked grin over his shoulder. "Afraid we're going to pillage your holds? You were the ones who admitted conspiring to steal from us."

The captain set down her pen. "Are you always this insufferable?"

"Oh yes," Harris said, mustering as much bravado as he could. "But once you get used to it, it becomes an endearing character quirk." He knew Irené was being sincere, that she really seemed to dislike him, but somehow that made teasing her more fun. *You should go to bed*, a voice whispered in his head. Unfortunately, he rarely listened to that voice, even when he was sober.

Irené stood from her desk. "Sir, we only have a few weeks. I don't believe I have the time to get used to your odd humour."

"That could be arranged, if you wished? Once all this is over, I'm a free man. I've always wanted to visit Edessa." He thought of the paintings he'd seen of the island nation, hanging in the gallery in Dunrigh. Warm seas and palm trees under a cloudless sky. Yes, perhaps that's exactly what he needed: a holiday.

The captain's face twisted at that. "Oh, please do, but not while I am there. I'm afraid I find your presence unbearable."

He barked out a laugh. "Ooft, don't mince your words."

"I shall mince more than my words," she said, folding her arms and looking down her nose at him. "Or I could have you thrown in the brig?"

Harris winked. "Would you chain me up, princess?"

Her lips twitched at that, despite herself.

Come on, flirt with me.

"Last warning," she said, coming out from behind the desk. "Go to bed, Harris."

"See," he said with a cackle, sloshing his whisky over his hand as he pointed. "You do know my name!"

Irené was across the room in three strides. As soon as she reached him, she leaned in close, giving him a lazy smile. "Do you think you're going to wear me down?"

Harris shivered as her scent hit his nose. A sailor should not smell this good. Her perfume was floral and fresh, putting him in mind of sandy beaches and blooming gardens. "Is it working?" he asked.

"Oh yes," she said, moving in impossibly close, until the fabric from her blouse was brushing his chest. If he leaned his face down a few inches, he'd be able to capture her full lips in his. Suddenly, there was nothing he wanted more.

Irené flicked her deep brown eyes over his face. When she spoke next, her voice had deepened, becoming huskier, as if she too was affected by the proximity. "I can't deny, I find you attractive. Since I first met you, I've imagined you in a myriad of... positions."

By the gods. Harris barely held back a groan. "Oh?"

One of her hands came up to cup his elbow. The callouses on her palm scraped against his skin, but Harris couldn't find it in him to mind as she said, "But do you know where I'd like you first?"

He gulped as he shook his head. *Anywhere for you.*

Irené smirked. "On your ass in the corridor." And with a shove, he was through the door skidding onto the floor, just like she'd wanted.

He stared up at her, open-mouthed, as she gave him a pointed smile. "So accommodating," she said, bringing a glass of whisky to her lips and taking a sip.

My glass of whisky, Harris realised.

"Thank you for the entertainment," Irené chuckled. "Next, I'd like you as far away from me as you can possibly get. Good night." With that, she slammed the door in his face.

Harris lay on the floor for a moment, his heart pounding in his chest, not quite believing what had just happened.

You've been bested.

And, gods damn him, he had loved every moment.

Chapter 18

Harris cracked an eye open and groaned as the hangover hit him full force. *When will I ever learn?* He wasn't even getting the good parts of a night of heavy drinking; he knew exactly what awful things he'd said and done. Ailsa. Irené. In the light of day, it was clear he'd been an eejit. He had some apologising to do.

The boat pitched, and he closed his eyes against a wave of nausea. Later—he'd apologise later, when he was halfway human again.

There was a shuffling near his head, like someone was trying their best to get up without disturbing him.

"I'm awake," he grumbled, looking down.

Cameron was standing beside his bunk, his trousers on but not done up. He wore no shirt, revealing scars which criss-crossed his chest. His hair was still sleep-ruffled, and he'd grown some stubble in the night.

"Bet you wish you weren't."

Harris tugged his blankets up further, hoping they'd swallow him up. "You don't have to look so happy about my current predicament."

"I can't wait for when my sister chews you out again," Cameron said with a shrug.

"Are you mad at me too?" He'd had an easy friendship with the soldier since they'd met.

It would be his luck if he'd ruined another with his antics.

But Cameron poked him in the leg. "Nah. If I'm honest, I had my own doubts about the demon, too. But I would never have said anything. It's up to her who she trusts."

Harris closed his eyes against the spinning room. "Smart man."

"I didn't hear you come in last night."

"I stayed up late."

"You should get up. Some breakfast will help you."

"I don't think I can," said Harris, pressing his palm into an eye. "The thought of walking about in an enclosed box with water pressing down on us and no way to escape isn't a pleasant one."

"You're in luck, pal," Cameron chuckled. "We're back on the surface."

"Now, that is good news," Harris said, kicking his covers off. Maybe he could turn into a seal and swim off. Or, at least, take a dip to cool his head.

It took a little help from Cameron but soon he was decent, if not nauseous. Harris followed the other man through the corridors, noticing that the air was indeed fresher. Up they climbed on spiralled stairs and through thick hatches until they glimpsed sky.

It looks like there's a storm on the horizon, Harris realised as his stomach turned over. Any other time, around any other company, that wouldn't be a worry. They could simply dive underwater again to avoid a squall. But he had a sneaking suspicion that the clouds weren't natural.

Say you're sorry, and she'll be fine. Get some food in you and breathe.

He paused at the top of the stairs, filling his lungs with the crisp sea air and listening to the squawks of seagulls. Yes, he preferred this to the cramped metal labyrinth below. Here, he could feel the salted spray on his cheeks and remember who he was.

Some of the crew had assembled on the deck, enjoying the fresh air, too. Harris guessed they were now on the fish-boat's back, above its gigantic eye-like windows. A railing had been constructed to keep people from sliding off the sloping metal into the sea below.

Harris tested the golden floor with his boot to determine how slippy it was, then carefully made his way through the relaxing crew to the edge. Cameron hung back, snagging a piece of fruit from a bowl and joined in with the lounging.

The deck was slicker at the railings, where the water had touched it. Harris peered down at the ocean and smiled. White-topped waves crashed against the side of the boat like passionate lovers. They were enough to rock the vessel, but Harris had been born with sea legs. The roiling in his gut quietened, as though, even in his human form, he could be soothed by sand and salt.

But it wasn't enough. What he would give to shed this skin and dive straight in. To feel the cold envelop him, even as his body kept him warm. He'd love to float for hours in the kelp forests, chase skittering crabs along the silty bed or crack open a shell to find creamy pearls.

His daydream was disturbed by a crew member crashing into the railing to throw up his breakfast. Harris remembered the tall, muscular man from Dunrigh; Orenzo, he thought his name was. The man retched but had the forethought to hold himself far out over the railing so none of his vomit would splatter on the boat's side.

"I'd have thought sailors would have stronger stomachs," Harris mused.

A curse was flung his way before the man lost his dinner overboard too.

Harris looked past the seasick sailor, and his laughter died in his throat. Ailsa was leaning over the railing too, at the front of the boat. Her hair was unbound, blowing in the breeze, but she did nothing to tame it. She was staring off at the horizon.

Apologies, Harris knew, were better said sooner rather than later. Otherwise they festered, going off like spoiled meat. He steeled his spine and half walked, half slid his way to her side, using the rail to keep himself from falling.

He knew that she'd sensed him coming; he hadn't exactly been subtle. Yet still she stayed. A good start.

"Hey," Harris said when he was beside her.

Ailsa didn't reply, save from a sharp nod.

Inside, Harris grimaced. "I'm sorry about—"

"-It's fine."

Harris tried again. "I've never met Maalik, but I shouldn't have said those things about him."

"No, you shouldn't have. You can't assume someone is bad because of what they are."

Just like people had always assumed she was evil for being a changeling. Harris pressed his lips together, understanding.

"When I heard it was a demon who had saved you, I was more than a little shocked. I've never met one, but they have a reputation for pure evil. I have met an angel, only once, and she had a great disdain for her fallen brethren. But that doesn't mean all of them are bad. If he's your friend, I need to get over my prejudices."

Ailsa said nothing, instead fixing her eyes at the end of the ocean, where it met the sky.

"But that's not the main reason I said those things last night. I'm going to be honest, Ailsa, honest with myself. I'd thought I wasn't jealous, that I could get over you and be happy you'd met someone else. But I think I proved myself wrong, in that moment."

Her mouth twisted unhappily. "Maalik and me, we're not together."

"But you wish you were," he guessed.

She sighed. "When I was with him, I was so focussed on getting away, getting to Ephraim and saving you. So I think it snuck up on me, how much I care about him." Ailsa licked her lips. "It's like I left a part of me back in that cabin."

If that's how she felt... he'd insulted a part of her last night.

"I'm sorry," he said again, meaning it even more now. "I want to be a good friend to you." He turned to go but her hand shot out, gripping his arm.

"I will kick your ass if you ever insult someone dear to me again. But I'd do the same to anyone else if they ever insult you."

Harris looked into the stormy blue-grey eyes of the woman before him and bowed. He walked away, before he did anything to break the tenuous peace between them.

Well, that went better than expected.

Harris slipped his way back towards the hatch, thinking of the bed far below and how he'd enjoy flopping onto it and losing himself to unconsciousness for a while. He couldn't see Cameron, he'd clearly gone back downstairs too, though he wondered if Ailsa's brother had seen Harris was approaching her and thought it best to get out of the way. He didn't blame

Cameron. Ailsa's powers had been downright terrifying last night.

Harris knew she'd been practising, but the magic had come as a surprise all the same. It was almost like she was made of it, like the electricity had coursed through her very veins. But it wasn't how powerful she was that scared him; she had seemed out of control.

Another thing to think about. If she was going to wield one of the treasures, she'd have to be ready. Otherwise, they'd need to find someone else. But that was not something he'd be bringing up anytime soon.

He'd almost reached the door when he glimpsed a familiar turquoise head. Irené had her legs over the side of the boat, swinging above the water. Unlike Ailsa, she was staring down at the waves. The huge osprey was back, perched on the railing above her. Its white belly feathers ruffled in the wind, and it turned a sharp, amber eye towards him, as if sensing his attention.

Maybe we can make this a twofer, he thought.

Speaking to Irené was different to apologising to Ailsa. He knew the changeling girl, knew her moods. The captain was still a mystery. And what had happened the night before... He cringed, thinking about how much he'd wanted to kiss her, how he'd wanted to take her into his arms and feel her strong body under his fingers. She'd tricked him, played on her assumptions about him. And had he not fallen right into that trap? He really was a lech.

Harris didn't even get a chance to open his mouth before she snapped her head up and snorted.

"Back for more, selkie-boy? I thought your ego would have been as bruised as your ass," the princess said with a smirk.

113

"What do you want?"

The urge to pull on that old swagger, to tease, was almost too irresistible. *No, be sincere.* "To say I'm sorry."

"Well, you've said it. Now leave," she laughed, pulling herself up. The osprey chirped before taking off from the railing, as though it too couldn't stand Harris. Irené turned and stalked off in the hatch's direction.

Harris watched her walk away with an open mouth, trying not to note the way her hips swayed, how she tossed her hair over her shoulder. That was it? Why did she hate him so much?

You should stop chasing after her. She doesn't want you around. But he knew as soon as he had the opportunity, he'd be back to following Irené like a seal pup.

Pathetic, he told himself, even as he hurried to catch up.

"Listen, maybe that wasn't enough for you—"

Irené spun, shaking her head like she couldn't believe he was still there. "Who are you really, Harris of Struanmuir?"

He blinked, saying the first thing that came into his head. "A clown." But even as he said it, he realised it was true. Court jester, Iona had called him once. Always making fun, taking nothing seriously.

The princess considered that. "No, you're not. At least, not all the time. You make jokes to hide your vulnerabilities."

He crossed his arms over his chest. "Go on. What else do you know about me?"

Irené rolled her eyes. "I know that if you will not stop acting like a little boy, you'd better stay out of my way." She turned to go.

"Wait—" Harris started, reaching out to her. But his fingers had barely grazed her arm when there was a boom and the entire world tipped sideways.

Harris pitched forward, landing face first on the golden deck. His head rang from the collision and the floor was still pitching up and down, like they'd suddenly found themselves in a storm. All around him the crew were shouting and Irené—

He spied her hands gripping the railing for dear life, her body hanging off the side of the boat. She'd obviously slipped underneath the barrier in the impact.

Harris pushed himself up, even as his vision swam, and dived for the edge, grabbing her forearms. Irené stared up at him in shock as he reached her, her feet swinging above the raging sea below. They weren't that far from the water, not enough to cause injury if she fell, but what had happened? Behind, Harris could hear the crew asking the same thing.

"Here," he said as he pulled her up so that she could get a foothold.

She gritted her teeth. "What was that?"

He didn't answer, holding her arms as she climbed back over the railing. Across the deck, he saw Ailsa, exactly where he'd left her at the front of the boat. She was leaning against the railing too, staring down into the water below. Even from a distance, he could see her face was ashen.

"Nadya, report," Irené barked out to her sailing master.

The slim woman who'd been with Irené in Dunrigh shouted back, "It came from the starboard side."

"Can you see what it was? Did we hit a rock?" Irené shrugged out of Harris's hold, dismissing him.

Nadya pulled a telescope from her belt and opened it out. "In the middle of the sea? I doubt it."

"It wasn't a rock," Ailsa called to them. Up above, the

clouds swirled. "There's something down there."

But before anyone could react, something bashed into the side of the boat again, sending them sprawling once more.

Chapter 19

Ailsa's arms were almost wrenched from their sockets as she grabbed the railing to avoid falling to the water below.

Behind her, the crew were running for the hatch, yelling to whoever was beneath.

"Get inside!" Irené shouted from her spot. "Now!"

Ailsa eyed the distance as the boat swayed in the swell. Water had swept up and over the metal, making it slick. If she was going to do this, there was a real chance she was going into the sea. And that didn't seem like a great option. She'd seen a shadow, but what had bashed the boat?

She craned her neck, trying to spot anything out of the ordinary on the horizon. The waves were mountainous, looking like they wanted to devour the little boat whole. Ailsa reached out her powers, trying to soothe the water with a calming wind, but her hands shook too much. Where was Iona? She'd be able to—

And then she saw it.

The fin was small enough—it could have belonged to an orca or a basking shark. Except it was yellow and scaled between the sharp spines. An enormous fish? Ailsa didn't have long to wonder as the body of the creature snaked out of the water. The fin was miniscule next to the rest of it, just for show. Water dripped off the striped back as it reared up and she could finally see the creature's head.

Ailsa had seen eels before, had even eaten one after a successful fishing day. The monster before her looked like a gargantuan version. Its head was the size of the vessel she stood on, while its neck was just as thick: muscular and powerful as it readied to strike. The eel looked down at her with one colossal blue eye and opened its mouth to reveal rows and rows of knife-sharp teeth.

"Ailsa!" Irené yelled.

The sound of her name set Ailsa's feet in motion. Rather than running for the hatch, she pushed herself from the bannister, sliding across the slick metal back of the fish-boat. The goliath eel watched her progress, unmoving, until she was mere feet from the door. As though sensing an easy mouthful was about to be lost, it swung its massive head into the side of the boat.

The submarine lurched, and Ailsa slipped in the wrong direction, towards the edge.

I'm not going to make it. I'm not going to make it.

Her fingers grazed the hatch, but not enough to find purchase. Then she was falling to the side, down towards the icy sea—

A hand locked around her wrist in a bruising grip. Ailsa snapped her head back to see Irené had managed to grab her as she'd passed.

"Come on!"

More hands darted out of the opening, and she was being pulled inside. The eel screeched and launched its colossal head at them, piercing teeth first, but they were all in and Irené's crew slammed the hatch shut and turned it. Just as they finished locking it, the monster slammed against the metal with teeth-shattering force. Ailsa looked up from her place on the floor, expecting the door to be crumpled under the weight but there was only a dent.

"Get us under," Irené ordered. "We'll have to outrun it."

"How?" Harris said from behind her. "That thing was massive."

The captain ignored him, shouting to her crew instead. "Get us to shore, hopefully it won't follow."

Ailsa yanked Harris's shirt to stop him from going after her. "Come on, we have to find the others."

They found Cameron first, outside the room he'd shared with Harris the night before.

"It would have been nice to have seen this one coming," said the selkie a little tersely.

Ailsa pinched him. "Meet us up on the bridge. I don't want you stuck down here if we have to evacuate."

Cameron paled. "Angus ran down to get Laire."

"I'll go," Harris said, jogging off down the corridor. "At least I can hold my breath."

The boat groaned, and Ailsa knew they were submerging again. Probably speeding away as fast as possible from that thing. "See you up there," she repeated, and she was gone, running to her own room.

Iona wasn't there, but she was in the second place Ailsa looked: the mess hall. All the tables and chairs lay sprawled across the floor, tipped over by the impact. Iona was crouched over a tiny figure in the corner. The boat shuddered again and the person moaned.

"She hurt her head," Iona said when Ailsa approached. Indeed, one half of the little girl's face was covered in blood.

Head injuries always look worse than they are, Ailsa told herself as she bent down. "What's your name?" *She can't be over ten.*

"Paloma," she said. "I'm the cabin girl."

"Can you stand? We have to get to the captain."

Paloma let out a weak sound of assent, and between Ailsa and Iona, they dragged her to her feet and out of the room.

"What was it?" huffed Iona as they made their way through the narrow corridors.

Ailsa glanced down at the little girl. "A creature. Looked like an eel but much, much bigger."

Iona stopped in her tracks, her face leeching of colour immediately. "A Stoor Worm?"

"Whatever it was, it was ugly." Ailsa shook her head, indicating they should have this conversation away from the injured cabin girl. Iona only hesitated a moment before her arms were circling Paloma again and she was pulling them forward with determination.

They had almost reached the bridge when another blow racked the boat and all three of them slammed into the metal wall. Ailsa swore as a rivet pushed into her back. When she opened her eyes, she found the cabin girl gazing up at her with delight.

"I've been in the company of pirates for a year and I haven't heard that one before."

Iona let out a noise that was half laugh, half sob.

"I'll teach you all the ones I know, once we're back on dry land again," Ailsa groaned, hauling them back up.

She could hear Irené barking orders before they were even

in the room. The captain was sitting in a chair to the side of the humongous globe while the sailing master, Nadya, steered.

The woman's arms were almost a blur as she pulled the sphere around and down and back up again. The other crewmen had assembled too, either checking the mysterious tools or standing watch the edges of the room.

No one noticed Iona, Paloma and Ailsa at first, until the little girl let out a cry. Immediately all eyes, except those of the captain's and the sailing master's, turned to them.

"Lola!" a woman with green hair cried and then she was upon them, sweeping the girl into her arms. "We couldn't find you."

"Sorry, Egeria," the girl said sheepishly.

"Doctor," Irené said, still with her unflinching gaze on the windows in front. "Please take Paloma and anyone else who's injured to your infirmary. She doesn't need to see this."

The little girl began to grumble, but one look from the green-haired woman silenced her. They exited the room, leaving Ailsa and Iona behind, standing at the top of the stairs.

Some of the crew returned to monitoring the sailing master, but most now turned their attention to an hourglass in the corner. Ailsa stared at the strange object watching its contents slowly trickling from one chamber to another. But, when she looked closer, it wasn't sand, but some sparkling liquid.

"Faster," Irené shouted and one of the crew in the lower deck pulled a lever. The shining liquid ran through the hole in the hourglass quicker.

"What is that?" Ailsa asked, though she had a sneaking suspicion already.

It was the closest crewman, a man with tattoos covering his

dark skin, that answered. "It keeps track of our fuel reserves."

We're going to run out, Ailsa realised, eyeing the little liquid left.

Irené turned to her whole crew as Nadya continued to steer.

"We need to decide. Do we power ahead, risking our fuel running out before we reach land? Or do we stand and fight?"

The quartermaster, Agustin, spoke up first, peering out of the yellow-tinted windows. "We'll reach land with our fuel, but only if we slow down. Or, we could burn our reserves on a sprint and hopefully lose the creature."

Irené's gaze went to a petite woman at one desk. "Amanda?"

The woman grimaced. "We have guns, but I have no idea whether they'll penetrate the monster's hide."

"They won't," Iona said quietly, descending the stairs. "The Stoor Worm won't be harmed by your bullets."

Irené regarded her, calculating. "Tell us what you know."

"Stoor Worms... they're in tales told to selkies when we're young, to stop us from straying from our land. They're created from malevolent spirits, from the souls of those who die drowning and in their final moments curse the world for their fate. Stoor Worms are always hungry. They can never be satiated. They have hides so thick nothing can pierce it and once they decide they want to eat you, they will hunt you down until they do so, or you can set foot on land, where they cannot go."

"Why have I never heard of this?"

"They're rare; it takes thousands of spirits to make one."

Irené considered this a moment, while the crew flicked their eyes between their captain and the fast-flowing hourglass. After a moment, she smiled. "We won't outrun it and we won't try to defeat it. We have something that no other ship has; something that no one else has tried." She stood, surveying the room. "You'd all better hold on to something." To the sailing master at her side, she nodded. "Take us down, Nadya."

Chapter 20

The tattooed man pulled a cord and dozens of bells rang in unison. A moment later, Ailsa could hear a distant peeling from the hallway. She wondered if the warning could now be heard throughout the boat.

"Ailsa!" Iona shouted up at her.

Ailsa whipped her head back to the room, where the crew had now flattened themselves on the ground, grasping at the floor. The bannisters...

She barely had enough time to throw herself down too, to wrap her arms around a pipe, before the craft juddered. Not from a hit, not from the Stoor Worm, but from the power cutting. The overhead lights flickered off, leaving the room bathed in darkness, save for a few red bulbs flashing at the corners.

"Now!" the captain commanded.

And then they were falling.

Ailsa's stomach turned over as they sped towards the seabed, while her ears *pop, pop, popped*—so hard that she thought her eardrums might burst. The muscles in her arms and hands screamed in protest from the effort of holding on, but she couldn't let go, or she'd fly up to the ceiling. Ailsa realised that they must be using the precious fuel they had left to propel themselves down— away from the Stoor Worm—to try to lose it.

Finally, Irené pulled a lever and they slowed their descent. How deep under the sea were they now? From the look in Iona's eyes, who was clinging on further down on the stairs, Ailsa didn't want to know. The selkie's thoughts were plain on her face. Shock. Wonder. Even she'd never been this deep.

Ailsa expected the lights to flare back up again, but they remained off. There was a stillness now, as if every single person aboard The Nymph was frozen. Ailsa peered out of the yellow windows with the rest of them, seeing only black.

No one spoke, not even a whisper. Irené hadn't needed to give the order, they all knew: make a noise, and the Stoor Worm could find them.

Ailsa thought of the boys somewhere beneath them. Harris had gone to find Angus and Laire. Cameron was supposed to meet them up here on the bridge; where was he? Did they hear the warning bells? Had they realised what was about to happen? Were her friends somewhere below, injured?

Focus on your breathing, Ailsa told herself. In and out. Slowly. *Don't make a noise.* She reached out with her powers, playing with the air to calm herself.

They stayed like that for a while, no one daring to make a sound. But, little by little, knuckles unclenched, faces grew hopeful.

It was Irené who called it. "I think we lost it—"

No sooner were the words out of her mouth than something smacked hard into the side of the boat, the sudden impact the most violent yet. Crewmen were thrown from their positions, screaming as they thudded into the walls. Ailsa hadn't let go of the pipe, but her head whacked against it, making her see stars.

She raised her eyes towards the windows on instinct, and

that's when she saw it.

The Stoor Worm hovered outside the glass, glowing red, illuminated by the little bulbs on the bridge. It widened its maw, revealing its sharp teeth again, and reared back.

It's going to break the glass!

Sick, icy dread ran up Ailsa's spine. All throughout the room, the red lights flickered.

"*Dios mio*," the quartermaster whispered.

"Nadya, evasive maneuvers!" shouted Irené.

But it was too late. The Stoor Worm struck the glass, its nose bashing into the window at full force. Ailsa held on to the pipe for dear life, watching as it prepared to hit again.

"Move us, now!" Irené turned to her mistress-at-arms. "Now would be a good time to get those guns out."

The short woman began pulling levers and pressing buttons on her desk while the sailing master jerked the globe to the side. The boat tilted, moving a few feet, and then it stopped.

"We're stuck." Nadya turned panicked eyes on her captain.

The Stoor Worm had stopped to watch them as they moved, but now they'd stilled, it reared back and crashed its huge, heavy head into the window. The whole boat shook, setting instruments sliding off desks and the crew members screaming.

Ailsa cast her eyes up to the yellow glass in dread. Right where the Stoor Worm had struck, the glass was cracked.

"It's just the outer layer," the quartermaster said, loud enough that they could all hear him.

But with the depth, the pressure, a few more strikes— surely the whole window would smash?

The captain turned her back on the windows and faced

her crew, her chin wobbling slightly. "*Mi familia*, it has been a pleasure serving with all of you."

Outside, the Stoor Worm opened its mouth in a silent shriek and reared back once again.

This is it. Ailsa closed her eyes, picturing a cabin in the woods, a crackling fire, a smiling mouth.

Are you going to give up that easily? Ishbel asked.

There was a tug inside Ailsa's chest, like the spirit guide was trying to shake her.

Use your magic!

But her powers weren't any good. Perhaps she could seal some air around them when the glass broke, but the Stoor Worm would keep coming. This far under the sea…

Ailsa raised her head, looking for Iona. The selkie's still gripped the bannister , but from the set of her jaw, Ailsa had a feeling she'd had the same idea.

"Can you use your magic through that glass?" Ailsa shouted down to her.

Iona whipped round. "It won't be enough to kill it."

"I just need it distracted."

By now, all the crew were looking at Ailsa and Iona. "What are you planning?" Irené asked.

"Where does this pipe go?" asked Ailsa, not letting go of the metal.

Irené frowned. "The engine, but—"

That was all Ailsa needed to hear. "Iona, if you can hold off the Stoor Worm, I'm going to give us a boost. Everyone: hold on." She signalled to Iona.

Ailsa and the selkie stood in unison, each keeping one hand tethered with the other raised in front of them. Ailsa sensed the power flowing through her, towards the window.

She sent a wall of bracing air to hold it together, as she felt Iona reach out with her own magic.

The water in front of the windows rippled and shimmered. The Stoor Worm attacked again, and Iona gritted her teeth, but the barrier of water held firm.

"Now what?" Irené asked, gripping her chair.

Ailsa's body crackled with power as she let it build and build. "Now we prove we're worthy to wield your weapons." And then she struck.

Not outwards, not towards the Stoor Worm, but down into the pipe. Towards the engine.

Ailsa's teeth chattered with the force, but she managed to get out, "Take us up."

The sailing master didn't need to be told twice. She pulled hard on a lever and the boat shuddered back to life.

Ailsa concentrated, sending every ounce of energy pulsing through her into the engine, powering it. The boat lurched and they were propelled towards the surface.

Instead of flying up to the ceiling, Ailsa's body was pressed into the floor. She fought against it, keeping her hand outstretched. The fissure on the yellowed glass spread. But she kept the air pressed against it, containing it. The crew held tight, ducking their heads as they did from the change of pressure. Iona had her arms wrapped around herself. Ailsa had no doubt that, far below, Iona's wall of water was slowly fracturing as they sped away.

Up, up, up they hurtled, until the colour of the water changed, casting the bridge in pale green light.

A little more, Ailsa thought as she felt something wet trickling from her nose to her lip.

Then they were through. They breached the cold sea,

emerging in a great wave. And still Ailsa didn't stop directing magic into the engines. "Get us to shore," she groaned.

Because she sensed it then, the weight of the Stoor Worm surging through the water towards them. Faster than she'd expected.

But they were faster.

She pushed the boat on as the crew held their breaths. A wave of dizziness lapped at her body but she kept her back straight, kept her hand on the pipe. Down on the stairs, Iona was throwing up her arms, directing her water magic back at the monster.

On the horizon, the coast came into view. Closer and closer they sped until they could see the houses. Until they could make out the doors.

With a scream, Ailsa funnelled her last reserves into the boat. The submarine almost skipped across the water.

Ailsa knew they'd crossed some invisible line of protection when she felt the Stoor Worm's presence halt. It stopped there, swimming back and forward, looking for a way in.

And then it was gone.

Ailsa sagged to the floor in relief.

Hands were on her, and Ailsa leaned into the touch. The familiar scent of sea-salt and citrus enveloped her, soothing her.

"You did it," Iona whispered, her smile leaking into her voice.

"*We* did it," Ailsa answered. And she let her head fall back against the deck.

Chapter 21

arris groaned as he pressed a man's unconscious body into the floor and let out a string of curses. He'd been on his way to find Angus when the boat had lurched and he'd heard a scream. The room he ran into was some sort of control centre. Two boys, barely teenagers, were huddled in the corner. As soon as he'd appeared, they'd pointed shaking fingers at a man slumped to the floor.

"The panel exploded," said the tallest boy with shaved hair. "I think he hit his head."

Harris found the man unresponsive, glasses askew, a few cuts and bruises, but otherwise fine. He'd just been knocked out. "He'll be okay. Just look after him," he said, turning to leave.

"Wait," the other boy called after him. "Please don't leave us; we don't know what we're doing."

Harris sighed. "Why are you on this boat, then?"

"We're apprentices. Señor Santiago is training us—"

"He's the ship's engineer."

"Is he going to be okay?"

I don't know, Harris wanted to say. But that wouldn't be helpful. Instead, he knelt back down beside the unconscious man. "He'll probably wake up any moment now—"

Another impact. The room shuddered. Harris threw himself over the man to keep him in place, as he watched the boys. The smell of urine permeated the small space.

"You're alright. We're going to be alright," Harris told them. *They're terrified, absolutely terrified.* What exactly were the rest of the crew doing up on the bridge?

"Are we going to die?" asked the smallest boy.

Somehow, you've found yourself as the only adult in the room. That was never a good idea.

Harris grinned up at them. "Where's your sense of adventure? I know you have it somewhere. You joined a pirate ship, after all. What would your captain say if she saw you like this?"

They blinked. Then the tallest one said quietly, "What do we have to do?"

"Run through everything you've been taught so far and think what's going to help."

"We can't do anything," said the smallest. "We've only been watching for a few weeks. We're just going to make things worse."

Harris shook his head. "You won't. You have to decide whether you're going to sit there and worry, or you're going to help. Because there is a chance we are going to die—there always is. If we do, at least you'll go down fighting. And if we don't, you can be proud of yourselves, because you helped." Harris shrugged as best he could from his position on the floor. "It's a win-win situation, really."

There was a tense moment when he thought he'd lost them, scared them too badly. Harris cringed internally, even as he kept the grin plastered to his face.

Finally, the smallest boy bit his lip and nodded.

That's when the bells began to ring.

They'd leapt up, turning dials and shouting commands

at Harris, until he'd dragged the unconscious man under a table that was bolted to the floor. The boys had barely made it under with him when the whole boat had shuddered and then plummeted.

Harris had whispered them tales of heroic deeds, embellished of course, as the boat quaked. He'd squeezed their hands as the control panel was electrified, sparks fizzing across the instruments. He told them repeatedly that it would be okay as they'd shot upwards.

Now, everything was still, quiet. And yet, they didn't emerge from their spot under the table. Harris's body was battered, like he'd just gone ten rounds with a goblin. The boys were shivering beside him. Then, with a groan, the man below Harris blinked his eyes open.

"Who are you?" he asked groggily.

Harris grinned down at him. "Don't worry. I know I look like an angel, but you're not dead." Then, with a wink Harris rolled off the man.

The two boys fell upon the engineer, telling him through tears of relief what had happened. Harris lay on the floor, listening to them chatter.

Perhaps it would be nice to avoid adventures for a little bit.

Once Harris had extracted himself from the boys and the concussed man, he went in search of his friends. But it was his sister he found first, on her way back from the infirmary. She looked rumpled, her usual neat copper hair now a snarl of knots encircling her head. Half her white shirt had been pulled out of her trousers and there was a bruise on her cheekbone that had only just yellowed, despite her healing abilities.

"You look worse for wear," he said by way of greeting.

Iona scowled. "And where have you been?"

"Down in the control room." Harris leaned against the wall. "Do I want to know what happened?"

"I'm sure you felt it. I was certain we were going to die and then…" Iona shook her head, looking off into nowhere. "Ailsa powered the ship—took us straight to the surface."

Ailsa had done that? The energy that must have taken. "Where is she?"

"The medic's seeing to her. She drained herself of magic."

Harris tried to imagine it, how the electricity would have coursed through her. "I didn't think she had that sort of power…"

"She's been practising," Iona said, biting her lip. "But I was surprised too."

"Well, at least we know we have the right person for the air treasure."

Iona dipped her head. "Have you seen Angus and Cameron?"

"I was on my way to find Angus but got a bit sidetracked. Want to come and see if he survived?"

Iona poked him in the ribs. "If we find a splatted prince, I'll feed you to a shark."

They wound their way through the corridors, down the stairs and through hatches, until they reached the cargo hold. All the while, Iona filled Harris in on what had happened up on the bridge, what they'd faced.

"A Stoor Worm, really?" Harris almost choked on his own spit. "I thought they were only legends."

Iona's mouth was a grim line. "I can't shake the feeling that it's all connected. The Stoor Worm, the Edaxi… We don't have the best of luck, do we?"

Harris couldn't help but agree. "Maybe we're cursed."

The first room of the hold was almost cavernous compared to the rest of the ship. Crates of food and other supplies were piled up neatly and various machines were hanging from the ceiling, which Harris couldn't even comprehend. But it was clear Angus and Laire were not there.

"Do you think they hid somewhere up here?" Iona asked, striding off to a wall of doors at the back.

Harris followed her, worrying that he might indeed find the prince injured. He knew that if Angus had been in this gigantic room, there would have been nothing to stop him from flying up to the ceiling during the dive. And if he'd been anywhere near one of those machines…

Harris eyed one on his left as he passed. It was some sort of vehicle, with four wheels like a wagon, except there wasn't a place a horse could go. Instead, its front jutted out in a long arm with spikes on the end. They were rounded, as though meant for scooping. Or gripping onto something.

Iona stopped in front of a hatch with a round window in the centre. Harris was about to ask her what she could see when she turned to him and held her finger to her lips.

Confused, Harris crept up beside her and peered through the glass.

The room was much smaller with a lower ceiling. It was barely large enough to hold the unicorn that was sprawled on her side. A net had been tossed across her back and the ends were tied to the walls, the floor, anything that would keep her in place. Then he saw them. Behind the unicorn, two men were huddled side by side, heads leaning in like they were talking. Harris recognised the hair: one pink,one brown.

"Should we check if they're okay?" he whispered to Iona.

His sister stepped on his foot. "Don't you dare." She watched them for a moment, then she grabbed his arm, tugging him behind her as she made her way back across the cargo hold. "Oh, I'm really going to enjoy being the third wheel when we leave for Kilvaig," she muttered.

Harris only snickered. Perhaps someone was having some luck after all.

Harris dropped Iona back at the infirmary, only ducking his head in before leaving her there. *I'll see Ailsa once she feels better,* he told himself with a grimace.

Not that he didn't want to see her, he just didn't know if she'd want to see him. She'd have to deal with him for a few days yet. It was probably best to let her recover. But the excuses didn't stop his mind repeating a single word as his footsteps pounded through the halls.

Coward, coward, coward.

Upstairs the scent of salty air was the same as before, even if the view wasn't. The whole hatch that led to the upper deck had been pulled off and tossed to the side—dented from the Stoor Worm's attack. Half the railing was missing with scrapes gouged into the golden plates. But the skies were blue, and the breeze was gentle. Seagulls squawked overhead, telling him they were near land. The calm after the storm.

Harris ducked out and slipped his way onto the deck, laughing softly when he could see where they were. Ailsa

135

had been pretty thorough. Not only had she powered them to the surface, she'd taken them all the way to the coast. The tiny port town was within swimming distance, if anyone was brave enough to jump into the cold water. The settlement was modest, stretching along the harbour; each of the buildings was painted in bright colours and draped with climbing plants.

He would have looked more, would have traced all the wee winding paths with his eyes as he basked in the briny smell, if he'd been alone up there. But there was someone else there, staring out at the town, leaning against what was left of the railing.

"Oh, sorry," said Harris, tracing his sliding steps back towards the hatch. "I didn't think anyone would be on deck."

Irené glanced over her shoulder. "I was just taking a break."

Harris nodded, about to go back inside, but Irené called out to him.

"I heard what you did. That you helped down in the control room."

He faced her, shrugging. "I didn't do anything." Besides cracking a few jokes and acting as a body weight.

"You kept those boys from falling apart," she said.

"They're good kids." Harris leaned back against the gnarled door, sticking his hands into his pockets. "They didn't really need my help."

Irené looked him up and down, her eyes burning a trail from his toes to his head. Calculating. "Diego and Cesar wouldn't stop singing your praises downstairs. You're their hero."

"You seem surprised."

The captain merely shrugged.

Harris bolstered his courage. "I think we should start over," he said, bracing for the inevitable dismissal.

"Who will you be this time?" Irené crossed her arms.

Don't make any jokes, just be honest. "Hopefully a friend?"

"In case you haven't noticed, I have many of those," she said, lifting her chin. "What makes you think I need another?"

"Everyone could use one more friend." He sighed. This wasn't going well. "Look, I'm sorry for offending you when we first met. I know I can be pretty annoying. In the past, I've found, if you feign confidence, eventually it works. I can sometimes cross the line and become insufferable. It's a trait of the fae, I'm afraid. My sister has just had more experience getting along with humans."

Irené watched him for a moment. "Have you ever heard the story of the king and Queen of Edessa?" she asked.

He narrowed his eyes. "No?"

"My father, Elias, was the crown prince of Edessa." Irené stared out to sea. "In his early days, he was quite a scientist. Not in a laboratory or workshop, mind you. He was an oceanographer. He would go sailing, recording the behaviours of dolphins and whales. Sometimes he'd risk his life, donning heavy metal suits and sinking to the ocean depths, with only a hose attached to supply air. But one day, deep down in the wreckage of a ship, the hose was severed and his suit filled with water. That was when my mother saved him." She smiled. "*Mi madre*, Marisol, is a xana."

"The sirens of the sea?" Harris had heard of them, of course, but he'd never actually seen one.

"Yes," said Irené. "The xana had a habit of luring sailors to their deaths once. Not for hundreds of years. Now they seek to share knowledge with humans."

Just as well. Harris's aunt had told him stories of the xana when he was a child. They were beautiful maidens with fish tails and haunting voices, able to sink entire ships with their songs. But unlike their cousins, the ceasg, they were known for their intelligence and creativity. Harris had dreamed, as a young boy, of swimming off to find their underwater palace, covered in murals of seashells and coral, filled with treasures from old shipwrecks.

"Few people know about my mother now, she's rarely near water in public," Irené continued. "My father has built her private fountains inside our Castillo and there she can be herself in secret. But once, she was always in her fae form. She lived under the sea and loved its creatures, as my father did. When my father had first started studying the ocean, she had been interested in his work and so she showed herself to him one night when he was watching the bioluminescence on our shores. She asked him if she could assist him, learning what he did and teaching him her ways. And so began a beautiful friendship."

"On the day that my father's air hose failed, she was nearby. She noticed almost as soon as it happened and tried to pull him to the surface. But his suit was too heavy. Only the people above would have been able to pull on the chains to bring him up. Sensing the air inside the suit was running out fast, she prayed to the goddess of the sea, Salacia, to spare his life. The goddess called to my mother and said she would save my father if my mother promised to return to the land with him."

"And your mother accepted," Harris guessed.

Irené closed her eyes. "He was her friend. She couldn't bear to let him drown. So she agreed. My father shot to the surface and my mother followed him, all the way to his ship and back to his kingdom." Irené turned her unflinching gaze on him again. But it had softened from her memories. "She did not save him because of romantic love; she didn't feel that for years. No, she saved him because he was her friend and she was his."

The princess pushed herself up and strolled over to where Harris was leaning. "I tell you this story for two reasons," she said. "First, as a half-fae, I understand your moods better than most. If you agree to be honest, I will not mind a little arrogance."

One corner of her mouth lifted, and Harris's heart beat a little faster.

"And second, you're right. A person could always do with more friends." Irené held out her hand to him.

Harris stared for a moment, not quite believing the way the conversation had turned. But then he shook himself, taking her hand in his and giving it a squeeze. "Deal," he breathed.

And so, the selkie and the pirate captain grinned at each other on the back of the battered submarine, declaring peace in the aftermath of battle.

Chapter 22

On any normal day, Iona would pull the water out of the jug using her magic, but pummelling the Stoor Worm had been a drain on her power. Instead, she poured the water the old-fashioned way and placed the glass on the table beside Ailsa's head.

The room smelled of bleach and medicine but nothing had been given to the sleeping girl lying on the bed in front of her. Ailsa hadn't exactly passed out, she'd just been so tired that as soon as her head had hit the pillow in the infirmary, she'd started snoring. Even while Iona had been off with Harris, Ailsa hadn't woken up, so the doctor had told her.

No wonder. Using that sort of power had to tire anyone out. Ailsa's sleepiness wasn't anything to worry about.

Iona looked down at Ailsa's side, where her right arm rested above the blankets. Now that *was* something to worry about. The skin there was raised in red welts, starting from under her shirt sleeve and radiating down to her hand. The marks were branching, as if they followed the veins under Ailsa's skin. They reminded Iona of forked lightning.

That must have been the hand that had held the metal pipe.

Iona flicked her gaze up to Ailsa's face. She looked much younger in sleep, her face relaxed, without her usual frown, and her chapped lips slightly parted. The changeling mark below her left eye was a mottled wine colour, but a faint scar on the other side cut from her eyebrow, across her cheek, and down to her chin. Ailsa had said little about that injury, just that she'd received it when she'd been captured by the Avalognian raiders. It had healed nicely; it was only really noticeable when the light hit it. Healed, probably thanks to her fae blood.

What are you? Iona wondered again, for the hundredth time since she'd found Ailsa on the beach, after she'd sunk those ships with her storm. Before then, she'd suspected Ailsa had some sort of fae blood, far back in her ancestry, but now it was clear: Ailsa was too powerful not to have at least one fae parent. She had to be something very special indeed. It was why Iona had easily believed Ailsa was Nicnevan's daughter after all.

Perhaps they'd never know. Iona thanked the gods they had Ailsa on their side. She'd be a formidable enemy.

The door creaked open and Iona raised her head, expecting to see the green-haired doctor but it was Cameron who stuck his head round the corner.

"I came as soon as I heard," he whispered, creeping into the room.

"She's fine," Iona told him, motioning to Ailsa's sleeping form. "Just got a bit tired out after saving us all."

Cameron crouched down at the foot of the bed. "I was on my way up to the bridge when I felt sick. Something tugged me down to the cargo hold, where Angus was."

"Another vision?"

He paled. "I don't think so, just a gut feeling. Harris wasn't there and Angus was struggling to secure Laire so she wouldn't hurt herself."

"My brother got caught up looking after some boys in the control room."

"I thought we were done for, when the bells started ringing, and then it felt like we were getting sucked down into the ocean." He wiped a hand across his face. "But we're safe. Apparently, we're getting towed into harbour."

"Do you know which town it is?"

"Inshmore."

"Huh, that was lucky." The exact town they'd been aiming for. "Does that mean we'll be getting off then?"

Cameron smiled ruefully. "I think even if we'd been a thousand miles from where we needed to be, Laire would still want to be off this boat."

"And you're still alright to come with us?" Iona asked.

He lifted his chin. "Of course. Besides, Ailsa didn't want me with her, and I didn't want to go with Harris."

Because if he went with Harris, he'd have to go back to Ephraim. Back to where he'd been imprisoned for so long, where he'd been tortured by the Faerie Queen.

"Angus and I will be better company, anyway. As long as I don't get in the way of you two," she teased.

Cameron looked at her sharply. "What do you mean?"

Oh dear. "Sorry, I just assumed... I just thought you two had been something to each other, once. I must have been mistaken."

He sighed, running his hand along the back of his neck. "When I first met Angus, I didn't know he was the prince. I remember the day he turned up to the training camp. He looked so scrawny in his fighting gear. I could tell, we could all tell, that he was younger than he'd said he was. But who were we to judge? Many of us in that camp were orphans with nowhere else to go. So we overlooked the fact he was below the age limit and did our best to make him one of us."

Cameron's gaze was unfocussed. "At the beginning, it was like I was taking a younger brother under my wing. But then he got stronger and fitter and I couldn't help noticing. I knew I liked boys then, that wasn't new to me, but I felt like a bit of a cradle snatcher."

Iona scoffed inwardly. He couldn't be much older than Angus. "How many years are between you?"

"Three."

Now she couldn't help her lips pressing into a smile. "I've heard of bigger age gaps." Amongst the fae, that was nothing.

He glanced down at his sister, still sleeping away soundly. "He was the first boy I held hands with. The first boy I kissed. I didn't actually find out he was the prince until his father rode in to take him away."

"Now you know. And, I've got to say, he seems happy when you're around."

Cameron shook his head. "He's royalty. I'm just a grunt."

"At the very least, you're his friend. Like I said, we'll have fun." She placed a hand on his and gave him a squeeze, feeling the ridges of dozens of tiny scars as she did so. Gods, barely a man and his body had seen such violence.

Stop that, he won't want you mothering him.

Cameron slid out of her grasp. "Thanks. I'm going to see if I can help any with fixing the damage. Would you send word when she wakes up?"

She gave him a weak smile. "Sure thing."

As soon as he was out the door, Iona went back to watching the sleeping girl in the narrow bed, suddenly very aware of how young and fragile all of her friends were.

Chapter 23

Ailsa had woken to find her pillow covered in drool and a selkie staring owlishly down at her. After trying, in vain, to convince Iona she was fine, she'd invented a message to send to Cameron. The redhead left her. But only after doling out a list of instructions on how to look after herself, which Ailsa immediately disregarded as soon as Iona was out the door. She had her own list.

Step one, new clothes, Ailsa decided. She'd been sweating in her sleep, the fabric clinging to her back and itching where it had dried. Step two was food.

Now, in a fresh shirt and leggings, Ailsa slipped through the corridors, hoping she'd go unnoticed. They had taken on a lot of damage during the Stoor Worm's attack. Everyone would probably be working hard to piece the boat back together.

But as Ailsa descended the stairs from the living quarters to the kitchens, she came face to face with half a dozen crew members. These were all people she'd seen before, people she vaguely recognised. By the way they stopped in their tracks, staring as she passed, she was in no doubt that they knew who she was.

Ailsa's skin crawled like their eyes were touching her. She had grown up used to people staring at her. It often preluded insults being hurled her way. Or other projectiles. Ailsa ducked her head, allowing her hair to form a curtain over the left side of her face, and hurried on.

As she walked, she examined her arm. She'd noticed the welts snaking down her forearm as soon as she'd woken but hadn't really looked properly until she'd been alone in her room. *Your body's looking a bit worse for wear*, she thought wryly. If that was the price to pay for saving everyone, she'd gladly do it again.

It suits you, Ishbel told her.

Ailsa was inclined to agree. Unlike her changeling mark, these scars had been earned. "Will they go away?"

Eventually they'll fade, but they'll never fully disappear.

Ailsa nodded, clenching her fist. "I didn't know I could do that. I thought I needed open air for my magic to work."

The spirit guide snorted in her head. *Silly girl.*

Ailsa waited to see if there would be anything after the insult, but Ishbel had gone quiet again. "Fine. A lot of use you are," she grumbled, stalking into the kitchen.

Like the rest of the boat, the room had suffered from their battle. An enormous pot had been knocked from the stove, coating the work surface and the floor in a thick orange mush. Chairs were tipped over and baskets of fruit and veg had been overturned, spilling their contents across the tiles. The cook was nowhere to be seen, so she tiptoed across the broken crockery and helped herself to an intact plate. She looked into barrels and inside cupboards, grabbing anything that looked ready to eat. A box in the corner hummed strangely and when Ailsa opened it, the interior was freezing, as though by magic. She closed it quickly, unwilling to pull anything out. Too risky. The pantry at the back looked a little more promising. Amongst the toppled supplies inside, she found a jar of olives

145

in oil, some cured meat and a loaf of crusty bread someone had already cut from.

Holding her plate in two hands, she crept through the door to the dining hall, just in case there was anyone there, but it was miraculously empty. Ailsa let out a sigh of relief before picking up an overturned chair and sinking into it to eat her meal.

As soon as the ham touched her tongue, filling her mouth with the tastes of salt and sweet, she realised how ravenous she was. Looking round once more to check she didn't have an audience, she proceeded to devour the food. She ate until her dish was clear, and then ran back into the kitchen for more, not bothering to fill another plate, instead eating straight out of the containers. She was tucking into a jar of pickled anchovies when she heard a cough behind her.

"Iona said you were up." Cameron closed the door behind him, taking in her wild eyes, the fork she'd discarded beside her in favour of her fingers. "Hungry?"

"Starving," she mumbled around a mouthful of fish. Because, even now, her hunger hadn't dampened. She cast her eyes down to all the boxes and tins she'd already devoured. They covered the whole central island. Ailsa lowered the anchovy jar with a wince. Who knew how many days' worth of supplies she'd just eaten?

"It was probably using your magic," Cameron said with a chuckle. "That much energy has to be replaced."

"You heard about it?" Ailsa asked, wiping her mouth with the back of her hand. *Hag's teeth!* There were spots of grease and sauce on her fresh shirt. She'd have to change again.

"Everyone's talking about how you saved us."

Ailsa groaned. "Great. Looks like I'll be hiding in my bunk

for the rest of the journey." She studied her brother more closely, noting the travelling clothes he now wore. "How far are we from shore?"

"We're already docked. In Inshmore harbour."

"Which means you'll be heading off?"

"Looks like it. Once we've got some supplies, of course. Are you sure you'll be okay by yourself?"

I was for years, Ailsa almost told him. But that wasn't fair. That wasn't Cameron's fault. "I won't be for long, remember?"

"Sure." He didn't look convinced. "We're heading into town in an hour. Will you see us off?"

"Of course."

Cameron just lifted one corner of his mouth before heading back out through the door. As soon as he was gone, Ailsa let out a sigh, resting her head on the wall beside her.

He wants to go with you, Ishbel echoed her own thoughts.

"You know that isn't a good idea." Ailsa bit her lip. "It's too dangerous for him."

You could just tell him where we're going. Then he'll know you are protecting him.

Ailsa grabbed a block of cheese and swept out of the kitchen, heading for her room and a new shirt. "If I told him, he'd never let me leave his sight."

I should have let everyone drown, Ailsa thought as she made her way down to the hold. Everywhere she went on the godsforsaken ship, crew members stared at her in open awe. The cabin girl Iona had found had placed a flower in Ailsa's hair. Where did she even get that? It took all of Ailsa's remaining strength to hold back the growl that had bubbled behind her lips. She was officially over being recognised. *As soon as Cam, Angus and Iona are gone, I'm holing myself up in the cabin.*

Her friends were waiting in a loose group when she stomped into the hold. They all had the common sense to avert their eyes, except for the captain who greeted her with a wide smile.

"There she is, the hero of the day!" said Irené. The osprey perched on her shoulder ruffled its wings. It looked too big to be sitting there, the claws too sharp to be comfortable, but the captain looked like she hardly noticed.

Ailsa reined in her bad temper again. It wouldn't do to send a stray spark in their host's direction. Even after the encounter with the Stoor Worm, she could feel her magic returning.

"I'm glad I could help," she gritted out instead, turning to her companions.

Iona, Cameron and Angus were in their travelling clothes, their rucksacks already hauled onto their backs. The prince was petting the unicorn's side as her eyes darted from him to the open hatch and the docks beyond, like she couldn't leave fast enough.

I doubt she'll be getting back in any boats soon, Ailsa thought with a stab of guilt. It couldn't have been comfortable down here while they'd been plummeting up and down.

Harris was perched on a crate, his shirt unbuttoned, revealing his freckled chest. His shoes were off too, and his trousers were rolled up, looking for all the world as though he'd just been sunbathing.

"All set?" he asked his sister.

Iona gave her bag strap a tug. "Raring and ready to go." She leaned in, giving him a hug where he sat.

"Don't do anything I wouldn't do," he said over her shoulder.

"Sometimes I actually think it's safer to do the exact opposite of what you would do," she chuckled, letting him go. Then she turned to Ailsa, clasping her shoulders. "Stay safe," she said, giving her a knowing look.

Ailsa bit the inside of her cheek and squeezed the selkie's arm.

Next, Angus was upon her, completely oblivious to the grim mood she'd just been in. He pulled her into a bone-crushing hug, spinning her in a circle as he did so. "See you in a few weeks," he told her.

As soon as the prince set her down, Ailsa gave his chest a half-hearted shove. "Idiot," she said, fondly. Angus always knew how to cheer her up, even when she didn't want to be.

Finally, it was Cameron's turn to say goodbye. He hesitated in front of her, weighing up his options, until Ailsa reached up on her tiptoes and slung an arm over his shoulders. She felt him tuck his face into her neck.

"Look after them," she whispered into his hair. *And yourself.*

Then, too soon, she stepped away. He gave her a wave before joining the others at the gangplank.

The captain slipped away to speak to the crew who'd just delivered some boxes of supplies from the town, leaving Ailsa alone with Harris.

"They'll be fine," he said, giving them a wave as they walked over the wooden slats.

Ailsa did her best to smile, coming to lean against the crate

Harris was perched on. "I hope so," was all she said. She looked down at the welts on her hand again and sighed. This was meant to be a quick journey round the coast. But wherever they'd been in the last few weeks, danger had followed.

What new wounds would they each have the next time they met?

Chapter 24

Iona looked over Cameron's shoulder impatiently. "Well?" she asked.

"The map says we should be there any time now," he sighed, shaking the parchment out.

"A warm bed and a hot meal, that's all I want," Iona grumbled. It had been raining ever since they'd left Inshmore. It had rained while they walked, while they tried to cook their dinner, and while they'd tried to sleep, the water cascading through the trees they'd tried to shelter under. Iona had done her best to repel the precipitation, but it was hard while it was still falling.

If only we had Ailsa to keep the clouds away.

Angus patted Laire's side and said nothing. His hood was up, head tilted down to keep the droplets from getting inside. It was no use though; the rain was a light smirr which crept under clothes and into bones.

They pressed on and sure enough, the welcome sight of chimney smoke greeted them above the treetops. Iona could barely hold herself back from running ahead.

"I think it's an inn," Cameron said as the three-storey stone building came into view. "But it's not on the map."

"Who cares? It looks warm," Angus mumbled. "I'll take you round the back first and see if there are any stables," he said to the unicorn.

She gave her head an indignant toss and walked off by herself as the prince stared after her.

"What did she say?" asked Cameron.

Angus rolled his eyes. "That she can take care of herself but if we find any raw meat, I've to send it out her way."

They hurried up the path and past the windows. Iona caught flashes of little round tables and a fire roaring in the hearth. *Perfect.*

The heavy wooden door was half open so they let themselves in. Immediately, a wave of heat washed over them. Iona looked around surreptitiously before clicking her fingers. All the water from their clothes and skin rose into the air, hanging there for a moment, before she flicked it out of the door.

Even better.

"Hello, are you open?" Cameron called, taking a tentative step into the hallway.

A set of stairs snaked up to the left and below them was a lacquered desk filled with books and papers. To the right, through another open door, was the pub Iona had spied through the window.

There was a crash somewhere in the back and then a young woman, looking slightly frazzled, appeared through the door behind the desk. "No, we're closed—" The woman stopped when she saw them, her gaze snagging on Iona. "I mean, we open in half an hour, but you can come on in and take a seat." She waved them through the door to the right.

Iona bit her lip. "Sorry, we don't mean to be a bother—"

"No, no. You're fine," said the woman, patting her dark hair, tied back messily in a bun. "Just let me get finished setting up and I'll get you a drink."

"Thank you," said Cameron, brushing past Iona to go sit in a booth.

Iona followed, taking in the pub decor now that she knew they could stay. It was bright and cosy, the early light shining through the antique windows. The walls were covered in pictures, antlers, and other collected objects.

Above the stained-glass window, two axes were mounted on the wall, the handles crossed over each other. A dozen tables with mismatched chairs were scattered about the bar, which was stacked with glasses. There was a faint smell of rosemary and gravy, as if someone else was cooking. Iona settled across from Cameron in a deceptively squishy seat.

Angus sighed happily. "If they have some rooms, we could use this place as a base and search outwards for the sword."

"It could take weeks. Do we have enough money?" asked Cameron.

"Didn't you know?" Iona said with a wink. "I'm incredibly rich."

"I didn't think selkies even carried money," he teased. "It's not like you have pockets when you're a seal."

"The money is in my clothes' pockets. When I'm a seal, it disappears wherever my clothes go."

Cameron chuckled. "And how did you get so wealthy?"

"Investments mostly. It's easy to accumulate a fortune when you live beyond a normal human lifespan. You see trends. Sure bets. Did you know there's a lot of money in seaweed, for example?"

"I hadn't heard."

"Oh yes, you can make almost anything from seaweed. Food, cosmetics, even medicine." Iona patted the side of her bodice, making a faint clinking sound. "So the rooms are on me. I feel like we deserve a little luxury, don't you?"

"You do both realise you're travelling with a prince of the realm?" Angus said with a frown.

Iona poked him in the side. "Well, next time you can offer to put your money up first then, my liege."

Chapter 25

humans, Harris realised, were easily entertained. They thought they were cultured and learned, but none of them could resist a seal flopping about in front of them.

"Look at him."

"He's so cute."

"Do you think it would be weird if I pet him?"

Harris lay on his side, curled so his tail was in the air, and let the crew admire him. It was the least he could do for his audience.

He was in the middle of the mess hall, surrounded by the off-duty sailors. They'd been travelling underwater for two days since leaving Inshmore, with nothing to see except metal walls and each other's faces. Harris had sensed they needed a bit of fun. Which was why he'd upended his glass of water on his head and promptly turned into a seal.

"Do the slide again!" someone shouted from the crowd.

Harris let out a bark and belly-rolled to the starting position. As soon as he'd changed his form, the cook had darted into the kitchen for some oil, spreading it across the floor. *Yes, easily entertained* Harris chuckled to himself before launching his body down the strip of slick floor. But it wasn't enough to just slide. No, if there was one difference between a selkie and a regular seal, it was that selkies had style. So Harris twisted as he slid until he was spinning nose over tail.

But the crowd's cheers died. Harris came to a stop at the bottom of the makeshift slide and peered up at them. They weren't looking at him anymore. Instead, their eyes were on something behind him.

"What," said the captain, "is a seal doing in my boat?"

Harris tipped his head back over his shoulder to find a very irate looking Irené. Her hands were on her hips and her mouth was pressed into a thin line.

Nothing to see here, just a cute, very lost seal. Harris began to slink away.

"You all know the rules," the captain said slyly. "If any errant sea creatures jump into this boat, they're fair game for dinner."

Harris's eyes widened as he willed his body to flop faster. But the crew had a new game. Harris looked over his shoulder again to see Irené shrugging out of her jacket.

"I suppose I'll need to catch him first," she said with a cackle before launching herself at him.

What followed was a scramble across the slick floor as Harris tried to dig his claws in and failed, while Irené slipped over the oil after him. The crew were laughing heartily, but did not lend a hand to either their captain or the seal. *Traitors,* Harris thought as he tried to duck between their legs.

Just then, Irené's hand wrapped around his back flipper; he was caught, the wind knocked out of him.

Harris grinned. *This'll teach you.*

Instantly, he shifted again, back into a man. Now with human eyes, Harris looked down at Irené, still holding his ankle. The captain's face was frozen between laughter and horror as she took in his new body. His new, almost naked, body.

"Why are you only wearing underwear?" she spluttered.

"I didn't want to ruin my clothes in case I had to shift back." And he was glad of it too. Despite having changed forms, his freckled skin was still covered in grease. He'd need a shower after this. The captain wasn't faring much better. Her trousers and shirt were sticking to her and the skin she had on show was shining with oil. She still hadn't let go of his ankle.

Things didn't seem so funny anymore.

"Okay, nothing left to see here," he called to the crew as he sat up, hugging his knees to his chest. "All of you can piss off now."

Irené smirked at him as the sailors dispersed with some grumbles. A blush crept into his cheeks as he held her gaze. *Why aren't there more ballads about brown eyes,* he wondered absently. Hers were luminous. Rich. Like sweet chocolate.

"I wouldn't have thought a captain would join in with such nonsense," he said, his voice breaking halfway through the sentence. *Smooth.*

"We're all allowed a little fun," she said, letting go of his foot. "I was coming to tell you we've reached the coast again so we can drop Ailsa off."

Harris's stomach twisted. Ailsa hadn't left her room since Inshmore, except to eat. He'd been hoping to spend a bit more time with her before she had to leave. *You'll see her in a few weeks,* he told himself.

"I'd better go make myself look decent."

The captain looked him over and let out a snort. "You've only got an hour."

Harris's good mood had vanished by the time he'd showered and made his way down to the hold. Another of his friends was leaving, and he had a terrible feeling Ailsa's destination was much more dangerous than where his other companions had gone.

She'd given him a swift hug and shouldered her bag, striding down the gangway without a backwards glance. He watched Ailsa as she walked, feeling his chest tighten. Off to gods-knew-where with a literal demon.

"She'll be fine," a voice said, startling him.

Irené had joined him at the railing. She too had washed, looking much more like the pirate captain he expected. She raised her chin, staring after Ailsa the way he had just been doing.

"She's a strong woman," she said.

Harris nodded, turning back to watch her progress. "She is."

"But you worry about her?"

"My sister went with Angus and Cameron. Ailsa is going alone. Of course I'm worried."

"You could go with her," Irené said. "It's not too late."

"She wouldn't want me. Besides, she's meeting someone."

"The demon?"

"Yes. I've only heard about him from my sister and Angus."

"Are you jealous?"

Harris blew out a sigh. "I could say no, but I'd be lying. But I just want her to be happy."

"Good," was all Irené said.

Ailsa had reached dry land where a path snaked up into the headland, away from the sea. Harris half expected her to continue without pause. Instead, she turned and gave a small wave before disappearing. It happened so fast, Harris could only get his own hand halfway up before she was gone. He tried to ease the turn in his stomach. *Stay safe.*

"Well, we should probably get going," Irené said. "I want to be out in open waters before tonight. It's safer."

Harris caught her wrist before she walked off. "Did you want me to leave?" he asked, his voice small. It had only just occurred to him that Irené could hope he'd gone with Ailsa.

She looked down at where his fingers encircled her arm, just like hers had been wrapped around his ankle only an hour before. "You're welcome on my boat as long as you'd like."

He smiled, letting go.

"Besides," Irené said with a grin. "We need a fae to find Ephraim, and you're as good as I'm going to get."

He smirked back at her. "I want to say something like *'I'm as good as you'll ever get'* but I'm trying to be less insufferable."

"Just because you're behaving yourself, doesn't mean you can't joke," she laughed, stepping gracefully away. "And believe me, selkie-boy, I've had better."

Harris felt his cheeks turn the same shade of red as his hair as he watched the captain disappear into the boat and out of sight. *She's your friend,* he reminded himself, before following her down below.

Chapter 26

Cameron rubbed the crease between his eyebrows and
tried his best to keep up with Iona's story. Not that the
tale wasn't interesting, but he was getting a headache and it
seemed like the pain was settling in for the long haul.

The noise didn't help. By the time the barmaid had brought
them a drink and Iona had paid for some rooms, locals and
travellers alike had arrived in dribs and drabs until almost
every table had a customer. Most were Eilanmòrians, going
about their business or meeting friends. A few looked to be
passing through, probably on their way to Dunrigh.

Cameron assessed those surrounding them, noting all the
exits. It was something they'd been taught to do in the early
days of their training. *Keep your eyes open and know your
surroundings.* There was a loud group of men behind Iona,
who seemed ready for a heavy night. The tallest of them came
back from the bar holding four tankards, one for each of them
and they cheered heartily.

In the corner, someone sat with their boots resting on the
chair opposite, a hood covering their face. They smoked a
pipe and looked like they were drifting off to sleep.

A thin woman sat beside the fire, glancing now and then
at the table of men. Her dark painted nails tore at a piece of
paper absently.

"Are you listening?" Iona asked him.

"Yeah." Cameron took a sip of his beer and rubbed his pounding temple. "Just have a headache. Do you think it's safe to stay here?"

"As safe as the woods. Probably safer."

"I just have this bad feeling."

The door creaked open and Cameron's eyes darted up instinctively. A gigantic man filled the entryway, clad in furs and weapons and gave the room a once over. A cold flash of adrenaline flickered down Cameron's spine, but, just as he braced himself for trouble, the giant whistled and a deerhound trotted in from the rain to stand, dripping, at his side. They selected a table that had been recently vacated and the large man sunk down into a chair and ordered an ale.

"You won't be any good to us if you're tired out by worrying so much," Iona said, placing a hand on his.

Cameron switched his gaze back to his companion. Now that she'd warmed up a bit, some colour had returned to her cheeks. He didn't want to imagine what he looked like at that moment. Probably like a wet tea towel.

"Yeah, you're right. I'm just antsy. I have this funny feeling, kind of like I'm seeing this for the second time."

"Maybe you've been here before and you just don't remember?"

The door swung open again and this time it was a familiar face that appeared out of the storm. Still, Cameron shivered. *It's just Angus,* he chastised himself.

"Laire about had my hand off with that bucket of meat," the prince said, swinging himself onto a chair. "Gods, it's minging out there. If only Ailsa was here to chase away the clouds."

"How did the scouting go?" Iona asked, waving down the heckled barmaid.

"There's a village east of here and then woods to the west. Nothing much."

The young waitress appeared at Angus's elbow. "I assumed you'd want an ale," she said, placing a tankard on the table in front of him.

Cameron watched the movement thoughtfully. The barmaid had yet to use her left hand, not even to steady herself as she put the heavy drink down.

"Do you both want another?" She shifted and Cameron realised the hand was missing.

No wonder she's run off her feet, he thought. "I can come up to the bar to collect them?"

The barmaid smiled at him in thanks before busying herself at another table.

He stood up and immediately regretted it. The room spun for a moment until another layer of throbbing settled itself onto his temples. *Just get over it,* he told himself sternly, pushing off from the table towards the bar.

By the time he'd returned, clutching a pint in each hand, the selkie was nowhere to be seen. He placed the spare beer in front of Angus and settled back into his chair.

"Iona's gone to check out our rooms," Angus explained. He gave Cameron a weak smile and lapsed into silence.

Cameron was sick of silence.

"Do you remember when we tried sneaking into the mess hall after hours?" he said, grinning over the top of his beer.

The tips of Angus's ears reddened, but he huffed out a chuckle. "What do you mean 'tried'? We managed, didn't we?"

"But we got caught stealing biscuits."

"*I* got caught," Angus corrected. "You could have easily run off. They hadn't seen you."

"Yeah, well, I wasn't about to leave you behind, was I?" Cameron gave his foot a nudge under the table and immediately cringed. *I'm playing footsie with a prince.*

"I'm sorry I left you behind," said Angus, "when my father came to collect me. I wanted to stay."

Cameron shrugged. "Listen, I understand, we all did. You didn't have any choice."

"I kept looking for you, you know? Every parade, every time we had soldiers in the castle, I was looking out for you." Angus snapped his mouth shut, as though he hadn't meant to say that.

"I was probably a hundred miles away, sweating my ass off in Edessa or Kemet," Cameron said, as he watched Angus's teeth worry at his lip. "It didn't take me long after you left to get myself into cartography. To be honest, I was hoping I wouldn't see you for a while."

"Oh," the prince said, his face falling.

"Only because I worried that I'd acted like a right tit," Cameron said quickly. "I didn't know I'd been snogging the prince."

Angus considered this for a moment, sloshing his beer about inside his tankard. Then he gazed up at him underneath his eyelashes. "And if you had known?"

"I dunno, I'd probably still have snogged you, but at a ceilidh or something. Not in a barn we'd snuck off to." Though sometimes he still thought about that barn.

Angus brightened. "Oh really? Like in some faerie tale?"

Cameron leaned in, resting his cheek on his fist. "Yeah, you were the handsome prince, and I was the poor irresistible stable boy."

"And now you're a world-renowned map maker and

brother to my best friend."

"Does that change things?" Cameron wondered. "I wouldn't want to make things difficult."

"Me neither," Angus whispered.

There was an ache in Cameron's chest that he knew had nothing to do with the sickness he'd felt earlier. It would be so easy to reach across the table and place his hand over Angus's where it rested on his beer. And then what? He was still a soldier and Angus was still a prince. But perhaps they could pretend differently, just until they were back in Dunrigh. "Well, we could tell each other how we feel and go from there. No promises."

The prince looked him in the eye and shook his head. "I'm afraid I can't do that," he said. "I want all your promises."

"Angus, I—"

"The rooms are ready," Iona said, as she sank into her seat. "And I suggest we go to bed as soon as possible."

Cameron sat back, swallowing a groan. They'd been so close. The next time they were out on the road, the selkie had better watch her back. "Why?" he asked tersely.

"I can sense that there's a fae around, but I can't pinpoint who it is. There are too many people in here." She blinked between them. "Sorry, was I interrupting something?"

"It's fine," Cameron gritted out. "We were just reminiscing about old times."

But then Angus did something that made him choke on his beer. He winked.

"Yeah, we'll continue reminiscing later," the prince said. And within those words was a promise.

Chapter 27

Harris peered out of the round window, marvelling at how everything was magnified by the glass. The last rays of sunshine pierced through the ocean, allowing him to see the coral and seaweed surrounding the boat where it moved over the sea floor.

Now that his friends were gone, he didn't feel like talking. Instead, he'd grabbed a bowl of food and had positioned himself at the small portal while he ate. It wasn't long since they had set off again for Ephraim, but for now Harris just wanted to pretend he was alone and enveloped in salt and water.

In the mess room, he could hear the crew of The Nymph laughing. In amongst it all was Irené's voice. It sounded like she was telling a story to the entire room, though he couldn't quite make out what the words were.

He wondered if this is how his friends had sounded to the crew when they'd been up playing cards. Did they sound this happy, this free? Or had the tensions been easy to hear for anyone?

He set his plate down beside him, suddenly not hungry.

His sister would always say he never worried about anything. But that wasn't true. Harris was just better than most at hiding it. Irené had been right. He hid his anxieties under jokes and laughter.

Everyone has ways of coping. At least I'm not drunk all the time.

A noise behind startled him. He whirled from the window to find Irené standing with her hip cocked and a plate in each hand.

"I thought you might want dessert?"

"I didn't finish dinner," he said, gesturing to his half-eaten plate.

Irené held the bowl out. "I won't tell if you don't."

He took the food, sniffing. It looked like a mound of slop, but it smelled of coconut and sugar.

Irené smiled before taking a seat beside him so she could look out of the porthole too. She raised a spoon to her lips, licking at the dessert absently.

Harris realised a moment later he was staring. He dropped his eyes from her mouth and cleared his throat. "What is it?"

"Rice pudding."

He scooped some up and stuffed the spoon into his mouth. It was creamy and delicious.

"You could go out there, you know?" said Irené wistfully.

Harris swallowed his mouthful and looked up. "Where?"

"The ocean. You're a selkie, you can swim out there, can't you?"

"Of course."

She stared through the window as the light danced on her face. "If I could hold my breath underwater, I wouldn't be wasting my time in a boat."

"You said your mother was a xana. Have you ever tried to use magic? Maybe you can?"

Irené placed her bowl on the metal floor beside her. "When my mother made the bargain to save my father, she gave up most of her magic. I think she had so little left, none of it passed to me."

"Just as well, you'd be horribly overpowered if you did. Imagine: a princess, the captain of one of the impressive vessels in Ossiana, and a xana?" he said, ticking off all her accomplishments on his fingers.

"Well, look at you: a selkie, ambassador to Eilanmòr—"

He raised an eyebrow. "—pain in the ass?"

"You said it, not me," she chuckled. "Sometimes I dream about the ocean, of swimming in it."

"You don't need magic for that."

"Will you show me one time? How you swim as a seal?"

"I don't know if that's a good idea," he said. "As you saw earlier, I'm terribly cute. You may be tempted to give me a belly scratch."

Irené gave him a light shove. "I'll try to resist."

"I'd better let you get back to your crew. I haven't heard them laughing for a while," he said with a weak smile.

She considered him for a moment. "They can wait. I was wondering if you wanted to see something cool?"

"Now, normally, I'd say *'I'm already looking at something cool'*."

Irené snorted. "I don't know how anyone could fall for that. Come on."

The hallways were dark as Harris let Irené lead him through the boat. She had one hand locked around his wrist to pull him along and he used the other hand to feel his way along the walls so he didn't bump into them. Down a set of stairs, then another, through doors and rooms with whirring equipment. Eventually, they reached a heavy metal hatch and Irené dropped his arm to pull at the round handle. It groaned before giving way, revealing a small, dimly lit room.

"After you," she said with a grin.

Harris stepped inside, half expecting the captain to shut him in by himself, but she followed on his heels. With a thud, she closed the door behind her and turned the handle. Once his eyes had adjusted, he gasped in shock.

Every wall of the room was made of thick, tempered glass. Outside the submarine, pale blue lights illuminated the water so that inside they could see the surrounding ocean. Harris stumbled, mesmerised, to one wall where fish were swimming past in groups. Bright white corals and fiery anemones swayed in the currents. A lobster scuttled along the sea floor with its antennae twitching. In the distance, a grey shark prowled, its mouth open wide for any small particles of food it could find in the water.

Harris watched with fascination. "It's beautiful," he murmured.

Irené came to stand beside him. "I'm sure you've seen it all before."

"Never like this." Harris reached out a hand to the glass, watching a ghostly jellyfish undulate upwards. "I've only ever seen underwater as a seal. It's so much richer with human eyes."

"Well, I'm glad I could show you this then."

"How is the glass withstanding the pressure?"

"It's very thick, but I won't lie; having this here is dangerous. I was advised against it."

"So why have it?" he asked.

"Life is about having a little risk. At least if the glass

cracked, the water would be inside in an instant. The door is airtight, so the rest of the crew would be fine." She placed one hand on the window, splaying her fingers out. "Sometimes, when I can't sleep, I come down here and just watch for hours and hours."

"By yourself?"

She shrugged. "I like the peace. And the danger. Few do."

"Mind if I sit for a bit?" he asked.

When she gestured in assent, he sank to the floor, leaning against one glass wall so he could look out of the other. After a while, Irené sat down beside him and they stayed that way in companionable silence, watching creatures float by on a gentle tide. He imagined he'd survive if the walls cracked open, turning into a seal as soon as the water hit. But he tried to put himself into Irené's shoes, tried to understand the appeal of flirting with death.

You've done it many times yourself.

"I just feel so small here," Irené said, answering his thoughts.

"I think I understand." Because here was a woman who was so powerful, with a presence so consuming, she would never be small outside of this room. He'd listed off her accomplishments before, but how many of them had she chosen for herself? "Sometimes it's nice to take a break from ourselves."

Irené fixed her dark eyes on him, and she nodded.

Chapter 28

Cameron had changed his mind about their selkie companion, he decided when she ushered them upstairs. Iona knew exactly what she was doing.

"There were only two rooms left," she said, holding up the keys. "It's a pretty small inn."

Yes, she'd have to watch her back alright. Cameron didn't know whether to curse her out or kiss her. "Looks like two of us will have to share," he gritted out.

Iona pressed her lips together.

But Angus just stood in the hallway, wringing his hands. "I could sleep in the stables with Laire?"

Well, if he was so against them sharing, Cameron wasn't about to throw himself at him. "No, I'll sleep outside—"

"Are you two kidding me?" Iona said, the roll of her eyes barely perceptible in the dark. "Just share the room. It's not like you haven't slept beside each other before; didn't you have to sleep in a dormitory when you were training?"

"I don't want to make you awkward," Cameron said, leaving it up to the prince.

Angus crossed his arms. "I'm not awkward; we can share."

"Right," said Iona. "Well, I'm heading to bed and you should too." She unlocked the door across the hall and chucked her bag in unceremoniously. "We have a big day of investigating tomorrow." She'd almost closed herself in when she stuck her head back out into the hallway and fixed them both with a stare. "Don't leave your room." And then, with a toss of her copper curls, the door slammed shut.

Cameron eyed the room opposite, where the door was already half open. Perhaps he should check it for traps first?

Don't be ridiculous. It's a little inn on the outskirts of nowhere. But Iona had seemed rattled by whoever she'd sensed.

Before he could suggest sweeping the room himself, Angus strolled inside, dropping his pack at the foot of the bed. *The* bed, Cameron realised as he followed. Singular. Cameron had the sneaking suspicion Iona had planned this.

Angus bit his lip as he took in the faded comforter. "Right, so—"

Gods, why were his cheeks heating? "Er, yeah—"

"You take the bed," Angus said quickly. "I'll sleep on the floor."

Cameron sighed, suddenly weary. "Are we really going to do this? We're two grown men, not a couple of blushing maids." Despite whatever was going on with his cheeks. "Let's just get over ourselves."

"Yeah, you're right," Angus said, scratching at his beard. "Sure, erm, I'm just going to get changed."

Cameron sat down on the end of the bed, putting his back to the prince, and rested his elbows on his knees. His headache was getting worse; little spots of light were pulsing in the corners of his vision. *Don't ruin this now.* The conversation they'd been having downstairs needed to continue. He just had to work his way round to it again.

I want all of your promises.

Cameron didn't know what that meant, but he liked the sound of it.

He's a prince.

You're just a soldier.

But for now, they were merely two men sharing a room. And a bed.

"I wonder if Harris and Ailsa made it round the coast yet," said Angus from behind him. There was the distinct sound of fabric hitting the floor.

Cameron rolled his neck, trying to dispel the headache. "They're in expert hands. Though, it seemed like there was a bit of tension between Harris and my sister the other night." He turned his head to look at the door and caught the shine of a mirror on the wall. Cameron felt his heart skip a beat. If he were to look at the glass, would Angus be reflected back at him?

"There's some history there," Angus said, the sound of another garment hitting the floor.

Cameron gulped. *Don't look.* "I kind of guessed that. But that's over, right?"

"Yeah, it started when we went to look for the Stone of Destiny." Angus's voice was muffled as he spoke, like he was pulling something over his head. "You wouldn't believe the flirting. But I think that's pretty standard for Harris."

"So she dumped him?" For Harris's sake, it better not have been the other way around.

"Essentially. He doesn't seem too upset." More clothes rustling.

"Hence the awkwardness?" Cameron felt hot. *Don't look, don't look.* "He could have at least held off from chatting up the captain till Ailsa was gone."

"Like I said, standard Harris, I'm afraid."

"And what about this other one, the demon she's going

to find? I get the impression she's got more than a save-the-world interest in him."

"Should I really be telling you this?" Angus laughed. "I bet you'd be a nosy big brother."

Cameron chuckled. "I missed out on years of being nosy, better make up for it now." Then, unable to help it, Cameron raised his eyes to the mirror. Angus was standing behind him, staring back at him, as though he'd been doing it for a while now. He had changed into an undershirt and loose, grey trousers, ready for bed.

"You didn't look up," he murmured.

Cameron knew what he meant. "I didn't want to be a creep."

Angus smiled and ducked his head. "I'm just going to head to the toilet. You should get changed too."

Cameron nodded and waited until Angus had closed the door behind him.

"Oh gods," he said, when he was gone, dropping his head into his hands. *What is wrong with me?* He was like a hormonal teenager again.

Quickly he stood, shucking his trousers and shirt. For a moment, he debated just sleeping in his pants like he usually did. *Perhaps not the best idea.* Cameron searched inside his pack until he found a clean-ish pair of leggings and dragged them on. He left his torso bare, instead slipping into the bed and pulling the covers up to his shoulders.

The problem was, he'd felt like that teenage boy with his first proper crush as soon as he'd seen Angus in Ephraim. It was hard not to; how many fantasies had he had over the years of a handsome prince come to save him? He'd never expected it to actually happen. And the way he'd turned up, clutching that sword, ready for battle? It was no wonder those fantasies still plagued him.

"Are you decent?" Angus murmured into the room.

Not even close, he thought with chagrin. "I'm already in bed."

Angus ducked his head into the room before coming in and closing the door behind him. The prince rummaged in his things, but Cameron pinned his gaze to the ceiling, refusing to follow the other man's progress around the room. *He doesn't need you gawping at him.*

Finally, the other side of the bed dipped and Angus eased himself in, turning so that his back was to Cameron. In the silence, Cameron could almost hear his own heartbeat. Indeed, the moon shining through the thin curtains illuminated the sheet on his torso, which moved with every pulse of blood through his veins. His temple pounded like a drum, too violently for the peace of the room. How was he going to survive the night like this?

Just when the stillness had gone on long enough to make him think his companion was asleep, Angus rolled over to face him.

Cameron wet his lips.

"I'm sorry I've made things uncomfortable," Angus whispered after a moment. "It turns out I still have a bit of a teenage crush."

"It's not uncomfortable—" Cameron said, his voice too loud in the small, dark room. *Who are you trying to fool?*

"But you obviously don't feel the same," Angus replied.

Cameron's head twinged. He rolled over so he could look at friend. "I've not been well," Cameron told him gently. "But, if I felt the same—" *I do, I do, I do.* "—things are different now than they were when we were in the training camp." *How am I going to explain this without pushing him away?*

Angus sniffed. "I don't see how."

"Back then," Cameron screwed up his face at the memory and pain in his skull, "I didn't know who you were. You were no different from any other runt-soldier in that godsforsaken hole. And now—"

"I'm a prince."

"Exactly."

"And that's put you off?"

Cameron ran his tongue over his teeth. "No, of course not."

"So you *do* still like me?" Angus asked and Cameron hated that quaver in his voice. How could he not see it?

"Of course I do, but we can't—"

"Can't." Angus shook his head, the movement rustling the sheets. "All my life has been filled with '*can't*'. *Can't* dance with commoners. *Can't* become a soldier. *Can't* like boys. Well, I've got news for you. I'm not even in the line of succession anymore. There's no way I'll ever be king. So what does that make me? I reckon I'm allowed a bit of '*can*' now, don't you?"

Cameron's heartbeat thumped in his stomach. "I swore to protect Eilanmòr and the royal family," he said weakly.

Then a hand was brushing the bare skin of his arm. "So protect me. Right now I'm in a lot of danger of a broken heart and I'm afraid you're the only one who can save me."

Cameron made a noise somewhere between a laugh and a growl and the weak reins he had on himself snapped. He surged forward, capturing Angus's lips with his own. Angus's beard scratched against his cheek as their lips moved. It was so familiar, this thing between them, almost like déjà vu or like returning to a place once loved but then forgotten. Angus's

175

fingers came up to thread themselves through Cameron's hair and then, the prince gave a tug.

Immediately, Cameron jerked back, a wave of nausea engulfing him. "I—" he began, trying desperately to explain, but he was already gone. The headache he'd been feeling all evening wasn't just a headache. He'd thought the night at the ceilidh would have been a one-off, but the familiar blurring of edges and sharpening of shadows invaded his vision.

The last thing he saw before he was pulled into the premonition was Angus's agonised face.

Chapter 29

"Iona," Angus called, slamming his fist into the oak door of her bedroom. "Wake up!"

It swung open, revealing a sleep-mussed Iona, wrapping her travelling cloak around her shoulders. "What the—"

"It's happening again." The words tumbled out of Angus's mouth in a rush. Shouts from other rooms drifted into the hallway but he found he didn't care who he disturbed. "Cameron, he's having another vision."

Iona pushed past him, Angus right on her heels. The scene that greeted them was much the same. Cameron was still lying on the bed, stiff and staring unblinkingly into the distance. His skin seemed to shake, like it wasn't quite attached to his bones anymore, and the muscles strained, causing his back to bow off the mattress.

Angus felt a lump in his throat, threatening to choke him but he shoved it down. *You can panic later. Right now, Cam needs you.*

Cameron had seemed fine only moments before. Angus could still feel the shape of his lips on his own mouth.

"When did this happen?" Iona asked, rushing to Cameron's side. The selkie brushed her hands over his arm and Angus bit back the words of warning and panic. *Help him, quick!*

"Just now; he's only been convulsing for a couple of minutes."

"And this is the same as last time at the ceilidh?"

"It's more forceful now," Angus admitted, running a hand through his hair to give his fingers something to do. "And it didn't last this long before."

"It looks like he's coming out of it now," Iona murmured.

Cameron's muscles were unclenching. He sank back to the mattress, giving a few twitches.

Eventually, his eyes gave a slow blink, and he inhaled a deep breath, like he'd been under water for a long time.

"Angus?" Cameron croaked.

The prince sat down on the edge of the mattress and grabbed the other man's hand. Cameron looked up at him with fearful eyes.

"I saw something."

Angus shushed him, squeezing Cameron's palm in his own. "Let's make sure you're okay first."

"No," Cameron moaned. "We have to get word, they're going to be attacked."

Angus's stomach plummeted just as Iona asked. "Who?"

"Harris. Irené. The whole crew. They're waiting for them in the forest."

"Who's waiting?" Iona asked urgently. "The forest around Ephraim?"

"It was hard to tell." Cameron screwed up his face, as if the echo of the vision still caused him pain. "There were many people, but they didn't seem human. And then there was a figure on a horse? I think it was the Forest of Frith, that's where they're heading, isn't it?"

"Was Ailsa with them?" Angus asked.

"I didn't see her."

So whenever this vision took place, maybe they'd already split up.

"There were so many," Cameron said again. "Too many. It's going to be a bloodbath. There's no way they can fight them all."

"Oh gods," Iona whispered.

Cameron stared up at them, still half-lost in the premonition. "We have to warn them."

"There's no way," Iona said, wringing her hands. "We're days away and it could happen at any time."

"I'll go," Angus heard himself saying. He couldn't look at Cameron's tortured face. What horrors had he seen? What horrors was he going to see? "I'll take Laire and we'll run as fast as we can."

"You can't." Iona shook her head. "You'll never get there in time. Even if you do, you'll be killed."

"I need to warn them," Angus told them resolutely. "Maybe we can fight."

"Angus," Cameron croaked, squeezing his hand again. "I'll come with you."

The prince shook his head. "I'll be quicker if it's just me. You can meet me in Ephraim when you're better. Let me do this."

"I'll, er, go and get Cameron some water," Iona said, her eyes darting between them, sensing they needed a moment alone. She swept out of the door and Angus turned his eyes back to Cameron's. He hadn't expected the fire he would see there.

"Listen to me," Cameron said. "If you don't come back—if something happens to you—"

"What?" Angus smiled. "You'll kill me?"

"I finally thought I was going to get to keep you." Cameron's voice cracked. "You can't take that away from me now."

Angus dipped his head, and then their lips were brushing together again. He felt Cameron try to deepen the kiss, felt the raw agony in his jaw, but he kept it chaste, until he pulled back slightly. "Let me do the protecting this time." Then, with one final press of lips against lips, he stood, grabbed up his pack and headed for the door. "Anyway, you're going to fancy me so much more now I'm playing the hero. By the time I see you again, you won't be able to resist."

"I'm already there," Cameron whispered.

Before Angus could lose his nerve and dive back into the other man's arms, he left, closing the door behind himself with a snick. For a few heartbeats, he paused, leaning against the wood and trying to convince his body this was the right thing to do.

Then Angus McFeidh went off to save his friends.

Chapter 30

Ailsa was hopelessly lost. She'd trekked the forest for hours the day before, and again since first light, but was no closer to finding where she needed to be.

You could just go straight to Maalik's cabin, she told herself.

But where would be the fun in that? Ishbel answered back.

I'm not out here for fun. This is something I have to do. Maalik is suffering. At least he had been the last time she saw him.

Do you remember where to go? Ishbel asked.

"You're my spirit guide. Guide me," Ailsa said out loud.

The voice in Ailsa's head paused for a moment, and she wasn't sure if Ishbel had withdrawn. But then Ishbel whispered in her ear. *Do you see that dead oak? You need to go in that direction.*

Ailsa scanned the woods until she saw the tree and adjusted her steps so she was heading straight for it. "How do you know where to go?"

We were there once before, don't you remember?

"Yes, but I still don't remember the way," Ailsa grumbled.

Ishbel let out a laugh, the sound reverberating inside Ailsa's mind. *When you are as ancient as I am, you can't avoid visiting such places.*

Ailsa's stomach rolled over. Her spirit guide was still a mystery. She'd been putting the pieces together, but it still wasn't enough. She knew Ishbel was old, and she knew she had magic. Maalik had said spirit guides were powerful souls, who chose not to cross over in death, but to attach themselves to fae they had some sort of bond with. But what was that bond? How had Ishbel chosen Ailsa? And what type of fae had Ishbel been in life?

So many questions, little one.

"Are you going to answer any of them?"

All in time. For now, I like to keep you guessing.

Ailsa reached the dead tree and skirted round it, hoping that she was still going in a straight line. She thought of her destination, of Ishbel's knowledge. "You weren't a demon, were you?" she asked in a small voice.

No, Ishbel answered. *I was what demons feared.*

"Just as well," Ailsa said, climbing over a tree root. "If they attack, I'll set you loose on them."

I will gladly fight for you.

Ailsa was comforted by that. At least part of her was up to task for what lay ahead.

The sun had only just popped up over the treetops. There was still plenty of the day left. Ailsa paused and said a quick prayer to whatever gods listened that she reached her destination before nightfall. Encountering a hoard of demons would have been terrifying in the light. She did not want to find them in the dark. She stretched her powers up towards the sky and just held them there, allowing the answering crackle of lightning to soothe her fraying nerves. Then she marched on, through the thick, pine scented forest, towards Hell.

Chapter 31

The early morning air was chilly and Iona pulled her cloak tighter over her nightdress, using it as a makeshift robe. Biting her lip, she knocked on the door, hoping she wasn't too early, or too late, but then a soft *"come in"* echoed from inside. She pushed at the wood and ducked her head into the dim room. Cameron was sitting up against the headboard, like he had only just woken up.

"Morning," Iona said. "How are you?"

Cameron passed a hand over his face. "Really crap, to be honest. But my head doesn't hurt like it did yesterday. Does that mean I won't be having another vision soon?"

"We can only hope." Iona perched on the side of the mattress, being careful not to jostle him. This close, she could see the bags under his eyes, his pale skin. It was more than tiredness. It looked like he'd recently recovered from a sickness. "But I dare say they are useful. You saved so many people in Dunrigh, and hopefully you'll save my brother and the Edessans this time."

"Or I could have sent Angus to his death." A muscle in Cameron's jaw ticked. "If something happens to him, it'll be all my fault."

"Angus chose to go by himself. I for one am very grateful you saw what you did."

Cameron shook his head, blinking away tears. "Am I

cursed? What's happening to me?"

"I don't know. But a curse can be a blessing with a fresh perspective." She squeezed his knee through the blankets. "All we can do is wait and hope. In the meantime, though, we can keep looking for the sword. Let's get some breakfast into you."

He sighed and then seemed to collect himself, like the good soldier he was. "Yeah, it doesn't help to lie here worrying. Might as well be up and worrying instead."

Iona gave him a half smile and left him to get dressed. She'd had almost as bad a night as Cameron had. His words had replayed through her head a thousand times. *They're going to be attacked.*

At many points in the hours after she'd left his room, she'd considered going back in to shake him awake for more details, but she knew that wasn't fair. Cameron had told them everything he knew. It was maddening that he only saw these visions in snippets. If only she could see it for herself, maybe she would have been able to decipher more.

She changed back into her travelling clothes before heading down to the bar. The crowds from the night before were gone. Now only the few patrons of the inn remained, nursing hangovers or readying for their day. She'd chosen a seat by the window and settled down to wait for Cameron when she noticed something strange on the table.

Here and there, on the woodgrain, were splodges of something. They were brown and at first Iona supposed it was dry gravy. Yet something felt odd about them. With a nail she scratched at one, peeling it off easily in flakes. She raised the finger to her nose; it smelled metallic.

"Oh, I'm sorry, I haven't got round to cleaning that table yet," said a brisk voice from behind her.

Iona jumped as an arm snaked round and brushed at the stains with a damp cloth, removing all traces of them. But just as it was pulled back, she glimpsed the cloth had been stained rust red.

"There, that's better." The waitress from the day before stepped back, chucking the fabric in a bucket of water at her feet. "It was a busy evening, and I didn't manage to make the room as polished as I usually do."

Iona looked the woman up, and down, noticing the way her eyes darted around the room. "That's okay," she said, to be polite.

"Well, what can I get for you this morning?" Something about the woman's smile didn't seem genuine.

Probably stress, Iona thought. Waitressing did not seem like an easy job. "I was going to wait for my friend before ordering, is that alright?"

"Yes," said the woman. "Absolutely fine, call me when you want me." Then, with a swish of her skirts, she was gone, off to serve other customers.

Iona stared out the window at the grey morning. The clouds looked set to either form a thunderstorm or to burn off from the heat of the sun. There would be no in between. The air seemed to press close, like a thin layer of gauze on her skin. *I wish I could shed this form*, Iona thought. It had been a while since she had changed into a seal. After all this, she was going to go back to Struanmuir and stay there until she forgot she was part human.

"You look a million miles away." Cameron appeared, looking worn and scruffy, and sank into the seat across from her. "What were you thinking about?"

Iona shook herself "Home. Do you ever miss where you're

from?"

He snorted. "No. Our village wasn't a friendly place."

"I gathered as much from Ailsa, but I wondered if you had a different experience."

He fixed his gaze on the salt and pepper shakers on the table and reached out to click them against each other. "They didn't help my mother when she was dying and then they stole me away from my little sister. I'll never forgive them."

Iona sighed, "I don't blame you." The server nodded in their direction to let them know she would be over in a moment. Iona sought for a change of subject. *He needs cheering up.* "So, if you could be anywhere else in the world right now, where would you go?"

"Back to bed?" Cameron said with a short laugh. "No, that's not my actual answer. I'd probably head back up to Visenya. I liked the snow. Did you know they strap wooden planks to their feet and use them to slide down hills?"

Iona smiled. "That sounds dangerous."

"I sprained an ankle, but it was loads of fun. Where would you go?"

Immediately, the image of a beach with a little cottage came to her mind. Iona pressed her lips together. *You can't go back there.* "It's not the where but the who that was there."

"What?"

"Never mind." Iona stared out the window. "What's our plan of action today?"

Cameron drummed his fingers on the table. "We should head to Kilvaig first, start asking questions."

"I doubt this will be as easy as asking where the sword is."

"It's a good place to start."

"Or it's a good way to let everyone know what we're—"

Before Iona could finish her sentence, she spied something crawling under their table and she gave a start. "What was—" She ducked her head to peer underneath and was met with the back of a small head, covered in blonde curls.

"Well," said Cameron. "What do we have here?"

The little girl scooted further underneath until she had her back to the wall. In her hands she held some sort of doll with red flowing hair, almost exactly like Iona's. The girl was bundled in a thick jumper and seemed well kept. Not an urchin then. But for someone so young to be by herself, Iona could imagine her parents were looking for her.

Iona was about to look away from the child to find her mother amongst the patrons when the girl raised her huge, round eyes to hers and Iona's heart stopped beating.

It was there, in the nose, in the very expression she wore. But most of all, in her eyes; one was blue, the other brown. The resemblance was so obvious, the girl couldn't be anything other than a blood relation. Iona gasped, and the girl raised her doll in the air.

But how did this child have his face when his son and grandsons looked so very different?

"Whose child is this?" Iona breathed, never taking her eyes off the girl. A million scenarios and possibilities tumbled through her head.

A distant relative? A coincidence? No, this child sitting underneath their table in an inn in the middle of nowhere was Alasdair McFeidh's flesh and blood.

"Who does this child belong to?" Iona called, louder this time.

Out of the corner of her eye, Iona watched the waitress from earlier appear. She seemed to be as flustered as ever, though there was a definite waver in her voice which hadn't been there before.

"Maggie," she said, looking under the table. "Come here, please."

The girl raised a chubby finger at Iona. "But mama, look."

"Now," commanded the waitress.

At the change in her mother's voice, the child scooted back out, grabbing at the server's skirts to pull herself up.

"Is this child yours?" Iona asked.

"Yes," she said, patting the little girl's head. "My daughter should have been out back playing but I think she saw you and thought you were like her doll."

The girl clutched the toy closer. "This is Ro."

"She's lovely." Iona tried to slow her pulse, tearing her gaze away from the child. "I'm sorry, it's... she looks like someone I used to know."

The waitress tucked her daughter further behind her and glanced between Iona and Cameron warily. "Would you like some food?"

"Yes, please, whatever you have for breakfast," he said, cutting in. "And the same for my friend too."

The woman cleared her throat. "Come on, Maggie, let's go and get food for these customers."

As soon as they were out of earshot, Cameron leaned forward. "You were acting really weird. Who does she remind you of?"

"Angus's grandfather," Iona whispered. "And she doesn't just remind me of him, she's the spitting image."

Cameron considered this for a moment. "Is it possible they're distantly related? It's not like Eilanmòr is a big place."

No, she wanted to reply. But that was almost impossible,

wasn't it? "Maybe," she finally conceded. "It caught me off guard. I haven't seen him for years and years; it was almost like meeting a ghost."

"Perhaps not the best reaction, though. People don't go about staring at children in polite society."

"Oh gods, was I really creepy?"

"A bit. That waitress will be watching you like a hawk."

The door banged open, making Iona jump. She was about to reply to Cameron when the hairs on her arms prickled and she felt it; the instinct that a predator was nearby. The other guests sensed it too. A hush spread across the inn, all chatter ceasing almost immediately. For a moment, there was silence, and then the sound of footfall echoed throughout the room.

Click. Click. Click.

Iona raised her gaze towards the door. The owner of the clacking steps filled the doorway, wearing heeled boots beneath a dark cloak. The hood covered their face, but Iona could feel the glare emanating from the shadowy depths.

Not right, not right, her instincts screamed.

Iona tore her eyes away from the thing and looked at Cameron. Without making a sound, she mouthed two words.

"Knife. Now."

Cameron had turned as white as spilled milk, but his hand was steady as he slid it under the table to his belt and the weapon there.

Then the creature spoke in a rasping voice. "I'm looking for a girl."

A man in the corner let out a nervous chuckle. "Aren't we all?" he muttered. Immediately, he clamped his hand over his mouth. The stranger turned their head towards him and Iona knew he was already done for. With supernatural speed, the monstrous figure launched itself at the man, knocking him off his chair. The whole tavern scrambled into action. Some customers let out screams, while others clambered to get as far away from the stranger as possible.

"The girl," it hissed at the man's horrified face. "A changeling girl with magic. Tell me where she is and I'll let you live."

The man babbled in dread. "I'm sorry, I'm sorry. I don't know. Just let me—"

But it was too late. The creature bent its face to the man's neck, and then there was the sickening sound of skin ripping and shredding.

Chapter 32

"Oh my gods," Iona gasped at the gory scene, her heart stuttering.

Cameron pushed up from the table and yelled at the other customers. "Everyone, get out!" Then, as they followed his orders, he turned back to Iona. "Come on, we have to help him."

Iona jumped up, grabbing Cameron's arm before he could rush at the creature. "There's nothing we can do."

The unfortunate man jerked underneath the monster, desperately clawing at the cloak. Mere seconds ticked by, and then it was done. His arms fell limp, and the creature raised their head, revealing a bloody mouth. It dropped the man's body and stood, seeming to stretch as it did. It turned to Iona and Cameron, the only other people in the room, and lowered its hood.

Underneath, the creature's face was a mess of blood and gore. It looked like a woman—a hauntingly beautiful woman—yet there was something wrong about the angles of her face. She was too sharp, too perfect. And then when she opened her red-stained lips, two long white fangs emerged, wicked and deadly.

"Where is the changeling girl?" the creature asked them.

"What is it?" Cameron whispered to Iona.

She shook her head, never taking her eyes off the stranger.

Now was not the time.

The monster stuck out a blackened tongue and licked the blood from her face. "Give me the girl or I will feed from you too."

Cameron raised the knife in front of him and Iona couldn't help but notice how small it was. There was going to be a fight and she wasn't sure who would win.

Distract it. Keep it talking. She stepped in front of Cameron, hands up in supplication. "What does the girl look like?"

The creature snarled. "She could look like anyone. That isn't important. Can't you smell her?"

Iona paused, sniffing the air. Underneath the scent of blood and food, there was indeed a hint of something else. Or something fae. Hadn't she sensed it the night before? "How did you know she was here?" she asked. Her eyes flicked outside the windows, trying to remember how far the nearest stream was. Was it close enough for her to call the water here?

"Rumours and half-truths," said the creature, taking a step forward. "The Unseelie have been looking for her for years. But you would know all about that, wouldn't you, selkie?"

Iona flicked her eyes back to the monster. "What do you mean?"

The woman smiled cruelly. "Your kind stole her. Now we want her back."

Iona's stomach plummeted. "You don't mean—"

"Queen Nicnevan's daughter," the creature growled.

"But Nicnevan is trapped."

"There are those of us who are still loyal. She will be freed and when she is, she will reward us for finding her heir."

Cameron brandished his dagger. "And what if she doesn't want to be found?"

"I do not care, human." The woman crouched lower, an animal ready to pounce. "I will kill anyone who stands in my way."

"The only death will be yours," said a voice from behind them.

Iona and Cameron turned, in time to see the waitress from earlier poised at the kitchen door. Her back was straight, her face fierce as she stared down the monster in front of her.

"Run!" Iona shouted at her.

But the creature had already locked on to its target. With a bloodcurdling scream, it rushed at the woman. Iona cast around desperately for some water she could use, but there was only the liquid inside the various glasses on the abandoned tables. With the creature moving, she could only send it flying in its direction, as ineffective as a butterfly against a lion. But then the waitress stepped forward towards the monster, and raised her arm.

In her hand she held a gleaming sword, but it was not formed from steel. Rather, it looked like it was made from polished gemstone. It glinted in the sunlight, sending reflections of red and orange across the walls. And then, without warning, the whole sword burst into flame.

The Sword of Light, Iona's thought as her mouth opened and closed in shock. It had to be.

Chapter 33

The waitress didn't even flinch from the fire, as the sword was suddenly set alight. Instead, she gritted her teeth and snarled at the monster. "Last chance to leave." She shifted so that the end of her left arm, where her hand was missing, could be braced against the hilt.

"You—" the creature began, but the server had obviously decided the chance was over.

She launched herself at the fae, swinging the sword down in a fluid motion. But before the blade even touched the monster, it was shrieking in agony. Iona watched as an enormous slice cut its skin from shoulder to hip.

The creature doubled over, panting hard. "How?" it asked.

How did the sword cut without touching?

Cameron made to run forward, but Iona grabbed his arm. "Give her room," she told him.

The waitress held it in front of her again—but now her arms were trembling badly. Blood trailed from her nose to her mouth and when she spat on the floor, it was red.

The monster's head snapped up, and its nostrils flared. "That smell." Then it leapt forward, running full speed at the woman, its clawed hands extended towards her throat.

"Watch out!" shouted Cameron.

He needn't have worried. Before the creature could get two feet from the server, she swung the sword again.

The monster's body hit the floor with a dull thump. Then its head landed beside it in a wet thud.

Iona and Cameron stood, panting, as they took in the scene in front of them. The monster's corpse lay in the middle of the wooden floor. All around, chairs were upturned, and plates lay abandoned.

And at the back of the bar, the waitress held the flaming sword in both hands, looking as if she wasn't surprised at all.

The young woman sighed, lowering the blade. Instantly, the fire winked out. She raised her arm to her nose and wiped at the blood. "Should have known bleeding was not a smart thing to do in front of a Baobhan Sith."

"A what?" asked Cameron, lowering his knife.

"A vampire," the waitress said. She eyed all the mess in the pub. "Well, since I doubt my customers will be back today, I think I'm going to have a drink." With that, she stomped to the bar, placing the sword on top and grabbing a tankard.

Iona held up her hands as she approached. "Do you know what it is you have there?"

The waitress pumped one of the taps a couple of times before holding the cup underneath and letting the amber liquid flow into it. "A magical sword?"

"I believe it's called the Sword of Light."

The woman sniffed. "You fae are all the same, so worried about names. It's a magical blade. It can create fire and it can deal blows without touching your opponent. Pretty useful."

"And it looked like it demanded payment for its usefulness," Cameron said. He pulled out a stool and sat down, suddenly more relaxed.

Iona pursed her lips. *I won't be getting too close to the weapon, or to the woman.* "How did you know I was fae?" she asked.

The waitress raised an eyebrow before taking a sip of her ale. When she finished, she said, "I could smell you."

Cameron grinned. "Funny, I think my friend here could smell you earlier."

Iona frowned. "What do you mean?"

"I mean," said Cameron, leaning forward on the bar, "that she's fae too."

The waitress snorted. "Impressive. And after I'd gone to so much trouble to hide myself."

"Your sleeve has ridden up," Cameron said, pointing to her arm. "I saw your mark."

"Ah," Iona said, at last noticing the woman's arm, where a birthmark the size of an apple wrapped around her wrist. "A changeling. I didn't sense you were anything but human."

"I use sage," the waitress explained. "If you burn it near yourself for a while, it covers up your smell." She set her cup down on the bar. "So, should I be worried? I don't usually like to be found by fae."

"Like I said, we didn't know you were here. We just needed a place to stay."

"So you didn't come to capture me?"

"Why would we do that?" But then Iona remembered what the Baobhan Sith had said about Queen Nicnevan's daughter.

Something must have changed in Iona's expression; the waitress's shoulders stiffened, her hand moving closer to the sword again.

"The monster mentioned something about Nicnevan..." Iona's voice trailed off. No, that was absurd, wasn't it? After meeting the Faerie Queen but a month ago, what were the chances of stumbling upon her lost daughter in an inn now?

The woman's voice was low and calm when she spoke next.

"I have someone waiting for me in the back and she has a weapon. All I need to do is scream."

"No!" Iona spluttered. "We mean you no harm."

"Do you work for her?" the woman asked, looking now at Cameron. He rocked back in his chair, holding up his hands.

"No," said Iona. "I'm a selkie. A good fae. I'm one of the Seelie Court."

"A selkie?" The woman chewed on her lip. "So you aren't here to take me?"

"We're not here to kidnap anyone. But, does that mean you're—"

The woman held up her arm to give them a better look at her birthmark. "My name is Eilidh Buchanan, though that last name doesn't really belong to me. When I was a baby, I was stolen away by a group of fae. They rescued me from evil."

"You're Nicnevan's lost daughter," Cameron murmured as if the pieces were suddenly fitting together.

Eilidh raised her eyes to him. "I'm not lost. I am hidden. I am safe. And I will destroy anyone who tries to ruin that safety."

Iona studied the young woman closely. She looked like most Eilanmòrians, with her dark hair, pale skin and light eyes. She could easily be Ailsa's sister, though Iona had always thought her friend was quite striking, with her sharp features and piercing irises.

This woman was plain—not ugly—but she had the sort of face that could be forgotten easily. *Well, that's the point, isn't it?* She'd dressed modestly in a light green dress with an apron over the top, almost blending into the surroundings.

Iona placed a hand on the bar, not quite daring to touch the woman. "We would never turn you over to Nicnevan, or the Unseelie."

Cameron shook his head in disbelief. "All this time we thought we were just looking for the Sword of Light. Now we've found the literal heir to the faerie throne." He stopped when he saw the look on Eilidh's face. "Of course, we'll keep that a secret. How did you get the sword?"

"Many people know the story of the night Nicnevan's daughter was taken, but they never seem to know the other part. Something else was stolen from her when I was." She touched the side of the sword with a pinky and it seemed to glow.

"Nicnevan had the sword?"

"As far as I've been told, she has an entire collection of magical objects. She didn't even know what it did. I don't believe she has been searching for it."

"How did you learn how to use it?"

"My guardian, Agnes, taught me. She raised me all these years." Eilidh looked at the corpse on the floor. "Would you like to join me in the back? It might be a little nicer through there and you can ask Agnes all you like about the sword."

Iona bobbed her head dumbly. She still couldn't believe they'd found the Sword of Light and the Faerie Queen's daughter in one morning.

Eilidh came out from behind the bar and crossed to the door of the pub. She pulled out a large key from her pocket and locked it. "There, now no one will disturb us before I can get rid of the body. Come with me." And with that, she stalked to the portal that Iona had assumed led to the kitchens and held it open.

Cameron rose from his seat and nudged Iona. "We shouldn't leave the sword here, should we?"

"No, could you grab it for me?" Eilidh asked.

So casual, Iona thought. It was like the other woman didn't care who had it. *Maybe that means she'll be willing to give it to us if we explain the situation.* Iona looked down at the sword before placing a hand reverently on its hilt. It was hot to the touch and gave her skin a small shock as she gripped it. Inside her pocket, the tiny cauldron seemed to shiver. "It feels strange. It won't take blood from me too, will it?"

"No, not unless you plan to injure someone with it." Eilidh held a hand out so that Iona could pass over the blade. "Agnes knows more about it than I do."

She ushered them through the door, where the corridor was narrow and clearly only used by staff. While the pub was bright and decorated with portraits and art, back here it was sparse. Many doors lined the long hallway, the first of which was fitted with distorted glass panels. Iona glanced through as they passed, spotting the outline of a range oven and an icebox.

Finally, Eilidh stopped in front of a room on the left and knocked twice. "All clear," she called out. Then she twisted the handle and beckoned them through.

Inside was a cosy sitting room, with a plump purple couch before a crackling fire. A floral sheet had been draped between the back of the couch and a nearby table, the edges weighed down by a few books. As soon as they entered, an older woman with long grey hair leaned out from underneath and looked at Eilidh with concern.

"Did anything happen?" she asked, her gaze sweeping her from top to toe.

It struck Iona that it was an odd question. Of course something had happened. Eilidh's face had bits of caked blood on it and she still held the gleaming sword in her right hand. But then, when another, smaller head popped out from underneath the blanket, she understood. The older woman was trying to ask what happened without frightening the girl.

"Mama," she shouted and flung herself at Eilidh's skirts. "What happened?" she asked, pointing to her nose.

"Oh, silly me," Eilidh said sheepishly, brushing away the blood, "I must have bumped it."

"And who are your guests?" The older woman used the couch to pull herself to her feet, and regarded them warily.

"I'm not entirely sure," Eilidh said. "But they have a few questions for you."

"This is Cameron MacAra of the King's Army," Iona cut in. "And I'm Lady Iona of Struanmuir."

The woman's mouth dropped open. "A Struanmuir selkie. Wasn't it two Struanmuir selkies who defeated Nicnevan a few months ago?"

Cameron nodded enthusiastically. "Yes, Iona was one of them. She saved me from the Faerie Queen."

"Well, we helped," said Iona. "Do you own the inn?"

The woman—Agnes—smoothed out her skirts with a steady hand. "Yes, this place is mine. Though I'd never be able to keep running it, if it wasn't for Eilidh here."

"That's not true," Eilidh said shyly. "Everyone comes for Agnes's food. I just serve drinks."

"And clean and do the finances and everything else," said Agnes with a fond smile.

"We have other staff who travel from Kilvaig every day. I don't have to change the beds thankfully." Eilidh brushed her hand through the little girl's hair absently as she spoke while the girl cast her unusual eyes between them all.

"It's a lovely place," Iona said softly, noting again the

resemblance between the girl and the man she once knew. "We were planning on staying here a few days while we looked for something." And then she realised the connection. If Eilidh was Nicnevan's daughter, then she was also the daughter of King Connell. And the granddaughter of Alasdair. Iona's head was spinning. Of course, it really wasn't a coincidence. This little girl was Alasdair's great grandchild.

As though he could sense she couldn't carry on the conversation, Cameron took over and said, "We're here because we heard rumours that an object we're looking for was nearby. And then, as luck would have it, Eilidh walked right through the door with it twenty minutes ago."

"Do you know what it is?" asked Agnes.

Cameron swallowed. "The Sword of Light. One of the Four Treasures. That's really all we know."

Eilidh cocked her head and Iona was reminded of a bird. "What do you plan on doing with it?" she said.

"A friend of ours warned us of a threat to Eilanmòr," answered Cameron. "The Treasures are supposed to be magnificent weapons we can use to fight it."

"They know about me too," Eilidh said. Then, to her daughter, she smiled. "Would you like to try some of Nanny's sticky buns?"

The girl squealed, and Eilidh lifted her into her arms. "I'll leave you to ask your questions, but I'll be right through the next door."

Iona watched the young woman leave, still unable to form a sentence. There had been a lot of shocks for one morning.

"I assume," said Agnes quietly from behind her, "since you're not dead, that you mean Eilidh no harm?"

"Like I said, we were merely looking for the sword,"

Cameron reassured her. "The Baobhan Sith was looking for her and that's how we realised who she was. We won't speak of her identity to anyone."

The older woman seemed to deflate. "Good. I've been trying to protect Eilidh since she was brought to me, but it has not been easy. Now and then, fae turn up on our doorstep, looking for her."

"It seems that she can defend herself," Iona croaked.

"I knew she would need to. Luckily, they didn't entrust her to just anyone. Before I was an innkeeper and a skivvy, I was in the King's Army, same as you," Agnes said with a chuckle.

"You were a soldier?"

She shrugged. "Of sorts. I worked by myself and removed targets that threatened the safety of our kingdom."

"You were an assassin?" Iona guessed.

The woman smiled and gestured to the couch. "Take a seat and I'll make it worth your while."

Chapter 34

As soon as Angus had explained Cameron's vision and swung onto Laire's back, he knew he'd made a mistake. He'd barely got a grip of her hair before she burst out of the stables and out into the night.

"Wow, you're fast!" he shouted down at her.

The muscles in her shoulders tensed. "I can go faster," she said.

"How fast?" He flattened himself against her back, savouring the smells of hay and horse. *There, that's better* he thought.

"I can be as swift as a shooting star. I can run so fast it's like flying," she said. "Can you handle that?"

"We need to get to Harris as soon as possible. Do what you must."

With that, Laire lowered her head and then she was running, running, running, until the trees were a blur. And still she ran faster. Impossibly fast. Angus could feel a tingle of magic in her body, building with each stride. He could hardly gasp in a breath as the wind whipped past him. Her hooves pounded against the road— it was all Angus could do to hold on.

Angus was unsure how long they travelled for, but eventually, when the sun was high in the sky, Laire slowed, then came to a stop. He unlocked his muscles and raised his face from her neck to take in their surroundings.

He didn't recognise the forest he was in, nor the mountain range rising behind them. Had they passed through those peaks on their journey? If only they'd stopped a little higher up, then he could see the way more clearly. Though he couldn't exactly complain. Laire had been running flat out for hours. They must be forty miles from Kilvaig by now.

"We need to get you some water and food," he told her, patting her neck.

"That's why I stopped here. There's a loch just beyond those trees." She trotted forward, with him still on her back, until he could see the water sparkling up ahead.

"How did you know that? Have you been here before?"

"Yes," she said. "And so have you. Don't you remember it?"

Angus narrowed his eyes. How could he have been here before? "I don't understand—"

"This is where we met," Laire laughed.

He slid off her back and looked out onto the loch. It looked like any other, with its tree-lined banks and clear water.

"Of course," Laire said, "it used to have a whirlpool, but that's gone, thanks to you and your friend."

Angus's mouth dropped open. "Are you telling me we're at the loch where we found the Cauldron of Life?"

Laire tossed her head and walked down to the water's edge. "Are you surprised?"

"That's in The Forest of Frith!" Angus felt faint. "That's a few days' ride away, at least. We were only going for a few hours."

"You said you had to get to your friend as soon as possible."

Well, thought Angus, rubbing his hand through his hair in disbelief. That settles it. He was never travelling by boat again.

"Water, food, rest," he croaked. "Then we need to be back on the road again." Maybe they'd reach the coast, and whatever danger lurked there, before Harris, after all.

Chapter 35

Ailsa had felt like she'd walked for days before she reached the entrance to the demons' nest, but that was normal with finding Hell. She knew it had only been a few hours since Ishbel had relented and shown her the way. Now, exhausted and sticky with grime, she stood in front of the same gnarled old oak Maalik had led her to all those weeks ago.

Pulling out a knife, she quickly nicked the side of her hand, flicking the blood at the tree. She paused, waiting for the payment to be accepted, then the tree twisted up out of the ground to reveal a hole.

Well, there's no point in staying here all night.

Ailsa slipped down the dark, dank stairs, straining her ears for any sounds ahead. Her heart hammered in her chest while her palms were slick with sweat, despite the cold.

The last time she'd been down here, she'd been a prisoner, summoned by a demon trying to prove Maalik was mistreating her—as any demon should treat the mortals sacrificed to them. But it had been impossible to keep up the ruse, and they'd been caught out. It was only when Ailsa let out a burst of her power, and she'd threatened to kill them all, that they'd let her go. Maalik's one friend, a demon called Calix, had convinced his comrades Ailsa was worth more to them alive than dead.

As she descended further into Hell, she noticed the

difference in atmosphere. On her last visit, there had been hundreds of demons in the long hall that led to the interrogation chamber. Now, as she reached the bottom of the stairs, she realised there was no one. Not a single person haunted the room. Without the close pack of the demons' bodies, it was even colder than Ailsa remembered. She hugged her arms to her as she skirted the outsides of the room. There were many corridors leading off the main one, and she tried to think back to where she had been led last time. But the demons' nest was labyrinthine—it wouldn't be easy to find her way by herself.

Perhaps I'll run into Calix, thought Ailsa. Maalik's friend would be a handy ally.

But until then, you'll have to find your way yourself.

Ishbel was right. She'd thought about this all the way here, had tested out different theories while sitting on the boat or walking through the woods. Closing her eyes, she inhaled deep and even, willing her heart to slow. She reached her senses out, searching for the thing she was there for. Lifting one hand into the air in front of her face, she waved it back and forward, slowly but surely dragging the air through the rooms and halls towards her and then away. She didn't know for sure where they'd be keeping it, but she had an idea. When the smell of metal and dirt wafted in on the breeze, she turned her head towards it and opened her eyes again. It had come from the second tunnel on the left. As quickly and as quietly as she could manage, she crept towards the smell.

The further she descended, the surer she was about her direction. She'd spent a night in the dungeons; the smell of the metal bars and the dirt from the floor, reminded her of their captivity. Maalik had been imprisoned, but the sacrificial bond between them had kept her tied there with him. Passing through the darkened hallways, she wondered again at the distinct lack of demons.

Perhaps they're all out? she wondered.

I don't like this, Ishbel whispered.

We can't go back now. Indeed, she wasn't exactly sure how she was going to get out of Hell without a fight. The chances of never running into any demons were slim, but she'd been hoping to only encounter a few this time. Now she had an advantage she didn't have last time: she had a weapon. It didn't matter who or what you were when dealt an axe to the back of your head. Or at least, she hoped.

Holding the hilt of her weapon, she turned a corner; she'd made it to the cells. Wiping her palms on her trousers, Ailsa began to search the stone rooms.

Each was as empty as the last.

Shouldn't there be guards?

I really don't like this.

Then, in the semi-dark of the dungeons, Ailsa noticed something out the corner of her eye. Something was glowing at the end of the corridor. A blue light flickered lazily in one cell. Ailsa inched closer until she could peek her head through the doorway. Inside, dozens of little orbs hung in the air, glimmering like sapphires. Ailsa fought back a gasp.

We did it Ishbel.

Ducking into the cell, she scanned the twinkling globes, looking for anything to mark them differently.

How am I supposed to know which—

But then she stopped. There was a jerk inside her stomach. She snapped her attention to the orb in the corner. As she drew closer, it glowed brighter, like it recognised her.

"This is it," she whispered out loud. With trembling hands, she reached out and tentatively picked up the ball of light. It was both solid and not in her hands, like touching liquid glass. The orb pulsed gently in her palm; she admired it for a moment before slipping it into her pocket for safekeeping.

Now that she had what she came for, Ailsa itched to get out of the tunnels. Her feet carried her out the cell and back up the corridor.

I can't believe we found it, Ailsa thought, a little light-headed.

Don't get too cocky, Ishbel warned.

But Ailsa was already thinking of the next step. *We have to make our way to Maalik's cabin. Then we'll have to convince him to come with us.*

It was only when Ailsa rounded the next corner that she realised her mistake. She'd overshot the exit, ending up somewhere she didn't recognise.

Which—

A hand clamped down on her shoulder. Ailsa turned to find its owner, a tall demon covered in scars, leaning down over her. His obsidian eyes glinted in the low light. A tongue darted out of his mouth like it was sensing the surrounding air. And then he smiled, revealing sharpened teeth.

"Well,' he hissed. 'What an interesting find."

Chapter 36

Ailsa had the strangest sensation she was floating away from her body as she was led down the corridors. It was like she was already dead, watching the scene from above. She noted the way the demon's hands gripped her upper arms, digging his nails into her skin. One of his golden horns had been torn off, a punishment Maalik had told her about last time. If he had displeased someone, chances were he would be even more desperate to win back favour. Perhaps by delivering a thief the others could torture and kill?

They don't know you took anything, she reminded herself. The precious cargo she carried in her pocket was hidden and secret. If she could only get it out of the demons' nest, all would not be lost.

Maybe if I see Calix, I can get it to him before they kill me?

Ailsa waited for the answering remark from her spirit guide, but nothing came. Ishbel was there though, watching and waiting.

The demon led her down, down, down again, deep into the earth. His body was hot, like a fever, but it wasn't enough to stop her shivering.

It's from the cold, not fear, she told herself.

Yet, the truth was stark in front of her: she was going to die, and it wouldn't be quick. Yes, she had a weapon, but it was currently swinging from the demon's belt. She'd been planning on taking anyone she encountered by surprise. That was out of the question now. And though her powers had grown since the last time she was in Hell, she was so far underground, it probably wouldn't help. The air was stagnant and useless around her.

Ailsa swallowed thickly, trying to drink in a breath, but the more she thought about the stiff air, the less she could fill her lungs. The corridors were getting narrower and darker, and she could almost feel them closing in on her. Maybe this would be how she died, hyperventilating, before she could even reach her destination.

The thought pulled a croaked laugh from her parched throat. It wouldn't be that easy.

Just as her vision darkened, the demon stopped them in front of a huge, red door that she recognised from before.

"Now for the fun," he hissed. The door pushed open and Ailsa saw where all the demons in Hell had gone.

The hall was packed with bodies, pushing and clawing at each other. The one holding her pulled her through a narrow gap. Demons pressed in on her, almost scalding her with their searing skin. They didn't seem to notice her, even when they were pushed out of the way; they all had their eyes focussed on the middle of the room.

The demon council stood silhouetted in front of the central fire, looking down at something. Most wore robes of rich burgundy but at least one was bare chested. On his back, three long scratches scored down his skin, revealing the molten core underneath. As Ailsa was pulled closer, she could see they were gathered in front of a broken and bruised, clearly dead, body.

The person's skin was a patchwork of the red draw of a new

burn and black char. Ailsa's stomach pitched as she realised it reminded her of barbecued meat. Blood matted the hair to the corpse's head, and she wondered if there had been golden horns there before. The body's blackened hands were pulled back behind them and bound by wire.

The demon holding her pushed Ailsa forward until her legs hit the rope separating the chamber. Her nose grazed against the invisible wall, magicked to keep the crowd at bay, as her captor readied his nerves. "With respect," he called out, "I found this human wandering our hallways..."

Immediately, the smallest of the demon council turned and fixed her eyes on Ailsa's captor. She was tiny, the size of a child. Ailsa fought a shiver as she spoke in her high-pitched voice.

"You are interrupting our interrogation." Then she turned to take in whoever the lower demon had in his arms, and her expression made Ailsa's stomach flip. The demon-girl smiled. "Ailsa! I wondered when we'd see you again."

The magical wall collapsed in front of her, allowing her captor to push his way through. He kept Ailsa's body between him and the council as a shield. *Smart man.* These demons were terrifying in a different way from the salivating rabble behind them. They were refined, calculating—like predators. The last time Ailsa had been brought to this chamber, they'd been sitting in high thrones, swirling glasses of liquid as they dealt out punishments. But something had changed since then. The body at their feet had obviously earned their wrath.

Ailsa looked up at the high roof, remembering how she'd almost electrocuted them before. The stained-glass windows she'd broken with her wind and lightning had been boarded up, blocking the sky completely.

"Ah yes," said the demon-girl, following her gaze. "You

can't use that trick again. You'll have to think of something else this time. But first, come look, dear Ailsa." She gestured down at the corpse and Ailsa was pushed closer still.

"We've been hearing all sorts of rumours." The girl leaned down to inspect the body. "Rumours of death and destruction and chaos up there in your world. This one was sent to recruit us." Then she reached out a hand to touch the corpse's shoulder with one clawed finger.

Ailsa watched in horror as the badly burned body moved.

"No, he isn't dead. I'm glad you are here to see what we do to those who displease us."

The charred demon moaned and rolled so Ailsa could see his side. Underneath all the burns, she could see his skin wasn't healthy. It had a distinct greyness to it, like it was spoiled and rotting. The demon's mouth curled into a grimace before his face slackened.

He passed out again, Ailsa realised.

"Perhaps you can confirm what he told us," said the girl as she stood again. "What do you know of the Edaxi?"

Ailsa blinked a few times, collecting her thoughts. She hadn't expected to hear about the gods, not down here. Hell was ancient and unchanging, like they wouldn't care what happened above ground, as long as it was bad. But what had the demon-girl said? *This one was sent to recruit us.* It appeared Ailsa hadn't been the first to realise there were very few fae with fire magic to wield one of the Four Treasures.

"I know they're four gods," Ailsa said slowly. "Minor gods, though they didn't used to be. They are plotting to take over Eilanmòr and then the whole of Ossiana." She left out the part about the treasures. The demons didn't need to know about four indestructible weapons.

"I see. Well, it seems they're building an army. But they can't make it onto Eilanmòrian land, not yet. That's why they've sent an envoy." The little girl licked her lips as she studied the body again. "Though, if they had access to Hell, they'd be able to pass through here to move from place to place. There are entrances to our queendom in every land in Ossiana? All you need to do is slip in one door, walk through our corridors, and open another, to find you've travelled thousands of miles. There is one catch, however." She raised her head again to Ailsa. "I can sense every single person who passes into or out of Hell. I knew the moment you snuck into our realm, and I could track your movements down into our dungeons. But there are no prisoners down there, dear Ailsa. So, the question remains: why are you here?"

Ailsa's heartbeat stuttered as she felt the weight in her pocket. Maalik's soul. They couldn't find it. Ailsa did not know if you could destroy a soul, but she was sure they were capable of it, given the chance.

She searched her mind, piecing together an excuse. "I was looking for a friend of mine. I thought they might have been sacrificed, like I was."

The demon leader clicked her tongue. "We all know that's a lie. But I'm glad; now we get to pull it out of you." She snapped her fingers and two giant demons materialised beside Ailsa. They batted the one holding her to the side.

"But—" he struggled to hold on, digging his fingers further into her arm. The demon closest to him reached out a hand and grabbed her first captor's face. Immediately, the skin under the palm bubbled like boiling water. The lower demon gave a shriek and dropped his grip, tearing away from the council chamber, clutching his face, taking her axe with him. Then the two burly demons grabbed Ailsa, pushing her forward onto her knees in front of the little Demon Queen.

Use your magic, Ishbel commanded.

Ailsa reached out with her powers desperately, pulling the stale air towards her. But it wasn't enough. Without fresh air, it was like handling syrup.

I can't.

This block is in your head. You're breathing air in right now, aren't you?

Ailsa tried again as the demon-girl considered her. She could almost feel the outside, so high above her.

"Did you know," the girl said in her high, chilling voice. "The worst, most painful way to die, isn't by burning. Your nerves damage too quickly that way, you stop feeling it. No, the worst way is by steaming. You're alive when the water slowly cooks your flesh. But we don't want to kill you yet, so we could just start with the bits you can live without." She snapped her head up, levelling her cool gaze at the guard behind Ailsa. "Go fetch me some water."

A hand came down on Ailsa's shoulder, pinning her in place as she struggled.

Help, she thought at Ishbel. *Do something!*

Find the air inside your lungs, the spirit guide ordered. *Find it and make a spark. You know how to do this.*

I can't. I can't. Panicked gripped her as waves of cold swept over her skin. Her arms were leaded weights hanging at her sides and her stomach roiled. *They're going to kill me.*

Yes, they will. But only you can decide how you meet death. Aren't you angry? Aren't you furious that after all you've been through, this is the way it ends?

"Yes," Ailsa choked out between heaving gasps. "Yes."

Good. Use that anger, that frustration. Let death know of your rage.

Ailsa's entire body shook as she tried to get it under control. All around her, demons were screaming and calling, ready for her torture and death, but she blocked them out, focussing instead on slowing her panting. And above all else, focussing on how much she hated those surrounding her, how much she despised this place, and what they'd done to Maalik.

You'll never see him again, Ishbel told her. *They'll take his soul and he'll never be free.*

It was that thought that tipped her over the edge. Because if she wasn't angry enough for herself, she could be for him.

In her heart, something clicked into place. And then, inside her lungs, something flickered to life. Lightning is created by air friction, Maalik had once told her. So she breathed out, allowing it to leave her lungs and enter her windpipe. And then, like striking a match, she let it explode.

Yes, whispered Ishbel.

The Demon Queen's face fell. "What—"

Every vein in Ailsa's body sang with electricity. It sizzled over her skin, lighting her up from the inside. The power was incredible, like she hadn't been properly alive until that moment. But Ailsa only allowed herself half a second to enjoy the sensation before turning her attention to the demon with his hands on her.

The lightning crackled out of her body and into his with half a thought and then he was down. His muscles contorted, his body writhing like a fish. But she didn't pause to watch him die. Instead, she raised her arms and rained her wrath upon the demons in the crowd. One by one, the magic snapped out, killing them where they stood.

They're not who you're angry at, Ishbel said.

Ailsa turned her attention back to the demon council.

"Wait," one of them said, fear etched on his features as he watched Ailsa stalk forward.

"Quiet!" the Demon Queen barked at him. Then she too turned her attention to Ailsa. "The only reason you're still standing is that I'm intrigued. You didn't display this level of power the last time we saw you."

Ailsa opened her mouth to reply, but the sparks lept along her tongue, making it too hard to form words. Instead, she levelled a glare at the demon closest to her, who had been edging out of her line of sight. This one was a woman, tall and muscular with horns that curled over her head. Ailsa shot a fork of lightning at the ground in warning.

You can't run.

"Was it Maalik who taught you to use your powers?" the Demon Queen asked, with a look of disgust plain on her face, as the others eased their way between her and Ailsa. "We should have known that he was playing us for fools. Once we've killed you, we'll be sure to find him and destroy him."

Well, there was no doubt now. Ailsa would either have to find Maalik and hide him, or she'd have to kill every one of the council members. Her body vibrated with the force of the charge, willing her to let it out.

Not yet.

The Demon Queen grinned from ear to ear. "Goodbye, little lightning girl." Then she snapped her fingers.

The screaming and shouting from behind paused for a moment. Ailsa turned in time to see the first wave of lower demons fall forward over the ropes. At the same time, they realised what had happened.

She's removed the barrier.

The shrieking started up again, louder than before, as the demons surged towards her. Ailsa spun once more towards the council, ready to run, but the demons in front were ready. Their skin cracked and glowed, revealing the magma inside. Then the woman with the curling horns rushed at Ailsa, making a gesture with her hand as she ran, and a ball of flames flickered to life about her fingers.

I'm going to have to fight all of them, thought Ailsa.

But her body was shuddering, even as she sidestepped her attacker and sent a wave of power at the woman, singeing her flesh with sparks. The magic was bigger than her body, bigger than her and it was growing. Ailsa tried desperately to hold onto the strands, to hold onto something that wasn't static or current. But there was nothing else there: no mouth, no skin, no body—just pure energy

Ishbel, help! Ailsa screamed in her mind. Did she even have a mind anymore? Had the lightning ripped through her, turning her to ash?

Distantly, she heard someone screech "Get her!" But then, that meant she had ears still, didn't it?

Then something hard knocked into what was left of her body and Ailsa felt the barest prickling sensation. The power was pulsing out of her in waves, and it was all she could do to hold on to it.

Storms have eyes. Do I have eyes? she wondered absently.

Then a voice spoke, gentle as a caress. *Hush now, I've got you.*

And just like that, the last sensations of her body blinked out, plunging her into darkness.

Chapter 37

Cameron pushed aside his ever-present headache and tried to focus on the meal in front of him. He'd listened intently all day to the older woman's stories, but all the excitement was taking its toll.

Agneta Dalgaard. He was actually sitting across from Agneta Dalgaard, one of the deadliest freedom fighters in history. He'd heard the stories, whispered around campfires in the training camps, of how she could slip inside a prison, free the people trapped there and slit the throats of every jailor before anyone had ever heard a sound. She'd made quite a name for herself fifty years ago, especially in her homeland of Avalogne, where they had set their sights on invading their neighbouring countries. *Traitor,* they'd called her. But for hundreds of Eilanmòrian prisoners, she was a hero.

He took in the woman across the table. Her skin was growing papery; her famous raven black hair had gone silver, yet there was a fire in her eyes, burning brightly still.

As soon as Cameron had learned who she was, he couldn't help pestering her for stories. *The Siege of Sandbrook, The Liberation of Venza, The Battle of Dalbrae.* The tales were famous, and he couldn't believe his luck, that he could hear them straight from The Reaper herself.

"While I'm sure my companion would love to hear more," Iona eventually cut in, when the outside world was dark and

Agnes—as Eilidh called her—had served them a simple meal of smoked fish and potatoes. "There is one story I want to hear above all others. How did Eilidh come into your care?"

And, sitting at the little wooden table, with the help of the changeling woman, Agnes told them.

"The coup had been planned for years," she began, "ever since Nicnevan chose the Unseelie Court over the Seelie. Good and evil fae are supposed to inhabit Ephraim together, balancing each other out. But the Faerie Queen found her dark creatures to be more fun. Then Nicnevan did something no one had expected: she fell in love. And not just with anyone, with the heir to the Eilanmòrian throne. The Seelie had hoped this would change the Queen's ways, but old habits are hard to break, and she drove her prince away. In a last-ditch attempt to win her love back, Nicnevan travelled to Dunrigh. Some time after she returned, she gave birth to a baby girl."

Cameron couldn't help it as his gaze flicked to the woman beside him. Eilidh tugged on her sleeve as her eyes darted from the doors to the windows and then back again. *How long has she lived in fear?* he wondered.

"The fae knew the only way they could ensure this child was not raised around evil, was to steal her away," said Agnes.

Iona's mouth twisted. "So they took you from your mother?"

Eilidh raised her chin. "And I'm glad they did."

"But Eilidh wasn't the only child to be taken that day," Agnes continued, frowning deeply. "The Seelie knew they couldn't keep a stolen baby secret for long, so they hatched a plan. All over the continent, fae gave up their daughters voluntarily to throw the Queen off the trail."

"Who could do that?" Cameron wondered. "Who would

give up their child like that, knowing they may never see them again?"

It was Iona who answered him. "You don't remember what Eilanmòr was like before," she said quietly. "The Unseelie had a chokehold on this country; no one was safe."

"It can't have been that bad—"

"You know all of those scary stories you heard when you were a child?" Iona asked, her face paling. "About kelpies snatching travellers and dragging them to watery graves? Or red caps slaughtering villages and dunking their hats in their victims' blood? Those are only the tales deemed suitable for young ears. Imagine what was left out."

A log snapped in the hearth, making Cameron jump.

"Iona is right," agreed Agnes. "The Seelie were desperate and willing to do anything to build a better future. The children were changed so they would fit in with the locals and then they were dispersed all over Eilanmòr." She reached out a hand to squeeze Eilidh's arm, above where her changeling mark was. "Nicnevan's daughter was brought to me. The Seelie knew I'd be able to protect her, a last line of defence."

"But you've still had to fight," Cameron guessed. "The Baobhan Sith can't have been the only Unseelie who has come looking."

Eilidh clenched her fists. "Agnes has taught me well."

What a life, Cameron thought, studying the young woman. Fighting for her freedom. Keeping secrets. "Have you always known who you were?"

"As soon as I could understand, I've known," Eilidh said. "It would have been too dangerous to not know. I've had to be very careful."

"Do you have magic?" Cameron asked, thinking of his

sister's powers. And Ailsa wasn't even a faerie princess.

At this, Eilidh's eyes lit up, for a moment. "I do. But I try to keep it hidden. Sometimes I can't help using it though."

"Were you ever tempted to go back?" asked Iona. "Ephraim? Your mother?" Even as she said those words, Iona's nose wrinkled, like she already knew the answer.

"Never," Eilidh said vehemently. "I wanted nothing to do with her. I've been living my entire life in fear that monster would find me. But then, recently, that all changed." She pressed her fingers to her chest, above her heart. "I felt... she's gone."

"Yes," Cameron said. "Iona trapped her."

"Trapped?" Eilidh breathed. "She's not dead?"

Iona frowned. "Not dead, but cursed. We thought our friend, Ailsa, could have been the lost princess. Nicnevan had kidnapped my brother, so we went to Ephraim, hoping Ailsa could rescue him."

"I was Nicnevan's prisoner," said Cameron. "Iona took a spell from me and pushed it onto the Queen."

Eilidh exchanged a look with Agnes. "Your friend, she's a changeling too?"

Cameron bit his lip. "When I was young, my baby sister died. Ailsa was left in her place."

"And you knew this?"

"We both did. Me and my mother."

"Your sister, Ailsa, is lucky to have you," Eilidh said with a weak smile. "As I am lucky to have Agnes."

"And your daughter?" asked Iona, her eyes gleaming.

Cameron rubbed a finger against the wood grain of the table and wondered what the selkie was getting at.

Eilidh's gaze climbed the stairs in the corner, to where the little girl was fast asleep. "Maggie is my everything. I would do anything to protect her."

Then Iona leaned forward and fixed the young woman with a hard stare. But there was something about her face, her expression, that made Cameron's hair stand on end. At that moment, as the candlelight flickering across her freckled skin, she didn't look quite human.

"Does that include saving the world?" Iona asked. "I think we need your help."

And so, the selkie told the lost princess a story—one which didn't have an ending yet.

Chapter 38

The demon sat on his narrow bed and watched the clouds darken through the window. The muscles in his shoulders and arms ached, but he did nothing to seek relief. It was good to feel something, even if it was pain. Better than the numbness that had been surrounding him like a fog this last month. His sore muscles were a reminder he'd finally got up and out of the cabin; to move on with life. There was no use lying in the house day after day. It wouldn't bring her back.

The wolf beside him whined and put his massive head on his lap. The demon let a blackened hand land on the beast's fur but that was as much as he could manage. Even getting out of bed had been an insurmountable task a few weeks ago, so the wolf didn't complain.

On the demon's shoulder, a tiny fae the size and shape of a hedgehog lapped at a stray drop of blood on his ear. The brownie hummed in contentment, licking at the red liquid. The demon didn't have it in himself to bat her away. It wasn't, after all, his blood.

There had been an outbreak of disease in a village to the west. As soon as the demon had walked into the settlement, he knew it was hopeless. The healthy had abandoned the dying, leaving them where they lay. The only unaffected person for miles was a schoolteacher.

When the demon had found her, the teacher had been

watching over a sick old woman. He had expected her to scream when she saw him, but she looked resigned, as if she had been waiting for the devil himself. She told him she had been sick too, but she had recovered.

"I'll probably get sick again," she said as she pressed a wet cloth to the old woman's head. "But I couldn't leave her like this."

"You won't get sick again," the demon told her. "You're immune now."

The teacher lifted one shoulder, looking as tired as he felt. "Will they recover?"

"No," he said. "I can help you, though. We need to burn the bodies. That way it can't spread further."

And so he'd spent the day and night lifting the dead to a pyre in the middle of town. Even as their bodies burned, more people died—until the schoolteacher was the only other living thing in the village apart from himself.

"Are you going to take my soul now?" she asked him as they watched the flames rise higher.

"The only soul I want is my own," he told her and left her in the village of ash.

Now that he was back home, he wondered if he should have invited her back so she could eat and wash and recover. But he couldn't bear to have anyone else in the house. He'd been selfish.

Hopefully she'll find the neighbours who escaped, he thought. *Hopefully, they won't kill her when they see her for fear of catching the disease.*

The demon rubbed his night-black eyes and fought the compulsion to lie down and never get back up again. It was hard, but so was everything else about life. If Ailsa was with

225

him, she'd tell him to stop moping.

His stomach twisted as he thought of the girl who had once been his bonded servant. A few weeks ago, she'd left. Then the wolf had gone chasing after her to Ephraim. The demon had felt utterly helpless as he waited to find out about her fate. But then Wulver had come back and had relayed the information as best he could: she was alive: she was safe.

But Ailsa hadn't come back. She had told the demon she would, but he should have known better than to hope. *Why would she come back after she'd been here against her will for weeks?* And yet, there was nothing to do but sit and wait. If only he still had his soul, he could leave the cabin and these woods and stop seeing memories of her wherever he looked.

The clouds were now the purple of a bruise and even that was a reminder of her.

"I just need to get into a routine," he told the wolf in his lap. "If I can get back into making my rounds, I'll feel better."

Wulver gave a huff.

Thunder boomed in the distance and the demon sighed. Even the weather was against him.

The demon shifted so that the wolf knew to move. The brownie squeaked in protest as her food source was jostled.

A cup of tea will do you good, the demon told himself as he unfolded from the bed.

But when he looked, there was no water in the pot.

Go and get some, it's not like it's far.

The demon grabbed the metal pail and forced his body out the door. before he could talk himself out of it.

Immediately upon setting foot outside, he sensed the pressure in the air from the storm. It hadn't quite begun to rain over the cabin, but it seemed like it needed it.

His limbs were heavy as he made his way to the well. It was amazing, really, how illness of the mind could manifest in the body. The muscles in his forearms ached from all the hours he spent clenching his fists without realising it. He'd often vomit without reason, like his stomach were desperately trying to get rid of whatever was making him sick. *I should write a book,* he thought absently as the lightning flashed against the trees. *Ways Your Own Brain Is Out To Get You.*

Only a few seconds after the lightning, thunder boomed loudly above. The storm was almost upon him. *Get the water and get inside.* It would do him no good to be caught out in it.

Stop being sad. The memory of Ailsa's voice was sharp in his mind. He could almost see her now, just there in the shadows, trying to taunt him into a smile.

But then a branch cracked up ahead and his heart lurched in his chest. There was someone between the trees. The figure swayed, losing their footing, and then righted themselves.

"Ailsa?" the demon whispered. It couldn't be.

The lightning flashed, illuminating her face for a split second. But it was enough. Her features were strangely blank, but it was her eyes which made his heart seize in terror. They were rolled all the way back into her head, with only the whites showing. The exact opposite of his. They didn't even blink as the raindrops showered all over her skin, her eyelids. Then they were plunged into darkness again.

"What's wrong with you?" the demon asked.

In the dark shadows of Ailsa's face, her lips split into an eerie smile. Thunder rumbled overhead. "Hello, Maalik," she croaked. And then she crumpled to the ground.

Chapter 39

"Ailsa? Ailsa, wake up!" Maalik had only just grabbed her as she fell, saving her head from cracking on the stones underfoot.

His mind flicked through the procedures for treating an unconscious patient, willing himself not to panic.

First, check they're breathing. He turned his head, hovering his ear over her mouth, and listened while watching her chest rise and fall. *Definitely breathing.*

Next, check for wounds. He brushed his hands underneath her neck, the small of her back, the back of her legs, checking there was no blood on his hands each time. *Nothing.*

Breathing is normal. No blood. He looked up at the sky, which was still spitting water. It wasn't safe to stay here. Better to get her inside where it was warm.

"Hold on," he said. "I'm going to lift you now." It was good practice to tell the patient what you were about to do.

With shaking hands, he reached under her body and scooped her up, noticing how unstable his legs were.

It's the adrenaline, he told himself. He fought through it, turning to walk back to the cabin with Ailsa in his arms, his bucket forgotten.

She mumbled something, wrinkling her nose and Maalik held her closer, trying to keep the rain off her.

When he reached the door, he kicked it open with one

foot. Wulver sat beside the fire, his hackles raised, until the wolf realised who had barged in.

"It's okay," Maalik said, laying Ailsa down on the couch. "I found her in the woods. She fainted."

A buzzing drew closer and Maalik scowled. "Give her some room, Muck."

The brownie zipped about a few times before flying to the top of her bookcase, watching the scene with tongue at the ready.

"We need to get her warm," Maalik told Wulver, who had raised himself to his immense height. "She's soaked through." The demon turned to grab some dry clothes from the chest beside the bed when a low chuckle sounded from the couch.

"They're dead," Ailsa said with a laugh that made Maalik's arm hairs stand on end.

He turned back to her. She was lying in the same position he'd put her down in, but her eyes were as empty as they'd been outside. Her face was split into a grin again, but there was something wrong about it, as if some unknown force was pulling on her face muscles.

"Who's dead?" Maalik asked.

"Those that tried to attack her," Ailsa replied. And then Maalik knew who he was speaking to.

"Ishbel?"

"*Yesss,*" she hissed.

His skin crawled. "Who did you kill? And why are you talking for Ailsa?"

"Poor dear, she couldn't handle the power, so I stepped in." Then her smile faltered. "They were going to kill her, Maalik. I couldn't let them do that. So I killed them."

"Who?"

"The demons."

"Which ones?"

"All the bad little demons in their nest," she said in a sing-song voice. "Ailsa went to find them."

He was going to be sick. He had just been sitting in this cabin, barely able to move, and she'd been in Hell. "Why? We barely made it out alive last time."

"She said they had something she needed."

"What?" he asked, barely able to get the word past his lips.

"Can't you guess, little bird?" Ishbel asked. When he didn't answer, she closed those blank eyes and said, "your soul."

Oh gods. "She tried to get my soul? Why would she do that?" he demanded. *She could have died. I could be living in a world right now without her in it.* The thought was reprehensible.

"Surely you must know? And she didn't *try* to do anything. *We* succeeded."

It took his mind a few moments before they'd caught up with his ears, and even then he couldn't believe those words. "Where is it?" he asked without really thinking what it meant.

"No, I won't take that away from her," said Ishbel. "She would want to see your face." Then she cracked an eye open, her white gaze blazing into his. "I would never let anything bad happen to her. Can you make the same promise?"

"On my life," he whispered.

"Good." Ishbel let her head fall against the pillows. "You can have her back then."

Maalik watched in horror as the body in front of him gave a twitch, like Ailsa was a marionette and her strings had been cut. Then she was still; the only sign she was still alive was her chest rising and falling.

He moved towards her hesitantly, not wholly sure she would even want his hands on her. *Check her vitals*, he reasoned, placing a palm on her neck. Her skin was warmer than it had been, her pulse was a steady thrum under his fingers.

Having ascertained she was alright, he took in the rest of her. Her hair lay limply against the pillow, still damp from the rain. Aside from the birthmark and the old scar that ran along opposite cheeks, there was a new blemish. This one ran from the corner of her mouth, across her jaw and down her throat. It looked like a burn, but under the skin, as if her veins had been singed. It almost looked like lightning.

His gaze slid over her clothes, which had been torn in places, to her arms. There, on her right arm, was a similar mark, though this one was faded.

What happened to you?

He lifted one of her hands in his, examining another scrape, when she stirred.

"Maalik?"

Immediately he was squeezing her fingers in his own, wondering if he should give her some space, but unable to follow through. "I'm here."

She blinked and Maalik was glad to see her familiar piercing grey-blue eyes again. "But I'm dead. Is this what it's like when you die?"

"You didn't die. You're not in Hell anymore." Of course, what would anyone else think when they woke up with a demon in front of them?

She inhaled deeply, as though testing her lungs out for the

first time in a while. "No, I can't be in Hell, you're here. But I *was* in Hell; I was in the demon's nest. And then they killed me."

"No," Maalik told her, smoothing back her hair. "Ishbel saved you. She said you killed all the demons in the nest."

She stared up at the ceiling. "They were going to kill me. Slowly." She shuddered, like she was replaying those last moments in her head. "I suppose she's not too bad to have around then." Then Ailsa turned her eyes, full of confusion, on him and Maalik had to hold on to the bed to stop himself from falling in. "But how did I get here?" she asked.

"You must have walked." His voice came out in an embarrassing wheeze and he had to cough to clear it. "I found you in the forest. Ishbel was still possessing you."

Ailsa let out a gasp and sat up, rummaging in the bag attached to her thigh. "Oh please, oh please," she chanted, and then a silver-blue glow lit up her face. "We did it," Ailsa whispered.

She pulled her hand out, bringing the blue light with it, and held it out to Maalik. "I believe this is yours."

His soul. Right there in her hands. But that wasn't important, not now. "You shouldn't have risked yourself—again—to get this. I can live without it, Ailsa." There were other, more precious things he couldn't live without.

"But now you have it, you can come with me. There's something important we have to do." Ailsa smiled as though he was being dim. His heart ached.

"Slow down. How do we know it won't be taken away again? I made a deal with the angel who healed you that I would give it up." As long as the soul sat there, separate from himself, it was always a possibility.

"It'll never be taken from you again." She reached back into her bag and produced a flask of clear liquid. "Drink up."

Maalik frowned. "What is it?"

"Water," she said. "From inside the Cauldron of Life."

For the second time that day, her words made it to his ears, but not to his brain. He rocked back onto his heels, shaking his head. "How—"

Then her hand was reaching out, grabbing his shoulder, steadying him. "It doesn't matter how. This water will restore your soul to you, if you choose to drink it." She gave a low chuckle. "And I really hope you do, otherwise I just took down all of Hell for nothing."

"Oh my gods," breathed Maalik, staring now at the liquid.

Ailsa let go, slumping back against the pillows, and smiled. "*Slàinte.*"

Chapter 40

There was a demon in Ailsa's room. The shadowy figure stood in front of a window, his back to her. It took a few moments for Ailsa to remember where she was and when her brain finally cleared, she half sat up in the bed and stretched.

I fell asleep.

"Maalik?"

"You should go back to sleep," Maalik croaked without turning around.

"Sorry, it's been a long day," Ailsa said, running a hand over her face. "I'm awake now."

Turning from the window, he settled himself into a chair at the small table. Ailsa raked her gaze over him. He looked... terrible.

She'd been too tired earlier, but now it was clear. Maalik looked wrecked. Like he hadn't slept in weeks or like some sickness had ravaged him. His face was pale and drawn. Deep bruises spread across the skin under his eyes. His blackened fingers curled around the chair, gripping the wood too hard. Even the muscles on his forearms shook with some unknown effort.

What happened to you?

Ailsa's heart broke seeing him like that.

"Are you going to tell me why you risked your life to come here with this?" he asked, gesturing to the soul and the water he still hadn't drunk.

Her mouth was dry as she struggled to answer. Struggled to push the worry away. "I told you I'd come back for you, whether or not you wanted me to. You're stuck with me." She frowned. "And I need your help."

He shifted in his seat then, sitting up straighter. "What happened after you left?"

"We got to Ephraim. Nicnevan killed Gris."

"I'm sorry."

"He had protected me my whole life, without me knowing. We were only just becoming friends again." Ailsa shook her head. He'd bet on her, and he'd been wrong. "Nicnevan isn't my mother. She knew as soon as she saw me."

Maalik bit his lip. "What did she do?"

"She tried to kill me too, tried to kill my friends. We fought." Ailsa's eyes glazed over, remembering that taunting, sneering face. "Iona trapped her."

"How?"

"The Cauldron of Life." The glass bottle was perched on the table beside him. *Why hasn't he taken it yet?* "She'd cursed Harris. And my brother. Iona used the cauldron to take the curse from them, so when she tipped the contents over Nicnevan, she got it instead."

"Your brother?"

Ailsa's lips flexed into a quick smile. There and gone again. "We found him in Ephraim. Nicnevan had captured him."

"That still doesn't explain why you're here."

"Dolor," Ailsa said, simply.

Maalik froze, clearly remembering what had happened when he'd last seen the goddess—when she'd broken Ailsa's back. And what Dolor had done to him.

She nodded. "Dolor and the other gods, they're after the Four Treasures. Iona has one of them, the Cauldron of Life. King Duncan had the Stone of Destiny, but it was stolen from him. We need to find the other treasures before the gods do."

Maalik ran his hands through his hair. Ailsa felt her own fingers itching. "Do you have any idea where they might be?" he asked.

"A friend of ours has heard varying reports, so we split up to check them all out. Our friend, Irené, and Harris went to Ephraim because it's rumoured Nicnevin has one. Iona, Angus and my brother left for Kilvaig."

He frowned. "I'm afraid I don't know where any of the treasures are."

"There was another place the stories had pointed to. Monadh. I'm going up there," she said lightly.

"Iona is with Angus and your brother. Harris is with your friend. And you're supposed to go to Monadh all by yourself?"

She gave him a winning grin, biting the inside of her cheek. "No. You're coming with me."

"Oh," was all he said, looking back at the bottle of liquid. His hand twitched towards it but then he dropped it back to the table.

Ailsa couldn't help the disappointment that ran through her, but before she could become too dejected, Maalik was up out of his chair.

"I almost forgot," he said, crossing to the bookshelf, leaning up against the far wall. "It's late..." He scooped something into his hands and sank back down onto the floor in front of the bed. "I don't have any wrapping for it either..." He seemed nervous.

"What is it?"

The demon dropped something into her palm. Ailsa bent her head to inspect it. Three light blue stones were nestled together on a delicate silver chain. Though they were rough, the gems sparkled in the candlelight. The aquamarines were so light they were almost grey, but in their depths were swirls of white. It was like water vapour, like clouds, frozen in time.

"Happy birthday," Maalik said, his mouth pulling into a smile.

Ailsa raised her face from the gift, knowing her mouth was hanging open but unable to do anything about it.

"You know," Maalik licked his lips, "when you said your birthday wasn't really yours? That it belonged to the child you replaced? We made up a new one for you."

"When was it?" Ailsa asked, looking back down at the gems.

"July 15th. Yesterday. Though, I'll admit, I've had this for a while. I bought the chain and the stones separately, from a woman who makes trinkets. I sometimes visit her to treat her arthritis. If you don't like it, I won't be offen—"

"No." Ailsa closed her fingers around it. "No. I love it. Would you help me put it on?"

Maalik took the chain from her to fix it to her wrist. "They reminded me of you, of your eyes."

"I can't remember the last time I had a birthday present," she whispered. "Thank you."

Maalik closed the clasp but kept his soot-stained fingers on her arm so he could position it with the beads facing out. His skin was warm and flushed, so it was a surprise when a shiver ran down Ailsa's spine.

Maalik raised his eyes to hers again. "You should get some sleep," he whispered. Somehow, it would have been too loud to speak normally. The room felt different from a few moments ago.

"So should you," she murmured back. "When was the last time you had a proper rest?"

The shrug of his shoulders was barely perceptible. "Probably about a month."

When I left? Or when he'd had his soul taken from him again?

But Maalik didn't move. "I forgot how bad it was. The insomnia. The dreams. I was handling it and then you came along, and I slept better than I had in years. I've seen Hell, even the places underneath where all the souls go to disappear. But somehow, this has been worse."

"What is?"

"Knowing what it could be like and then losing it again."

Sleep. He means sleep. He can't mean me.

"You have to keep trying."

A shudder ran through him then. "I see their faces, every night, when I close my eyes."

King Alasdair and his daughter. Maalik had killed them and he'd become a demon. "You have to let them go. You can't go back and undo it."

"If I could, I'd die a hundred deaths to bring them back. I don't deserve to have my soul back."

"We have a chance now," Ailsa growled. "To save all of Eilanmòr, all of Ossiana. You can't bring the dead back, but you can save the living. My friend, Angus, that's Alasdair's grandson. I saw his great-grandson in Dunrigh a week ago. Those are the people we're trying to save."

Maalik looked stunned. "I didn't really make the connection when I met him."

"You need to stop hating yourself." She tried to make her tone soft again. "It won't do anyone any good."

"I don't know how." His shining black eyes stared down at her. He looked so lost.

Be brave. Ailsa cupped his chin, his skin heating her palm. "I'll teach you. I know something about hating myself. I won't pretend it's the same, but when my mother became sick, everyone in my village said it was my fault. And then, when she died, my brother was taken away by relatives he hated, because they were all so scared of me. When I found out I really was a changeling, I wondered if they'd all been right about me. I thought I was Nicnevan's daughter, and by extension, was evil, like her. But I've learned some things since then.

What you are doesn't make you evil; it's your actions. And no one is beyond redemption. Yes, you did something evil. But ever since then you've done everything you can to make amends. Most people would have wallowed. I wallowed. For the longest time, I cut myself off. But you, Maalik, you went to work. You learned to heal people without magic. You put your life at risk to care for others. I know the other demons would have killed you if they'd seen how you'd treated me when I was bonded to you. And yet, you couldn't help being kind. You may never get to be an angel again, but you can be good."

He'd stilled as soon as she'd touched him, but now he gave a slow nod.

"And anyway," she said. "Who wants to be an angel? The only one I met was a total dick."

Maalik choked out a laugh at that. "Thank you."

"You should drink that," Ailsa said, gesturing to the flask of seemingly innocuous water. "Then we can get going."

Maalik stared at the flask again. Ailsa opened her mouth to encourage him again, but then thought better of it. He needed the time to convince himself—to decide he deserved it.

"I'll sleep on the couch." Maalik moved to stand, but she gripped his wrist tightly.

"We can share?" Ailsa motioned to the empty mattress beside her. "For old times' sake? Of course, if you don't want to—"

"No, I want to." Maalik bit his lip. "Let me get out of my dirty clothes."

Ailsa let go of his skin and settled down into the bed to wait for him. The demon didn't go far, crossing to the wall where the old chest of drawers stood. Ailsa quickly averted her eyes when he pulled off his shirt, but not before spying the tanned skin, the muscles as they rippled across his back. Not before she saw the dark metal, melted to his shoulders in the shape of shrunken wings.

She closed her eyes, fighting against the rage that had almost consumed her before. *How could anyone do that to him?* To Maalik, who hadn't stopped trying to heal people, even as his angelic powers had been ripped from him?

The bed sunk beside her, and then there was a hot body at her back.

"Sorry, I—"

"You're nice and warm," Ailsa said in a hushed voice. So that he'd know she wanted him there.

Maalik hesitated before throwing an arm over her side, pulling her closer. They'd fallen asleep like this a few times before. More often, he'd placed his head on her stomach as Ailsa had run her fingers through his hair. Not tonight, though. Tonight, he'd hold her after she fought through Hell to bring his soul back. After she'd killed every demon and almost lost herself in the process.

With the almost feverish heat and the quiet of the cabin, sleep tugged at Ailsa's eyelids.

"It's okay," Maalik whispered against her hair. "You're safe here."

Ailsa sniffed, letting the smells of cotton sheets and crackling fire and old books fill her nostrils—- the smells she associated with Maalik, with her demon—and let herself be soothed to sleep.

Chapter 41

Wherever Ailsa was, it was warm and comfortable, and she did not want to get up. She fought to hold on to sleep, like she'd often fought to hold the blankets against herself while Cameron had tried to pull them off her, telling her to wake up. There was peace here, and she hadn't known peace in so long.

She was pressed up against something—someone, she corrected after realising their chest was rising and falling against her cheek. Well, that was new.

Ailsa blinked fully awake and assessed her position. She'd rolled over in the night, snuggling her head into a shoulder, throwing one leg over a hip and a hand under a shirt—

Ailsa froze, her cheeks heating.

"Are you awake?" Maalik asked above her.

She shuffled back, extracting her hand from his stomach and immediately missing the heat. The fire in the cabin had died down overnight, making it chilly. She'd obviously followed the heat from his body in her sleep.

"Sorry," she muttered, rubbing the sleep from her eyes.

"Don't be."

Ailsa thought she detected a chuckle in his voice. *He's laughing at you.* She sat up, levelling her gaze at the demon.

Maalik was stretched out on his back across the mattress, one arm slung behind his head. He gave her a smile, the corners of his eyes crinkling. "I haven't slept that well in a while."

Even if I tried to assault you in my sleep. Ailsa cringed. "What time is it?"

Maalik glanced to the side, to the clock above the fireplace. "Only seven. Still early. Are you hungry?"

Ailsa made to rise, but he clicked his tongue. "I'll make something, you stay here."

He was up, and across the room before she could protest. But something snagged his attention on the table and he came to a stop in front of it.

His soul.

It glowed blue beside the vial of cauldron water. When Maalik reached out a hand towards it, it grew brighter still.

Ailsa settled back down against the pillows, chewing on her lip as she watched him. She knew better than to say anything, to break the quiet of the moment. If Maalik wanted to take the liquid, it would need to be his own choice.

Please, please.

Making his decision, he moved with fluid grace as he picked up the soul and pressed it into his chest. At the same time, he lifted the bottle to his lips and took a swig, his throat bobbing as he swallowed.

Ailsa didn't know what she had expected. A noise? A beam from heaven? But the coming together of body and soul was nothing like that. One minute the ball of light was gleaming against his shirt, the next it was gone, like he'd absorbed it. Maalik shuddered and placed the vial back on the table, using the wood to help steady himself.

"How does it feel?" Ailsa murmured.

"It's... cool. Like drinking a cold drink." He huffed out

a laugh. "It's been a while since I've felt anything but heat." Maalik looked up, still with those same black eyes. "I suppose we'll have to wait and see if it makes a difference."

Then, as if he hadn't just reunited with a vital piece of himself, he made his way into the kitchen, choosing a pot, then a bag of food from a cupboard.

Ailsa shook her head. She'd imagined a bit more of a celebration, but perhaps they'd manage that later.

The door to the other room creaked open and Wulver's face appeared as something small and furry shot out. The wolf fixed Ailsa with a stare that seemed to convey he'd had a long night.

Muck zipped around Maalik's head before coming to rest on Ailsa's blanketed feet, purring as she rubbed her face onto her toes.

"Good morning to you too," Ailsa said, scratching her behind the horns. The fur there was as soft as duckling feathers. "Did Maalik lock you away?"

"Over-excited brownies are not conducive to a good night's sleep," Maalik called from the stove.

The smell of onions cooking wafted from the kitchen, making Ailsa's stomach clench in hunger. "We should get going as soon as possible," Maalik said, focussing on the frying pan. "Who knows how long it'll take to get to Monadh. I think I know a shortcut, but we'll have to find it first. We'll eat and then get ready."

"So you're coming with me?" she asked, barely believing her luck. The night before, he'd seemed so reluctant.

He looked at her over his shoulder, keeping his tone light, even as the muscles along his back seemed to stiffen under his shirt. "As long as you still want me to go?"

She nodded, trying to convey as much sincerity as possible. "Of course."

Ailsa relaxed back into the pillows to the sounds of domesticity. She couldn't help wondering when the next time they'd have this would be. Peace, comfort, quiet; they could all be things of the past, if what Irené had said was true. Then a thought crept up, and she blurted it out before she could stop herself.

"We could go anywhere. We could just run away." Nothing was tying either of them to Eilanmòr anymore. Maalik could literally go anywhere. Ailsa could go with him.

But she knew it was impossible. Not because of a bond, or a spell, or even because of poverty. No, she had people who trusted her now. Trusted her and needed her to fight for them. With them.

Maalik turned slightly, his hand still on the spatula. "Do you want to run away? It's your choice."

"No, I don't."

"Well, then we'll go to Monadh. We'll look for these weapons."

"You could still run." Ailsa swallowed thickly.

He turned those black, unreadable eyes on her. "I'm going where you're going. If you'll have me."

Ailsa gave him a small smile. "Good, because I wasn't really going to let you go that easily. I risked my life for that soul, it belongs to me now."

It was a joke, but it came out wrong, and Ailsa found herself willing the words back into her mouth. *You've admitted too much, too soon. What if he doesn't feel the same? What if—*

"It's yours. As long as you want it." The words were hoarse. Broken. Maalik turned his eyes back to the food. "This is ready."

And Ailsa knew two things. First was that he felt the same way she did. Second, her demon thought himself incapable of being loved—that he didn't deserve it.

"Great, I'm starving," she said breathily.

Well, Ailsa thought, slipping out of bed and over to the table, *I have the entire journey to Monadh and back to convince him otherwise.*

Chapter 42

The early morning mist still clung between the trees by the time they were ready to leave. Ailsa considered sweeping the fog away but left it as it was. The sunlight shone through the vapour, reminding her of cosy mornings under blankets.

If only, Ailsa thought. One day soon, she'd allow herself a lie in. Once the world has been saved.

As they were heading out the door, something small and fuzzy whacked into Maalik's back with a thud.

"Are you saying goodbye or are you hoping I've changed my mind about you coming?" Maalik asked the brownie.

Muck buzzed about his head, emitting a high-pitched *'weeeeee'*. Ailsa wasn't sure what exactly that meant, but after a few rounds Muck bumbled over to Ailsa's shoulder, giving it a nudge, before zooming off to find Wulver. The great wolf padded to the front door, taking up much of the space inside the cabin. Muck landed on his back with little grace.

"Stay safe," Maalik told him.

The wolf lowered his head into a bow. Muck sank herself further into the fur on his neck and he gave a small whine.

"They'll be fine," Ailsa told Maalik as they walked off down the rough path.

"Of course they will. I'm just worried about my cabin, if there'll be anything to come back to after all this."

They trudged on in silence, smelling the pine air and

listening to the gentle chirp of birds overhead. There were no footsteps, save their own.

Ailsa glanced sideways at her companion, almost hearing the cogs whir in his head. "You know, I never thought I'd enjoy wandering through a forest, but this is actually pretty nice."

Maalik gave a half smile. "It is nice."

"Then why do you look worried?"

"It's been a long time since I was trapped here. I'm wondering what it'll be like to take a step outside these woods. To smell the sea."

"Well, what are we waiting for?" She skipped ahead, the sunbeams through the branches kissing her skin. "The faster we go, the faster we reach the coast." It was still far: days and days away. But perhaps a race would cheer him up. Or take his mind away from his brooding for a bit.

Maalik's full lips curled into a proper smile now. "Are you challenging me to a race?"

"Only if you can keep up, old man." And then she was off, kicking her feet behind her as she sped through the forest. The bag she wore bounced against her back until she held the straps in both hands. She could hear footfalls behind, so she pressed on, willing her legs to go quicker. Ailsa drank in the cool air into her lungs and then had an idea. She willed the wind to change direction so it was pushing against her back, making her faster and faster.

Is this what flying is like?

On and on she ran, soaring over fallen trees and darting between boulders. After all these weeks cooped up in Dunrigh, it was freeing to stretch her legs, to feel her lungs burn. A stab of pain lanced through her side, but she pushed through the stitch, almost enjoying the ache.

"Ailsa!" Maalik shouted from somewhere behind her.

He didn't sound panicked, merely out of breath. She slowed, skidding through the pine needles until she came to a stop at the top of a rise. From there the path snaked down through the trees, probably to a river. If they followed that, hopefully they'd make it to the coast quickly. Or they'd make it to wherever Maalik's shortcut was.

The sounds of panting came through the woods and she turned to watch the demon loping through the trees. There was sweat on his brow, despite the cool morning, but Ailsa supposed that was partly from his inner heat. He grinned ruefully as he jogged up the hill, coming to rest against a tree trunk with his hands on his knees.

"Do you know," Maalik said, huffing out a laugh, "how fast you were going?"

Ailsa shrugged. "I beat you, didn't I?"

"How?" was all Maalik said, leaning his forehead against the tree.

"I used the air to push me along." She swept her arm up, sending a gentle breeze around him.

Maalik's mouth popped open in astonishment. "You've got a much better handle on your powers than you did a month ago."

Ailsa looked down at her own hands, where the beginnings of one of those strange welts began at her wrist. "It's not been without some mistakes, but I've been practising."

Maalik pushed off the tree, coming to stand at the top of the hill with her. "We just covered an hour's worth of ground in a third of the time."

"Well, that's good; maybe we can run the entire way."

He snorted. "I don't think I can keep up with you. Anyway,

we don't have to. I know a guy."

Ailsa motioned down the hill and gave him a grin she knew she only reserved for him. "Lead on."

Chapter 43

harris woke to sunshine pouring in the small round window, which meant two things. First, that it was going to be a pleasant day. Second, they'd already surfaced, and he had slept right through it.

He stretched as best he could in the narrow bed. After Cameron had left, he'd kept the same room and the same top bunk. He enjoyed reading the things the previous occupants had scratched in the ceiling.

Miri was here.

Amo a Laura.

What snores like a bull and smells like a pig? My roommate.

There was even a crude picture of a male appendage which had clearly been drawn by someone who had either never seen one or someone who needed to be checked by the medic.

Unless something strange had happened and they were far off course, they'd now be at their first destination.

And then on to Ephraim.

It would be weeks before they'd be back on The Nymph, if they didn't decide to travel back to Dunrigh by land. This was Harris's last chance to make his mark.

Stretching an arm down to the side table, he grabbed the dagger he'd been carrying these last few days and unsheathed it carefully. Harris was sure he'd been given a smaller knife than everyone else. But then again, he didn't blame anyone for that. Sticking his tongue between his lips, he scratched the very point into the wood above him. Who would be the next person to see his message? Would it take weeks or even years until someone was lying in this bed again?

Finally, his crude words were complete. He dropped his head back onto his pillow and surveyed his handiwork.

Perfect.

Then, brushing the shavings off his clothes, he swung out of bed to get ready.

The waves were choppy, despite the azure skies overhead, as the little dinghy was lowered from the side of the boat. Overhead, Irené's giant osprey circled, having followed them from the last time they'd surfaced. She'd whistled to him when they'd emerged from the boat, chucking him a piece of fish in greeting.

"Now you have to invent a way to bend the sea to your will," Harris joked to the woman beside him.

"I would never want that," answered Irené as they made their landing. "Then we'd have no fun."

Gone were the casual trousers, the loose braids; Irené was in her full captain's regalia now. Her dark coat was back on and underneath she wore a tight red waistcoat and belt full of pistols. Harris had seen guns before, but they were usually massive contraptions that had to be loaded with gunpowder to do anything. These were hand sized, in ornamental brass and leather. He didn't doubt they were just as deadly, if not more. Still, she'd also strapped her cutlass to her waist. It gleamed wickedly in the sun. Atop her head was her usual black, wide-brimmed hat. Her turquoise braids had been partially tucked into her collar, as though she hadn't bothered to flick them out when she'd shrugged on the coat.

Harris's hands itched to fix them for her, but he stopped himself. *Don't touch other people's hair.*

"How far inland do we need to go?" Irené asked him.

Harris eyed the treeline as there was a splash of another boat landing behind. "A few hours west from here. Not far."

"It's that easy?" she asked, unimpressed.

"You can only get there if you know where you're going," Harris replied. "Fae have this... sense inside us. We know where Ephraim is; it's innate."

"Just as well we have you then," she said.

They made their way across the water, with Irené's gunner rowing, until the bottom of the boat hit sand. Then it was time to get their feet wet. As soon as the cold water hit his bare toes, Harris smiled in delight. How long had it been since he was touching the sea, feeling the grains and bits of shell beneath his skin? He paused for a moment, marvelling at the way the ocean kissed his shins, how it eddied and swirled about him. *I could turn into a seal and swim off.*

He looked up to find the captain staring. "What?"

"You look happy," Irené said.

"Do you want to know why?" he laughed. He kicked the water towards her.

Irené shrieked, but it twisted into a cackle as she dodged out of the way. Her hat toppled off her head and onto the waves, but she didn't bend to pick it up. Instead, she joined him, kicking the water in his direction until they were splashing around, completely soaked. When her gunner, Orenzo, shook his head, she kicked the water at him too.

"Hey!" he shouted as his trousers dripped from the splash.

"These are my best clothes."

"The sun is shining, and we made it," Irené said, dimples in her cheeks. "I'm enjoying the moment."

Harris turned his head, laughing, to see if the rest of the dinghies had made it to the beach yet. And that's when he saw them. Behind the small boats filled with Irené's crew, three longships were outlined on the horizon.

Chapter 44

"Raiders," Harris shouted, grabbing Irené by the elbow. "We have to get to shore."

The captain wasted no time, switching effortlessly from the laughing woman of a moment before to a fearless leader. *"Todos a la playa, ahora!"*

They crashed through the waves, pulling the boat along until it could go no further, propped against the sandbank. Then Irené was swinging around, grabbing her cutlass in one hand and one of the little pistols in the other. Harris, too, pulled out his knife, though he knew it wouldn't do much good. Out beyond the breakers, the longships cut through the ocean quickly, gaining on The Nymph's crew.

"Cover them!" Irené shouted, and the five sailors that had been on their own boat fired their guns in unison. But it was no use. The longships didn't hesitate, barreling towards their targets.

"Wait," Irené commanded, holding her gun aloft. "We'll only hit our crew."

The Edessan dinghies reached the shallows and the sailors piled out to pull the boats up the beach. Harris's heart thudded in his chest as he watched their crew splash across the sandbar. The longships were forty feet away, then thirty, then twenty. But just as he thought the raiders would run the Edessans down, they came to a stop as their hulls ran aground. It was only then that Harris got a good look at the inhabitants.

There had to be a dozen people in each boat, but they were not Avolognian raiders. They rose from their crouches, swaying in the waves as they stared at The Nymph's crew. Each bore markings across their faces. At first, Harris thought they were tattoos, but then he realised they were bands of rotten, black flesh.

"Do you remember you told us about what the Edaxi do to people they meet?" asked Harris.

Irené flinched. "The Soulless."

The people inside the longboats dropped over the side, landing in the sea. And then they left the vessels behind, shambling through the water haphazardly, as if unbalanced. Each wore tattered clothing and a slack expression.

"Are they dead?" asked Irené, fear choking her voice.

"No, they're alive," said Harris, raising his knife higher. "But I think that's worse."

The Edessan crew had all made it to the beach, abandoning their boats and running behind Irené and Harris to form a line.

Irené lowered her gun again, aiming for the middle of the pack of ragged people. "*Disparo.*"

The pistols discharged in a cloud of smoke, downing a few of the Soulless, but they kept coming, their steps speeding up as they too made it to the sand.

Harris gripped his knife as Irené and her crew ran forward to meet the rotting bodies. He stayed on the captain's heels as she fired her gun and slashed repeatedly with graceful movements. Harris came face to face with one of their opponents and, without pause, sank the dagger into their neck. They crumpled to the sand with a low moan.

I've just killed someone.

Harris stared down at his hands, now covered in blood.

I've just killed someone.

But then the next enemy was running for him, and he was slashing at their chest. This time he didn't have the luxury of stopping as they fell; another foe already upon him. Around him, screams permeated the air. Were they winning? Was everyone dead?

Harris's stomach plummeted as another Soulless launched themselves at him and he was knocked to the ground with them on top. *A woman,* he realised, as she tried to claw at his face. He kicked her off, and she splashed into the waves. How had they gotten so close to the sea again?

I'll have to kill her too, he thought as nausea threatened to choke him.

But then he watched in horror as the woman he'd been fighting turned her head instead to her right. To where Irené was firing her pistol at a group of Soulless. Everything moved in slow motion as the cursed woman's hands moved to her hip and she pulled out a dagger of her own. Then she was rising from the water, walking with sure steps now towards the captain.

"No!" Harris shouted, pushing himself up. His feet kicked against the sand, finding no purchase at first, but then he propelled himself towards Irené and the woman. Irené's back was turned as her gun fired once, twice. The Soulless woman raised her dagger. It glinted in the bright sunlight as she brought it down towards the captain's shoulder.

Harris knew, in that moment, he couldn't fight off the attack, he could only block it. So he threw himself between the woman and Irené as the knife came down on his side.

He landed with a splash in the shallow water. The sound caught Irené's attention and then, with one blast of her gun, the Soulless woman's side was shredded. The impact knocked her backwards until she landed in the sea as blood pooled around her.

Irené looked down at him, not lowering her pistol. "Are you hurt?"

Harris hissed a laugh, "Barely a scratch."

Irené set her jaw as her eyes darted over his face. "You didn't need to do that."

"I'd be a really crap friend if I let her stab you."

Irené's lips parted like she would say something more. But then a shout rang out from across the beach and her head jerked up.

"*Capitana!*"

Irené pushed to her feet, straining her gaze to find the crew member who had shouted. "Will you be alright?" she asked him absently.

"Of course," Harris told her. "Go, you're needed."

With one more glance down at him, she marched off across the sand. Harris waited, watching until she was far enough away. Then he let out a groan, clutching his side.

You really are an eejit, he admonished himself. As he had suspected, his hand came away covered with blood.

The battle raged on, but Harris was detached somehow, as though the Soulless knew he was no threat now he was down. Only the osprey, Duende, seemed to notice him. He landed in the sand beside him, twisting his head so he could regard Harris with one eye.

"Are you planning to eat me?" Harris croaked.

But the osprey just stared.

Choosing to ignore the bird, he dragged himself across the beach, until he could lean against a pile of packs the crew had dropped. He rooted inside all of them, but he had no luck that day: there was nothing inside to help him.

Harris's head swam, and he knew it wasn't good. He'd left a trail of blood up the sand, like a gory snail. *Heal,* he told his body. But, after some inspection, he realised the wound was large, bigger than any he'd had before. This one would take days to close. Maybe, if he could find a nice cave, have a lie down...

It was only when the screaming stopped that Harris realised he must have fallen unconscious for a moment. He cracked his eyes open to find a collection of people standing on the beach with their arms by their sides. The crew. The battle was over and the Soulless were finally at rest. Harris grimaced at that through his chapped lips. They'd won.

But then a woman was running towards him, her head blocking out the sun. Harris tried to push himself up, but his limbs weren't obeying commands anymore. *I'll have to stay here then.*

"Harris!" Irené shouted as she skidded across the sand. Duende flapped his wings, scattering grains over his legs, like he was telling her to hurry. Then she was on her knees, shaking his shoulder. The movement jostled his wound, the pain enough to clear his foggy head.

Irené's fingers went to his own, to where he had pressed them into his side.

"Why didn't you tell me you were injured?" she asked harshly.

"I would have got in the way," he rasped.

Irené's dark eyes were enormous, terrified. "Harris, this

259

wound looks bad; it's almost punctured a lung. You've lost a lot of blood."

"I'm a selkie. We heal easily." But he was already slipping away again.

"Yes, but how are you supposed to swim with only one lung?"

His head lolled back. "But it was only *almost* punctured. Nothing to worry about."

"We'll get our medic to see you right away." She squeezed his arm. "You are—"

"I know, completely insufferable."

"That too, but I was going to say *brave*. I'm in your debt."

His eyelids were too heavy. *Don't fall asleep, keep talking to her.* "Now Captain, was that a compliment?"

Irené let out a harsh laugh. "I'm afraid you must have a fever too."

He wanted the last thing he saw before he passed out to be Irené, illuminated from behind by the sun, the rays making a crown about her worried face. But then something to the side caught his eye. From out of the treeline came a unicorn, of all things. *Not real,* he told himself, and then Harris lost his tenuous grip on consciousness.

Chapter 45

Ailsa squinted up at the man in front of her. "You still look like a demon."

Honestly, Ailsa didn't know what he expected. He'd only wrapped a tartan scarf around his head. Yes, it covered his small golden antlers and the shadows it created hid his obsidian eyes a little, but then there were the blackened hands, the skin which cracked in glowing fissures whenever he was annoyed. Like right now.

Maalik pressed his lips together into a flat line. "I'm not done yet."

When they'd eventually reached the river after a morning of hiking, Ailsa had expected them to follow it downstream as it cut its way through the forest and out towards the coast. Instead, Maalik had led them up a tributary, walking against the trickling current of the smaller river. Half an hour later, she'd understood why; perched on the side of the bank was a little thatched house. *I know a guy,* Maalik had said. But obviously not well enough to go as he was.

"Why are you even bothering anyway, didn't you say you knew this person? Surely he knows you're a demon?"

"It's been a long while since I was this far away from my cabin. And since then I heard he's started a family. I don't want to scare the children."

"I'm afraid I can't help you there." Ailsa swept her gaze over the demon, trying to imagine she didn't know him. Would she be frightened if she had met him like this? Dressed in normal clothes, in the bright forest, she liked to think not. But hadn't she screamed when she'd first seen him? She cringed at that memory. "Should I go instead?"

Maalik sighed. "He doesn't know you. It'll be quicker if I go." He reached into his pack again, pulling out burgundy fabric and sweeping it round his shoulders. A cloak. He raised the hood, adding another layer.

"That's probably better. I can hardly see your face. Though, you must be roasting?" Indeed, a single bead of sweat emerged from his hairline, trickling down the side of his face.

"It's only for a moment." He turned back to the cottage, nestled between the tall pines.

A plume of smoke puffed out from the house's chimney and the smell of baking was so strong it made it all the way to their hiding place amongst the ferns. On one side of the house, an enormous wheel turned, pushed by the river below. Maalik had said his friend was a baker, but Ailsa couldn't fathom why they would need to speak to him. Especially when their packs were already full of food. *Perhaps the man has a horse we could borrow*, Ailsa thought, hoping that wasn't true. The last time she'd ridden a horse, all the way from her beach to Dunrigh, she'd been sore for days.

"Okay, wish me luck." And then the demon was off, slinking through the trees. Ailsa tracked his progress as he kept to the shadows, getting closer and closer to the house, to the little door at the side. She shifted her eyes to the front door as he grew nearer but saw no movement. Hopefully, he'd stay hidden. His disguise really wasn't very good.

Finally, he was at the building. His head darted around,

checking the coast was clear, and then he knocked hesitantly at the wooden door. Ailsa waited with bated breath until it swung open. She couldn't see who stood just inside the house, but since Maalik wasn't backing away, she thought it must have been his friend. Their conversation was quick and before long, someone emerged. The man closed the door behind himself slowly and carefully, as if he was trying to make as little noise as possible. And then he was ducking down and following Maalik back through the woods.

Ailsa counted to ten and then Maalik emerged from between the trees with his hood and scarf thrown back.

"Come on, he says he can help."

From behind her demon, a man appeared. The man was younger than she expected, probably in his early twenties, like her brother. He hadn't bothered to take off the apron he wore, covered in flour and oil stains, and he wore his blonde hair tied in a loose ponytail behind his head. His gaze flicked immediately to Ailsa's birthmark, burning like a brand.

Ailsa readied herself to fight or run.

But then his smile was genuine as he said, "I didn't think Maalik even knew any girls." His eyes darted back to the cottage, and he licked his lips.

"Calum, this is Ailsa. Ailsa, meet Calum. You're not allowed to hit him, even if he deserves it."

The man folded muscular arms across his chest. "Too right, I'm risking my neck for you two."

What had Maalik asked him? "We don't want to cause you any trouble—"

"You'll only cause me trouble if my wife notices the canoe is missing."

Ailsa blinked. "Canoe?"

Maalik lifted one shoulder. "That river goes all the way to the north coast. I figured it would be quicker than rowing."

"We can't take your boat. I don't know if we'll ever be able to bring it back," she said, remembering the last boat she'd borrowed, still probably sitting on the beach on the Isle of Faodail.

"We never use it, anyway. My wife likes to try new hobbies, but she gets bored quickly. If you want a loom or a finger piano, you can have those too." He smiled widely, despite his grumbling, as though he didn't really mind.

Well, I won't refuse free transport. "Lead the way," Ailsa said, relenting.

They darted through the trees until they reached the riverbank, scrambling down over rocks and roots, until they were directly beneath the house. The great wheel groaned as it moved with the force of the water.

Calum saw Ailsa studying it and grinned. "It's pretty cool, isn't it? It helps to grind the wheat kernels we buy in so we can make flour. My grandpa built it, but I've done a bit of tinkering with it too. Now it powers our lights."

"You have electricity?" Only the richest and most advanced could afford electric lights. She hadn't been surprised to see them onboard The Nymph. But here, in the middle of the woods?

Calum almost seemed to glow himself at her questioning. "We even have electric heating. I ran some pipes under the floor."

"That is cool. They don't even have that in the castle in Dunrigh."

"Ailsa is no stranger to electricity," Maalik said.

"Ah, you're an inventor too?" asked Calum.

Ailsa squirmed under his attention. "It's magic, not science."

Calum's eyes lit up. "Electric magic? I would love to ask you some questions—"

"I'm afraid we have to get going." Maalik's voice was hard, but then his mouth pulled back into a wince.

What's that about?

"Of course," the baker said at once, looking between Ailsa and Maalik. "Here's the boat." He waved them down to where the canoe was tethered to a post with rope.

"Maybe we'll be here again soon," Ailsa told the baker as Maalik went ahead, untying the craft and placing his pack into it. "Thank you for letting us take the canoe. If your wife ever finds out, thank her for us too."

Calum grinned, his eyes still darting back and forward between her and the demon. "Don't let him boss you around."

"I would never," Ailsa told him. "I know how to handle him."

From below, she heard Maalik grumble something which sounded like, "*I'm* the bossy one?" before he called up to the baker. "Thank you."

Calum waved, tucking his other hand into his apron. "Take care." And then he was sneaking back up to the house.

"What's wrong with you?" Ailsa asked when they were alone. That whole interaction had been weird as soon as she'd told Calum she had magic.

Maalik's face twisted as he held the canoe still for her to climb in. "I don't like the thought of random people knowing about your powers."

"He wasn't random," she said, sitting down. "I thought he was your friend."

Maalik grunted as he pushed the boat off from the bank. Then he was jumping fluidly in before his feet could get wet. "The fewer people know what you can do, the better," he finally said when they were floating out into the river. "I'm not sure if you realise this, but your power is strong. Stronger than most fae."

"And?"

He raised those night-dark eyes to hers. "And the Edaxi will be looking for the fae with the strongest powers to wield their weapons."

"I bet there are loads of fae with air powers outside of Eilanmòr."

"Yes."

Ailsa cocked her head, Maalik's rudeness forgotten. *What are they?* She wondered. *What am I?*

Maalik must have noticed her stare. He chuckled, his dark eyelashes sweeping his cheeks. "Back in Kemet, there are the Jinn. They can shift their shapes or even become invisible. Or in Akrosia there are Nephele, cloud nymphs; or Furies, flying women who really don't like men." He regarded her then. She could almost feel his eyes trailing from her legs to her face. And then he smirked. "Or you could be a Wyvern?"

She gave him a dubious look. "Aren't those the same as dragons?"

He lifted the paddle from the bottom of the canoe and placed it across his lap. "Dragons have fire magic; Wyverns have wind magic. But apart from that, they're the same."

"Are you calling me a giant lizard?"

He snickered. "Do you want me to check you for scales?"

"How would you like to be pushed into the river?" she said, leaning forward so they were almost touching. "Maybe I'll go find a dragon, if they've got fire magic, and replace you."

Maalik snorted. "Good luck with that." Then he dipped the paddle into the river and dragged it along the rippling water. "You're supposed to turn to face the same way in canoes you know."

Ailsa swatted his knee before turning, looking downstream now. They'd already picked up speed. Not quite enough to beat that horse she'd been thinking about, but certainly faster than walking, and more comfortable. A bright green dragonfly zipped past her face, and Ailsa wondered if it was mocking her. *Wyvern indeed.*

"Can we follow this river all the way to the coast?" she asked, grabbing the other paddle. A stray grey feather floated in front of her face; she flicked it away, scanning the sky for whatever bird had dropped it.

"We can, but we're not going all the way," said Maalik from behind her. "I have another surprise. For now, relax and trust me."

Done, thought Ailsa, dropping the paddle back in the canoe's bottom.

Chapter 46

harris's eyes were lead weights as he tried to blink them open. If the pounding in his head was any sign, he had been unconscious for a while. And it hadn't been a restful sleep. A noise echoed around him and it took a moment to realise it was coming from him. The moan had rattled out of his own chest.

"Hush, you're okay," said a woman's voice.

Harris tried to turn his head to see who it was, but his neck was too stiff. He felt something cool being pressed against his brow and he leaned into the touch, suddenly realising how warm he was.

"Go back to sleep," the woman said.

He tried to fight it, tried to drag himself up and out of the dark sickness. But then the woman sang something soft and haunting. There was a strangeness to the sound, and Harris's skin prickled. *Magic,* he thought, before he lost all trace of thought and slipped under again.

The next time that Harris woke, there was a pressure on his hand. The side of his body felt like it was on fire, but some of the stiffness was gone. His tongue darted out, trying to wet his chapped lips, but he didn't have any moisture in his mouth either. His throat croaked as he opened his eyes, searching for something to drink.

The room he was in was dark, save for a candle beside him, dripping waxy tears into the wooden table. It was enough to illuminate the bed he was in, though. He lay amongst covers and pillows of embroidered velvet, much too luxurious for The Nymph.

"Where—" Harris tried to say, but his voice came out more like a creak. He looked down at his hands, trying to find another clue to his whereabouts, and wondered if he was delusional. The pressure had been someone else's hand covering his own. Long, dark fingers curled around his palm. His eyes tracked the skin from the hand to the wrist to the arm. Finally, his gaze fell upon the woman, fast asleep and leaning on the side of the bed.

Irené had changed clothing since the last time he'd seen her. Probably because she had been covered in his blood. Now she wore a simple white shirt, which looked like it was meant for someone much broader, billowing about her slim frame. Her turquoise braids spilled out over the blankets on his legs and her face was towards him. His eyes flickered over her features, usually harsh and calculating, now smoothed out in slumber. Her eyelashes fanned her cheeks as she inhaled through parted lips.

How long have I been lying here? Harris wondered. He could tell he'd been sick, which probably meant his wound had become infected. The sudden urge to push up off the bed came to him, but he squashed it down, willing his legs to stay still.

He wasn't usually the one being nursed back to health. Only a few weeks ago, he'd looked after Ailsa in the same way.

It was uncomfortable being on this side. Not just because his body ached, but because there had been hours, or perhaps days, that he'd missed. Days where others watched him dream.

He turned his head and brushed the side of his mouth against his shirt. At least it didn't seem that he'd been drooling.

Irené's breathing quickened, and then her eyes shot open. She groaned before lifting herself off the mattress and letting out a snort when she realised Harris was awake.

"Seems like you're not as weak as you everyone thought, selkie-boy," she said with a half-grin, despite the dark circles under her eyes. "My crew were sure you were done for. They even took bets."

"Oh, really?" Harris croaked. "And did you join in?"

"Yes." Irené's smile faltered. "I've just become very rich."

"You bet I would survive?" Harris asked. "Captain, I didn't know you cared. Is that why you've been tending to me?"

Irené wiped a hand over her face. "I couldn't have lived with myself if you'd died. You saved my life." When she looked back at him, her eyes were glassy.

Harris watched her as she battled to rein in her emotions. Silently, he held his arms open, praying that she didn't run away. *Please.*

Irené's lip trembled and then she was climbing onto the bed and into his arms. Harris wrapped his body around hers as best he could, and she clung to him. "I thought you'd died at one point, your breathing was so slow."

"It's going to take a lot more than a dagger to stop me," he whispered into the crown of her head.

Irené nodded. "I'm sorry for being so emotional. I'm tired."

"How long have I been unconscious for?" *How long have you been worrying?*

"Three days," she mumbled.

"And where exactly am I?" It was so hard to tell in the room's dark.

Irené raised her head, revealing tear tracks down her cheeks, and took a deep breath. "You're in Ephraim," she said.

Harris's stomach dropped. "How did we get here?" They needed one of the fae to let them in.

"Just when the fighting stopped, Angus turned up, and led us here. Or rather, his unicorn did."

Harris squeezed her tighter. "It isn't the safest of places to bring so many humans, but at least the Faerie Queen is trapped. Where is Angus? I need to speak to him."

"I'm afraid he's been busy since we arrived. You see," Irené bit her lip, "He freed Nicnevan."

Chapter 47

Angus threw open the door made of branches, balancing a tray in one hand. This walk had become a bit of a habit over the last few days, and he was in danger of becoming complacent. *Through there is one of the most terrifying people in Eilanmòr,* he reminded himself. *She captured your friends, tortured them and killed one of them.*

But the Queen of the Faeries was looking a little sorry for herself of late. Opening the second door, Angus revealed his captive. He'd only poured a few drops of the cauldron's water on her, enough that she could talk and eat, but do little else. Her body sat against the back wall of the cell, made of mostly wood and stone, looking like something from a children's story.

Nicnevan raised her head, the movement slow and strained, like a branch moving in the wind. "Is it that time already?" she asked.

Angus shivered. Even her voice had been touched by the spell. She sounded more like a whisper of air through reeds than a woman. "It's almost evening."

"Has your cook learned anything new since yesterday?" she asked, wrinkling her nose.

Angus shut the door behind him and carried the tray towards the Faerie Queen. "I'm afraid it's soup and bread, again."

"I suppose I can hardly complain. Most captives would not be treated as well as I. To be fed by the hand of the prince of Eilanmòr is a great honour indeed."

Angus set the tray down in front of her. This close he could see all the crystals in the stone which made up her cheek, all the buds sprouting from her hair.

He didn't know why he'd volunteered to watch Nicnevan. He could say that he needed the distraction after he'd found Harris so close to death on the beach. But it was more than that. The Faerie Queen was a legend he'd heard about since he was a little boy. He'd never imagined the man who'd been in love with her had been his very own father. There was obviously so much about his own family history that he didn't know. With both his mother and his father now dead, Nicnevan was possibly the only one who could shed light on his past.

"Careful," he said, dipping a spoon into the soup. "It's hot."

Nicnevan opened her mouth, revealing she had a leaf for a tongue and shiny marble teeth. He tipped the soup into her mouth and she drank it down, licking her lips with each spoonful. He studied her silently as she ate, as he always did, wondering what his father had seen in her.

For sure, she was beautiful. Even under the spell, Angus could tell her features were delicate and fine, her eyes sharp. But this woman had a heart of spite. *How could his father have fallen in love with her?* It was a question that repeated through his mind every moment he was with her. He had no answer, though he was doing his best to find it.

The soup was done, and he picked up the bread, tearing off a chunk. But Nicnevan gave an almost imperceptible shake of her head. If he hadn't been so close, he would have missed it.

"Are you finished?" he asked.

"Give me a moment to digest that awful slop." She sighed. "You can start if you like."

Angus leaned back and took a deep breath. "I wanted to talk about how you were chained to the tree."

"How I was betrayed, you mean?"

They'd come to an agreement over the last few days. After he had fed her, Angus could ask thirteen questions of the Faerie Queen. In return, he'd give her another drop of cauldron water.

He had no guarantee she was being honest, but that was always the case when dealing secrets with anyone. So far, she'd been surprisingly pleasant. Angus didn't trust it.

"What did my father say, when he did it?" he began. "I'm trying to understand his reasons."

Her leaf-tongue poked out, licking a stray drop of soup from the corner of her mouth. "You humans are always so frightened of the fae. And when you fear something, you try your best to control it. That's what it was. Control."

"Did you indicate that you would seek revenge if he didn't trap you?"

"It was a surprise to me. Your father told me he was coming to run away with me. I would still have made him a king if he had."

Behind Angus's back, he counted the questions on his fingers. Two so far. "So he was going to give up the crown of Eilanmòr?"

"We knew his subjects would not have liked having me as a queen. Despite what everyone thinks, I was not intent on seizing Eilanmòr for myself. I'm quite happy ruling over my fae."

"But your child would have inherited the crown, though?"

The ivy snaking around her upper arms recoiled. "If Conall had abdicated, it would have gone to his sister's child. You have a cousin, do you not?"

"Moira?"

Nicnevan smirked as best she could. "Was that a question?"

"No," Angus said quickly. "But now, since my father *was* king, your daughter is in line for the throne?"

"Actually, since she was born before your brother, she would be queen. You would move down to third in line, I'm afraid."

"Fourth. My brother has a child." Baby Douglas was barely a few months old, yet so much rested on his little shoulders. "Was my father married to my mother before or after he chained you to the tree?"

"After. They were betrothed when I visited him in Dunrigh. I assumed it was an arranged marriage."

"It was, though they became friends. You didn't answer my first question. What did he say?" *Surely that still counts as the same question?*

Nicnevan sighed. "He told me he loved me, but he couldn't be with me. But I ran to him, pleaded with him to take me back. I am not proud."

"And then he tricked you?"

"Do you really want to know?"

Angus's stomach twisted. This was a subject that clearly caused her great pain. It didn't matter who she was; he didn't enjoy inflicting it. Still, he had to know. "Yes."

"Then we made love, right there on the forest floor. It was only afterwards that he chained me. Isn't that awful?" she asked, yet her mouth quirked into an almost smile.

"It is," he agreed. "He should never have done that to you."

"Oh, the worst part came next." Her voice turned to a rasping hiss. "He stole our daughter from her crib and rode off with her. I heard he was assisted by some traitorous selkies, and my baby was passed from hand to hand like little more than a package. I have spent the last nineteen years trying to find her again."

Angus hated to say it, but he could see why she was so angry. To be betrayed like that by the person you loved and then to have your own child stolen. It didn't excuse her actions, but... he understood. "How did you know Ailsa wasn't your daughter? She didn't even know."

"Like I said, when a changeling rests their eyes on her true mother, their glamour is removed and they change back into who they should have been. There is no birthmark. I'm afraid your friend's mark is very prominent."

"And they change their looks?"

The wood on her shoulders creaked, and he imagined she was trying to shrug. "Hair colour. Eye colour. Nose size. All these things could have been changed by those who took her, to hide her away."

"What did she look like, when she was born?"

Her eyes glazed, like she was truly seeing the child in front of her. "She was the most beautiful baby in Ossiana. She had tufts of blonde hair which stuck straight up on her head. And, as she was a faerie, she had pointed ears, like mine."

Still a few questions to go. "If she turned up now, would you still want revenge?"

"Conall is dead, yes?" Angus knew he didn't imagine the glee in her face.

"Yes, but his sons are alive," he said carefully.

Nicnevan considered this. "You know, you look so much like him. It should make me blind with fury, to see him in your face. And yet, I can't help but wonder how much you also look like my daughter. You are her brother, after all. What would you do, if she were found?"

"I would love her," Angus said simply.

"And what would your brother do, when he realised she had more claim to the throne of Eilanmòr than he did?"

"I couldn't tell you that."

Nicnevan's lips pulled back into a sharp grin. "We could make a vow, you and I."

Angus narrowed his eyes. "And what would we be vowing to do?"

"I would vow to never take revenge against Eilanmòr for your father's crimes, if you would vow to protect my daughter when she is found."

"And if she decides she wanted to be queen of Eilanmòr?"

She fluttered her dandelion fluff eyelashes. "You would support her, of course."

But Angus was already shaking his head. "I cannot fight against my brother."

It was only when Nicnevan relaxed back did he realise she'd leaned forward. *I need to be more careful with how much cauldron water I give her.*

"Two paths lie in front of you," she said. "In one, you vow to me to defend my daughter. She may decide she wants to be queen, or she may decide she doesn't. In either case, I will vow to never seek my revenge. Or, in the other path, you could refuse to take this vow, in which case I will rain down destruction over all of Eilanmòr, if I am ever free."

Angus wiped his palms against his trousers as something

inside him screamed, *danger, danger, danger.* "Or I could kill you."

"Oh, but then why haven't you done it already? You need me for something. Something so important that you've come all the way to Ephraim, and you've settled in for a long stay. I wonder, when are you going to tell me why you are here?"

He opened his mouth to reply, but she cut him off.

"I don't want to hear it now. You've run out of questions, little prince. Come back in the morning with my breakfast and your vow and then we'll talk." Then she closed her eyes and set her mouth in a grim line.

Angus pushed himself off the floor, never taking his eyes off his captive, and reached into his pocket for the vial of water he'd decanted. "I'll see you in the morning," he said, before unscrewing the lid. He allowed a single drop to land upon the queen's ear. The skin that the water landed on blushed a rosy pink, before settling into the pale green of the rest of her face.

How am I ever going to get out of this?

Chapter 48

harris wiped a hand over his face and wondered when he'd become the voice of reason. "What were you thinking?"

Angus shifted, looking uncomfortable as he stood at the foot of the bed. "I wanted answers. You weren't exactly conscious so I could ask permission."

"She is an evil Faerie Queen," Harris ground out between clenched teeth. "She has more magic in her pinkie than I do in my entire body. Who did you think was going to save you if she turned on you?"

"That's why I've only been letting her have drops of the water. Besides, I have an inkling Nicnevan is the least of our worries. It wasn't her who sent those people to kill you all."

"And you know that how?"

"Because they all looked just like my father did before they died. This isn't a faerie's doing. They were sent by gods."

"He's right," Irené chipped in from her spot beside the bed. "This is exactly what we were warned about. An army, half-living, half-dead, controlled by four gods intent on taking over the universe."

Harris breathed out through his nose. "Have you at least learned anything from Nicnevan? Does she have any of the Four Treasures?"

"I haven't asked yet, but I'm working on it," Angus said. "I'm trying to gain her trust."

Harris snorted. "Nicnevan trusts no one, not after—"

"Not after my father betrayed her," Angus cut in. "But maybe I can appeal to her better nature. Has she always been evil? She's not merely the Queen of the Unseelie. She's also the Seelie Queen."

"None of the Seelie have followed her in a long time. She became corrupted by power. It's why they helped your father trap her."

"When they stole her daughter." Angus suddenly looked a million miles away. "My sister."

"Did she say anything about her?"

"Yes, she mentioned her," said Angus, dropping his gaze to the floor.

Harris reached down to the bedside table for some water but stopped when he realised his cup was empty.

"I'll fill that up for you," Irené said, taking the cup from his hand. Their fingers brushed for a moment longer than necessary before she rose from her seat with a wink in his direction.

Harris couldn't help but watch her as she walked gracefully to the door, pausing before leaving to cast him a glance over her shoulder.

As soon as she was gone, Angus whistled. "And what exactly happened in the time since I last saw you? It seemed like Irené absolutely detested you before we got off The Nymph at Dalbrae. Now I feel like a gooseberry."

"We're just friends," Harris said, flumping back onto his pillows and crossing his arms.

Angus leaned against the bottom of the bed. "She didn't leave your side when you were healing."

"That's what friends do."

"But do you want to be more?"

Angus is trying to distract you. But he couldn't help replying, "I think I've made it clear since I met her, I do."

"Is she different from the other girls?" Angus pressed his mouth into a firm line. "Is she different from Ailsa?"

"I've never felt this way about anyone before. She sees right through me, calls me out on all my crap. She's also the most determined and daring person I've ever met. Most people, myself included, let life happen to them. Irené happens to life. I just want to be along for the ride, in whatever way I can be."

"I don't want an international incident because you couldn't keep it in your pants," Angus said, heading for the door. "Don't screw this up."

Harris bared his teeth. "Right back at you."

Angus lowered himself onto his plush bed and put his head in his hands. Harris was right. What had he been thinking, trying to reason with Nicnevan by himself?

But I've learned so much from her already. If anyone else had tried, would they have got the same results? Nicnevan had offered peace, if only he would vow to protect her daughter.

What if she wants the crown of Eilanmòr? There were a lot of maybes between now and then. *Maybe Nicnevan's daughter is found. Maybe she comes to Ephraim. Maybe she wants to be queen of both humans and fae.*

The thing is, she's been hiding all these years. That could mean she never wants to be found. Or, that if she is found, she doesn't want the power.

Angus toed off his boots and swung his feet up onto

the blankets, trying to imagine championing an unknown woman if she tried to take his brother's throne. *Your sister,* he reminded himself. Though she was unknown, she was his family. Surely he could convince her not to fight?

Gods, he was tired. He hadn't slept well the last few nights, despite the comfortable bed. His thoughts kept travelling back over the hundreds of miles to an inn outside of Kilvaig. To a boy there who may or may not be having visions of disasters to come. If he took Nicnevan's vow, would Cameron see destruction in his future? Or peace?

Chapter 49

Iona drummed her pen against the crisp white paper in annoyance. Her head was on the kitchen table, a corner of the paper under her cheek. Her copper hair was arranged like a veil over her face and the letter she was writing, as she tried to block out the night-darkened world surrounding her. But it was no use. The tap in the corner *drip, drip, dripped* into the sink and the wind battered the sides of the inn, scattering her thoughts like dandelion fluff.

She groaned and sat up, dropping the pen and folding her arms over the offending note. The problem was, she was trying to write to Harris to tell him she'd found Nicnevan's lost daughter, without actually saying it. She was also mentally running through all the ways she could try to convince Eilidh to come with them to Ephraim and make the letter redundant.

Iona had tried many times over the last few days to walk the line between nagging and begging. There were so many reasons Eilidh should come with them. First, the best reason, she could help them save Eilanmòr. If they had Eilidh, they didn't need to rely on another earth fae. Second, she could meet her brother. Or brothers, if she came back to Dunrigh afterwards. Iona had only mentioned once that she could take the faerie crown for her own. The look Eilidh had given her was a mixture of disgust, fear, and fury.

After trying these tactics, she moved on to warnings. She'd

outlined the threats Eilanmòr, and indeed all of Ossiana, faced. Iona wasn't proud, but she'd resorted to describing what had happened to King Connall before he'd died. The madness. The disease. Afterwards, she had felt bad. He was Eilidh's true father, after all. Not that she'd known him, of course.

There was one positive in all this: Eilidh and Agnes had agreed that Iona and Cameron could take the Sword of Light. It should have been enough. After all, it was why they'd come.

Iona mentally ticked off everything they needed. *The Sword of Light: check. The Cauldron of Life: check.* They were still missing the Spear of Truth, but hopefully Ailsa or Harris would find that. The Stone of Destiny was gone. *For now.*

Duncan was still in Dunrigh, trying to root out who had betrayed him. Then they needed fae to wield the treasures. Ailsa had air magic and Iona had water. The demon seemed like the only option for fire, but at least they had someone. That left earth. Surely Harris and Irené could find someone in Ephraim, who could help them? Any fae with earth magic, even a weak one, was better than none. Still, her mind went back to the young woman sleeping somewhere above her.

With her ancestry, Eilidh would be powerful, without a doubt. And with a little guidance, who knew how strong she could become.

Iona started from her thoughts when a floorboard creaked behind her.

"Sorry, I didn't mean to startle you," said Cameron, sliding into the chair beside her. His faded pink hair was rumpled like he'd been asleep, but the bags under his eyes showed it hadn't been restful. "I was going to get a glass of water, then I saw you were up."

Iona blew out a breath. "I was trying to write a cryptic

letter to my brother about our current situation."

"They should be at Ephraim by now; if all has gone well." Cameron looked off into the black windows, his eyes glazed. "Do you think Angus made it in time?"

"We can only hope and carry on like he did."

"So many people to worry about. Angus, Harris, Ailsa. I'm not used to it."

"I am, especially with having Harris as a brother," Iona said. "I worry that the night we played cards on the boat will be the last we all spent together."

"Like you said, we can only hope everyone is fine until we hear otherwise."

Iona gave him a tight smile. "At least Ailsa is away from whatever is happening in Ephraim. She wasn't in your vision."

"No. Monadh is pretty safe, right?"

"You tell me, Mr Mapmaker."

Cameron stood looking for a mug. "I've only been once, and that was to New Hope. The locals were nice enough." He filled the cup at the tap but didn't drink it. "I'm not really sure how they'd react when faced with a changeling and a demon, though."

"They'll be fine. Ailsa can look after herself."

He looked over his shoulder. "And the demon?"

"I have no idea, but he's a demon, isn't he? You'd think he'd be pretty dangerous."

Cameron leaned against the countertop. For a moment, Iona thought he wasn't going to say anything, and she tried to scrape some words together to fill the silence. But she was just too tired.

"You know," he finally said. "All these things are out of our control. In my experience, it's best to focus on what you *can* control. So, what is that?"

Iona frowned. "Well, I could ask Eilidh to come with us again?"

"What she does isn't up to you. What's next?"

There really was only one decision they had to make, a decision which they'd been putting off for days in the hopes they'd win Eilidh round. "We could stay here," Iona reasoned. "Or we could go to Ephraim ourselves."

"And since the only reason we've stuck around is Eilidh…" Cameron trailed off, allowing her to say it for him.

"We should go to Ephraim." Iona sighed. "Tomorrow morning."

Cameron hummed. "Are you going to be alright with that?"

"I suppose I'll have to be." Actually, now they'd decided, she already felt lighter.

"We can always come back to visit. I know you've grown fond of her. And her daughter."

It was true. Little Maggie reminded her so much of the girl's great-grandfather. Of Alasdair. "Being with them, it's like a link to my past."

"I know," Cameron said sympathetically. "You'll see them again one day."

"After all this mess."

"Even more reason to get to Ephraim quickly and save the world." He raised his mug of water to her. "To the things we can control."

She responded by raising her pen to her brow in a salute, and he drank.

"Well," Cameron said, "since we're heading off tomorrow, I'm going to get back to sleep."

Iona managed a small smile. "Me too, in a bit."

Once Cameron had shuffled back up the stairs, Iona took her pen to the paper once again. She knew it was stupid, that they were heading off the next day anyway and didn't need a letter, but she couldn't help writing it for herself. Underneath 'Dear Harris' in big swirling letters, she wrote six words.

We'll see you soon, love Iona.

And then she folded the paper and headed up to bed.

Chapter 50

Of all the journeys Ailsa had taken in the last few months, floating downriver on the little canoe was by far the nicest. *It's almost like we're on holiday*, she'd thought at one point, as they sailed lazily through the forest to the sounds of birdsong and trickling water.

It was on the first day that Maalik had stopped paddling, becoming suddenly still as he stared ahead. "This is it: the boundary. I couldn't go beyond that line before…"

Before he'd got his soul back.

Ailsa had reached back to grab his hand as they let the river pull them along, only knowing where exactly the border was because he'd stiffened and then let out a sigh of relief as soon as they were through.

"It worked," he breathed, as if saying those words too loudly would attract the attention of the curse again.

That night they'd slept under the stars, on the edge of the woods. The next day, they did it all again.

On the third day, Ailsa had become mildly frustrated by their slow pace. "The last time I was sailing down a river in a boat, I had a selkie to push me."

"Lucky," said Maalik. "And he didn't offer to come with you after you'd saved him?"

Ah, now that is a loaded question.

"I didn't want him with me," she sniffed. "Besides, he was

too busy flirting with a princess when I last left him."

Maalik dipped his paddle back into the water to push them away from the bank again. "I'm sorry. I know you had a… special friendship with him."

Ailsa bit the inside of her cheek. "We kissed one time. And when we got back to Dunrigh, we worked things out," she said, looking over her shoulder at him.

"Ouch, that sounds like you dumped him." *Was that a smile tugging at Maalik's lips?*

"I didn't dump him. We both realised we were better off as friends." Ailsa sighed. "He's not what I need right now."

He was quiet for a moment. "What do you need?"

You. "I need… I need to love myself first. I don't want to go mooning over the first man I ever met, who ever showed any interest.

"And do you love yourself?" he asked.

Her nose wrinkled. Did she? "I'm getting there," she said slowly. "I've stopped trying to be worthy of other people. I want to be someone I respect. And then, hopefully, whoever loves me will love the real me. Harris wasn't ready to give all of himself. He was always going to have one eye on me and another on the horizon. On the next prize." *Maybe that's changed, though,* Ailsa thought, remembering the way he'd looked at the captain.

"Well, I'm sorry again," said Maalik. "You deserve so much more than that prick was willing to give you. I know he's your friend, but I still think he's a prick. Anyone would be lucky to have you."

Anyone? She waited for him to say more but Maalik only clenched his fingers against the edge of the boat and lapsed back into silence.

Ailsa's heart sank. Sometimes she was so sure he felt the same way she did—that there was something there between them. But whenever she got close, he would push her away.

They travelled downstream as the sun rose above the treeline, paddling now and then when there were rocks or tricky sections, but mostly floating along as the river meandered through the countryside. The trees had become sparser, giving way to fields and grassland. Ailsa was sure she'd even glimpsed the sea at one point. It shimmered on the horizon, still so far out of reach. She'd resigned herself to another day of travel when Maalik steered them towards the bank, running the hull of the canoe into the sand there.

"This is us," he said, placing the paddle on the floor of the boat.

"But we're still so far from the coast." Ailsa squinted around, finding nothing but fields and a ramshackle old castle. "Are we stopping for a rest?"

"I told you I had a shortcut." Maalik grabbed his bag and his cloak and Ailsa followed suit until she was carrying everything she owned again. Then he was stepping out onto the bank and making his way through the tall grass.

"I see nothing," Ailsa said as they made it onto the field. Indeed, it was a sea of green. Clearly this place belonged to someone. The grass had been trimmed neatly, the surrounding dry-stone walls looked cared for.

Maalik didn't respond. Instead, he trudged over the ruined tower in the corner and ducked his head like he was searching for something.

"Have you ever been here before?" Ailsa asked, watching him with her arms crossed.

"No, but I've read about this place. Unless I'm mistaken,

that is Crone's Tower, part of Castle Ardnakaig." The word was stilted, like he'd never said it aloud before. "Legend says it used to belong to Eilanmòrian royalty."

"Angus's family?"

"No, this was before the McFeidhs."

It was old then. As far as Ailsa knew, Angus's family had ruled Eilanmòr for hundreds of years. She didn't even know who they'd taken over from and whether the transferring power had been because of marriage or war. *Probably war,* she thought. *You don't gain an entire kingdom through peace.*

Although, she realised, looking north to where she knew the sea, and their destination lay, the island of Monadh had once been part of Eilanmòr. Angus's however-many-times great-grandfather had annexed it, offering it as a home to refugees from a far-off land. *That was nice of him.*

"Harris told me once that there was a land bridge between here and Monadh," she said absently. "It fell into the sea and since then they've had unusual weather."

Maalik straightened, holding something in his palm. "I guess we'll find out about that soon enough." He held the object out for her to look at.

Nestled in his hand was a smooth stone. Had it been intact, Ailsa could almost have mistaken it for a strange flat egg. However, the cavity in its centre broke that illusion. The hole went all the way through, revealing Maalik's blackened skin beneath it.

"What is it?"

Maalik hesitated before slipping behind her, and Ailsa's heart immediately pounded a stilted rhythm. He brought his arm around her, lifting the stone in front of her so she could peer through it. "It's a hag stone," he said into her ear. "If you look through it, it's supposed to reveal something that can't normally be seen."

For a second, Ailsa wondered if the demon was having his own private joke. *Magical stones?* She'd heard that one before. But what did she have to lose? There had been stranger things.

Instead of taking it from him, she placed her eye to the hole. At first, the only thing she saw was the old, ruined castle. Then Maalik was steering her round with one hand on her shoulder, pressing her back into his heated body. She almost closed her eyes, revelling in the warmth, but as soon as the hollow was directed to the middle of the field, she let out a gasp.

"I see enormous slabs of rock, sticking out of the earth." They definitely hadn't been there a moment ago. The stones were taller than the demon beside her, arranged in a circle on the grass. The surrounding atmosphere shimmered, like air on a hot day. "But how are we going to get to them?" she asked. After all, they couldn't exactly walk through the hole in the pebble.

"Look again," said Maalik, his breath tickling the little hairs on her neck. "Without the hag stone."

She shivered before allowing him to lower the stone from her eyes and let out another strangled sound. There the slabs of rock stood, even without the magical stone. *How?* She wondered as Maalik let her go, marching across the grass to them.

Ailsa followed, still not quite believing her eyes. "What are they?" she asked, tipping her head back to look at them.

"Standing stones. But see these markings?" he said, indicating some patterns that had been carved into the first one. "They allow you to move between others like them."

"They transport you?"

He grinned. "Like a door from one place to another."

"Like the Stone of Destiny," she said faintly.

Maalik's mouth twisted. "Almost. As far as I've read, the Stone of Destiny can transport you anywhere you can think of. The standing stones can only transport you between others with the same markings. Plus, you can't exactly put these in your pocket."

That left one question. "And are there standing stones on Monadh?"

"I believe so."

Ailsa brushed her hand against the side of the hard rock. It was cool, almost freezing. Odd on such a warm day, with the sun beating down upon them. "Then let's go."

Maalik scratched his chin as he studied the stones. "You have to go through the right one." Then he stopped, staring at her. No, staring at the slab she was touching. "I think you're a good luck charm."

"Does that mean this is the one?" Ailsa dragged her fingers over the markings. But it wasn't rock she felt under her skin now. Instead, it gave way, like molten silk. "It's strange," she said.

"Hold your breath and walk through," Maalik said from behind her. "Nothing bad will happen to you."

Ailsa's stomach flipped as she first pushed her hand into the stone and then her arm. *What if he's wrong? What if this takes me somewhere else? What if I'm trapped in the rock forever?* Nausea clawed at her throat. *It's a leap of faith*, she decided. *Trust Maalik.* Her body sank into the liquid bit by bit, but she kept her head back until the last minute. Then, with one more look back at her demon, she plunged her face into the portal and stepped through.

Chapter 51

*E*ilidh sipped at her tea as the sunlight warmed her skin through the window. She had woken up a few times in the night with the same old dream of the day she'd lost her hand. Eilidh had been so young, she didn't know if it was a memory or her imagination, but it haunted her all the same. Now she felt tiredness pressing down on her. But that was nothing new.

Luckily, Agnes had taken her at dawn to play in the kitchen while she cooked, which left Eilidh a little time to herself. There wasn't any point going back to bed, though. They'd have customers to serve tonight. Besides, today Iona and Cameron were leaving. They finally took no for an answer.

The selkie and the soldier were nice and all, but listening to them try to convince her to go with them was tiring. It didn't matter how many reasons they had for going, there was one big reason to stay. Maggie had to be protected at all costs. As soon as she'd been born, Eilidh had stopped worrying about the Unseelie finding and taking her and started worrying about them taking her daughter. After all, would it matter to Nicnevan if she was reunited with her own child, or her grandchild? Eilidh doubted it.

Footsteps on the stairs interrupted her thoughts, and she shook her head to banish the last dregs. *You can't worry all the time.*

"I think we have everything," Iona called down before appearing in the hall. She'd braided her hair and was back in her travelling clothes and cloak. The Sword of Light was wrapped in cloth and strapped to her back, underneath her pack.

Cameron emerged behind her, dressed similarly but looking pale and sickly.

"Are you alright?" Eilidh asked him. "You look like death."

"Same old. Haven't been right since—" He stopped, closing his eyes for a moment.

"We don't need to go yet," Iona told him, placing a hand on his shoulder.

He shrugged it off. "I'm fine."

"At least stay for lunch." Eilidh placed her cup down and turned for the door.

"No," growled Cameron, with more force than Eilidh had ever heard him use.

She stopped and turned back, staring at the man in front of her. He seemed to be swaying ever so slightly on the spot. No, something was definitely not right.

"Sorry," he said. "Could we have something to go? The sooner we leave, the sooner we'll get there. I think I'm just worried about our friends."

Eilidh narrowed her eyes but said nothing, her instincts warring with her experience of serving guests. *The customer is always right*, Agnes would often say. Or, at least, they *think* they're always right. There was never any point in arguing with them. "I'll make up a packed breakfast," she said before disappearing through the door to the kitchen.

The scents of cinnamon and baking bread hit her nose straight away, making her mouth water. Her guardian must have known she was having a bad day. Cinnamon rolls were her favourite.

"Are they staying for food?" Agnes asked from the sink.

At the table, Maggie smiled around a mouthful of bread. Eilidh bent down over the little girl and gave her forehead a kiss before rooting in the cupboards for some paper bags. "They want some to take with them."

"Stick some fruit in the bag and then we'll wrap up some pastries," the older woman said. "Still not tempted to go with them?"

Eilidh grimaced. "Of course not. I need to look after Maggie."

Agnes sniffed. "I could look after her. I raised you, didn't I?"

"And how many times did you have to kill a fae who came looking for me? I'd rather my daughter didn't have to learn to slay faeries like I did."

"She'll need to learn to look after herself, eventually."

"Not when she's a little girl. That's what I'm here for." Eilidh wiped a hand over her face. "I don't want to talk about this anymore."

Agnes stopped what she was doing and fixed her with a sharp eye. "I worry about you, my love. You've been dealt a hard hand, in more ways than one. You've spent your whole life trapped here because of fear. What if this is your chance to live a little?"

"I am living. I live for her." Eilidh smiled at her daughter, but her heart ached in a way it hadn't in ages. "One day, when it's safe, we'll all go on an adventure together. Just not to Ephraim."

Agnes pressed her lips into a tight line but said nothing, going back to her washing instead. Eilidh sighed. Perhaps it was hard for an ex-soldier to believe, but she was actually happy in this inn. This was her home, and she had her loved ones right here. And if she wanted some freedom, there was plenty of forest to stretch her wings in.

"I'll go hand this over," she said, balancing the bags on her arm with the missing hand, while the other came to hold them to her body.

"Tell them to wait," Agnes called. "I'll make Maggie a bit more presentable."

Eilidh winked at her daughter, who was now covered in flakes of pastry, and pushed through the door into the dining hall again.

Iona and Cameron sat at the nearest table with a piece of paper opened out between them. As Eilidh got closer, she realised it was a map. Cameron was studying it, looking worse than he had been a moment ago.

"Here, this should last you for a bit," she said, placing the bags on the table, careful to avoid the map. She was just about to lean back when Cameron jumped, clutching at his head.

"What—" she began, but then his hand shot out, clasping her arm in a vice-like grip.

Iona stood, pushing her chair away. "Cameron?"

The soldier let out a moan and Eilidh watched in horror as his eyes rolled into his head. She tried to pull away, but he held on fast.

"He's having a premonition," Iona gasped.

Eilidh's heart pounded in her chest as she watched him shake. Then images flashed before her eyes. One moment she saw Cameron, the table, the hall, and the next she saw fire and mud.

"I can't," Cameron whispered, broken.

And then Eilidh was pulled into his vision.

Chapter 52

Death and destruction and violence and chaos. The picture appeared in front of Eilidh's eyes in bursts of colour and light.

Not real, not real, she told herself. But somewhere it was. Or it would be soon.

Feeling a pressure on her arm, she looked down to find Cameron's hand holding her. He too was looking out at the scene with awe-filled eyes.

They were in a forest, but many of the trees had been felled, lying on the ground like fallen soldiers. People swarmed over them, coming together to wrestle, bite and stab at each other. Blades flashed and bones crunched, but it was impossible to focus in on any one person as they were injured or killed. Instead, the sounds of death merged together in a hideous symphony.

Arrows fired over a tall hedge, which Eilidh was sure wasn't there a moment ago. Focussing in on it took effort, like it was shrouded in mist.

"I know where this is," Cameron gasped. "This is Ephraim."

Eilidh jumped as a woman was tossed to the ground in front of her. She looked up at Eilidh like she could see her, mouth open in disbelief, until an axe landed in her back. The woman dribbled blood and her eyes rolled back into her head, before she collapsed and didn't move again. An immense man in leather armour ran to her and grabbed the axe out of her skin with a sickening squelch before turning and running off into the crowd of bodies to find his next target.

"Who—" Eilidh began, but then there was another wave of people running through the trees towards the wall of branches.

They didn't pause, even as they were struck or stabbed or hit with some sort of magic. They didn't seem to feel a single thing. As they drew closer, Eilidh could make out individuals. Their skin looked like it was rotting. Their eyes were dull and blank; their mouths open in screams as they ran. As soon as they reached the hedge, they tore at it with their hands and teeth. And then, from behind the horde, a figure on horseback emerged.

The man glowed with red light, as if the rusted, metal armour he wore was on fire. He had no helmet, only a hood pulled over his forehead, leaving his face exposed. Black coal had been smudged at his eyes, which sparked with madness as he beheld the scene. His too-long legs bounced against his stirrups, like he couldn't wait to launch himself from the horse and into the fray.

He passed by, only a few feet from where Eilidh and Cameron stood. At first, Eilidh thought he was oblivious to their presence—but then he turned his head to stare directly at them, his scarred face lit up while his lips split up his cheeks, curling into a wicked and deranged smile.

"There you are," he said, his sing-song voice echoing as if the words were being said by many people all at once. In amongst the speaking, Eilidh was sure she could hear more screams. "I can't wait for you to join us, truth-seer." His gaze shifted to Eilidh, before he let out a cackle and swept his hand out. The whole forest cracked and all around them trees were falling. They smashed down indiscriminately on those fighting, leaving mayhem in their wake.

"Time to go," said Cameron, pulling Eilidh to him. Then she was falling. Down, down, down. Further than the ground. Beneath the earth and space and the universe.

And then the vision ended.

The next thing Eilidh knew, she was kneeling on all fours, emptying her stomach onto the tavern floor.

"It's okay, I've got you," said a female voice beside her.

Hands were rubbing her back and holding her hair from her face. Another wave of nausea hit and she gagged once again, but nothing came out, except bile.

"Mama?" Maggie's voice came from the kitchen door.

Eilidh snapped her head up to see Agnes holding her daughter, frozen in place. She tried to fix a smile on her face, but feared it was a little too wobbly. "I'm alright, just a little poorly. Agnes, would you take Maggie back to the kitchen for me?"

"Of course," said the older woman. "Would you like some water?"

Eilidh nodded and Agnes disappeared through the door with the little girl. As soon as they were gone, Eilidh let her smile drop and sat back against the table leg behind her. "What was that?"

Iona stood to the side, looking down on her and wringing her hands. But it was Cameron who answered her.

"I'm sorry, I didn't mean to bring you with me."

"Was it a dream?" Eilidh croaked. *So much blood.*

"A vision of the future."

"How do you know that?"

"I've had a few of them," said Cameron. "The first one was in Dunrigh. I saw an explosion in the castle before it actually happened."

"What did you see?" asked Iona.

Cameron bit his lip. "It was the same as last time, except I could make out where it was. Someone was attacking Ephraim."

Iona reached for his knee, giving it a squeeze. "But if it was the same attack as you saw, surely that means it hasn't happened yet?"

"There were so many people fighting." The soldier looked like he was going to be sick himself. "Whoever was attacking Ephraim was winning."

"Maybe the Unseelie are still occupying the faerie court?" Iona suggested.

He dropped his head into his hands. "I don't know."

"And who was the man?" Eilidh asked. "Do you know him?"

Iona tilted her head. "What man?"

"He was on horseback," said Cameron, "and he was behind the people attacking the gates. He could see us."

"He said '*I can't wait for you to join us, truth-seer*'," Eilidh added.

"In a friendly way?" Iona winced. "Like, '*hey, pal, can't wait to see you*'?"

Definitely not like that. "It was very ominous."

Iona's nose wrinkled. "Then I have a feeling that we know who was attacking who. And which side we're on. The plan was for Harris and Irené to wait in Ephraim for us. We have to assume that's where they are."

"There's something else," Eilidh said, the images flashing before her eyes again. "Some of the people attacking looked bad. Their skin was all rotten, and they were running blindly forward."

Iona paled beneath her freckles. "Just like the king. Or like the people I saw in the village near the cauldron. I think it's starting."

"What?" asked Eilidh.

"Everything we told you about," said Iona. "The gods, their army. They're going to attack Eilanmòr."

A wave of tremors swept over Eilidh's body. "There were so many of them."

Cameron flexed his hands, as though clearing pins and needles from them. "They'll find more as they go. Whatever they do to these people, it turns them into mindless drones. They're neither dead nor alive— the perfect soldiers. Iona, we need to go to Ephraim now. We have to warn them."

"We already sent Angus."

Cameron shook his head. "Then we have to help them."

A little voice floated through from the doorway. "Mama, water."

Eilidh looked over at her daughter. Maggie's blonde hair was still mussed from sleep and she had a napkin tucked into her dress to catch any food that missed her mouth. She held up a mug, a carved wooden one that she used so she could drop it and it wouldn't smash. Eilidh crossed the floor to her and took the cup before setting it down on the bar.. Instead, she cupped her daughter's face in her hands and swept her gaze over her rosy cheeks, her turned-up nose, her big eyes, one blue and one brown. Memorising them. Then, she turned back to the selkie and the soldier. "If this is what we're facing, I'll go with you to help in any way I can."

"You're coming with us?" Iona said with surprise.

Eilidh looked at her daughter. "Go see Granny Aggy. I'll be through in a sec."

Maggie turned her innocent gaze on Iona and Cameron but, after a pause, did what her mother had said. Eilidh waited until the door had swung shut behind her to stand.

"I'm doing this for her. I'm sick of hiding, of waiting for the next threat to come along. And if this war is going to be as bad as you say, as bad as it looked, then nowhere in Eilanmòr will be safe."

"We should go, as soon as possible," said Cameron.

Eilidh nodded. Better not to prolong her departure, anyway. "I need to tell Agnes and pack some things together."

This is going to be hard.

Chapter 53

*E*ilidh had only had her heart broken once. This was so much worse.

Maggie's eyes streamed as she clutched at Agnes's skirts. The tantrum she'd thrown was ending, replaced by quiet sobs. Eilidh's arms itched to scoop her up and never let go. To drop her bag and cloak and curl up in front of the fire to read a story or stroke Maggie's hair.

Don't lose your nerve now.

A little time apart would hopefully ensure forever together afterwards. Besides, it was quite possible that with Eilidh away from the inn, the threat from random fae would cease. They always came looking for Nicnevan's daughter, not her granddaughter.

"Be safe," Agnes told her, reaching to give her an awkward but fierce hug around the little girl.

Eilidh gave the older woman a watery smile. "You've taught me well."

"Of course I have," Agnes chuckled. "You weren't raised by a fool."

"No, but I feel like one."

"You'll be back before you know it." Then the older woman raised her chin to where Iona and Cameron stood, hovering near the door. "You had better return her in one piece. I don't want any more body parts missing."

Cameron gave a soft smile. "Noted."

There was only one last thing to do. Eilidh reached inside for her magic, sensing it fluttering somewhere near her ribcage. The problem with her fae power was that it felt so good. Over the years, it had been almost impossible to resist shedding her skin and taking flight. Now, standing in the inn, she gave herself permission. She plucked out the magic and let it spread all over her body until her form shifted.

All at once, she had forty-eight eyes to see, twenty-four beaks with which to peck. And wings that let her fly up, up, up into the air in all directions.

Down below, the selkie and the soldier were staring up, mouths hanging open.

"Magpies," Iona breathed. "You're a shifter, like me."

"Two dozen magpies," Agnes confirmed. "You can imagine my shock the first time it happened."

Eilidh fluttered about for a moment, revelling in the freedom. Then the birds came together, shifting back into her body once again. Except for one.

She breathed in through her human nose and raised her hand out in front of her. In it was one of the birds. "I can shift into other animals, but they're my favourite." It sat perfectly still, its glossy black and white feathers not so much as twitching as it watched Maggie and Agnes with its beady eyes. Eilidh could barely see through them, as if looking from a great distance.

"This one will stay with you," she said, holding the bird out to Maggie.

The little girl had stopped crying. She held her own pudgy hands out in wonder and as soon as she was close enough the magpie stood and hopped over to her. Eilidh gave a shiver as she felt her daughter's fingers on her feathers.

"Be careful with her," she said. "She's a delicate wee thing."

"Are you sure about this?" Agnes asked. "You've never left one behind before."

Eilidh gave a faint smile. "I'm already leaving my heart behind, what's another part of me?"

Cameron made his way to the door, still looking a little shocked. "Ready to go?" he asked, opening it. Then, seeming to understand she needed one last moment alone, he stepped through, Iona on his heels.

Agnes held Maggie against her as the little girl petted the bird. "I'll take care of both of them."

"Thank you." Eilidh blinked back the tears which threatened to spill. *Gods, this is hard.*

With one last, long look back at her family, Eilidh straightened her shoulders, then followed the selkie and the soldier out of the door. The further she walked, the stranger it was to be apart from the bird. It wasn't uncomfortable, just different. Like putting a ring on the wrong finger. Eilidh looked back, unable to help the tear which trickled down her face as she saw her daughter and Agnes watching her progress from the window.

"How many days until we reach the faerie court?" she asked, giving Maggie a wave.

"We don't have a unicorn," answered Iona unhappily. "We'll try to buy passage on any passing wagons, but we need to be careful. Three or four days?"

"Well," said Eilidh, wiping the saltwater from her eyes. "Let's get to it. The sooner we get there, the sooner I can come home."

And with that she marched down the path, on her way to the last place she ever thought she'd choose to go.

Chapter 54

*S*omeone has muddled my mind, Ailsa decided as she blinked against the bright sunshine. One moment she'd been moving into the standing stone, the sensation like being submerged in cold water, and the next she was on the other side. There was no time between, or at least, she couldn't remember any. She raised her hand to block out the light and drew in a breath through the humid air. It pressed down on her like a weight, so different to the fresh air of Eilanmòr. Ailsa could almost taste it on her tongue, and she wasn't sure if it was pleasant yet.

There was a shimmering sound behind her and she turned to see Maalik stepping through himself. His face was screwed up and his eyes were closed. Ailsa couldn't help but smile fondly as she reached out to take his hand before he could take a tumble down the hill they were on.

"You made it," she said, squeezing his flushed palm.

Maalik's long eyelashes fluttered open to reveal those night-dark eyes, and he gazed down the slope in wonder. "I wasn't sure it would work."

Ailsa snorted. "Now you tell me." She gestured to the village below, not letting go of his hand. "Are we in the right place?"

"It seems right," said the demon. "Didn't you say the climate was weird?"

The place they'd found themselves in was certainly strange. While Eilanmòr was covered in forests, Ailsa didn't think she'd seen so much green before in her life. The foliage here piled on top of itself, like there were many layers of plants, each vying for attention. Fallen branches had been colonised, covered in vines until not a single sliver of brown was left. Even the forest floor had a thick layer of moss that spread down the hill like a carpet.

The village at the bottom was the only respite from all the greenery. Red sloping roofs marked the buildings, but Ailsa couldn't see inside beyond the high wall around its perimeter.

"Well," said Ailsa. "We'll never know unless we go look." Through the trees, the sky overhead was a thunderous grey. She reached her powers up, trying to push the clouds to the side but there were even more beyond them. With a sigh, she gave up. *I can't work miracles.* "Come on, before it rains."

But Maalik hesitated. "I'm not exactly good in a crowd."

"You're joking, right? I'm a changeling, remember?" Ailsa waved at her face, where her mark stood out against her pale skin.

Maalik pointed to his chest. "Big, terrifying demon, remember? I won't be able to go two steps without someone screaming."

Ailsa considered this. "We'll just have to cover you up a bit."

"I'm scared," Maalik admitted, looking down upon the settlement with worry creasing his forehead. "It's been so long since I've had to do something like this."

"I'll be right here, holding your hand." Ailsa gave him a half smile. "We need to get to an inn, then we can hide in there for the rest of the day."

"Okay. Don't let go, right?"

"Right." Ailsa squeezed Maalik's soot-covered palm and waited while he adjusted his hood so that it covered his antlers and created a shadow on his face. In contrast, she pushed her hair behind her and raised her chin. Maybe everyone would be so shocked by her mark they wouldn't bother to look at Maalik? Then they walked down the pillowy, moss-covered path and into the village.

Luckily, the heavy wooden gate was open when they reached it. Vines grew across the surface, like it hadn't been touched in a while. Together they slipped into the sandy streets, marvelling at the unfamiliar sights. Wooden buildings perched on short stilts, simple except for the red sweeping roofs sitting on top like fancy hats. Each was lit by lanterns, the light needed under the grey skies and tightly pressing jungle.

The town was bustling with people, but most of them were too busy to spare them a glance. There seemed to be some sort of market being set up. Some villagers were erecting stalls, while others hung banners from string attached to the buildings.

The few who looked their way quickly averted their eyes. Ailsa wasn't sure if it was her face or the fact that she gripped the handle of her axe. Maalik kept a step behind her as she weaved through the crowds. At last, they spotted a sign for an inn and half ran up the little stairs to the entrance and inside.

The inn was almost as busy as the street. Ailsa fought through the crowd to the little desk against the wall. Behind it sat a squat and balding older man. He smiled when she produced some coins and took a key down from the rack behind him.

"You came at the right time," he said, showing off a gap between his front teeth. "Tonight is the Lunar Festival. Make sure you go out and enjoy."

Ailsa offered him a non-committal shrug and then pushed Maalik towards the stairs. "Third floor, fourth room," she muttered, until they found the door, painted a bright pink and decorated with swirls. The key stuck in the lock but with a bit of shoogling, it twisted and they entered.

"How much did you pay?" Maalik asked as soon as they were inside.

Ailsa didn't answer. She was too shocked by the room they were in. The space was bigger than the cottage she had lived in growing up. The walls were covered in painted murals; animals and flowers were woven together, taking up the whole space. The ceiling had been removed, revealing the beams of the roof. From two of the wooden rafters hung pieces of fabric, dyed bright colours. In the corner, a set of low wicker chairs circled a small table. There was only one thing missing…

"Where's the bed?" Ailsa asked.

Maalik dropped his bag and strode towards the hanging fabric. "These are our beds. They're hammocks." He stretched one of them out, revealing a kind of bag shape, held together by rope.

"Those don't look very comfortable," Ailsa said with disgust. *I'll sleep on the floor.* Her attention went to the wall furthest from the door, which was covered in wooden slats. Light from outside poked through between the strips, creating patterns on the floor. A string hung down from the top of the wall and Ailsa tugged on it. The shutters changed their angle, letting more light and noise through from the town below them. A pleasant breeze snuck in through the holes, bringing with it the smells of the food being cooked in the market stalls.

"Looks like this part is a door," Maalik said, fiddling with a handle. And then, one part of the wall opened up. Outside was a small balcony, barely big enough for a chair. Maalik stepped through and Ailsa followed. A railing ran along the side of the building, preventing anyone from accidentally falling into the street below. Ailsa rested her arms on it, finally able to stop and admire the village.

In the time it had taken them to pay and get into their room, the market had almost completely sprung up. Little tents lined the street, looking very much like bigger versions of the paper lanterns they had seen earlier. Inside, the vendors were cooking their street food, or setting out their wares. At the corner of one building a troupe of performers huddled together. Then, as one hit a mallet against a gong, the smallest of the group was thrown into the air, somersaulting before being caught by their friends. Above the thick jungle, she could just make out misty mountains looking down, as if watching the show.

"Wow," Maalik breathed. "It's amazing."

Ailsa couldn't help but agree. "Have you ever seen anything like this before?"

"It's been a long time." He bit his lip. "I've just realised how long I was in that forest for."

"I know we said we'd hide here for the rest of the night, but what if we could go into the market without anyone seeing us?"

"How would we manage that?"

Ailsa gazed up at the mountains again, and the cloud which obscured their peaks. "Some clever accessorizing and a touch of magic."

Chapter 55

Maalik and Ailsa stepped out onto the street and held their breaths. It was dark now but the lights from the lanterns should have been too bright to hide from. Instead, they shone like dull beacons in the thick mist. It had been a simple thing for Ailsa to pull some of the fog down from the mountains into the streets of the village. Certainly not as difficult as her attack on Hell.

The second part of her plan had been easy, too. She'd snuck out to the stalls to buy a couple of face masks. Hers was made from teal silk and covered her lower face, including the mark on her left cheek. Maalik's mask was actually a scarf, made from black dyed cotton. Once Ailsa had wrapped it around his face a few times, there was enough fabric to create shadows. When he pulled his hood up, his eyes were almost completely covered.

The last task was the most difficult: convincing Maalik to come outside with her. Yet, he'd taken her hand, his face pulled into a grimace, and had followed her. Now she had to show him he was safe.

"Come on," she said, tugging on his blackened fingers. "I smell something good and I need a reward for all my hard work." She swept her other hand through the mist, which was so thick it swirled with the movement.

Maalik adjusted his scarf. "We'll get something to eat and

then we can go back inside, yes?"

"If you like," Ailsa answered.

They quickened their pace until they found the main street and Ailsa couldn't help but grin. There was no way Maalik could resist looking at every booth. Through the fog, the lights from dozens of stalls shone dimly. The smells of spices and cooking mingled in the air, making Ailsa's mouth water. Other stalls seemed to hold trinkets and fabrics, but it was too hard to tell exactly what treasures were laid out. Somewhere nearby, musicians plucked at string instruments, accompanied by a pounding drumbeat. The silhouettes of people darted by, but without being right beside them, their features were totally obscured. There was plenty of space between them, though, and Ailsa found she could easily keep their distance.

Maalik stumbled forwards, as if in a trance, pulling Ailsa along behind him. "Can you smell that?" He stopped in front of one booth, where the vendor was stirring something in a heavy frying pan over a blazing fire. "Noodles. Dumplings. Fried rice. Ailsa, you have to try this."

Ailsa smiled, glad to see her companion excited. "We'll have a little of each. Courtesy of the Crown of Eilanmòr." She jangled the purse at her hip.

As soon as the vendor heard the coins jingling, he looked up from his pan and beamed. "Please, friends, what would you like?"

"Do you have anything that's vegetarian?" Ailsa asked, glancing at Maalik. She could almost see his dark eyes lighting up under all of his layers.

The cook shook the frying pan and sloshed something liquid inside. "We don't serve meat, only tofu." He tipped the pan, causing the contents to catch fire. Ailsa jumped, which earned her a chuckle from the demon beside her.

"We'll take two bowls, please," Maalik said. But then he paused, looking down at his hands. Ailsa swooped in smoothly, paying and taking the bowls from the vendor to prevent Maalik from having to show his soot-stained palms. The demon nodded his thanks and together they ducked into the shadows of an alley.

"How are we supposed to eat this?" Ailsa asked.

Maalik pulled down his scarf and raised the bowl to his lips. "I'm pretty sure there are more polite ways, but I reckon we can get by without utensils."

Ailsa shrugged and copied the demon, pulling her mask away. She brought the bowl to her mouth and took a swig of the soup. Flavour instantly hit her tongue. It was sour and spicy and everything she didn't know she'd wanted. The cook had cut the vegetables up small so she could swallow them without too much effort. Ailsa pointedly looked anywhere but at Maalik as she slurped the noodles, and she hoped he was doing the same. The sauce stuck to her lips and chin messily, but she didn't pause to wipe it away. Then she came across something strange and spongy. She chewed a bit before deciding it wasn't for her. Once she was done, she held the bowl out to Maalik, who tipped her leftovers into his and finished the rest.

"I haven't had tofu in so long," he said once he was done.

Ailsa looked up at him and let out a little laugh. There were splodges of sauce all down his chin. She lifted a thumb to his face. "Here, you've got it all over you."

But then, just as she made to wipe the sauce off, Maalik's tongue darted out, licking at it. The tip of his tongue caught her finger and Ailsa's stomach gave a twist, as she watched his skin turn a darker shade of umber.

"Sorry," he said. "I didn't realise you were going to wipe it away."

"It's fine," Ailsa squeaked out. "Shall we get something else?"

The demon nodded and fixed his scarf back into place, before stepping back out into the street to return their bowls. Ailsa wiped the end of her thumb on her shirt as she willed her heartbeat to return to normal.

Chapter 56

"I can't believe you ate that!"

Ailsa grinned up at her companion, then made a show of smacking her lips together. "It wasn't that bad."

"I wouldn't have been able to put a single cricket in my mouth, let alone a stick of them."

"Yes, well, you're vegetarian."

"Even so. You're very brave."

She'd kept him out for hours until some vendors had begun to pack up their wares. They'd tried food at every stall, browsed through trinkets, and watched performers dancing in the fog. At one street corner, they'd come across a woman who breathed fire. Maalik said it was a trick, but Ailsa couldn't be sure. She had seen stranger things in the last few months.

Now, they'd called it a night. The inn was quiet as they ascended the steps, most of the patrons having gone to bed already. But Ailsa didn't want to be quiet. She hadn't laughed this much in weeks. Even her limbs were lighter.

"Did you see the stall with the puppets?" Maalik whispered.

"Yes! They kind of creeped me out though—too alive." They came to their door and Ailsa fumbled around in her pocket for the keys. "I wish we could stay here for a few more days."

Maalik cleared his throat. "But we have to go in the morning. Fate of the world and all that."

"Iona, Harris and Angus will have that all covered, though."

She produced the key and stuck it into the lock. "We're the backups. I bet there aren't any treasures up here."

The door opened, revealing a room illuminated by the lanterns outside. It almost looked cosy. Ailsa wandered in, dumping her bag and moving to the windows. "It really is beautiful here."

Though he didn't make a noise, Ailsa could sense Maalik come up behind her. "The entire world is beautiful. I used to love travelling to different countries, when I could fly."

Ailsa glanced up, catching the demon staring wistfully down at the street. She held her breath for a moment, debating whether to reply. Finally, she said, "Maybe one day we could go somewhere else together?"

"I suppose we could, now that I have my soul back. But won't you want to go back to Dunrigh, with all your friends?"

"I'm not from Dunrigh like Angus. And I reckon Harris and Iona will probably go back to Struanmuir. Besides, I would really like to see more beautiful places. With you if you'll have me?"

"Of course," Maalik said softly. "If you want me by your side, I'll be there."

Ailsa bit her lip. "Great. Now, how are we supposed to get in these things?" she asked, gesturing to the hammocks.

Maalik chuckled. "I'll give you a hand?"

He wants to help you get into bed, Ishbel whispered in her ear.

You can't call that contraption a bed, Ailsa thought back, trying to stave off embarrassment at the spirit's suggestion. But it was too late. Her cheeks grew hot and Ailsa could only imagine the skin on her right cheek now matched the deep red of the birthmark on her left.

Maalik tilted his head. "Are you okay?"

"Fine," Ailsa coughed. "Are you going to give me a boost?"

Maalik searched her face for a moment, and she fought the urge to duck her head. Instead, she gave a half smile, willing her blush to fade.

Maalik's tongue darted out to lick at his bottom lip before he reached past her, opening up the fabric so that it resembled a chair. "Take a seat."

Ailsa slid her cloak off and kicked her boots into the corner before turning so she could lean against the shelf he had created, bringing her in closer contact with his body. *Gods*, he was hot.

Not in that way, she thought to Ishbel, who had let out a tiny cheer.

His skin was almost scalding. Ailsa looked down at the demon's arms, where the flesh had cracked, revealing his molten core underneath. His body usually only did that when he was upset, but Ailsa got a sense that wasn't the case right now. She breathed through her nose and decided not to mention it.

"Right, now you swing your legs up and at the same time you tilt back and to the side," he almost whispered in her ear.

Ailsa hesitated. "Will you catch me if I fall?"

"Always," Maalik breathed.

Ailsa's heart tried to leap, but she pushed it down; caged it in her ribs. She swung her legs up like he'd instructed and leaned back. The demon held the fabric still as she moved, stopping her from spilling out, until she was nestled inside, with all of her limbs tucked in safely.

"There," said Maalik, gazing down at her. "That was easy, wasn't it?"

Ailsa could only nod.

He gave the hammock a little push, causing her to swing gently back and forth. "What do you think?"

"It's snug," she said. Indeed, she didn't know if she could get out again. "But I can't wait till we have a proper bed again."

Something passed over Maalik's face. "Me neither," he said. But the words were odd, almost husky. He cleared his throat and bent down to where she lay. "Sleep tight." Then, without warning, he dropped a kiss to her forehead and straightened up.

From somewhere beside her, Ailsa could hear the noises of him getting into his own hammock, but she didn't turn to watch. Instead, she fixed her eyes at the wood beams above and lay utterly still. Her pulse was pounding so hard she could feel it in her stomach. All from a forehead kiss.

And from all your flirting, Ishbel said.

Ailsa wrinkled her nose. *Shut up. Shouldn't you be away somewhere minding your own business?*

You'd want me to miss all the entertainment?

I want some privacy. And to be rid of your teasing. He wasn't flirting with me.

Ailsa could almost see Ishbel shake her ghostly head. *I'm not sure which one of you is the biggest idiot sometimes,* she said, before her presence melted away.

"Think you can sleep?" Maalik asked her, now fully in his own cocoon. "It won't be too unfamiliar?"

Ailsa settled in deeper, the embroidered fabric brushing against her skin. "You forget I've slept in much stranger places."

"Yeah, me too," Maalik agreed with a sigh. "And no doubt we'll sleep in stranger, after tonight."

Ailsa considered this. After tonight, they'd be trekking into the mountains. Even from the town, she could see they were lined with a dusting of snow. There wouldn't be hammocks with warm night breezes where they were going. "Maybe we should try to buy some warmer clothing before heading off tomorrow."

"And a tent," said Maalik.

They lay in silence for a while, but Ailsa found she wasn't as sleepy as she'd thought. From the sounds of Maalik's breathing, he too was awake.

She scratched idly at an itch on her arm, finding a grey feather digging into her skin through the hammock. "Tell me something about your past. Before you were an angel," she said, pulling the feather from the fabric and dropping it to the floor.

His voice floated through the room. "Before I died?"

Ailsa frowned. "Well, if you put it that way I might start getting creeped out."

He gave a dark laugh. "Did I ever tell you I had siblings?"

"You might have mentioned some sisters," she said, searching her memory. "How many siblings did you have?"

"Three sisters, one brother. Ramia, Zahra and Hafsah were all older than me, and never let me forget it." He chuckled. "Ramia wanted to be a dancer. She was good at it, too. Zahra loved to cook and always helped my grandmother with meals. Hafsah was the closest in age to me. She used to walk around with a magnifying glass and a bag, collecting things she wanted to study later. My mother would always tell her off for bringing insects and frogs into the house."

"And your brother? I don't think you mentioned him before."

"Khalid, my twin." He paused. "Are you surprised?"

Ailsa blinked. "I just didn't imagine you as a twin."

"We looked identical. I was born a few minutes before him, so technically he was the youngest in the family. I was very protective of him."

She smiled. "That doesn't sound like you at all."

"We were pretty wild as children, and my brother was fearless. He always convinced me to go along with his crazy schemes."

"That's the job of younger siblings. I was the same with my brother." She tried to imagine it. Two little Maaliks.

"We both wanted to be soldiers or adventurers, so our time was usually spent fighting or exploring. My father used to say he knew where we were by the dust clouds we kicked up."

But that was long ago. "Do you know what happened to your family after you died?" Ailsa whispered to the dark room.

The beam holding Maalik's hammock creaked, and she imagined him settling deeper into the fabric. "It was a while until I could come back, but I found out a little. My sisters survived the war against the shaitan. They all grew up, married, and had children of their own. Sometimes I would visit their children, but it wasn't really allowed. I was a holy warrior after all."

"And your brother?"

"When we were running from the shaitan and I was killed, my brother had gone to visit with my uncle. When he heard what had happened, he did something incredibly brave and incredibly stupid."

"What?"

"He went to the underworld to resurrect me."

Gods. If the underworld was anything like Hell… "How do you do that?"

"He took a potion which made him both alive and dead," said Maalik. "When he got to the underworld, he begged the god Anubis to have me returned. But Anubis didn't listen and instead judged Khalid for the afterlife. The Kemetians have forty-two sins. For a soul to go to heaven, the dead person must have committed less than the god who is judging. They take out your heart and weigh it against the god's."

Ailsa blanched. "Your actual heart?"

"It's a representation of it."

Thank the hag. "So, how did he do?"

"He was only twelve, so he didn't have many sins. The ones he had committed were pretty minor. He'd cursed, eavesdropped, little things like that. His heart was light, and he was deemed worthy— Anubis told him he could go to heaven. But Khalid hadn't really died. He'd meant to go back to the land of the living. So he gave up. Just as my brother turned away from Anubis, the god of death grabbed his heart and marked it. It turned black and shrivelled." Maalik's voice cracked. "When I found my brother, years later, he was happy and healthy. He couldn't believe I'd been given a second life. He almost didn't tell me the story of his brush with death. But when he did, I realised what had happened."

"What?" Ailsa breathed.

"He'd been made immortal," said Maalik.

"Do you mean he's still alive now?"

He huffed a laugh. "Yes, unless something has changed, Khalid is in Kemet, surrounded by his grandchildren and great-grandchildren."

"Oh yes, I forgot I'm travelling with an old man." *Should*

that bother me more? Ailsa wondered.

"When I died, I was given the body of a warrior, so that I could fight for my gods. I stopped aging, frozen in time. Khalid has aged, he looks old. But he's fit and healthy and enjoying life. No daggers can pierce his skin, no disease can infect him. I imagine one day, Anubis will come for him, and he'll go on living, just in heaven."

"He aged, but can't die," Ailsa said slowly. "You haven't aged and you're dead."

"Technically, yes to all."

"So you could go back to Kemet. You could see him again."

Maalik's hammock rustled. "I would never want him to see me like this," he answered sadly. "He almost gave his life for mine. If he found out what I'd done, what I'd become... I couldn't bear to see his disappointment."

"No one could be disappointed in you," she whispered, wishing she could take his hand again. "You're loyal and brave and kind."

Maalik cleared his throat. "Thank you," he said thickly. "Maybe one day I'll live up to that. Prove you right."

Ailsa leaned her head back against the fabric and closed her eyes. "You do, every day. Maybe one day you'll believe me."

Chapter 57

Angus snuck through the faerie kingdom, hoping he wouldn't be seen between the dark trees. Ephraim had changed so much in the month since he'd last been there. Where it had once been teeming with strange and monstrous creatures, now the woods were almost deadly quiet. When they'd arrived, he'd been shocked to discover most of the residents had left when Nicnevan was cursed.

Her Unseelie Court abandoned her when she was weak.

The fae that had stayed seemed to be neither good nor evil. The mischievous pixies and crystalline animals had mostly kept to themselves since the crew of The Nymph had taken over.

The balls of fae light they'd made still hung around the trees, illuminating the path, but Angus kept to the shadows. He didn't need anyone catching him as he headed back down to the dungeon behind the waterfall for the third time that day.

Angus had served Nicnevan her breakfast and her dinner as he usually did, asking his questions, exchanging them for drops of cauldron water. But he'd been distracted, thinking over what she'd said about her daughter and the vow she'd proposed. She hadn't asked about it again, but it whirred inside his head as he tried to sleep. If Nicnevan wanted something from him, surely he could get something from her?

It was that thought that drove him out of bed and through Ephraim in the dead of night. One member of royalty speaking to another. It was basic diplomacy, really.

Angus slunk down the path to the dungeons, finding the place deserted. Four treasures, four fae. That's what they needed. They had the Cauldron of Life and water, fire and air fae. Now they needed a powerful earth fae.

"I have a counter-offer," Angus said, after he'd slipped into the only occupied cell. He was out of breath,but wasn't sure why. "I'll take your vow to defend your daughter, if you agree not to take revenge against Eilanmòr and you agree to fight with us to defend Ossiana."

Nicnevan raised a brow, looking imperious from her place huddled on the floor. She was exactly as he'd left her last, except there was more colour in her cheeks and now her neck looked to be made of skin rather than stone. "That seems like a very broad oath. When are you defending Ossiana? Who are you defending it from?"

He came to stand in front of her, clenching his fists. "We can put a time limit on it, if you like? You could fight for Ossiana, in all battles, for the next year?"

"Who are you defending it from?" Nicnevan repeated, sharper this time.

Angus took a deep breath. "Four gods."

"You are telling me you are battling literal gods?" When he didn't answer, she snorted. "You are all going to die."

"Everyone is going to die if we don't. Or they'll be enslaved and tortured at the very least. Everyone, including you. Unless you think you are immune?"

"And how am I supposed to help you fight if I am trapped like this?"

This was why he had wanted no one to see him. "I'll free you," he said.

She smiled wickedly. "Oh, I don't think your little friends will like that."

No, they won't. But soon we may not have a choice. "As long as I have your assurance you won't hurt us, they'll have to get over it."

"That wasn't part of your vow. You must be very careful whenever you make a deal with a faerie." She spoke as one would to a small child and Angus fought the urge to snap at her. "We like to take advantage of loopholes. Would you like to try again?"

Angus squared his shoulders and tried to slow his words. "You must never seek revenge against Eilanmòr. Agree to fight with us against the Edaxi and their allies, in all battles, in the next year. You must never harm me or anyone I call a friend. If you do all of this, in exchange I will set you free and I will defend and support your first-born daughter."

Nicnevan licked her lips with her leaf-tongue. "Very good. Now, you may go."

Angus blinked. "What?"

"You had time to think over your vow. Now I need time to think over mine," she said.

"We're leaving in a few days." He'd expected Iona and Cameron to be in Ephraim already, even if they hadn't found the Sword of Light. Once they arrived, they'd be heading back to Dunrigh to continue their research.

Nicnevan's lips curled. "That is not my problem. For now, get some sleep, prince."

Angus left the Faerie Queen in her dungeon, trying to guess her answer and fretting over what he could have said differently. But that was the point, wasn't it? Nicnevan already knew her answer. She just wanted to make him worry.

Angus grumbled as he climbed back into his bed, trying to content himself with petty thoughts of serving her staler bread the next day.

Chapter 58

"Too fast!" Harris stumbled, clutching at his side with a pout.

Irené looked back at him over her shoulder. "I'm sure Valla is thinking of dropping you right now, so if you want help getting to the food tent, I suggest you stop whining."

Harris glanced sideways at the man holding him. The Visenyan was sturdy, a good crutch, except he seemed to be doing everything he could to make this harder for Harris. When Irené had suggested he could have some help to get out of his room, he'd thought she would be the one with her arms around him.

"Your crewman wants me to rip open my wound again," Harris moaned.

The other man rolled his eyes.

"We're almost there," Irené told him, pointing to the white fabric up ahead. "Did you get to explore Ephraim when you were here before?"

"Not really, unless you count the dungeons."

"Then you're in for a treat."

The pale canvas hung between the trees like sails, creating a great canopy for anyone to sit under. Harris couldn't help gawking as he was half-carried inside, marvelling at how tall the space was.

Up in the wooden rafters he spotted Duende, who gave a

chirp but didn't alight from his perch. Low tables dotted the area, surrounded by heavily stuffed, embroidered cushions.

Many of Irené's crew were already seated, enjoying the food the cook had made and relaxing. But it was the absence of other creatures which caught Harris's attention.

"There are no fae," he said as Valla dropped him onto a pillow. He narrowed his eyes at the big man, who didn't react as he walked off, putting as much distance between himself and Harris as possible.

Irené selected a seat across. "There have been none, save for a few wisps and pixies, since we arrived. The place looked abandoned. Angus thinks they fled when you defeated Nicnevan."

Harris poked his side gingerly. "Speaking of, has Angus come to his senses or is he still going down to the dungeons?"

"He visits her every morning and evening," said Irené. "He insists he go alone."

"What an eejit. Does he think he's hosting a tea party?"

"Perhaps he's making headway."

He snorted. "I doubt that. You can't reason with an evil old hag."

"What exactly did she do to you?"

"Let me list my grievances." Harris held out his fingers. "One, she got her ceasg to kidnap me. Two, she got a Nuckalavee to kidnap me, and that was a lot more unpleasant."

"What is that?" Irené asked.

You're better off not knowing. "Half horse, half man. No skin. Smells like death."

Irené wrinkled her nose but said nothing, allowing him to continue.

"And what was next? She held me in a jail cell for days.

Then she pulled me out at regular intervals to have her cronies torture me." He raised his chin. "And lastly, she turned me into a statue. That's all the things she did to me personally. She also threatened my friends and killed one of Ailsa's. She's a monster."

"And yet," Irené said, bringing her thumb to her lips and biting it idly, "she's the best hope we have in fighting the Edaxi."

Harris sighed. "There is no hope; we need to find someone else."

"She's probably the most powerful fae with earth magic in Ossiana."

First Angus and now her. "She is dangerous, Irené. We could never trust her. Was this your plan all along?"

"My plan is to save the world. And I will do anything I can to achieve that." She stared off at a table full of her crewmates, her shoulders tensed. "I read that one of the Four Treasures was kept in Ephraim: the Sword of Light. That was why I wanted to come here."

"And have you looked for it?"

She rubbed at her temple. "Angus asked Nicnevan. She said it went missing years ago."

Harris rolled his eyes. "She's lying."

"Maybe. But so far my crew have found nothing."

"So, back to this nonsense about her fighting with us," he said. "You realise if that's going to happen, we'd have to give her the Stone of Destiny?"

Irené pursed her lips. "That is the treasure tied to earth magic, yes."

"Do you know anything about Eilanmòrian folklore? The Stone of Destiny is enchanted to protect the king and his subjects. *From* Nicnevan. If she gets it, that protection is gone. What is going to stop her marching into Dunrigh and killing everyone?" *What's stopping her taking all of Eilanmòr for herself and her Unseelie Court?* And then, surely, she'd remember those that had trapped her. They'd have to leave the country forever.

"I heard fae like to strike bargains," said the princess. "Perhaps Angus will convince her."

Harris considered this. Not that he thought the prince incapable of doing so, but hadn't it been his own father that had chained Nicnevan to the tree in the first place? Perhaps someone else would get on better. "I want you to take me to her."

Irené barked out a laugh and leaned away from the table. "Absolutely not. You're in no state to face her, even if she is trapped."

"If anyone is going to convince her of anything, it would be me."

"How did that go for you last time? Believe it or not, I have faith in Angus."

Harris wiped a hand over his face. "I want to do something. I've been useless for days."

"Just days?" she asked with a snigger. "Sorry, force of habit. I enjoy teasing you."

Harris couldn't help wondering what else she enjoyed about him. "We're friends now. Friends tease each other."

She nodded. "Friends also call friends out on their nonsense. Friends also look out for each other. We have time. Heal. Give Angus a chance. And if he's gotten nowhere in a few days, you can swagger in and turn on that charm."

Harris smirked. "I don't know. I'm starting to doubt my

abilities. I've been rejected twice in the last fortnight."

Irené's mouth opened as if to say something. Then she closed it again, sucking on her bottom lip.

Harris watched in fascination until she grinned, a dimple kissing the side of her mouth. "Would you like to know a secret?"

"Yes." *Tell me all your secrets.*

"The night of the explosion was not the first night I ever saw you. You probably don't remember this, but at the king's coronation, I walked past you and Ailsa. Do you want to know my first thought? Who is that redhead and is he single?"

Harris wiped his palms against his trousers and rested an elbow on the tabletop. "You didn't think that."

"I did," said Irené with a wink. "You gave me this cheeky grin, and I got butterflies."

"And then you met me and immediately knew better?"

She raised a brow. "Unfortunately, you can be quite annoying when you're trying to be charming. I like you much better when you're being yourself."

I like you.

Harris opened his mouth to ask how much better she liked him. But a little girl had appeared at the princess's back. He recognised her as the cabin girl from the boat.

"Capitana," she said, huffing out a breath. "There are people at the gates."

"People?" Irené stood, all traces of the blushing woman gone, and put her hand on the girl's shoulder. "What do you mean?"

The girl looked nervously between Irené and Harris. "They don't look human."

Harris leaned against the table and pushed himself up,

remembering he'd been stabbed a few days before when pain sliced through him. "Maybe I should look," he said with a frown.

"I suppose you want me to help you?" Irené sniffed. But then she was by his side in an instant, wrapping her arms round his torso. "Lead the way, Paloma."

Harris winced all the way down the winding path through the woods, but tried to bite back any grumbles he had. Having Irené holding him was by far preferable to Valla. Besides, they were both too focussed on whoever the strangers were to continue arguing with each other. Not too focussed to enjoy the moment though. Or to notice the way Irené flicked her gaze to him now and then. This close, Harris could see the flecks of amber in her eyes. It made him wonder what else he had missed in her appearance.

Get your head on the task, he admonished himself.

Suddenly, the tall hedgerow which marked Ephraim's boundary flickered into view. It was spelled invisible from a distance, so no one could find the faerie kingdom unless they knew how to look. Irené had stationed some of her crew to walk the perimeter, but now they stood to attention in a group, hands resting on their cutlasses as they watched something on the other side.

A gap in the branches and brambles revealed the strangers. There were five little people huddled together. 'People' wasn't the right word though; they weren't human. Beneath their matching cloaks of moss, their skin was pond water green. Huge sunken eyes peered out from underneath their hoods, darting between the crew like they didn't know who to watch.

"They won't say why they're here," the sailing master, Nadya, muttered.

Harris snorted. "And I wouldn't either if I had expected to walk into my ancestral home and instead found a bunch of ugly humans at the gate." He pulled away from Irené and half-hopped forward. As he grew closer, he could see the strangers shivering under their cloaks. "You don't need to be afraid, my friends," he said.

One figure inched forward. "We heard the queen has been defeated. We came to see for ourselves." The small man's voice was soft, like he didn't dare hope too loudly.

"Nicnevan is detained," Harris confirmed. "Ephraim is open to you." Then he turned back to his companions. "Let them pass," he called.

Irené signalled to her crew, and they stepped back, creating a gap for the creatures to walk through. With one last long look at Harris, the strangers took his offer and entered the faerie kingdom. As soon as they had shuffled past the humans, they broke into a run, fanning out into the forest and disappearing amongst the foliage.

"What were they?" asked Irené, stunned.

Harris smiled. "Ghillie-Dhu. Forest spirits."

"Are they safe to be around?"

"They are Seelie; good fae. Since Nicnevan was crossed by her lover, they've stayed clear of Ephraim. Now that we've defeated her, they feel safe to return again."

Irené stared after them. "She won't be defeated for long. Need I remind you that Angus is slowly setting her free."

"Another reason he shouldn't be doing that. Good fae like the Ghillie-Dhu deserve to have their home back, without worrying about the evil fae queen."

"Should we expect more to show up?" asked Irené.

Harris beamed. "Certainly."

"What if they decide they don't want us here?"

"We won't be staying long. And besides, you've got a selkie with you. I can put anyone at ease," he told her with a wink.

Irené's response was to bat him on the shoulder, not hard enough to hurt his wounds. Still, Harris complained all the way back to the tents, revelling in having her arms around him again.

Chapter 59

Ailsa stared at the jungle in front of her and wondered how she could have ever believed magic wasn't real—there could be no other explanation for the strange sight.

The trees covered the land ahead—until they didn't. It was like there was some invisible wall and the trees stopped there. Beyond that…

"Is that snow?" she asked, pointing to the white beyond the treeline. "We don't have to go through that, do we?"

Maalik grimaced. "That's the way up the mountain."

They'd left the village in high spirits, with full bellies and new hiking and camping equipment. Their packs were full and sweat coated her back, but Ailsa knew they'd need all the layers soon. She hoped the misty, snow-coloured mountains weren't as high or as cold as they seemed.

Now, after hours of trekking, they'd reached the end of the rainforest. She just hadn't expected it to be so abrupt.

"Where do you want to have lunch?" Maalik asked. "Hot or cold?"

Ailsa eyed the dividing line between tropical and glacial. "We could go for body in the cold and legs in the heat?"

In the end, Ailsa took one step into the freezing winterscape and quickly decided that one more hour in the jungle would be best. She tucked herself into the sprawling roots of a gigantic tree while Maalik climbed up to drape a net from a branch to stop the biting insects.

"Ugh, will the bugs ever shut up?" Ailsa asked, pulling out some fried pastries they'd got in the village.

"I believe they're called cicadas," said Maalik, dropping beside her and taking one for himself.

"I don't care what they're called; they're the loudest things I've ever heard. It sounds like they're screaming."

"Don't worry, soon there won't be much in terms of insects." He bit into the triangular pastry, chewing slowly. "Are you worried about climbing up there?"

Ailsa looked to the mountain range, where one peak towered above all the rest. It seemed impossibly steep and distant. "I've never climbed a mountain before. Is it hard?"

"I've read about some dangers, but you probably don't want to know."

"Try me. It's good to be prepared."

Maalik's mouth twisted. "There's two problems: the cold and the altitude. The cold can lead to hypothermia up there, especially if you aren't wearing the right clothes. There's less oxygen higher up too and it can play tricks with the brain. I've heard of climbers sitting down on the slopes of mountains and never getting back up. I've also heard of them removing all their clothes, thinking they're too hot when in fact they were freezing. We'll need to keep our wits about us."

"No pressure then," said Ailsa.

"I mean, exactly, the air pressure will be much lower—"

"Not what I meant," said Ailsa with a fond smile. "But I'm glad I have someone so smart with me."

Maalik ducked his head.

When they'd eaten their lunch, Ailsa donned her heavy layers and hefted her pack onto her back. They'd never climb the mountain sitting in the jungle, though after Maalik's assessment, she dragged her heels as she walked to the snowy edge.

"We'll have to come up with a way to keep ourselves entertained," Ailsa decided as she waited for Maalik to catch up. A drop of sweat trickled down her back.

"Like what?"

"Angus made up some stupid poems when we were searching for the Stone of Destiny, but I'd rather we did something else."

"I think Angus and I would get on," said Maalik, bumping her shoulder.

Ailsa snorted. "Ready?"

They hesitated at the jungle's end, staring off into the white expanse before them. *Say goodbye to warmth*, Ailsa thought to herself before stepping over the threshold.

Indeed, the new landscape was freezing. Quickly, her sweat chilled, and she pulled her fleecy collar up around her neck. Ailsa made it a few steps across the snow before she realised Maalik hadn't followed her from the treeline.

"What?" she asked, turning around.

The demon pointed to her feet.

Between them, Ailsa's snowy footprints were glowing blue, as if lit from within.

"Weird." Ailsa crunched a boot into the snow and lifted it. The ice immediately turned a soft azure, becoming brighter by the moment. "What is it?"

"I have no idea," breathed Maalik, placing his foot into the powder. When he removed it, the same blue light appeared. But Ailsa's old footsteps were fading away. They watched them disappear until the snow was a dull white again.

"It's pretty," Ailsa said, walking out into the cold. A few paces out, she stopped and turned, marvelling at the illuminations. "Are you coming?"

"The only thing is," Maalik said, following her. "If we had to hide from someone, they'd know which direction we were heading."

Ailsa shivered. "You shouldn't say something like that." Memories flashed in her mind of running through forests, being chased by a monstrous presence. "Surely there isn't anyone all the way out here?"

"Except for who we're trying to find," Maalik said, toeing a chink of ice.

"Maybe they'll spot us before we reach the top of the mountain. Maybe they'll come to meet us." Though, if the rumours were true, and those that lived at the peak were witches, Ailsa wasn't sure she wanted them to drop in on her and Maalik.

"I don't think either of our luck is that good," he replied. He reached down to touch the ice with a finger. "Interesting. It must be activated by an increase in temperature. The heat from the undersoles of our shoes is reacting with something in the snow."

"Yeah," Ailsa muttered, trudging on ahead. "Magic."

They trekked through the snow and ice on a steady but shallow incline. Ailsa knew they'd been travelling for hours, yet the mountains still looked so far away. They sprawled like sleeping giants on the horizon, daring them to get closer. The sun didn't help; it was peculiar here, not following its usual course across the sky, instead sitting lazily and unseen on the other side of the mountain. They only caught the faint aura of light it gave off. The moon, though, hung in the sky like a gleaming coin, watching their progress as they scaled the next rise.

Just as Ailsa's toes were going numb from the cold, the landscape dipped into a fog-filled basin and she groaned in frustration. It was one thing to keep climbing, but to lose progress by going down again was almost worse. *This better not be too deep*, she thought as they slid down the snow into the mist.

Maalik said nothing as they descended, as though he was too exhausted from the day's climb and lugging his heavy pack. But now and then he'd reach out, steadying her with a hand on her elbow if she slipped across the ice.

Eventually, they reached the basin's bottom, and Ailsa gave a sigh of relief. The air was wet with mist, almost humid. Odd with it being so cold. That's when she realised. "Steam? But it's freezing."

Ahead, something large and dark appeared through the fog. A wooden structure sat half buried in snow. Like the buildings of the town they'd stayed in the night before, its roof was curved and soft lanterns swung from the rafters. Steps led from the snow up to the door and light flickered in the windows.

"A bathhouse," Maalik said, puffing out a breath. "There's probably a thermal spring under the ground. We may avoid the tent for one more night."

Ailsa didn't reply, following close behind Maalik as he made his way to the building. Yes, a hot bath sounded appealing after a long day of hiking in the frozen terrain, but so did snuggling up to a hot demon.

Chapter 60

The woman who ran the bathhouse was not human. Emerald scales trailed down the sides of her face and neck; they were beautiful and shining in the dim lantern glow, but Ailsa did her best not to stare. Likewise, the woman flicked her gaze over Ailsa's changeling mark, over Maalik's black eyes and golden antlers, and welcomed them in.

"It's not often we get new guests," the woman said, the words coming out in a soft hiss. "Do you need a room?"

Maalik tipped his head. "For one night and we'll be off again early."

The woman drummed her fingers on the wooden desk in front of her. "You're climbing mountains?"

"Just one," said Ailsa.

"The Mother," the woman breathed. "You're climbing the highest mountain?"

Ailsa shrugged, unsure what had caused the change in tone. "We're looking for—"

"—we're looking for some beautiful views," Maalik cut in. He squeezed Ailsa's elbow, and she bit her tongue.

"I would choose a different mountain," the woman said, her lips twisting. "The Mother is too dangerous to visit for the sake of a pretty view."

Maalik pretended to consider this. "Perhaps you're right. Shall we get the map out tonight and have a look at our other options?" he asked Ailsa.

Ailsa cleared her throat. "Yeah, sure. It's not like we're tied to anything."

The bathhouse keeper relaxed. "There are plenty of others I would recommend. For now though, enjoy the baths. Each has different properties intended to relax. I'll have your rooms set up—"

"We just need the one," Maalik said. "My wife and I can share."

Ailsa blinked, and then nodded. She hoped she hadn't done so too enthusiastically. *Wife?* Was that merely part of his cover story?

"Great," said the woman, passing over a key. "This one is ready, then. Enjoy your stay."

Ailsa allowed Maalik to steer her through a door and down a dark corridor, the woman's eyes on them as they left. She was dying to know what that had been about, but she didn't dare ask Maalik until they were in their room.

Maalik found the door with the symbol which matched the key fob and then ushered them inside. Compared to the last room they'd slept in, this one was much more moderate in its sizing. Two beds with white sheets were sunk into the floor. They sat against opposite walls, with their sides pressed against an immense, floor to ceiling window.

Ailsa took in the scenery beyond in surprise. Green shrubs had grown in the snowy landscape, looking like a miniature version of the jungle they'd been in that morning. Through the branches, she glimpsed water; round pools were cut into the rock and from them steam rose in vast clouds.

She tore her gaze away from the window and rounded on Maalik, speaking in a hushed whisper. "Why didn't you want to tell her where we're going?"

"I had a bad feeling," he whispered back, running his hand through his hair. "The fewer people who know the better."

"And what if something happens to us? She'll tell everyone who comes looking that we climbed a different mountain."

"If something happens, no one is coming to look for us."

Ailsa bit her cheek and crossed her arms. "Do you think she's hiding something?"

"Maybe." Maalik dropped his bag and rolled his shoulders. "Or maybe it's actually dangerous, and she's concerned for us."

"Nothing is ever safe anyway," said Ailsa, "not really." Then she raised an eyebrow. "Wife?"

"Yeah, we're on our honeymoon." Maalik's mouth twisted into something between a smile and grimace. "Sorry, I thought it would stop her from asking more questions."

"It was a good idea." Ailsa's voice came out too breathy, and she had to cough to cover it up. "What do you think— would honeymooners go for a swim? My muscles are aching."

"Yes, I imagine it's very romantic," Maalik croaked out.

Ailsa didn't know what to do with her hands. "Let's go then."

Chapter 61

They found some fluffy towels and a couple of robes hanging on the back of the door and made their way to the baths, still fully dressed. Maalik's palms were sweating, and he knew it had little to do with his higher-than-average body temperature.

Why had he said Ailsa was his wife? He really needed to get his schoolboy crush under control. Luckily, she hadn't seemed offended.

You're going to ruin everything if you're not careful, he admonished himself. This past week had been the best of his life. Not only had he left that godsforsaken forest, but travelling with Ailsa, laughing with her, sharing these new experiences, had been a dream. As soon as his soul had been a part of him again, he'd been lighter. Every moment afterwards had been like flying again.

If you're not careful, you'll fall. He didn't have wings anymore, and the ground was hard.

He followed behind Ailsa, arms ready to catch her if she slipped on the mist-soaked stairs which led down to the pools, but she glided down effortlessly, eyes on the water.

"How hot do you think it'll be?" she asked him, placing her things beside the edge of one pool.

"Hot enough to melt the snow."

Ailsa took a deep breath and then pulled her fleece over

her head. Immediately, Maalik turned around, examining a little wooden sign at the side. Words were written there in an unfamiliar language. The letters were joined with a bar at the top, the rest of them hanging down like vines. In fact, now that he was looking, he could spot a sign beside each of the half dozen pools. The owner had said something about each one being a different relaxing experience. Maalik kneeled in front of the one Ailsa had chosen and sniffed. The water was faintly perfumed with a floral scent. Seemed harmless enough.

He turned to tell Ailsa about his findings but closed his mouth as soon as he saw her. She'd stripped down to her vest and was now toying with the band on her leggings, as if considering pulling those off too. A thin strip of goose-bumped skin was visible on her stomach, and her shoulders were trembling. She'd pulled her hair up and tied it with a piece of cord. *I don't think I've ever seen all her hair away from her face and neck,* he thought, his eyes straying to the gentle curve of her collarbones. When they'd gone swimming in Eilanmòr, she'd kept her hair down, letting it pool about her like a curtain.

"I can't decide whether to go without the leggings," she said. "It's so cold and I'm too tired to spread the hot air around with magic."

Maalik swallowed. "Up to you."

Ailsa bit her lip for a moment and then dropped her hands, dipping a toe into the water. Maalik breathed out a sigh of relief. He wasn't sure he could have played it cool if she'd suddenly been only in her underwear.

You're a scoundrel.

He kicked his own shoes off, then lost his own jacket and trousers until he too was in his long-sleeved undershirt and shorts. Then he followed her in quickly, submerging his lower half, hissing as he did so. It was hot, almost scalding. The water prickled at his skin as he took a deep breath, working up the courage to duck down fully. He was already boiling, especially with the thick shirt he wore. He'd bought it in the village, especially for climbing. The vendor had said it was made of rabbit wool, perfect for keeping the heat in, but not so good for cooling him down. Even now, he could feel his skin opening, threatening to reveal his molten core and he wondered if his clothing was going to go up in smoke. But if he removed it, she'd see the monstrosity that was his back.

Ailsa floated nearby, watching him. "You can take your shirt off if you want to. It's just us here. And I've seen what you have underneath before."

Maalik looked around, considering this. "What if it's worse than you remember?"

"It won't be," she said, fixing him with a steady gaze. "But it's your choice."

Maalik nodded before slowly peeling the jumper off and placing it to the side. He heard Ailsa's breath hitch but when he looked at her again, her face was composed.

He gave her a half smile before sinking into the pool and wincing as it covered the mutilated wings there. It was wonderful torture to feel the water envelop the mottled skin and the heavy metal remnants of his feathers.

"Does it hurt?" asked Ailsa with concern.

"It aches. They're very heavy."

"Come here."

He opened his eyes, watching her as she floated across the pool to him. "What are you doing?"

"Do you trust me?" When he bobbed his head, she said,

"Trust that I don't judge you. Trust that I have my own scars and I understand the burden."

He swallowed thickly. "Your scars aren't there to remind you that you're a murderer."

She narrowed her pale blue gaze. "My scars remind me I survived. Yours do too. You survived and since then you've done everything you can to atone for them. You have to stop hating yourself. It doesn't do you or anyone else any good."

How had a swim turned into this? How could she be so nice? "I can't, Ailsa. I deserve to be hated."

"That's not true. I wouldn't be friends with you if you did," she said, flashing him a smile.

He hung his head. "I feel like a monster."

Ailsa sighed. "Sometimes I do too. I especially did when I was growing up. But who said monsters are always bad? Lately, I've realised you're only a monster if you do things that are monstrous. And if you keep doing those things. Every monster can be redeemed."

"Can I be redeemed?" he blurted out.

"I saw it in every face of the people you helped. You already have."

Maalik gave a shaky laugh. *I don't deserve her.* "Thank you." But already he was feeling better, as if another weight had been lifted.

Ailsa swam closer, until she was a breath away from him and then reached her hands up to his shoulders, massaging the muscles there. She seemed to sense he wasn't ready for her to touch his back, to get too close, so instead she stayed in front, knocking her legs against his under the water. Ailsa worked on his muscles, easing their tightness and he couldn't help the groan that slipped past his lips. She froze at

347

the sound and Maalik cursed himself until she resumed her kneading, harder than before. Maalik closed his eyes again so he wouldn't be tempted to stare and stare at her face. At those ice-chip irises, or that gently sloping nose, or her plush lips.

I am done for.

Maalik wasn't sure how long they floated there, but soon Ailsa's ministrations became gentler and her breath puffed out in a sigh. *No, not a sigh*, he realised. *A laugh.* He opened his eyes to find her sniggering quietly to herself. As soon as she noticed him watching her, she let go, pushing away into the water, all while sniggering at something.

"What's so funny?" he asked. She only laughed harder. "Are you alright?"

"Of course," she gasped out.

But her eyes were glazed, and her grin was too wide. "No, something's wrong," he said, inspecting her. "We need to get you out of this pool."

Ailsa giggled—actually giggled—and raised her hands to her head, spreading them out to resemble antlers. "Oh, I'm Maalik and I know everything."

This was not like Ailsa at all. He cast about wildly for some help, spotting the bathhouse owner cleaning one of the enormous windows that looked out onto the pools. "Excuse me," he called as his companion began blowing bubbles in the water. "I think something strange is happening to my friend?"

The woman dropped her cloth into a bucket and shrugged. "It's fine. Sometimes the hot springs do that. The minerals go to some people's heads. Didn't you read the signs?"

I knew I should have asked before we got in. "It's not permanent, is it?"

"No, she'll be okay once she's dried off and had a sleep."

And with that, the woman left, taking her cleaning supplies with her.

"Maybe we should get out then," Maalik said mostly to himself.

"Why?" Ailsa pouted. "It's so nice!"

"I wouldn't think you'd want to be incapacitated like this." Though, if there really was no danger, he couldn't help but admit it was nice to see her laugh.

"I could still beat you up, don't worry about that. I feel... light." She tucked her legs up, spinning round in a circle. "Like all my worries are floating away."

"Well then, I'm jealous." She really was adorable, like this.

"It's not working for you?"

"No." *And I'm glad. One of us needs to be sensible.*

"That's a shame. I'll have to cheer you up in a different way." She had to do an odd sideways step to get to the side of the pool, and then she reached an arm onto the rocks, trying her best to keep most of her body submerged.

"What are you doing?"

With two fingers she grabbed onto the piece of fabric which tied one of the robes together. "Cheering you up. When I was young, my brother and I used to go swimming and we'd play a game where we'd throw something and we had to race to find it again under the water." She pulled the tie out of the loops and held it aloft, careful to keep it out of the water.

"Those dressing gowns don't belong to us."

"Nothing will happen to them. And if I tie this around a rock, it'll weigh the fabric down enough that we can use it for our game, see?"

He shook his head. "I don't think we should play a game where you have to have your head under water. You'll drown."

"You wouldn't let me drown," Ailsa said, twirling the cord in the air. "Fine. What should we do instead?"

"Just enjoy the heat a little longer and then we'll get out soon." Maalik leaned his shoulders against the side. "We've got a big day of climbing tomorrow."

"Or… we could play a different game," said Ailsa. Her lips curled into a wicked smile. "One where I don't dunk myself underwater? Here, hold still." She bobbed closer and raised the fabric to his face.

"What are you doing?" he asked suspiciously.

Ailsa giggled again. "Using this to cover your eyes." With deft fingers she secured the towelled cord at the back of his head in a bow. Her fingers brushed against his ears, the nape of his neck, and he shivered.

Maalik pressed his mouth into a thin line. "Why?"

"It's part of the game," she said from somewhere beside him. "Now, I'm going to touch your finger against something, and you have to guess what it is." She gripped his palm under the water.

"This is a bad idea…" And yet, didn't he always wish for opportunities to touch her? *This is different, she's drunk on the fumes.*

"Shh, let me have my fun," she murmured. Then she lifted his hand, pressing it against her skin. "Okay, what's this?"

He sighed, giving up. "Your cheek."

"Yes. That was an easy one. What's this?"

"Your nail?"

"Right." Ailsa pulled his hand under the water and touched his finger against her again. "What's this?"

Maalik gulped. "I don't know, Ailsa, but I—"

"How can you not know that? It's my collarbone." He

could almost hear her lips curving into a smile as she pulled his hand down, down, down. "Okay, here." Then she pressed the pad of his finger into a fleshy spot.

Maalik yelped, jerking away as he ripped the fabric off his eyes.

She burst into laughter. "It was the back of my leg. I rolled my leggings up."

His heart was hammering against his ribcage. "It felt like somewhere else."

Ailsa snorted. "Oh really? Where?"

"I won't dignify that with a response." He shook his head, trying to calm his pulse. "You are a minx when you're intoxicated."

"Oh, really?" she said, giving him a saucy wink. "I'll remember that one later."

"I think it really is time to get out and dry."

She pouted. "Spoil sport."

The sudden desire to bite her lip came unbidden to his mind, knocking the air out of him.

She is your friend. Look after her.

Maalik waded back to the side of the pool and Ailsa followed behind. He winced at the cold as he lifted his torso out of the water, reaching for the robes. He swung the first one over his shoulders, stepping out fully, then turned round and held the other out to her.

"I don't want to get out; it's cold."

"Don't be a baby."

Ailsa took a deep breath. "One, two." Then she screamed the last number as she jumped out of the pool and wrapped herself around his torso. "Three!"

The dressing gowns were soft, but definitely not warm

enough. Already she was shivering as the cold seeped into her bones.

"Here," he said, lifting her into his arms. Immediately, she stopped shivering as the heat from his body seeped through the fabric. *At least I'm good for one thing.* "Let's get inside."

"Maalik?" she said as she tucked her head into the crook of his neck. "I thought I should tell you I would like to kiss you."

If only, if only, if only.

"It's just the hot springs talking," he said gently as he started walking back up the steps towards their room. "You'll feel differently in the morning."

"No, I always want to kiss you," she murmured into his skin.

Don't believe it.

They made it back to the door with no other revelations and he opened it with his elbow, depositing her gently onto the bed as soon as they were inside. It was warm in here, enough that she wouldn't catch a chill in her wet clothes. *She'll have to sleep in them until she's better.* He did his best to slip a dry towel underneath her. Once he was done, he moved to leave her, but she caught his arm before he could stand.

"Why don't you want to kiss me?" she asked.

She probably won't remember this anyway, might as well tell her the truth. He looked into her eyes and said, "Because I can't take advantage of you. Because if I start, I won't ever want to stop."

"You wouldn't have to," Ailsa said.

He breathed in deep through his nose, fighting temptation. "You need some sleep. I'll see you in the morning." He stumbled out the door and closed it behind him, leaving her there. As soon as he was in the hallway, he leaned his forehead against the wooden wall and tried to take control of his body. *Burning. I'm burning.* But he'd burned before; it hadn't felt this good last time.

Maalik shook his head, clearing it from the fog which threatened to cloud all his better judgement, and went to procure himself a new room.

Chapter 62

A ngus stared down at the Faerie Queen as she rolled her long neck. Her shoulders were no longer covered in bark and the skin on her cheeks was green instead of stone grey. In the few days he'd been visiting her, she'd almost recovered fully above her chest. Which meant, at the rate they were going, she could have the full use of her arms in a week.

"I brought you dinner," he told her, setting the tray down. "Sorry it's late." Harris had been watching him all throughout the meal and he'd felt too guilty slipping away until it had grown dark.

"I'm not hungry," Nicnevan drawled. "But, please, sit. I've been thinking about you all day."

Angus swallowed hard, but did as she asked, dropping cross-legged onto the dirt floor. "Have you thought about our deal?"

"Later," she said. "I have some questions for you, prince."

He leaned back on his hands. "I suppose you have thirteen chances."

She licked her lips slowly, and he noticed her tongue was once again pink. "When was the last time you cried?"

Of course, she was bored and wanted to toy with him. "I don't know what game you're playing b—"

"Answer the question," she snapped.

Fine, she always answered him. Perhaps he owed her this.

"Probably a few days ago. I was worried about a friend of mine."

"That Ailsa girl?" Nicnevan wrinkled her nose.

"No, her brother. He was one of your captives." The words came out hard, as he was reminded of exactly what she'd done to Cameron.

"Ah, the soldier. So, you knew him before you rescued him?"

"We did our army training together," Angus admitted. "He was my friend."

"Just a friend?" Nicnevan fluttered her eyelashes. "I promise never to harm another hair on his head if you answer truthfully."

"Just a friend," he gritted out. "But I want him to be more."

"Hmm. I don't imagine that would go down well with your family?"

"My father wasn't keen when he found out. But it doesn't matter now. I'll never inherit the throne and my father is dead, so I can do as I wish."

"If you were my son, I would never let some silly human traditions stand in the way of your happiness." Her lip curled, totally at odds with her words. *Had that been anger on his behalf?* "Next question," she said. "What are you afraid of most?" When he didn't answer, she rolled her eyes. "I won't use this against you later."

"I was always afraid of open water. You can't see what's under you. But now my greatest fear is one of my friends being hurt." Angus raised his chin. "What is your greatest fear?"

"Being alone," Nicnevan said simply. "Do you ever wish you were fae?"

Angus blinked. *Could it be that the Faerie Queen didn't have any ulterior motives? Was she actually trying to get to know him?* "I've never really thought about it. But I suppose it would be nice to have powers."

"Every fae is different, of course. But most of our magic is tied to the elements. Selkies and ceasg can manipulate water, for example. But within that, there are unique talents. Faeries have earth magic, and I can control plants."

"I think I would want to help people."

"Very noble." She paused, considering. "Do you have any hobbies? Aside from putting yourself in danger."

"I play the fiddle. And I like to dance."

She clicked her tongue. "Music is a magic of its own. Did you have any pets when you were little?"

"We had some deerhounds. When I was about seven, I found a kitten abandoned round the back of the stables. I snuck it up to my room because I didn't think my father would let me keep it."

Her jaw twitched. "Did you name it?"

Angus couldn't help but smile. "Yes, Thistle, because she was so prickly. She was an angry little thing at first. Once I'd stolen her some milk, she was a lot happier, though."

"Did your father catch you?"

Angus was starting to wonder if he was being interrogated. Her focus on him was unwavering, sharp. "Yes. He was actually going to let me keep her and then he realised what she was. She wasn't a domestic cat; she was a wildcat. Not a great pet. He made me take her back where I found her."

"Were you upset?"

"Yeah, I cried myself to sleep, worrying she'd die. But I'm fairly sure she survived. I kept seeing a wild cat around the castle grounds for years after that."

The Faerie Queen looked down her nose at him. "It seems you have a love for wild things. I noticed you have a unicorn with you before."

He'd said before that he was Laire's pet, but sitting in the dungeons, he didn't feel like making the same joke. "I rescued her, and she seems to have attached herself to me."

"A beautiful creature. Unicorns are notoriously aloof. They rarely let others near them." Nicnevan sighed. "I believe I am done for the day."

He blinked. "Was that thirteen questions?"

"Not quite. I need time to think of some more."

Angus stood and opened up the bottle of cauldron water again until a drip landed on Nicnevan's shoulder. Then, on a whim, he let another drop land. Immediately, he cringed. The Faerie Queen was wearing down his resolve to hate her. Had this been her plan?

He turned on his heel and was almost at the door when she called out to him again.

"Wait, I have one more question, prince." Her voice was deeper, thicker, as if overcome by emotion. But, no, that was impossible, wasn't it?

He paused on the threshold of the cell. "Yes?"

"If you had been in your father's place all those years ago, would you have done the same?"

He knew exactly what she meant. "If I thought you intended to attack Eilanmòr, I would have tried to stop you. But I would never have taken away your baby."

She closed her eyes. "No, I don't suspect you would have. Thank you."

Chapter 63

Ailsa woke alone and damp in one of the white beds. She felt like she'd slept for days, but when she tried to cast her mind to the evening before, there was nothing.

Where's Maalik? she wondered, sitting up.

He left, Ishbel told her. *After you threw yourself at him.*

Ailsa swung out of bed with a groan. What had she done? "Is he mad at me?" she asked her spirit guide.

No, I think he was trying to be a gentleman.

She got dressed quickly, then padded down the hallway in her socks to look for him. She found the bathhouse owner changing some sheets in the room three down from hers and the woman directed her outside.

"Did you have a fight?" she asked.

"I don't remember," Ailsa grumbled.

"Everyone reacts differently to the baths," the woman said with a shrug. "Are you well, though?"

Ailsa rolled her shoulders and shook her arms. Now that the woman said that, yes, she did feel different. The aches and pains from yesterday's hike were almost gone, and she felt the most rested she'd been in a while. "I suppose so," she answered, still annoyed at whatever the springs had made her say.

"There's no rush to leave; you could always stay another night," said the bathhouse owner hopefully.

"We need to get going," said Ailsa with a frown. "You know, for the views."

"Well, help yourself to some food in the kitchen." The woman went back to her chores.

Taking a detour to slip her boots on, Ailsa stalked outside to look for the demon, finding him sitting on a boulder amongst the steam, like something from a faerie tale.

"I'm sorry," she blurted out as he turned to face her. "I don't remember anything and cannot be held responsible."

Maalik almost seemed to deflate. "Nothing?"

"Nope," she said, crossing her arms.

The demon's mouth twisted. "You laughed a lot, and I took you back to the room. I thought you'd be more comfortable without me hanging around."

She could sense that there was more to the story, but to save herself from embarrassment, she decided to take him at his word. "Should we get going soon? We have a lot of mountain to climb."

Maalik sighed and rose from his perch but a movement behind him caught Ailsa's eye. She fought the scream that bubbled to her lips as a small, older woman emerged out of the foliage, as though she'd been hovering there, out of sight, for a while. Maalik didn't notice her at first and almost continued up to the bathhouse, oblivious, until Ailsa caught the demon's arm.

"Pardon," said the old woman. The middle of her face was covered in wrinkles, but the sides bore scales, like the bathhouse's owner. Where the younger woman had long, black, silky hair, the woman in front of them had long since greyed. Her eyes were milky, like there was a film over them, but she still darted them between Maalik and Ailsa, lingering over her birthmark. "My niece told me you're climbing the mountains. You're not going up The Mother, are you?"

Ailsa exchanged a look with Maalik. "And what if we are?"

The old woman wrung her hands. "You deserve to know what's up there. She won't tell you, but I can't let you go unprepared."

This was the start of every cautionary tale. "You're not going to tell us something like *those who go never come back*, are you?" Ailsa asked blankly.

The old woman brought a finger to her lips. "Not here. Come with me." She motioned for them to follow her round the back of the house and set off at a stooped walk.

"We could just leave," Maalik said nervously.

Ailsa rolled her eyes and went after her.

They skirted the bathing pools and little gardens, walking through clouds of steam, until the old woman led them to a wooden building. It was nothing more than a roof on stilts, attached to some boards which made a narrow floor. Most of it was taken up by a carved statue in the centre. Ailsa peered at it, trying to work out if it was supposed to be a bear or a man.

The woman reached up to the rafters and pulled down a dish with some long matches attached. She scraped the edge of one against a beam but instead of erupting into flame, it smouldered, giving off the smell of perfume. She tucked the end that wasn't alight into the dish and hung it back up carefully. "Since my people came to Monadh, we've heard stories of folk going missing amongst the peaks. There are savage beasts that live on the slopes," she said, pointing to the statue. The creature's stone teeth curved out of its mouth and Ailsa couldn't help but imagine them tearing through skin.

But, after everything, she found she didn't have the energy for fear. Ailsa sighed, throwing her hands up. "There's always something. Beasts, monsters, fae. It doesn't take away from the fact we have to get up there."

"Surely we have an advantage on the slopes," said Maalik. "We're fae after all."

The woman hissed as she said, "My brother, who built this bathhouse, used to guide climbers on The Mother. He found the mountain does strange things to fae, steals their powers until they can descend. Don't stay on the slopes too long."

Magic stealing, freezing cold, altitude. Ailsa's stomach plummeted. "Do you know anything else about the mountain? We're looking for the people who live at the peak."

The old woman's face paled. "The witches? Some say they live in a crystal palace atop The Mother and others say they live amongst the clouds. If you seek them, they may not be in the place you are expecting."

"Of course." She gave the old woman a tight-lipped smile. "Well, thank you for the warning. I only wish you could give us some good news."

"Indeed, I have some. There was only one person my brother encountered who did not succumb to the mountain's effects." The woman smiled, revealing two pointed fangs. "And she had a mark just like yours."

Chapter 64

Another changeling had passed through here. Unless the mark the old woman had seen was a normal birthmark. *There's only one way to find out.*

Ailsa reached into her bag, pulling out an orange she'd picked up from the bathhouse. They'd left the woman, packing quickly and heading out onto the frozen slopes again. Ailsa's body felt like it had cycled a hundred times between being chilled down to the bones and boiling from carrying the heavy pack by the time they stopped for a break. Now they were tucked into an overhang, sheltered from the biting wind enough that they could sit down, huddled together.

"I doubt we need to worry about curses. At the rate we're going, I'll die of old age before we even make it to the top of the mountain." She dug a nail into the skin of the orange, making a perfect half-moon.

Maalik brought his hand to his eyes, shielding them from the aura glowing over the peaks. "I don't think we have far to go. We've already gained a few hundred feet."

Ailsa breathed a sigh of relief. It was the most he'd said in hours. Ever since they'd left the bathhouse, he'd been deadly quiet. *What exactly did I say last night?* Ailsa had wondered over and over as they'd climbed.

She peeled the orange skin back, but underneath was just more rind. "I'm not doing very well with this," she said, tearing at the fruit.

Maalik snorted. "Give it here." He pulled out a little knife and placed the orange on the snow between his legs, cutting one end off and then another.

"You're making a mess," Ailsa said as the juice leaked out over the ice.

"There isn't a way to keep this neat." He sliced the knife again, this time down the side of the fruit. Then with two hands on either side of the gash, he pulled it open, revealing neat slices all in a row.

Ailsa snorted. "Show off."

"Here." He pulled out one slice, the sweet juices running down his fingers. Ailsa's eyes followed the trail of one drop as it ran over his black stained knuckle, then settled in the soft space between his index finger and thumb.

Maalik held the slice up but frowned when he saw her looking at his hands. "Sorry, you probably don't want to eat anything I touch," he said with a cringe.

Ailsa caught his wrist before he could lower the fruit. She leaned forward, sensing his eyes on her as she went to take the slice from his fingers, using only her mouth. Her lips wrapped around the sweet fruit, barely brushing his skin before he let her take it. As soon as she bit down on it, the flavour exploded across her tongue: sharp and saccharine. Then she chewed on the flesh before swallowing it down with a smile.

Ailsa opened her eyes to find Maalik staring at her, mouth agape. "It's good," she said softly.

The demon smiled softly before bringing his own hand to his mouth. Darting his tongue out, he licked at the juice there.

Ailsa averted her gaze. "We're sleeping in the tent tonight. Hopefully, you'll keep me warm."

"It's what I'm good for," Maalik said, his voice taking on a bitter edge.

But the higher they climbed that afternoon, the paler Maalik grew, until they had to stop again, hunkering down into the snow. The wind whipped past them, sending dusty snowflakes into the air, coating their clothes with a layer of frost.

"Are you alright?" Ailsa asked the demon as his teeth clacked together. She reached out a hand to feel his pulse and gasped when her skin touched his. He was cold.

"I'm sorry, Ailsa. I'm really struggling," he said, as his body was racked with a shiver.

She blew her breath into her hands before cupping the sides of his neck. "It's not your fault. The old woman was right, it must be some sort of magic."

"Are you okay?" he asked, searching her face.

She was aching; she was hungry; she was cold, but... She reached out with her powers, feeling the bitter air surrounding her. It swirled this way and that, doing her bidding like it always did. "The same as I did when we left this morning." She concentrated, trying to find some warmer air near them. The only heat she could find was around her own body, so she willed the air particles to carry it from her and over the demon. His shivering slowed.

We'll have to stick close. Though she was already exhausted from hiking. Holding her concentration was going to take some effort.

Maalik's jaw worked under her fingers. "I think you should leave me behind."

"That's not happening," she said, stroking a warm finger across his jaw. "We can go as slow as you need."

364

They set off again, two huddled figures in a vast, white landscape. Soon night fell, plunging the temperature even lower.

"A little higher," Ailsa said, her muscles straining. Moving was the best way to keep warm. But Maalik's body was done. He sank to the snow, curling in on himself. Ailsa placed her hand on his forehead. His skin was like marble. "You're freezing—"

"Just… can you set up the tent?" He could barely get the words out. His shivering was so intense. "As quickly as possible."

Ailsa nodded, fighting her panic. "Tell me what to do."

"You need to insulate me from the cold ground. If you can put the roll mats down, that should help."

She pulled off both their packs, rooting about inside for everything they needed. Though she too felt the cold, her fingers were steady as she dug out the roll mats, the tent. The canvas popped up easily, and she rushed to secure the ropes, before helping his shuddering body inside and chucking all of their supplies in after him. The inside was blue and glowing from the weird snow it sat on. As soon as they were in, she did up the door, blocking out the wind. It howled around their shelter, as if cursing them for evading it.

"Pull out all the clothes and blankets we have and wrap me in them," said Maalik, his voice weak.

Ailsa did what she was told, watching him all the while. *Gods, he didn't look good.* "I could rub your arms?"

He shook his head. "You can't heat me up too quickly. My blood will rush to my skin and when it hits the air, it'll cool me down quicker."

Her hands stroked over his face as she fought the urge to

sob. "You're still so cold. I could give you my body heat?" *Is he going to die?*

"I don't want you getting cold too."

She shushed him. "I'm fine."

"Get under the blankets with me then."

Ailsa bit her cheek before unbuttoning her jacket.

His body was wracked by another violent shiver. "What are you—"

"It'll be easier to share body heat if you can actually get to my body."

He shook his head. "That's taking advantage—"

"I assure you, there's nothing even remotely sexy about you dying. So, pipe down and let me help you." She lifted the mound of blankets from his feet before tucking her jacket and then her doublet in over him. Then she pulled her shirt over her head and tossed that over him, too. At last, she was left in only her vest, trousers and woolly hat. She chanced a glance down at Maalik, but he had his eyes closed.

How many times did she have to strip off in front of him before he got used to it? With some shuffling, she crawled under the covers without disturbing them too much and wrapped herself around the demon's shaking body.

His skin was ice, and she fought down a yelp, fighting to stay still instead of flinching away.

"Sorry about this," she told him, before undoing the buttons which held his own jacket together. He said nothing as she undressed him, but he gasped when she pulled his shirt out of his trousers and pushed it up to his chest. Next, she counted down from three in her head, before lifting her vest up to reveal her own stomach and pressed it against his. Ailsa wound her arms about his body, inside the layers of clothing, and pulled herself in so that she was hugging him.

"There, that should help." In fact, the shivering was already less violent. She rested her forehead against his collarbone, willing the heat to flow from her skin to his. "We have to turn around," she whispered. There was no way she was going to lose him to hyperthermia, of all things. "There's no guarantee what we're looking for is even at the top of the mountain."

Maalik didn't reply, as though he didn't have the energy anymore.

Ailsa closed her eyes, relaxing as best she could against her freezing demon. But she knew she wouldn't be able to sleep, not with him hovering between life and death. "Stay with me," she breathed. *Could things be any worse?*

Then, as though in answer, she thought she heard a distant howl pierce the dark.

Chapter 65

Angus pulled out the bow from the case and eyed it warily. He wasn't sure what Nicnevan's game was, or why she'd requested he bring her the box from her quarters when he'd brought her an early morning meal. "It's a fiddle," he stated dumbly, brushing a finger over the lacquered wood.

"Yes, a very special one." Her face was unreadable as she watched him. "Take it out."

Angus grasped the neck gently and pulled the instrument out. The body was decorated with ornate patterns of leaves and vines, painted onto ebony wood. The bridge glinted gold, and the strings were almost iridescent. "Do you play?" he asked.

"No," Nicnevan said. "That violin is goblin crafted, made for a very special musician, who sold his soul for the gift of music. Unfortunately, he only played it once. It has been in my possession ever since."

"It's beautiful."

She sniffed. "I want you to play it for me."

"Is it cursed?" he asked flatly.

A smile played at her lips. "You are always so suspicious. It is an excellent trait to have. But no, it isn't cursed."

"Why do you want me to play it?" he pressed.

"It has been a long while since I have experienced beauty. Even before I was trapped like this, I was so hell-bent on revenge that I had little time for music and art. The Unseelie do not enjoy such things either."

"I'm not that good."

"Indulge me."

Angus placed the chin rest to his neck and breathed through his nose. The first pass of the bow across the strings was merely a test, but the sound made the hairs on the backs of his arms stand on end. That one note was more beautiful, more magical, than any song he'd ever heard. Tears sprung into his eyes and he peeked up at the Faerie Queen.

Her face was no longer impassive. She watched him greedily, like a spider to a fly. "Keep going."

Angus almost put the instrument down, but the sound had been too wondrous not to repeat. He drew the bow across the strings again, starting up a simple tune he'd learned when he'd first started out. But playing on the enchanted fiddle sounded more like he was commanding an entire orchestra. Soon, he lost himself in the music, closing his eyes and letting his muscles remember the piece. The sound swelled until it was in every fibre of his body. The melody flowed through his blood, coaxing his heart to sing along. Then, with reluctance, he allowed the song to finish with one last drawn-out note.

As soon as he stopped playing, the jail was silent. Angus opened his eyes and lowered the instrument from under his chin. "That was—"

And then he stopped.

Nicnevan was staring at him, tears streaming down her cheeks. Her arms were still trapped, so she couldn't wipe them away.

"Are you alright?" he asked.

She jerked her head in a nod. "Thank you," she said simply.

Angus placed the instrument back in its box and closed the lid before scooting nearer to the Faerie Queen. "I'll play for you again later." Then he pulled a clean cloth from his pocket and dared to bring it to her cheek.

Nicnevan closed her eyes, giving him permission.

Neither of them said anything as Angus gently blotted the tears on her pale green skin. Finally, he sat back on his heels. "There you go." Then he pulled out the bottle of cauldron water and repeated his usual ritual. Nicnevan breathed in deeply as the drops landed on her shoulder, allowing her to shrug it.

Chapter 66

Ailsa wiped the crust from her eyes and examined her demon carefully. Colour had returned to his cheeks and his breathing was even. His pulse was strong under her fingers and he was warm. Not hot like he usually was, but enough to give her some relief.

"Maalik?" she whispered, squeezing his arms. She wasn't sure whether it was wise to wake him or if she should let him sleep more, but they couldn't very well stay in the tent all day. They'd have to decide: up or down?

He stirred, wakening with narrowed eyes. The sun was shining outside, casting the tent in a warm glow and he blinked against it. "Ailsa?"

"How are you feeling?" she asked, biting her lip. *I thought you were going to die.*

"Better than last night," he said, sitting up. The blankets and clothes fell off him. "Whatever you did, it worked."

"Good. That means we can head back down."

"You're joking, right?" Maalik said. "We must be more than a third up the mountain by now."

"You almost froze to death," she growled, her voice too big for the tent. "I'm not risking you for a stupid trinket."

Then he was grabbing her chin, tipping her head back so she would look at him. "I didn't dress warm enough yesterday; I wasn't expecting to lose all of my heat. I'll put on some more layers today and I'll be fine."

"And what about the noises?" she asked. Even to her own ears, she sounded hysterical.

"What noises?"

"You didn't hear the howling?"

"It was probably the wind," Maalik sighed. "Look, I know that you're worried about me, but we need to see this to the end. If the Spear of Truth is at the top of the mountain, we have to find it. Believe me, the Edaxi are much more dangerous than a little cold."

A little cold. Ailsa would have snorted if she wasn't feeling so hopeless. "I could go by myself."

"You said yesterday that wasn't happening. Do you want me to leave?"

No, of course she didn't.

"Why don't I start walking up with you?" he said, stroking her cheek. "If by lunchtime I'm still struggling, we'll make camp and then tomorrow I'll go back myself."

"Fine," she said, leaning into his touch. "But I'll be watching you like a hawk so don't even try to pretend you're okay if you're not."

His smile lit up his face. "I wouldn't dream of it."

Despite her worrying, Ailsa couldn't help being hopeful. He seemed so much better now as he helped her pack away the clothes and blankets. He shook out his sleeping bag, sending a cascade of little grey feathers into the tent—probably from the stuffing—and took one between his thumb and finger. Then, with gentleness, he placed it behind her ear. She returned his grin before swatting him away so she could pack her own bag.

Please be right, she prayed as they folded down the tent. Ailsa watched Maalik's body closely for any shivers, before sending some warmer air swirling around him. *I can't do this without you.*

Chapter 67

*E*phraim, Harris decided, was getting crowded.

After the Ghillie-Dhu arrived, there had been a constant stream of fae, tempted back to the faerie court with rumours of the defeat of Nicnevan. *What would they do,* Harris wondered, *if they knew a human prince was slowly setting her free again?*

"What—who do we have now?" Irené asked, elbowing Harris in the ribs. They were yet again at the entrance to Ephraim. Irené had stationed some of her crew as a welcoming committee of sorts, but she had taken to popping down whenever she could, Harris in tow to act as a translator when needed.

He bent closer to her ear. "They're Crodh Mara. Faerie cattle." The nearest cow tossed her head, rustling the flower crown woven through her copper fur.

Harris bowed and waved a hand behind him. "You're very welcome here."

The lead cow opened her mouth to bellow out a long and low sound, then she ambled up the path to Ephraim. Her seven companions followed along, keeping in a tight group, flattening the grass and moss on either side.

"I think I've seen everything now," Irené muttered.

Harris grinned. "There are stranger creatures than these out there."

"Ghillie-Dhu, urisks, loireag, and now faerie cattle," she mused, turning to make her way back from the gate. "And you're sure they're all friendly?"

"They're all Seelie. But I wouldn't let my guard down. Just because we're good, doesn't mean we don't like to play tricks."

"You know, from my experience in diplomacy, the gathering of so many requires one thing."

"And what is that?"

She grinned. "A party."

Harris stopped walking. "You want to throw a party for cows and pixies?"

"And for my crew. The last one they attended didn't end well. I think we could all do with letting off a little steam. And if we form bonds of friendship with the faerie folk, so much the better."

"Because we have a war to fight?"

"Exactly my thoughts. We need every human and fae to fight with us."

Harris's stomach twisted. "These fae can't fight."

"They can provide us information then. They could be our eyes and ears across Eilanmòr."

He shrugged. "It's a good idea."

"So, you'll help us prepare?"

"If there's anything I know, it's parties. Count me in."

Movement to the right caught his eye, and he halted Irené with a hand on her shoulder. A dozen tiny fae poked their heads out from behind the toadstools that lined the path out of Ephraim. Their eyes took up more than half of their faces as they stared up at them. Little snub noses sniffed at the air and the leaves on their bodies quivered, making a rustling noise.

"Oh, how sweet," Irené whispered. She lifted her hand as if to hold it out to one. Harris immediately grabbed her forearm and yanked her back.

"Don't," he said.

Irené frowned but stepped back. "Why?"

"There are hundreds in the trees. As soon as you get close enough, they'll swarm you."

The princess snorted. "Fae really are obsessed with kidnapping, aren't they?"

"Yes," Harris agreed, with a fiendish smile. "We are."

Chapter 68

Ailsa had watched her companion climb all day. Maalik was tired. She could see it in the way he fought to take each step, but the extra layers had done their trick; he no longer shivered. Still, she stuck close, sharing any extra heat her body produced, sending the warm hair over him in a caress.

But now that he wasn't fighting for his life, it became clear something had changed between them. He kept glancing her way, all throughout the climb, opening his mouth as if to say something, then snapping it closed. It was driving her crazy.

What happened back at the bathhouse? She asked Ishbel again.

The spirit guide snorted. *I told you; you threw yourself at him.* But she didn't elaborate further.

Ailsa groaned internally. She couldn't go on like this, not knowing what exactly she'd said, not knowing his reaction. Not knowing if he felt the same as she did.

You're on a quest for a magical object, on a mountain that is trying to kill you. Now is not the time to be thinking about a crush. But wouldn't it be better to get it out in the open and move on? Even if he rejected her, at least she'd be able to stop worrying.

Before the sun set, Ailsa insisted they set up their tent. It was better to let the rays heat the interior, for them to still be warm when they were fiddling with the poles and ropes. The tension was a thick wall between them as they worked but Ailsa tried to ignore it. *Get him safe.*

As soon as they were set up, she bundled Maalik into the canvas structure and secured the door so that none of the biting wind could enter. Then she shrugged off her bag and began pulling out her bedding.

"Are you alright?" asked Maalik, copying her with quivering fingers.

She looked sharply at them. "Are *you?*"

"I'm much better than yesterday. Just sore." He stretched out his arms, and Ailsa listened as his joints popped. He squeezed his shoulder muscles, and she wondered if she should offer to massage his aches away again.

He probably doesn't want you to touch him after whatever you did the last time. And yet, hadn't he held her, stroked her face, fed her pieces of fruit from his own fingers?

"How long do you think we have left?" Ailsa asked, moving to give him space.

"Another two days. I think we'll reach the summit by nightfall on the day after tomorrow."

"Right," she said, nodding. "We should probably eat and get some rest then."

She could sense his eyes on her as she pulled out a tin she'd been carrying and cracked it open. With Maalik's powers reduced to ash, they'd been having to consume the food cold; the small fires she'd made with a flint and tinder were barely enough to melt the snow to drink.

Yum, she thought sarcastically, scooping the food with a spoon: cold beans. Still, it was edible, and she was starving. Ailsa closed her eyes, savouring the meal as it hit her empty stomach. When she opened them again, she found Maalik staring at her.

"You're doing that thing again," she said. "You look like you've got something to say."

The sun was setting outside now, casting his face in half shadow. "There are a million things I want to say to you, all the time."

She swallowed the last mouthful and set the tin to the side. "So, say them."

"I'm constantly asking myself why you came back for me, why you wanted me with you, why you still want me with you when I'm such a burden." He held up a hand to stop her from denying it. "I want to tell you all my secrets, all the little thoughts that pop into my head and I want to hear yours too. We've not known each other for long, but I can't imagine a life without you now."

"You don't have to," Ailsa told him fiercely. "After we find the Spear of Truth and we get off this mountain, you're coming with me, or I'm coming with you. Whatever comes next, we do it together."

He nodded, swallowing thickly and his jaw worked again. "I still have so much more to tell you, but some things are easier to say in the dark."

Ailsa bit her lip. "Then I'll lie beside you every night until you're ready."

Maalik's eyebrows pulled together but then he was sinking down into his sleeping bag like he was willing it to be true.

Once he was settled, she pushed her own blankets closer and lay down until they were both on their backs, side by side. Then, before she could lose her courage, she wrapped her hand around his and squeezed.

For a moment, the only sounds in the tent were of their breathing, and the wind whistling outside.

This is it, Ailsa told herself. *Be brave.*

She waited a moment, listening for Ishbel's voice to comment, but found her gone for now. Perhaps she was giving them some privacy.

"What did I do in the bathhouse?" she asked. "Tell me the truth."

Maalik stroked her thumb with his in a soothing rhythm. "You laughed, played a few games, made some jokes." He inhaled. "You asked me to kiss you."

Great. "And that upset you?"

"No, but you were drugged up; you didn't know what you were saying."

"And if I hadn't been, and I'd asked you, would you have done it?"

She didn't think he would answer at first. He paused, and she tensed for his reply. *He's going to say no. He's trying to think of a way to let you down gently.*

But then he took their clasped hands and raised them to his chest, so that she could feel his heartbeat thundering inside, and said, "Yes."

She gasped shakily as the word echoed inside her head.

Yes, yes, yes.

Now do something about it.

Ailsa moved as though she was trying not to spook a frightened animal, sensing that if she was too fast, he'd pull away, and it would be even harder to catch him next time. She leaned over his still form, and with one trembling finger, reached out and stroked the arm closest to her. In the moon's light, she could see Maalik's hair stand on end.

Ailsa nudged as close as she dared and waited. Then, with a rustle, Maalik rose up on one elbow until their noses were almost touching. Ailsa's pulse drummed in her veins. She hoped he couldn't hear it like she could.

"Tell me to back off," Maalik whispered. "Tell me to roll over and go to sleep."

Ailsa touched the tip of her nose to his and wet her lips with her tongue. "I won't."

"Please, Ailsa. I can't—"

"We've been dancing around this for weeks. Surely you know how I feel about you?"

"Whatever you think you feel, you're going to change your mind."

"Maalik." *Say it.* "I love you. And don't you dare tell me I don't know what I'm saying. Don't you dare tell me you don't deserve it. You aren't a bad decision made decades ago. You are deserving of love."

"Ailsa…"

"Go on then." She raised her chin, staring him down. "Tell me you don't love me back."

"Ailsa, I—"

"Go on," she growled.

All his breath left him. "I can't."

"You listen to me, Maalik. There is not a purer, more deserving person of love than you. And as long as I am on this earth, as long as my heart is still beating, I'm going to show you what you mean to me and, so help me, you're going to bloody feel loved." She shook her head, willing the words to reach him. "Tell me how to convince you."

Maalik shook his head as he stared at the ceiling, his brows pinched together, tears leaking down his face.

"I love you," Ailsa whispered again.

Maalik reached out a blackened hand and covered her own. "My heart, my soul, my entire being is yours," he said simply.

Yes.

She surged forward the last few millimetres, until her mouth met his and finally, *finally*, they were kissing. How long had she been waiting for this?

His lips were soft and warm, and best of all, they kissed her back. With a groan, he reached for her, pulling her into his arms, until they were chest to chest.

But it wasn't enough.

More, Ailsa thought, hoping she hadn't actually said the word out loud. She found herself rising, pushing and pulling, until she was seated in his lap. Maalik moaned, sitting up to meet her and deepen the kiss. Ailsa licked inside his mouth hesitantly and then his tongue met hers and it was her turn to whine. Maalik's fingers trailed down her sides, leaving shivers in their wake until they reached her hips and squeezed.

She'd had a kiss that was like drowning, another that was like fire, but this? Her body throbbed with feeling, like every nerve ending was alight, tingling with electricity. Their pulses thundered in time with each other, and the very air crackled between them. And yet, she felt safe, felt cared for down to her core. It was the perfect storm.

Maalik kissed over her jaw and she threw her head back, giving him access to her throat. He trailed open-mouthed kisses down her neck, to the place where her shoulder met her collarbone, and then grazed his teeth against the sensitive skin, bringing another moan to her lips.

Pushing him away, Ailsa tugged off her fleece, and then

her shirt, only taking her gaze away from those fathomless eyes when the material obscured her view. All the while, Maalik stroked her hips, her thighs that were still wrapped round him.

"You're going to get cold," he breathed.

"Warm me up then." Ailsa pulled her vest over her head, hearing his gasp over her pounding heart.

He licked his lips before reaching behind his neck and pulling his own clothing off, piece by piece. It was on the tip of Ailsa's tongue to stop him, to tell him to keep himself safe. But the tent was heated from the sunlight they'd captured and from their heavy breathing. *We're doing this*, she thought as he took his undershirt off, revealing glorious swathes of dark skin and shuddering muscles.

She reached out with a finger, trailing it up his chest, over his shoulder and down his arm. Then, with gentle slowness, she took his hand in hers and placed it against her bare stomach.

"You're beautiful," he whispered.

And then they were kissing again, drinking each other in as they pressed their fevered skin together. *I'll never get sick of this*. Ailsa trailed her hands up his back, breathing out her feelings as he brushed his lips against her cheek, tugged on her ear with his teeth.

"I love you."

"Ailsa," he groaned out, nuzzling her neck.

But then her hands brushed something soft on his shoulder blades. She ran her hands over the feathery material, trying to work out what she was feeling. But then her fingers sunk into it, grazing silken fibres.

What was that? She opened her eyes and cried out.

Maalik stopped what he was doing, raising his face to hers. "What?"

She traced the feathers under her fingers, felt along the bones carefully. "Maalik," she said in wonder, turning his chin so he could look. "You have wings."

Chapter 69

Maalik stared dumbly at the structures fanning out from behind his back, still holding Ailsa tightly to him. *I must be dreaming,* he thought. Everything he'd ever wanted was right here, in this tent, perched halfway up a mountain. There was no way this was real.

"I've been finding feathers," Ailsa murmured. "Ever since you got your soul back, they've been everywhere."

The wings were exactly as he remembered them, though smaller, barely fitting inside the canvas. White primaries, light grey secondaries, with a trim of charcoal feathers near the hollow bones. But even as he watched them, they folded in on themselves, shrinking smaller and smaller until they were once again against his back. The largest feathers sunk into his skin, turning back to metal, but the smaller ones remained in a fluffy strip across his shoulders.

"How?" he asked, willing them back.

Ailsa's mouth twisted, considering. And then she brought his chin up. When he tried to pull away, she held him tighter. "Humour me with something. Close your eyes."

He sighed but did what he was told. He sensed her leaning in to whisper in his ear.

"I love you," she said. "And you're worthy of that love. I'd save the entire world, just because you're in it. There's nowhere I wouldn't follow you and there's nothing you could say that would change my mind. My heart, my soul, my entire being is yours," she echoed his words back to him hoarsely. "Open your eyes."

He blinked away the tears which had built up as he'd listened to her words and found her smiling down at him.

"Look," she said.

He turned his head to find the wings were back, fanning out from between his shoulder blades once again. "How?" he repeated.

"I'm not sure," said Ailsa. "How do you feel when I tell you things like that?"

"Like I'm flying," he answered, and then he understood.

"I think you're turning back into an angel," said Ailsa as the feathers melted back into metal again. "And I'm pretty sure you can thank me."

Later, Maalik lay in his blankets with a sleeping Ailsa tucked into his side. He rested his head against his arm and stared up at the thick tent fabric, marvelling at everything that had happened.

He could still feel her lips against his, the softness of her skin under his fingertips. There had to be a catch, something to sour his joy. It came to him slowly but surely, as he listened to the woman beside him breathing gently.

If I turn back into an angel, I won't be able to fight with her. They needed a demon, a fae with fire magic.

He dropped a kiss to the top of her head. "I'd save the world for you too," he whispered. "Even if I must be a monster to do it."

Chapter 70

When Harris had agreed to help, he hadn't realised Irené wanted it all arranged so quickly. Yet, here he was, the morning after she'd voiced her idea, wrangling grogans and brownies and trying his best not to show his irritation.

"I said, I wanted lanterns around the tent, not for the tent to be set on fire."

The little fae rushed for buckets of water as their bonfire grew, eyeing him suspiciously.

"What? I don't have water magic. I can't help you."

There was much chattering, but it seemed like they got the message. Harris turned from the mess, hoping that they'd sort it out themselves.

The smell of spices wafted from the next room, which Harris hoped meant the cook had got on with the food. A few tarrans had offered to help, but he'd told the little spirits they were too young to be handling knives.

Outside the canvas, some hags stirred something in a large pot. He sidled up to them and glimpsed a golden and sparkling liquid before they snapped their gummy mouths in the air, in an obvious threat.

"Alright, alright," Harris laughed. "I'll leave you to it." He'd have to warn the crew about the faerie wine they were making.

But then again, perhaps not. It wasn't harmful, just incredibly potent.

Irené did say they could all do with letting off steam.

Back in his room, Harris found more fae fighting over pieces of cloth. He shooed the pixies away— they only caused trouble—leaving behind a short fae woman dressed in a beautiful gown.

Her skin was a cool lilac, complemented by the duck-egg blue of her dress. On it, flowers and leaves had been stitched in silver threads.

"Do you like it?" she asked in a high voice, noticing his stare. "I can make one for you too?"

"Maybe another time," Harris answered with a bow. "I'd prefer something more traditional tonight."

"Very well," she said, pulling a roll of tape out of her pocket. "I'll have to measure you." Her gaze roamed from the crown of his head to his toes.

Harris stepped into the middle of the room and held out his arms.

She blinked owlish eyes up at him and gave him a coy smile. "You'll have to strip. I can't measure your body with so many layers."

Harris hesitated for a moment and then pulled his shirt over his head. His trousers were next, sliding off his legs and puddling on the floor.

"And your underwear?" the woman asked.

"I'll leave those on," Harris answered, pressing his lips together.

She tilted her head back and forth. "Suit yourself."

The woman was measuring around his middle, tickling his skin with her fluffy hair, when Angus walked through the door, looking tired and wan.

"Oh, sorry, am I interrupting something?"

Harris said "no". At the same time, the fae woman hissed out a quiet "*yesss*".

Angus looked between them in confusion, then seemed to give up, leaning against the wall and sticking his hands in his pockets. "Are you still annoyed with me?" he asked.

"Of course," Harris said. "But we wouldn't be best friends if one of us wasn't always a little annoyed at the other."

"Really? So, you're going to let me come to your party?"

"Are you joking? It wouldn't be a party without you. Are you going to save me a dance?"

"Sure," Angus said, as the fae woman let out a huff. Angus's eyes snapped to her as she measured around Harris's hips.

"I hope you don't mind me saying this, but you look like you're going to keel over at any moment." Harris gestured to the bags under Angus's eyes.

"Tired is all," he replied. "Can't sleep."

"What are you worried abou—" Harris began but then the woman was measuring his inseam and not bothering to be gentle about it. "-I don't think you need those measurements," he ground out. "I just want a kilt."

"I want to be thorough," she purred, licking her lips. But then she glanced at Angus and stood up. "I suppose I've got what I need for now. I'll be back later with your clothing."

"Great, thank you." Harris smiled as the woman let herself out of the room, her hips swaying as she walked.

"I can't decide if I ruined your fun, or if I saved you," Angus said.

"What do you mean?"

The prince snorted. "She was absolutely coming onto you."

"She was measuring me for clothes." He flopped onto the bed, throwing his arm over his eyes.

"She wanted to get into your pants," Angus retorted with a laugh.

"Well, I didn't let her."

"That's not like you."

Harris raised his head and narrowed his eyes. "How dare you, sir."

Angus crossed his legs in front of him. "I think I know why, though."

"Oh?" Harris asked flatly.

"The captain. You like her."

He sucked on one of his teeth. "She's an attractive woman."

"It's more than that," said Angus. "Ailsa is attractive, and it didn't stop your eye from wandering when you were chasing after her."

Harris winced. "It's been brought to my attention that I've been a bit of a cad."

"So, does that mean you're chasing after Irené?"

"Irené has made it very clear I have no hope in hell. We're just friends."

"But you won't be looking at other people soon?"

"I'm looking at you right now." *You look like a smarmy git too.*

"I'm flattered, but as I've said before, you're not my type."

Harris dropped his head to the mattress. "I want Irené to think well of me."

"She does."

"She didn't," he corrected. "But then she saw right through me."

Angus crossed the room, sitting on the bed beside him. "What you're saying is, 'no one understands you like Irené'?"

"I'm not some lovesick fool," Harris ground out.

The prince shrugged. "You said the L word, not me."

"Don't you have somewhere to be? Perhaps a nap is in order?"

Angus sighed, lying down beside him. "I can't sleep. I'm worried about, well, everything."

"Tonight we're having a party," said Harris, ruffling the other man's hair. "And you'd better not spoil my fun." Then he had an idea. "Beside the big tent, there are three women and a pot. Go get yourself a cup of what they're making. It'll make you feel better."

"Yeah?" asked Angus, sitting up. "Maybe I need a night to unwind. Do you want some?"

"Nah, I'll catch you in a bit."

Angus patted him on the shoulder and left Harris to wait for the dressmaker, not turning back once to see the selkie's wicked smile.

Chapter 71

arris stepped out onto the staircase which led down from his room and sighed in the honey-sweet air. There was something about a fae party that was always more exciting than a human affair. He'd never been to a ceilidh in Ephraim before, but he'd heard all about them from his aunt and cousins. Before Nicnevan favoured the Unseelie Court, all fae had been welcomed. Perhaps now, despite all the threats to Eilanmòr, it could be a place of unity again.

Indeed, he'd never seen so many different fae and humans all in one place. The forest paths below were teeming with ghillie-dhus and nuggles and cu siths, along with Irené's crew.

From what he could tell, the dressmakers had been busy outfitting all the guests in a few hours. His own kilt had turned up thirty minutes ago. The habetrot that had measured him up earlier delivered it herself. Harris couldn't stop thinking about Angus's teasing as she prattled on about the stitching and his hairy legs. Thinking back, he'd probably been a bit abrupt with her when he'd thrown her out of his room with a "thanks".

She'd done wonderful work, though. The threads she'd chosen for the fabric were mostly black, with stripes of mustard and blue cutting across each other. He ran his fingers over the kilt, marvelling at the softness. Harris had added a white, open shirt on top and his favourite old boots on his feet. He didn't want to be too fancy, after all.

Movement to his left caught his attention, and he turned his head in time to watch Angus emerging from his own room. He was ready for the ceilidh too, in a kilt the purple and green of the royal family. Except it looked like he'd forgotten his socks and shoes.

"Are you alright?" Harris called out.

Angus swayed, keeping one hand on the wooden treehouse beside him. "Fine. I tried that faerie wine," he slurred.

Harris couldn't help but laugh. "Stay there, I'll come get you. I don't want you falling down those stairs."

By the time Harris reached the prince, he was sitting down on the steps with his head in his hands.

"I'm not sure drinking on no sleep was a good idea."

"Come on, you'll feel better once we get some food in you."

Harris half-led, half-carried Angus down the stairs and into the chattering crowd. Everyone was heading towards the big tents, so they let themselves be carried along. Now and then, Harris had to tell Angus to lift a foot, to avoid a twig or stone, but the forest floor was carpeted by a thick layer of moss and Harris was sure Angus wouldn't regret foregoing shoes too much.

The crew members he could see weren't dressed in traditional Eilanmòrian garb like he was. Instead, it seemed the clothes makers had made them beautiful gowns and tunics that could only be Edessan.

The patterned fabrics draped their bodies in a rainbow of colours and revealed much more skin than the long-sleeved shirts he and Angus wore, as though they were more suited to a tropical climate. Harris doubted they'd get cold though. While he'd been in his room, bonfires had been set up near the tent, so the canvas would trap the heat.

As they approached the vast, white structure, a bell rang and all the humans and fae flooded inside after them. There, long, low tables were lined up, side by side and in the middle of everyone sat steaming piles of food. Harris caught a whiff of the spiced dishes, and his stomach grumbled.

"This way," he said to Angus, pulling him to a table on the left. As soon as they were beside the low wooden structure, he dumped the prince onto a plump floor cushion and sat down beside him.

All around them, sailors and fae alike were dropping onto pillows. The Edessans Harris saw were eyeing their guests with a mixture of suspicion and curiosity. Indeed, he spied Nadya, the sailing master, reach for her glass, only to realise she'd brushed up against a sprawling cat sith. The faerie feline purred, causing it's night-sky fur to shimmer like a thousand shooting stars. Nadya blanched, snatching her arm away while the cat sith rolled over onto its back. Still, there was a spark of awe there in the sailing master's stare.

Give them a few hours and they'll all be dancing together, Harris thought.

"Thanks," muttered Angus, half sprawling across the wooden surface. "Do you think we're allowed to eat?"

"You had better," said a voice behind them. "I won't make any speeches until after it's all been eaten."

"Irené—" Harris began, turning in his spot. His gaze first caught on the fabric of her dress—a deep red with black and gold suns. It was crossed over at her torso, highlighting her slim waist and revealing her delicate collarbones. Her hair was still tied back in braids, but they'd been magically dyed black and red to match her dress.

On her head, she wore a golden crown that looked like a sunburst, or a halo he'd seen in paintings. Her lips were stained a dark burgundy and Harris found himself thinking it would make a mess if she were to kiss someone.

"Harris?" Irené said, cutting through his thoughts.

"Sorry, you surprised me," he said, shaking his head to clear it. "What did you say?"

"Mind if I join you?"

"Of course." He motioned to the seat across from them. "I need someone to help me babysit the princeling. Drank too much faerie wine."

"You told me to drink it," Angus grumbled.

As soon as Irené was at her place, she picked up her plate and spooned food onto it. The bangles at her wrists jangled as she lifted cloches and added rice and vegetables to her bowl. Then, suddenly, she froze, looking up at Harris.

"What?"

You were staring again. "Erm, sorry, I was just wondering what the food is."

Angus snorted beside him. Harris responded by kicking him under the table.

"Right," Irené said with a smirk. "This one is salted fish, and this one is jerk chicken."

"Is it good?" Angus asked, ladling some onto his own plate as he asked.

"My chef made it, so yes." Irené helped herself to some once Angus was done with the spoon. "Careful though, it's hot."

"We have plenty of curry dishes in Dunrigh. I'm used to spice."

"No offense, but I suspect they've watered down the taste for you Eilanmòrians."

Angus looked dubious as he raised his fork to his mouth and licked at the sauce. Immediately, his face reddened and he let out a laugh. "Wow, you weren't joking."

"How did your chef get all of this?" Harris asked, tucking into some fish. It dissolved in his mouth, leaving behind a tangy flavour and heat which made his eyes water.

"He said he asked for it and some of the fae got it for him. The spices and rice he brought with us. I told my crew we might be here a while."

They talked as they ate, sharing ideas and jokes and arguing over silly things like books and music. It turned out Irené had strong opinions on bagpipes, which led to Angus almost rising out of his chair to state his case.

"You can't possibly believe that!" he said, throwing his hands up in the air. "Sometimes you need loud music. And there's nothing louder than a set of bagpipes."

"They sound like elephants with stomach aches," Irené laughed. "If I never hear another bagpipe again, I'll be happy."

"They're our national instrument! I have half a mind to throw you out of my country."

"Oh really? *Your* country? Well, maybe I'd better leave. At least I won't hear any droning in Edessa."

"Right," said Angus, laughing himself now. "I'm going to go find a set of bagpipes so I can educate you in what good music sounds like. I'll see you both later when the dancing starts." And with that, Angus marched off, his kilt swishing as he walked.

"He's going to find one, you know," said Harris.

Irené smirked. "I have to confess, I don't actually mind bagpipes. I like winding him up."

He barked out a laugh. "Me too." He watched her over the

rim of his glass. Her shoulders were back, her head was high. She looked every inch a queen. "Can I make an observation? You seem happier here."

Irené considered this. "I suppose I like your faerie court. And I like that my crew are being cared for, that they're safe."

"Is that all?"

She bit her lip. "I like having friends who don't see me as merely their captain. It can be exhausting, being in charge. Even as a princess, I was expected to know what to do all the time. But with you and Angus, I can just *be*."

"I'm glad to hear it. I'm glad we're friends too."

"Are you?" Irené said lightly. "Stopped seeing me as a bit of skirt to chase?"

"Oh well, your skirt is pretty nice," Harris said with a wink. "No matter whether I think you're the smartest, funniest, most beautiful girl I've ever met. I would never want to make you uncomfortable. You said you wanted to be my friend, so that's what we'll be."

Irené's dimples were showing. "Really?"

Harris nodded. "I wouldn't do anything to jeopardise—"

"No, I mean, you think I'm smart and funny?" She twirled a braid around her finger and for a moment Harris was mesmerised by the movement.

"And beautiful, yes."

Irené raised one perfectly groomed eyebrow. "But is there anything else? Relationships aren't built on smart and funny and pretty alone."

Harris swallowed. "I guess I admire you. You could have sat in your palace all your life. Instead, you became a sailor, defending your home country. You also could have stayed at home instead of warning us about the threat."

"A threat to one country in Ossiana is a threat to all."

"Not everyone sees it like that."

"And you don't mind that I'm built a little differently to other girls?" she asked, waving a hand down her body.

"Like I said, you're beautiful."

Irené placed one hand on the ground behind her so she could lean back, considering him. "I'm starting to like you, Harris. In a more-than-friends way. But we still have a long way to go. I like a slow burn."

He almost spat out the drink he'd been sipping. "Are you saying I should try to woo you?"

"I'm saying: don't be an idiot, act like a gentleman and then we can see where this goes," she said with a sniff. "Of course, this is all dependent on whether you want that too?"

He raked his eyes from the crown on her head down to her collarbone, dipping no further. "Here's to seeing where it goes." Harris raised his glass in the air.

Irené smirked, copying his gesture with her own cup. "I'd better get a dance out of you, selkie-boy."

"You can bet on it," Harris said, returning her smile.

Chapter 72

It took a few hours and some water before the faerie wine left his system, but soon the bubbling was gone from Angus's veins as he sobered up.

I'm going to kill Harris. But he didn't really mean it. The wine had been a fun excuse to let down his hair, a pause in the worrying he'd been doing, but now those fears were back at the forefront of his mind.

Everything's fine, he tried to tell himself.

Angus watched from the tables as Harris led Irené in another dance. He'd counted four songs since they'd started twirling together, as if they were so lost in each other that they hadn't noticed the music had changed.

Angus smiled softly. It was nice to see his friends happy. Gods knew they all deserved a bit of joy.

What he would give to have Iona and Ailsa and Cameron here right now. Especially Cameron. The last time they'd danced, Cameron had had a vision before the end of the song. He'd wondered if it was an elaborate excuse to get away from him, but then Cameron had started to shake and he'd known it was real.

Not everything is about you, he chastised himself. It was just bad luck that every time he'd managed to get close to his old flame lately, they'd been interrupted.

Angus rubbed his knuckles against his chest, over his

heart. Maybe he needed a walk.

After he'd found some shoes, he made his way out of the colossal white pavilion, dodging merry sailors and twirling sprites. It was good that everyone had come together; it felt like laying the foundations of peace. How long had the humans in Eilanmòr feared the fae? Perhaps this was the start of friendship.

The night was cool on his still heated skin and he basked in it for a moment before setting off towards the entrance to the fae kingdom.

When he hadn't been down in the dungeons with Nicnevan, he'd found his feet returning to the gap in the towering hedge. He'd attempted to lie to himself about why. *I'm helping to keep a lookout. I'll ask the sentries if they need anything.* But he knew the real reason he'd gone there so often: he was watching for Cameron and Iona.

When he arrived at the gate, there were only two crew members. One of them, the green-haired medic, sat against the structure, reading a book by the light of the lanterns overhead. The other was one of the young apprentices Harris had saved on the ship. He was swinging from the branches of a gnarled oak, looking thoroughly bored.

"Have you come to replace us?" said the boy as Angus strolled up.

"I hadn't planned to," said the prince. "But if you want to go to the party—"

The boy dropped to the floor, sprinting towards the lights and music with a *thanks* thrown over his shoulder.

Angus sighed. *I suppose I'll be on gate duty then.* "Don't you want to go?" he asked the doctor.

She dragged her eyes from her book. "I'd rather sit here. In the *quiet*," she added, giving him a pointed look.

Fair enough, no talking.

Angus sat down at the opening and resigned himself to a few hours of watching the dark forest beyond. The moonlight cast strange shadows, which flickered and moved with the surrounding trees. Several times he was sure he was seeing figures out there, darting through the gaps. *It's your imagination. You might actually be going crazy with worry.*

The problem was, he'd pored over the maps he'd found, tracing every possible journey from Kilvaig to Ephraim, calculating distances and factoring in breaks. And Cameron should have been there by now. His mind kept picking over the potential scenarios.

Perhaps they couldn't find the sword and lingered longer than we'd planned.

Maybe Cameron is still unwell, and they've had to stay in the inn.

They could just be taking their sweet time.

But underneath the rational thoughts, a voice whispered all the things that had gone wrong.

They've been attacked. They're injured. They're dead.

Angus shook his head. It didn't do anyone any good to catastrophize. Tomorrow he'd get Laire, and they'd travel back down south together to look for them.

Something flickered at the corner of his vision and Angus snapped his head up, scanning the trees for the source. Just as he was sure he'd imagined it, he saw the same thing: dancing firelight somewhere in the dark. Rising to his feet, he watched the flames grow brighter and closer.

It's more fae coming to join the party, he assured himself.

But then the flames spread out, growing larger and larger

through the tree-gaps and Angus realised with panic that the forest floor was on fire.

"Doc, are you seeing this?" he asked the medic.

She lifted her eyes from the book and gave a frightened gasp. "A fire? Surely it can't get through the gates. You'd think they'd be spelled against something like that."

"We should still raise the alarm," said Angus as the sounds of crackling drifted towards them. He'd seen forest fires before, seen how much destruction they could inflict. But this fire wasn't acting the way he expected. It stayed low to the ground, not touching the trees. Almost like it was controlled.

Just as Angus's stomach plummeted at the thought, something large appeared out of the flames. It grew closer, silhouetted against the fire, until Angus could make out a head and arms. The figure lumbered over fallen trees and debris, as if unaware of the danger behind.

"Who are you?" called the doctor into the night.

But then the figure was joined by another. And another. A hoard of people advanced out of the blaze, towards the gates to Ephraim.

"We need to tell someone," Angus said, watching the strangers with horror. "I don't think they're here for the celebration."

Now the first figure was close enough he could see her features, illuminated by Ephraim's lantern-light. Her eyes were blank, her skin rotten and bruised; her clothing hung off her, shredded. And in her hand, the woman carried a knife.

"Run," he told the green-haired medic, fear gripping at his chest. "Go get the captain."

But before the doctor could rise, something else—something larger—stalked out of the smoking forest. It strolled steadily forwards until Angus could see it clearer.

A man sat atop a tan horse, dressed from his shoulders to feet in rusted armour, but with a tattered hood over his head. Even under the bulk of the metal, Angus could see his body was rail-thin. His long legs juddered as the horse moved, as though he couldn't keep them still.

At his flanks, another group of men followed. They did not shuffle like the others. Instead, they marched, holding glowing torches in their hands.

The doctor sprinted back to the pavilion, leaving him alone to watch the group grow steadily closer until he could see their faces. Whole, unblemished. The man on the horse pulled back his hood revealing a scarred face, smudged with coal, and a knife-sharp smile, splitting up his cheeks.

Not right, Angus thought. An ancient fear shivered up his spine. "Who are you and what do you want?" He positioned himself in the middle of the hedge's gap, wishing he'd brought a sword. His stomach was roiling, his palms sweaty, but he tried to stand up straight, staring them down.

"What we want is access to Ephraim," said the man on the horse in a sing-song voice. Though he hadn't shouted, Angus still heard every word clearly in his ears, like the man was right beside him. "We've been waiting a long time to get here."

"Who are you?" Angus repeated, his voice wavering.

The man's answering laugh was manic. "I am destruction. I am war." He held up something small in between his skeletal fingers and Angus froze. He would have recognised that purple crystal anywhere. *The Stone of Destiny.*

The man grinned, widening his eyes so Angus could see the madness in their depths. "I am chaos, and I've come for you all."

Chapter 73

Angus's breath came out in gasps as he sprinted towards the waterfall. Ever since he'd heard Irené talk about murderous gods and magical weapons, the threat hadn't seemed real. It was too far away; intangible. But now, here they were. They'd run out of time.

He passed under the thundering water; the spray clinging to his hair and clothes and running down his face like sweat. His feet pounded against the stone of the caves, echoing off the walls. It didn't matter if he made a racket, if he announced his presence early. The time for tiptoes and softly spoken questions was over. As soon as Irené's crew had arrived at the gate, he'd known exactly what he needed to do.

Finally, he rounded the corner of the biggest cell and yanked open the wooden door. Nicnevan sat against the wall where he'd left her. Her fingers and lower body were still stone and tree, but he'd given her enough movement to read by torchlight or to make herself comfortable. Now she turned, fixing those catlike eyes on him as he skidded towards her.

"What—"

"We're being attacked," Angus huffed. "The Edaxi—they're here."

Nicnevan narrowed her eyes. "They dare come to Ephraim?"

"They don't care who rules where or which place is sacred.

They're here to destroy and enslave." He pulled out the bottle of cauldron water. The contents sloshed about inside and Nicnevan's gaze tracked the movement. "I am going to free you and you're going to fight with us."

"And your vow?" she asked.

"I promise I will support, protect and defend your daughter." *There isn't time for debates over wording. That would have to do.*

Jutting out her chin, she said, "And I promise to take all my wrath, all my fury and direct it not at Eilanmòr but at the deities who threaten my land and my people."

"Good enough for me," Angus said, and then he poured the rest of the liquid over the Faerie Queen and set her free.

Angus raced back to the gate, guided by the firelight. Their enemy hadn't been careful with their torches; the flames were spreading now, incinerating trees like giant wicks and spewing smoke into the sky above. The forest echoed with the sounds of groaning wood and snapping tinder. But the burning trees didn't frighten him half as much as what he'd just left behind.

What did I do?

The chances were he'd just set an evil loose on the world. *It may be the only way to save it.*

His kilt swished about his legs; he hadn't changed from the party. Irené's crew, however, had shed their silks and picked up their cutlasses. He found them all at the hedge, with a few fae dotted between the sailors. Together, they watched the waiting army outside. The strangers stood poised, unfazed by the raging inferno at their backs.

He pushed his way through, stumbling to the front of the group to find Irené, still in her red dress and crown, staring down the man on the horse across the divide.

The god, Angus corrected.

"Ephraim won't let you in," Irené called, hands on her hips. "It's warded against you."

"I'm not here for Ephraim," the God of Chaos said and again, his melodic voice sounded as if he was only a breath away. "Did you know, we couldn't even set foot on Eilanmòr until we had this stone?" He twirled it between deft fingers. "Lucky for us we found an ally to take it from you."

Angus scanned the people behind the god again, this time taking in their appearance, their clothing.

"Mirandelle believes in our cause," said Chao as the soldiers shifted. "Though they're not the only ones. You raised suspicions, princess, when you met with the king of Eilanmòr. What did you tell him, I wonder?"

"That's none of your concern," spat Irené.

"It doesn't matter. I know everything you said in that library, including your and your friends' plans to find the Four Treasures."

"They aren't here," said Harris, coming to her side. "We've looked everywhere and couldn't find any."

"But there's a second half of the puzzle, isn't there?" The horse repositioned itself impatiently under him. "We still need four magic users."

No, thought Angus, looking over his shoulder. If Chao had come all the way to Ephraim, he had to be looking for the most powerful fae in Eilanmòr. And who was more powerful than the Faerie Queen? The Faerie Queen he'd just released.

"There are only pixies and doonies here," said Harris. All around Angus, the fae shrank back behind the sailors. "They can't wield your weapons."

Chao smiled lazily, showing too many teeth through his fissured skin. "We have an earth fae already. But I need someone with water magic."

Harris blinked. "Me? I don't have any special powers other than shape-shifting."

"Not you," sneered the god. "Her." Then he turned burning eyes onto Irené. "A princess, a captain and half xana? That seems powerful to me."

Irené had gone still. "I don't even have powers."

"You will, once we convince your body to show them." He tucked the Stone of Destiny away and pulled an enormous mallet from behind his back. It looked impossibly heavy, but Chao swung it to his side as if it were a toy. "But before that, I believe a fight is in order."

As if by command, the Soulless that had been hovering on the fringes of firelight began drifting forward again, moaning as they went. Behind the god, the Mirandelli soldiers drew their swords.

Angus surveyed at the crowd they'd assembled on their side of the barrier. Irené's crew were fearsome, but there weren't enough of them. The few fae that had come looked fragile, soft. They were hopelessly outnumbered.

At the gate, Harris grabbed Irené's hand, staring down the God of Chaos. Then, Chao gave a cry, and he too was stalking towards Ephraim, laughing as he rode.

We're going to die, Angus realised, watching the enemies draw in tighter. *I need my sword.* But he couldn't get his legs to move.

"This is not how we treat unwanted guests in Ephraim," said a female voice behind him. The crew and the fae stopped watching the enemy advancing. Instead, like a wave, they turned to find Queen Nicnevan standing amongst them.

She'd changed into an elegant dress made of black feathers. Her short hair gleamed golden above her pointed ears and her lips had been painted a deep purple. She looked like every nightmare Angus had ever had, embodied in flesh. It seemed like he wasn't the only one to think so, as the surrounding fae screamed.

But this only seemed to please Nicnevan. Her smile was razor sharp as she swept past them all towards the enchanted hedge, sparing a wink for Angus as she passed. He thought he saw Harris clutching at Irené. His face paled, but then the Faerie Queen halted in her tracks. Outside the gates, the Soulless and the soldiers broke into a sprint, crashing over the undergrowth and bearing down upon the thin wall of branches.

"Too slow," sneered Nicnevan and then she raised her arms. More roots flew out of the ground, weaving their way into the structure until the gaps were all filled in—until Angus could no longer see the approaching army. "Well," she said, once she was done, looking over her pale green shoulder at the open-mouthed onlookers. "Am I to fight a god by myself or are you all going to make yourselves useful?"

When no one moved, Irené raised her voice. "You heard her! Battle stations! *Ahora!*"

The queen gave the princess an approving nod as something unspoken passed between them, while all around, the pirates and fae scrambled to ready themselves for war.

Chapter 74

arris stared in horror at the barricade, holding on tightly to Irené's hand. There was no way the branches could keep an army out forever. And in the meantime, they were trapped in Ephraim with the most powerful fae in all of Eilanmòr. And the most evil.

Nicnevan still had her arms thrown up, strengthening the wall, but he could tell it was already being attacked from the other side. Her body and the branches shook, as the barricade was pounded from behind.

The sky above them was darkened; the stars blotted out by smoke from their fires. By some magic, the flames weren't coming closer, but the ashes floated down upon Ephraim, bringing with them the acrid smell of burning sap.

"What do we do?" he asked.

Irené extricated herself from his grasp. "I need my weapons and you need to help. Round up any fae that are willing to fight. " Then she reached down, tearing the silk of her dress without care, and began shouting orders to her crew.

Harris swallowed, unwilling to leave her after the threats Chao had made but knowing she wouldn't let him coddle her.

Once we convince your body to show them.

Harris's gut roiled. *What did the gods plan to do to her?* He hoped they'd never find out.

The Edessans had already set to work, gathering swords

and lining up to fight, t most of the fae had disappeared, frightened off as soon as they saw Nicnevan. Harris skirted past the sailors, ready to look for them, when he spotted Angus watching the queen with an open mouth.

Harris's blood boiled and before he knew it, he was across the clearing and had the prince pinned against a nearby tree.

"What the hell did you do?" he growled.

Angus's eyes blazed. "I made a deal. She's going to help us."

"You made a deal with the Faerie Queen?" Harris shook his head in disbelief. "You're a bigger fool than I thought. What does she get out of it?"

"That's my price to pay," said Angus calmly.

Harris let go. He knew he'd only kept him against the tree trunk because Angus hadn't wanted to fight back. The prince was stronger than him, a trained soldier. *So let him fight and deal with him afterwards.*

"If we survive this, I'm going to kill you," said Harris, turning from him in disgust. "I hope you know what you just did."

"I bought us some time," Angus replied. The prince stalked off, grabbing the sword that was offered to him as he joined the pirates.

Harris watched him for a moment as the prince readied himself. Then he went in the opposite direction, to root out more fighters stupid enough to fight alongside an evil queen that, until now, had been their enemy.

⬡⬡⬡

By the time he'd convinced the sorry group of fae to join the battle and found some pieces of armour to cover his party clothes, the sun was rising, casting the sky in a burnt orange above the smoke.

Harris ducked as another round of arrows from the Mirandelli soldiers flew over the barricade, but as soon as they landed, he was up again. "Fire!" he shouted, and a storm of rocks and pebbles were unleashed on the enemy.

But it wasn't enough. They hacked at the gates, pulling the branches and limbs off and throwing them to the ground. Even Nicnevan couldn't keep up with the sheer number of attacks.

"You need to be ready to fight," she called to Irené, still adding foliage to the wall.

The captain raised her cutlass. Someone had fetched her coat, which she'd pulled on over the remains of her dress. The crew of The Nymph stood in rows, poised, with their weapons drawn. "We form a blockade. As soon as the barricade collapses, we try to keep them from Ephraim. Push them into the forest, we'll have our battle there."

They'd left their vulnerable in the treehouses of the faerie kingdom. The cabin girl, the apprentices; they would stay behind with the fae who chose not to fight.

"If Chao is after me, we'll lead them away from Ephraim." That had been Irené's plan. Harris didn't like it. In fact, his plan was to do what the fae knew best: kidnap humans. As soon as anyone got too close to Irené, he was going to snatch her up and leg it back to Ephraim, where he could hide her. He just had to stick close enough to seize an opportunity.

The wall shook again, but this time Harris could see what was causing it. The God of Chaos was beyond the gate, wielding the massive mallet. He swung it above his head and then brought it down towards the wall, the impact reverberating across the clearing and snapping the branches.

"I'm going to have to drop it," shouted Nicnevan. "Are you ready?"

Irené gripped her sword tighter. "See you on the other side," she said to her friends. "Do it. Now."

Nicnevan dropped her arms and immediately the wall disintegrated under the weight of the Soulless. They tumbled to the ground and then the crew were on them, stabbing and slicing their way through the bodies. Harris shouted to the fae beside them and then they too were running forward. The faerie cattle threw their massive weights into the crowd of enemies. The pixies swooped in, slicing their rotting flesh with their sharp fingers.

But it was the Mirandelli soldiers beyond that Harris had his eye on. If anyone was going to snatch Irené away, it would be them. *Besides,* he thought, skirting the grappling crowd, *if anyone deserves a painful death, it's those traitors.* He slipped past the Soulless and the sailors, keeping an eye out for Irené as he did. Then Harris climbed over the remains of the wall, and into the burning forest, gripping his dagger as he went.

Chapter 75

*E*ilidh smelled the smoke first. They'd still been miles away from Ephraim, according to Iona, but the scent of battle was thick on the wind. More than trees were burning.

They'd been walking for days, travelling far too slowly because of Cameron's near constant headaches, and now they knew they were too late.

With little more than a word to her companions, she shifted into her flock of birds and flew high in the air, trying to get a glimpse. But the forest was thick; it was impossible to see more than smoke.

Coming back to her body, she relayed what she'd seen and the general direction.

"We have to hurry," Iona said. "And be ready to fight."

Cameron drew the dagger from his hip. "I'm as ready as I'll ever be."

Eilidh hesitated. "Don't you want to use the sword?" It was still sheathed and strapped to Iona's back.

"I'm not sure," he said, eyeing it. "You said it should only be used by fae with fire magic."

"I've been using it for years. It hurts, but if it's going to save our lives, I'm willing to pay the price."

"But you're fae," snapped Iona. "Cameron is human. The poem said, '*mortals handle them not*.'"

"I'll take it," Eilidh said, undoing the buckles. She pulled it from Iona's back but didn't undo the wrappings. They still had miles to go before they'd reach Ephraim, and she wasn't about to feed the weapon her blood before finding the battle.

The closer they got to the faerie court, the stronger the smells of burning became, until they were almost choking on it. But the fire seemed to have been halted by an invisible force, not spreading throughout the forest.

Now and then, they'd see figures darting through the trees, silhouetted against the smoke, but they seemed to be running away from Ephraim, so they paid them no mind. From up ahead came the vague sounds of shouting and screaming but they were too distant to make out words.

Just as she was about to speak, Iona tripped, landing on the forest floor with a bump.

"Are you alright?" Eilidh asked, rushing to help her up. Her nerves jangled as she cupped the selkie's elbow.

"I—" Iona began, but then she froze.

Eilidh looked at the thing Iona had tripped on and smothered a shriek. Lying on the ground, half covered in leaves and debris, was a corpse. The body was bloodied and beaten. It was unclear which side they'd been on.

"Look," Cameron breathed.

Eilidh's gaze followed his, and what she saw made her stomach plummet. Now that she'd seen one dead body, it was like the others magically appeared. There had to be hundreds, all spread across the forest. But beneath the horror, there was something odd about them.

"They look old. Like they were killed years ago."

Each of the corpses was covered in thick blankets of moss, explaining why they hadn't noticed them at first. They looked enchanted into sleep, like something from a faerie tale Agnes had told her. One thing was evident: the battle had been here, but it had moved.

Eilidh fought down a shiver. "How far from Ephraim are we?"

"It should be right ahead," Iona said, stumbling onward.

Eilidh pulled out the Sword of Light from its layers of fabric and held it aloft. If they were near Ephraim, they were near the battle. Immediately, she felt the tell-tale singing in her blood, like it was rushing to join her weapon. And then it was ablaze; another flame in the inferno.

She followed behind Iona and Cameron, jogging briskly, taking care to weave between the trees. A soot covered figure came running out of the forest, a dagger poised in their hands. Eilidh swung the sword down, cleaving her enemy in two with the weapon's power. They didn't pause to watch the body fall to the ground.

Soon it was obvious where the fight was raging. The sounds of clanging metal and agonised screams cut through the forest, filling her ears until she could hardly think. The ground shuddered, almost throwing them off their feet. The sour taste of magic hot her tongue and she spat it out as they ran nearer to the battle.

"Stay close," Cameron shouted.

Eilidh looked down to avoid another corpse but wished she hadn't. The person wasn't dead yet. They writhed around, trapped by the plants creeping up their arms and legs. Like in Cameron's vision, their skin was rotting and their eyes sunken. The body let out a tremendous screech as moss smothered their skin.

Oh my gods, it's killing them. Indeed, wherever the lichen touched, the skin burned and died, eating them alive.

"Don't touch the plants," Eilidh called out to Iona and Cameron, who were now racing ahead.

"I have a feeling I know who's controlling it," Iona shouted back. "If the plan worked, she's on our side."

Eilidh stopped in her tracks. *She? They couldn't be talking about—*

"Come on!" Cameron urged.

Eilidh fought down her terror and ran to catch up. She focussed on pumping her legs and her arms, on getting closer and closer to the fight. *You can worry about who they mean later.*

Chapter 76

arris had lost track of how many Soulless he'd killed, sneaking up on them from between trees and slitting their throats or stabbing them in the gut. Stabbing people in the back wasn't exactly the most honourable way to fight, but it improved his chances of survival vastly. He tried to reason that, if he were in their shoes, he'd rather be put out of his misery. Still, his hands never stopped shaking as the battle raged on.

He'd also lost track of where the conflict was taking place. The fires hadn't advanced to Ephraim's gate, blocked by some magical force, yet the smoke had poured in around them, making it difficult to see. Irené's crew had fought to push their enemies into the untouched forest surrounding the faerie court's borders, trapping them between the barricades and the choking flames. Worryingly, he hadn't seen the God of Chaos or Nicnevan in at least an hour. He'd also lost sight of Irené and Angus.

Now, running through the smog and over the fallen, Harris scanned the trees. *Where are they?*

One of the Soulless, an older man judging by his grey hair and his wrinkles, stumbled out of the forest, swinging something in his hand. Harris dodged, but his foot caught on a log and he was falling, the Soulless landing on the forest floor beside him. The man snarled, spittle flying as he pushed himself up and Harris realised his weapon was nothing more than a fallen branch. The man looked at Harris with unfocussed eyes.

"Can you hear me?" Harris asked, rolling away from him. "You don't need to do this." But it was as if the man hadn't heard him.

He swung the makeshift club down, missing Harris again by mere inches. But he'd also left his torso exposed.

"I'm sorry," said Harris and then he brought the dagger up and into the man's chest. The metal sunk into his skin, through cartilage and gristle. Harris gave a quiet sob. The Soulless fell back from the force of the impact and the knife came away with a wet slurp. *I'm going to be sick,* Harris thought as the blood trickled down his hand. Looking them in the eyes was so much worse.

Find Irené. He pushed himself off the ground, searching for any signs of the captain. But it was Angus he found first, swinging his sword in an arc down on one of the Mirandelli soldiers. The prince was covered in grime and dried blood, but he looked unharmed. At the Angus's feet was The Nymph's engineer, eyes closed and clutching a wound at his belly. Harris fell to his knees in front of the man. *What's his name?* He thought desperately. But no matter how much he racked his brain, he couldn't remember.

"We need to get him to Ephraim," Harris told Angus. But then, in a blink, the Edessan's chest stopped rising, and he was gone.

"Leave him," Angus said, grabbing up Harris by the arm. "There are other people to save."

The screams and smoke surrounding them, made it hard to tell who was friend and who was foe. The world was a blur of stabbing and slicing as the selkie and the prince fought back-to-back. Harris watched his companion out of the corner of his eye.

He's good, Harris realised. The prince was in his element, swinging his sword like it was a dance he'd been doing all his life. It was so at odds with the gentle man Harris knew. *At least he's on our side.*

A cluster of Soulless shambled towards them, their rotting flesh falling from their faces. *There are too many.* But then a tidal wave of green swept between the trees, mowing them down where they walked. Harris and Angus stared dumbly as the strange material covered everything in its path, slowing until it only lapped at their feet.

Angus crouched down, poking at it with an extended finger. "It's moss."

A blanket of vegetation, binding and smothering all of those in their path.

There could only be one person responsible.

"What are you gawking at?" Nicnevan drawled, lowering her arms. Tendrils of vines had wrapped themselves around her body as if seeking the sun. She drifted over the choking bodies gracefully, barely glancing at them as she passed.

Harris fought the urge to turn and run as he watched the Faerie Queen approach. She smirked at him like she could see all his fears laid out in the open.

"Hello, selkie."

A flicker of movement behind her caught Harris's eye. But before he could shout, Nicnevan swirled, sending a tangle of branches and thorns to pin her attacker to a gigantic oak.

I suppose I'm glad she's on our side too. For now.

The soldier blinked in shock, looking down at his stomach,

where he'd been speared through with a limb. His uniform was fancier than the others Harris had seen. An officer then. There was no denying Mirandelle had declared war on Eilanmòr now.

Angus approached the man, passing close by Nicnevan as he climbed over the branches and bodies. Harris gave her a wide berth.

The prince tipped the soldier's head back with his sword. "Are you here on King Merlo's orders or are you deserters?" he demanded.

Blood bubbled from the side of the Mirandelli's mouth. "One day this land will be ours and we'll have our justice," he croaked.

Harris scoffed. "Translated: *'we've been sent here'.*"

Angus pressed the sword a little harder. "What did Chao offer you?"

"A chance to reclaim what belongs to us and start a new world without the fae scum in it." He spat on the ground, the glob of blood not quite reaching Nicnevan's feathered skirts. The Faerie Queen twisted her fingers, and the thorns tightened around him, bringing a whimper to his lips.

"He's going to die anyway," admonished Angus. "You don't need to torture him."

Nicnevan folded her arms. "He's talking about genocide; I'd say that deserves a little torture."

Harris briefly wondered if he should give himself up to the God of Chaos to avoid this woman in front of him.

"We didn't just make a deal with Chao," groaned the man. "When the rest of the Edaxi make their way here, Eilanmòr will be nothing but dust."

"I think I've heard enough," said Angus, lowering his

sword. "Come on, we—"

But the soldier chuckled darkly, gulping in air in crackling gasps. "You shouldn't have left Ephraim unprotected."

Icy horror shot through Harris as he understood. The soldiers and the Soulless had been a distraction. "Where is Chao?" Harris asked Angus.

The prince must have reached the same conclusion he had. "We need to get back."

Nicnevan's lip curled as tendrils of vines dragged themselves up the dying soldier's body and surrounded his neck. "I'll clear a path for you," she said tightly. But the Faerie Queen would not move until the Mirandelli's face turned purple, and the breath was squeezed from him.

Chapter 77

They raced across the forest, back to Ephraim, with their hearts in their throats. Nicnevan ran in front, sweeping her wave of choking moss out before her. How she managed to be selective, to keep it from killing their allies, Harris didn't know. But he was grateful as they passed the sailors, gazing after them in wonder as their opponents were swallowed by the green mass.

They found Irené nearer the gate, fighting two Soulless at once. Harris watched as she sliced through one of them, their head falling to the side, while she raised her pistol at the other's chest. Before she could pull the trigger, Nicnevan's foliage flooded over them, dragging them to the ground.

"You took away my kill," she said in greeting.

"I'm sure there are plenty left," said Nicnevan, breezing past.

Harris caught the princess's arm, checking her over for injuries. "Are you hurt?"

"One of them bit me," she ground out, lifting her hem to reveal a bruise on her calf. "You don't think I'm going to turn into one, do you?"

"I think you're safe."

"Irené," said Angus, dragging her attention from her wounds. "We think Chao got into Ephraim."

She sucked in a breath and then she was off in the gate's

direction, grabbing Harris's hand and pulling him along behind her. "Come on."

Together, they flew over the leaf litter, through the barricade, and back into the heart of the faerie kingdom. Harris's heart threatened to burst out of his chest. *Don't be too late.*

Inside, Ephraim was deathly quiet. The screams from outside the walls sounded far off and indistinct, as though they were underwater. The thick smoke that had stuck to their clothes, their hair, hadn't made it past the wall. Harris took great gulps of fresh air as he ran, but it wasn't enough to stop the fear and nausea rising from his gut. *Where is Chao?*

A high wail cut through the silence and Harris pumped his legs faster, overtaking his companions. *It came from the pavilion.*

He rounded the corner, and the enormous white structure came into view. Harris scanned the exterior of the abandoned tent as he raced towards it. Had it only been a few hours ago that he and Irené had been dancing inside?

And then he was through the opening, skidding to a halt as he was met by a terrifying sight.

Chao had chosen a spot right in the centre of the makeshift dancefloor to wait for them, as if readying for some grotesque performance. He was off his horse, and yet he towered over the three figures kneeling at his feet like a giant spider surveying its catch.

Tears and snot streamed down each of the children's faces and the youngest boy was taking big hiccupping gulps. The apprentices Harris had saved raised their eyes to him as he entered, crying harder now that help had arrived. But the little cabin girl was looking off to the side, her face blank.

Harris followed her gaze and felt his heart drop. Near one of the long tables lay the body of Nadya, the sailing master, face down in the dirt. Though Harris could not see wounds on her from where he stood, there was bright blood on Chao's enormous mallet, which he'd tossed casually beside her.

The god didn't raise his head as Harris and then Angus stormed into the tent, instead staring intently at something in his hands. But then, when Irené entered, Nicnevan close on her heels, he snapped his eyes up and his face split into a depraved grin.

"Good of you to join us, princess," said Chao, lowering his hands so they could all see what he held in his long, thin fingers.

He twisted the heavy, metal revolver this way and that, admiring it like a new toy. "I found this on your companion. It didn't seem like she needed it anymore."

Irené let out a growl and raised her cutlass, but Harris snapped out a hand, grabbing her coat before she could run at the god.

Chao snickered. "So much spirit. Now, you'll like this: we were about to play a game." He brushed his fingers over the head of one of the boys, and the apprentice curled in on himself, trying to get away. The god didn't seem to notice. "You Edessans are so ingenious," he continued. "Isn't it wonderful all of the ways humans have designed to kill each other?" Chao looked down the barrel and for a moment it looked like he'd pull the trigger.

Can a god die? Harris wondered, his heart in his throat.

But then Chao flipped the weapon, handling it deftly, before opening the gun's cylinder and emptying the bullets into his palm. He slotted two back inside again and spun it.

"Six chances and two bullets." Then he held the end of the pistol to the oldest boy's head. The children's cries doubled in volume.

"No," said Irené, lowering the sword she'd raised. "You don't need to do this."

"But it's fun," said Chao, narrowing his coal darkened eyes. And then he pulled the trigger.

The gun exploded with a loud bang and Harris felt himself and those beside him flinch. The smoke cleared to reveal the boy, his eyes screwed shut, but still kneeling on the ground.

"That's one." Chao laughed, turning now to the cabin girl.

He's going to just keep going. Harris's heartbeat thrashed in his ears.

"You're sick," he spat, still gripping onto Irené's coat. *Don't do anything stupid,* he thought at her back.

But it was not Irené who darted forward next. Harris could only watch in terror as Angus ran at the god, lifting his sword to strike.

The movement caught Chao's attention and the next seconds unfolded in slow motion. The God of Chaos raised the gun from the sobbing cabin girl to the prince instead. Angus's steps faltered, but it was too late. Chao squeezed the trigger.

"No!" shouted Harris. At the same moment, there was another explosion.

He turned, ready to watch his friend fall, to watch the metal pierce his skin. But then there was a blur and something slammed into Angus's body, knocking him out of the way.

Somehow, the Faerie Queen, who had been standing beside them silently throughout their standoff, had been quicker than a god, quicker than a bullet. Nicnevan landed on top of Angus as the smoke cleared, a look of pure shock on her face.

It was another empty, Harris thought desperately. But then he saw the blood.

The Faerie Queen rolled off the young prince onto the forest floor, clutching her side. A red stain was already spreading from her body over the leaf litter, leaving a sticky mess on her feathered dress. Angus dragged himself to her, his hands fluttering over her wound. "Why?" he asked, his voice wavering.

Harris had gone numb. Nicnevan had just sacrificed herself for Angus.

"Two," said Chao, moving the pistol back to the cabin girl's head. The little girl shrieked, covering her ears, trying to keep out the surrounding horrors.

Irené dropped her sword. "No!" she shouted again. "Tell me what you want, and you can have it, just leave them alone."

The God of Chaos raised his chin, madness sparkling in his eyes. "I told you what I want already."

"And if I come with you," said Irené, pulling herself from Harris's grasp. "You'll let them go?"

No.

Chao twirled the pistol over his fingers again. "For now."

"You can't do this," Harris told her. *She couldn't go with him. There had to be another way.*

"We have a deal," said the captain, raising her chin.

Harris tried to grab for her again, but she stepped out of his reach. "Don't," she said, raising her watery eyes to his. "You'll find me. I know it." And then she crossed the few feet before he could say another word, until she was standing in front of the god.

The children's cries echoed inside Harris's mind.

Chao smiled, lowering the pistol. "Excellent choice." He reached his fingers into his rusted armour, bringing out a crystal on a chain. Then he twisted the Stone of Destiny with one fist, he held the other out to the princess. Irené's lip quivered, but her hand was steady as she took his. Behind them, the back of the pavilion shimmered.

"I'll get you back," Harris shouted as Irené was pulled towards the portal. He didn't know how, but he'd find a way.

Chao stopped in his tracks, turning to look over his armoured shoulder at the quaking children. At the prince, leaning over the dying queen. At the selkie, with his dagger still drawn. "I look forward to you trying," said the god. Then, with barely more than a twitch, he sent his divine powers spearing out straight for Harris, as Irené screamed.

Chapter 78

*E*ilidh carried the Sword of Light in her hand, its flames illuminating the smoke filled forest. She sliced away at more attackers, but as though they'd been given a silent command, those remaining stopped in their tracks, either slipping off through the trees or dropping to the floor where they stood. The battle was over, but she wasn't sure if that was a good thing.

She drifted towards the remains of a high hedge, as if in a dream. Branches were strewn across the path, pulled down by scrabbling hands or the wind, she wasn't sure. With a deep breath she stepped through the gap and felt the air change. It caressed the bare skin on her arms like a lover. Eilidh shivered. So, this was Ephraim?

The setting of so many of her nightmares certainly looked that way right now. Yet, it was clear that, before the battle, there had been some sort of party. Lanterns hung from trees and plates of food lay discarded on the ground. Indeed, many of the bodies she'd seen had been in beautiful clothing, much too grand for fighting in.

She wandered in a daze, taking in every glistening leaf and glowing lantern. But then her foot hit against a discarded wine glass, its stem snapped, and Eilidh suddenly realised she was lost.

Iona was nowhere to be seen, and neither was Cameron.

She raised her head, scanning the forest. The place was as quiet as a tomb, save for the wind whistling through the trees. Panic seized her. *I don't want to be alone in this place.*

You could run. Run back to the inn and forget you were here. Hide like you've been doing your whole life.

But then she glimpsed a flash of copper hair in front of a huge, white pavilion and staggered towards it in relief.

"Wait, Eilidh," someone called.

Why? she wondered, but as soon as her gaze landed on the man in Iona's arms, she understood.

He had hair like the selkie's, but shorter. Though it looked like he'd thrown on some armour for the battle, it had been peeled away, either by force or in order to get to his wounds. Dirt stuck to his fingers, like he'd just been crawling. His undershirt was ripped from his collarbone to his stomach, revealing a nasty gash.

But it was his face which had Eilidh gasping in shock. Underneath the fabric he was holding to his eye, it was covered in blood.

Eilidh lowered the sword, and the flames guttered out. "What happened?"

Iona ignored her, pulling something out of her pocket and talking to him in a low voice. He struggled, trying to push her off him, trying to get up, but she held him down against the mossy floor firmly. Then, with a twist of her wrist, the thing in her hand grew to the size of a mug. It had a peculiar shape, as though it had been carved from stone.

"Is that—" Eilidh asked.

Iona tipped the cauldron to her brother's mouth and pouring the contents in.

Immediately, he stopped shifting around, allowing the

429

magic to work. The cut down his chest seemed to pull itself together until there was nothing but blood left.

Iona's voice wavered as she asked, "Your eye?"

With a groan, the man removed the cloth. The remains of a wound were still knitting together, running from his forehead to his nose, through his right eye, which was swollen shut. Eilidh held her breath as she realised what had happened. *Please heal him,* she thought at the cauldron's magic.

It took half a minute for the cut to mend, and then he slowly opened the eye. It was milky white.

"I can't see anything with it," Iona's brother whimpered.

"It's okay, it's fine," Iona tried to soothe. "We'll get it fixed." She looked like she was going to throw up. Eilidh understood the feeling well.

"There's no time," he said, sitting up. "They took Irené."

"Who did?" Eilidh asked. "Who attacked you?"

"Chao," he croaked. "The God of Chaos."

And Eilidh understood. The man in Cameron's vision. That had been the god. And he knew who she was.

"Iona!" Cameron shouted from nearby. "We need the cauldron!"

The selkie squeezed her brother's shoulders. "Do you think you can stand?"

But Harris was already pushing up. He hobbled towards the sound of Cameron's shouts, inside the great tent. Iona grabbed her brother's arm before he could get far, tossing it over her shoulder.

Eilidh followed at a distance, drifting like an unmoored boat. She didn't know anyone here, couldn't comprehend the grief and the pain. *Why did I even come?*

They picked their way into the pavilion, over abandoned

plates and bunting, until Cameron's frightened face came into view.

"Angus..."

Eilidh's stomach dropped. *Had their friend been killed?* But, no. As she drew closer, it was clear the man in Cameron's arms was breathing. Eilidh recognised his face from the one night he'd been at the inn. Now it was twisted in pain as he clutched his head. Though there wasn't any blood, not that she could see.

Iona dropped her brother's arm carefully, letting him carry his own weight again, and reached for the cauldron. "It's okay, I'm here. Drink this and you'll be fine—"

"No," Angus moaned. "It won't work, it wasn't magic. She was shot—"

She? Who is he talking about?

Eilidh snapped her head up to look around. But the tent seemed empty at first. Then she noticed them.

Someone was face down on the floor, half obscured by a long table. Their back was still; long since dead. The other person looked like nothing more than a pile of feathers, discarded in a clump of wildflowers. But then Eilidh noted the movement. They were still breathing.

She floated forward, ready to help. And then, in the same moment she noticed the woman's golden hair, her pointed ears, her green tinged skin, she jolted to a stop.

"What—"

A wave of power crashed into her, sending stars skittering before her eyes. Until the wave was in her skin, like every fibre of her being was vibrating with it. She tried to shift, but she was stuck to the spot. She worked her jaw, but no sound came out, even as she screamed inside her head.

"Eilidh?" Iona's voice drifted over to her.

Can she not see it? Could she not sense the change in her?

Every cell, every molecule fizzed with it, sang with it. Like she was exploding. Like she was being rewritten.

What's happening to me? Eilidh looked at the woman on the ground in terror. *Was she doing this?*

Queen Nicnevan gave her a broken smile as she stared into the eyes of her only daughter.

And Eilidh began to change.

Chapter 79

Iona stared in horror as Eilidh's skin shuddered.

Then she was rising from Angus's side. It was only as she reached for the young woman that she saw who Eilidh was looking at.

Queen Nicnevan lay on her back on the floor, under the high canvas. From the odd angles of her limbs, the blood soaking her feathery dress, Iona knew she was severely injured. But the Faerie Queen was smiling, even as tears leaked from her violet eyes. All around her body, flowers were sprouting, curling over her like the earth was saying goodbye.

"*Mo cridhe*," Nicnevan whispered through dark lips as she looked up at her daughter. *My heart.*

Iona cast about for something, anything, that would act as a shield. She'd told Eilidh her mother was trapped, and she had been the last time she'd seen her. But Nicnevan was no longer made of stone and bark. *She's dying*, Iona told herself. But she was still dangerous.

Eilidh gasped, tearing Iona's attention away from the Faerie Queen.

"Eilidh?" she asked. And then she saw it.

The young woman's skin was glimmering. Faintly at first, but then bright enough to cast the whole clearing in a golden glow.

Then her face changed, the bones shifting and re-knitting

themselves. Her nose sloped down into a point, and her cheeks rounded.

The freckles dusted across her face disappeared, like stars blinking out one by one. Eilidh touched a hand to her hair, and it lightened, turning shades of brown, then gleaming blonde. Just like Nicnevan's.

Eilidh scrambled to pull her sleeve up to where her birthmark should have been. Instead, there was nothing but unblemished skin.

"Eilidh," Iona breathed again. She reached out a shaking hand to tilt the young woman's face up, taking in the changes with watering eyes. Her lips and her cheeks were fuller and pinker, like she'd been running and underneath her newly flaxen hair, her ears were perfectly pointed.

Eilidh blinked up at her, revealing yet another change.

"Your eyes," Iona realised. "They're like your grandfather's."

Indeed, while one was still blue, the other had turned hazel. Alasdair's eyes.

"What's happening to me?" Eilidh whimpered.

"You saw your true mother," came a wheeze.

Iona immediately wrapped a protective arm around Eilidh and snapped her gaze onto the Faerie Queen on the ground.

Nicnevan's breaths were coming in gulps as she clutched her wounds, but still she smiled. "When a changeling looks upon their mother, they revert into their true self."

Angus appeared at Iona's elbow and before she could stop him, he had flung himself down at the queen's side. He grasped one of her hands at her stomach, coating his own in her blood. "She saved me. We need to help her!"

But Nicnevan only let out a tired chuckle. "Nothing can stop my death now, but I can go to it peacefully." Then she lifted one hand from her abdomen and gripped Angus's forearm, smearing it with gore. Her eyes became sharp as she said, "Remember your promise, prince."

Angus gaped at her for a moment. But then he nodded. "I won't break it."

Then the Faerie Queen dropped his hand, stared up at her daughter, and let out her last breath.

Chapter 80

The wind bit at Ailsa's and Maalik's skin as they climbed. Now and then, the gusts sounded like howling, like the mountain was a living thing, ready to buck them off its back. The sun had been rising when they'd stumbled out of their tent, dismantling it as quickly as possible, but somehow, after only five hours of walking, it seemed to be setting again.

Ailsa huddled into her cloak's hood, desperately trying to calm the gale that blew against their backs. But her body was like lead. Even taking the next step took all her effort. Her powers were a mere memory.

"We're nearly there," said Maalik over the wind. "A bit more climbing."

Ailsa raised her eyes, taking in the point where slope met sky, high above. Every time she thought they had reached the top, she was disappointed to find it rising up into the sky again. They'd been walking for so long it seemed like they'd soon touch the stars.

"You said that an hour ago," Ailsa grumbled. But she focussed again on her boots, taking another step and then another, breaking the task down into small increments. "Should we set up the tent again?"

"There's no point, we'll be at the top before dark."

Up and up they climbed, moving as if through a thick syrup, lungs straining to fill themselves in the thin air. The twilight leached the colour from their clothes, the sky, until everything was in shades of grey.

"Are you sure we'll reach the top soon?" Ailsa huffed.

Maalik placed his hand on his chest and surveyed the landscape again. "Yes, look, it's just over that ridge."

"Stop," said Ailsa, unclipping her bag and placing it on the ground. "You wait here, and I'll climb up to look. If the peak is there, then we'll continue but if it isn't, we'll set up camp."

Her demon flashed her an exhausted grin. "Good idea."

Now that her pack was gone, Ailsa's steps were lighter over the snow. She scaled the slope, heart pounding as she climbed to the place where it flattened out. If the top was there, what would they see? Would the witches live in a castle like the legends said? Or would that be an exaggeration?

Right now, I'd take a shed and a nice fire, thought Ailsa, scrambling over the ice. But as she reached the peak, a sound from below froze her blood.

A shriek, louder than the ones she'd heard the other night, drifted out of the darkness below. She whipped her head round to search for the source and saw a dark shape looming in the distance behind Maalik. The demon had also turned so she couldn't see his face, but everything in his body told her he had noticed it, too.

Ailsa watched in horror as the thing drew closer and she could make out its features in the semi-dark. The thick fur which covered its body was the same white as the snow, camouflaging it against the ice.

At first Ailsa thought it was human, but as it got closer to Maalik, she realised it was much larger. It walked on all fours, using powerful, long arms but when it was less than thirty feet from the demon, it reared back, beating its chest and baring long, dagger-like canines as it howled again.

The creature from the statue in the bathhouse.

As soon as it made the sound, Ailsa was sprinting back down. "Go!" she shouted down at Maalik.

But he was stumbling, barely able to stand, let alone run.

Ailsa dashed back down the steep slope, her feet slipping and sliding over the snow. The monster bared its sharp fangs and let out an ear-splitting roar before it dashed for the demon.

"Maalik!" Ailsa shouted.

The beast rushed forward, closing the distance. Ailsa pushed her legs to run faster, her lungs screaming as she neared Maalik's trembling body. She reached him just before the monster, wrapping one arm around his middle while raising the other, bracing for impact.

An impact that never came. The creature smacked into something invisible inches from her body, a wall of impenetrable air.

"Ailsa, your magic."

While moments before she'd felt like a well that had run dry, now it coursed through her veins like never before. Ailsa drew in a breath, storing it up inside herself. And then, throwing her hands out, she released it all at the creature. The wall of air rushed at its body, a tidal wave of energy. The power exploded with a boom, flinging the body of the beast like it was a child's toy down into the darkness below.

"Quickly," she said, pushing him upwards. "There could be others."

They struggled up the mountain, chased by more and more screeches from below. *How far away were they? How fast could they run?*

Ailsa brought the air up from behind them, ice cold but enough to boost them towards the ridge. *Come on, come on,* Ailsa thought, willing them up faster and faster. *A little more.*

And then they were at the crest, the snow-covered landscape levelling out. Ailsa pushed her legs on, feeling the burn, until she could see they were indeed at the summit.

Her steps faltered. She'd expected a flood of relief, to celebrate, once they'd reached the peak. But Ailsa's stomach turned over as she took in the mountain' top.

"I'm so sorry, Ailsa," whispered Maalik, his words almost snatched away by the wind.

She blinked, not believing her eyes. There was nothing but a barren plateau covered in frost. No witches. No buildings.

"We're in the wrong place," she breathed.

Behind them, dozens of howls rose, echoing the wailing in her heart.

Chapter 81

Angus had always imagined the fae as unbreakable, but in the end, death claimed everyone the same.

A few of the remaining fae helped him carry Nicnevan out of the pavilion, and there the folk left their late queen, on the mossy grass. Just another body. Even the Edessan sailors skirted round them on their way back to the treetop houses, avoiding Angus's eyes. Honestly, he couldn't blame them. There were so many dead and stories of the Faerie Queen were told far and wide. Both Harris and Cameron had been her prisoner for weeks. She'd been their tormentor. *Evil. She's evil.*

But it didn't seem right. She was, after all, a queen. And as royalty, she should be afforded a proper funeral, like Angus's ancestors before him.

He collected the kindling and the larger pieces of wood from the forest surrounding her, laying them out so they were ready. It took hours to get enough. No doubt his friends were in the enormous pavilion, tending to the wounded. He'd get there, eventually.

Once he had his pile, he turned back to the body of the Faerie Queen. She looked as if she was sleeping, with her eyes closed and face relaxed, but below her head her body was covered in blood.

That could have been me.

Nicnevan's body was light as he lifted her, laying her out gently onto the wood. There was some stiffness already in her limbs, but her skin hadn't lost its colour, not yet. He brushed a stray strand of golden hair away from her face and peered down at her one last time.

She saved me.

Had she done it because of his vow? Somehow, he didn't think so. It had been pure reflex, jumping in front of that power, shielding his body with her own. So why had she done it? Angus thought back to the few times he'd spoken with her, down in the cell. How she'd started off with rules and threats, but they'd gradually eased. She'd asked about his life, had shared his joy when he'd played the fiddle for her.

"Why did you save me?" he asked her.

Of course, he received no answer. The Faerie Queen was dead, and he'd made her a promise that—

A twig snapped, making him jerk round. There, a blonde woman stood with her arms wrapped around herself.

"What are you doing?" asked Eilidh.

He looked her up and down. If he hadn't seen her change, he'd have no idea the woman in front of him was the same waitress from the inn. Everything about her had changed, except the clothes that clung to her body, a little tighter now.

Her eyes were wide, piercing, as they looked him up and down. He'd seen the portraits of his late grandfather, remembered his rare irises, one brown and one blue; like they were seeing two sides of the world. Which, he supposed, Eilidh was. Half fae and half human. Half a faerie princess and half a human princess.

He stood abruptly, reaching into his sporran, where his flint was hidden. "I'm saying goodbye."

"Did you know her?" she asked tentatively.

Did I? They'd spent hours questioning each other but Angus had never known her true motives. "Not really."

"But she saved your life," Eilidh said, staring down at Nicnevan. "Sacrificed her own for yours."

"Yes." *But why?*

"I hated her; I still do." Eilidh shook her head. "She was a nightmare: the monster under my bed when I was young. And then, as I grew older, she was the reason I couldn't go anywhere, do anything I wanted. I've been hunted my entire life, and I feared my daughter would be hunted too."

"You must be relieved?" Angus gave her a weak smile.

"Yes, and no. I can't help but wonder what it would have been like to know her."

He sighed. "I wonder that too, what she was like before my father—" he stopped dead, remembering, "our father. Before he betrayed her. Or before the power corrupted her."

"Before I was taken," Eilidh agreed.

"She loved you," Angus said. "She loved you so much."

Eilidh's mouth twisted. "She loved me so much she was willing to tear the world apart for me. That isn't a healthy love."

"You don't think she would have let you go, if you'd told her outright you didn't want to be here?"

"I didn't want to take that risk. Not after my own baby was born. I wouldn't tear the world apart for her," she said fiercely. "I would build it."

"You know that you're my sister," he said. "My elder sister. My *brother's* elder sister?"

She hummed in assent.

Just say it, just say it. "That makes you first in line for the throne. The rightful heir of Eilanmòr."

Eilidh blinked. "Shit." The word was so unexpected, Angus couldn't help but choke out a laugh.

"Yeah, my thoughts exactly."

"I don't want it," Eilidh said, gripping her arm with her hand. "I don't want any title."

Relief flooded through him. "Not even Queen of Ephraim?" he asked, almost giddy with it.

"Never," she vowed.

"Then who will rule? Your daughter when she comes of age?"

"Someone else." Eilidh bit her lip. "Someone who was raised fae."

Angus breathed the fresh air in deeply, because he could. "I made a vow to your mother, that I would protect and defend you for the rest of your life." Angus grimaced. "Or, I suppose, the rest of my life, since you're bound to outlive me with your faerie blood."

She tore her gaze away from the Faerie Queen. "Why would you do that?"

"It was payment for her alliance. But," Angus bit his lip, "I've always wanted a sister."

"Too bad you're stuck with me now," Eilidh said with a small smile.

Angus sniffed, the sound a ghost of a laugh, and positioned his flint and tinder. "Are you ready?" he asked.

Eilidh smoothed down her dress. "Do it."

It took a few tries to light the ball of hay and twigs, but soon it caught. *Goodbye*, Angus thought, before dropping the smouldering tinder onto the makeshift pyre. The fire spread over the wood, licking Nicnevan's clothes. Angus and Eilidh stepped back into the shadows of the trees, but kept watch as the flames grew.

"What now then?" asked Eilidh.

Angus considered this. "We lost a battle, but we've got a whole war ahead of us yet. I'll head back to Dunrigh, try to lend a hand when the fighting starts."

"I'm not going home," she decided. "Not until I finished what I started. Maggie's safe there, for now."

"We have the Cauldron of Life and the Sword of Truth; we need to get the other two treasures."

"And someone to handle them."

He nodded. "You're earth. Iona is water. My friend Ailsa is air and, if all goes well, we have a demon on his way to take the sword."

"And the Edaxi have your friend?" asked Eilidh.

"And the Stone of Destiny." He clenched his fists. "By the Hag, I hope that's all they have."

Angus jumped when he felt pressure on his hand, but then Eilidh's fingers threaded round his until they were palm to palm. They watched the flames climb higher, engulfing the body of the Faerie Queen. "We'll get there. Together."

If Ailsa succeeds, Angus thought.

It was all on her now.

Chapter 82

Ailsa stared down the mountain, her mind running through the many miles they'd covered on the way up, trying to imagine traversing them again. Emotions ripped through her, rubbing her raw inside, trying to find a way out. She sank to her knees, crunching against the snow, the crushing weight of despair pushing down upon her.

I could give up.

The thought itself was horrifying. If Maalik hadn't been there, would she have done that? Would she have relented and let the mountain claim her; one more missing person? But she wasn't alone. Maalik stood in silence, giving her a moment and reminding her what she had to live for.

So instead, she stored up all the pain, all the frustration and worry, and channelled it into anger. It boiled under her skin, sizzling through her veins as she sank her fingers into the ice. And then, raising her arms out, she roared her fury down the slope. The air thundered from her body, sending the loose patches of snow tumbling to the bottom. The screeches from the strange mountain creatures were instantly muffled, and Ailsa wondered if they'd been trapped by the avalanche.

Well, that's one less thing to worry about. At least she'd got a second wind with her magic.

Maalik dropped to the ice beside her, staring down the slope too. "Downhill is always faster," he said.

Ailsa gulped in a deep breath and bit her wobbling lip. "I can't believe we came all this way for nothing."

"At least now we know." Maalik placed a hand on her shoulder and she leaned into it.

"I'm sorry I dragged you all the way up here," said Ailsa. "I don't blame you if you never want to follow me anywhere again."

Maalik snorted. "I'm always going to follow you until you decide you're better off without me." He kissed the top of her head. "Would you believe me if I said I've enjoyed myself?"

"You enjoyed almost dying of hypothermia?" Ailsa said, hiccupping. "You're mad."

"I enjoyed being with you. But now we have to get down safely so we can enjoy another adventure together. Do you think you can do that?"

Ailsa wiped a shaking hand over her face, mustering her energy. The sky was fully dark now; filled with bright stars. She glanced up at Maalik, finding the lights reflected in his black eyes. "We just need to get off the summit," she said, shuddering. Looking down into the dark, she spotted her pack, disregarded on the snow. At least she'd be able to slip down without the weight for a few feet. "Then we'll set up the tent and think about climbing down tomorrow."

"Exactly," said Maalik, rubbing her back. "One step at a time."

Then, with the demon's help, she pushed herself to her feet. The wind wailed around the mountain top, as though mocking them. Ailsa pressed her lips together, holding in the curses bubbling up. Her days of climbing were over after this. If the witches were indeed at the top of a different mountain, someone else could find them.

She scanned the eerie, grey land one last time before she turned to begin her descent. But something to the left caught her eye.

"What is that?" she asked, her heart pounding.

A moment ago, the summit was empty save from snow. Now a peculiar dark shape was sticking out of the ice. It was taller than Maalik, and a few times as broad. Her legs carried her towards the curious object, wondering at first if it was another one of the standing stones. But no, the shape was more rectangular, with squared off edges. It was hard to see in the dim light, but as the glowing snow under her feet reflected onto it, she realised what it was.

"It's a door," she said.

Chapter 83

In the dark, the portal almost blended into the sky. *I'm hallucinating,* Ailsa thought. But it looked solid.

Maalik's steps crunched behind her. "Was this here before?"

"I didn't see it." What had happened since they'd reached the top, finding it empty?

The demon stared at the door, his forehead creasing as he raised his gaze up above it. "Do you think you could send your magic at it?"

Just like she'd thrown it out a moment before. Perhaps that was the answer.

Ailsa filled her lungs with the cold mountain air. It prickled her as she sucked it in, like plunging into freezing water. Please let this work, she thought. And then, with as much force as she could manage, she blew it towards the door. Not just the air, but her disappointment, her rage, her hope.

The darkness above the portal flickered. And then it dispersed, revealing a towering peak. Except, instead of the mountain, it looked like—

"A palace?" Ailsa whispered.

She watched in amazement as more and more of the structure materialised, looking like every faerietale castle she'd ever imagined. The building towered out of the mountain top, its rose-coloured stone walls covered in a layer of sparkling frost. No, not just stone— *crystal.* The whole structure was made of polished quartz, from the solid base all the way up to the spiralling turrets, reaching towards the stars. And all over the palace, tiny windows flickered with firelight. Someone was home.

Maalik took a step. "This is it," he breathed.

Ailsa walked forward on quaking legs and hesitated before the door. Then, steeling her spine, she rapped her knuckles against the wooden.

Knock. Knock.

The sound echoed across the mountain top and Ailsa wondered if she should have waited, if they should have been more hesitant. But something inside her felt right. This was the place they'd been looking for. They couldn't turn back now.

She held her breath, waiting for an answer but then, with a long groan, the portal creaked open as if pushed by the breeze.

"You don't think it's a trap, do you?" she said, stepping back into Maalik's chest.

The demon paused, before stepping round her. "I'll check it out first."

She watched as Maalik ducked his head round the door and froze. The scent of flowers drifted from the opening and Ailsa was sure she felt heat coming from inside.

She leaned forward, ready to snatch Maalik's cloak at any moment. "What is it?"

But Maalik didn't answer. Instead, he reached back, tugging her inside with him.

My gods, Ailsa thought, stepping inside the door.

The walls of the entryway were made of smooth, pink marble. Pillars supported a vaulted ceiling, each covered in lush, climbing ivy, dripping across the surfaces like millions of emeralds. A set of wide stairs led up to another floor where balconies looked down upon the door. A magnificent chandelier hung from a chain, casting the foyer in a bright light, so different from the mountain top they'd just been shivering on.

Ailsa stepped inside, mesmerised. It was like walking into another world. The palace was much warmer than the tundra they'd been climbing in, almost tropical in comparison. She vaguely heard Maalik closing over the door behind them, but knew he'd left a gap when a freezing wind snaked over her body, causing her to shiver. She spun around the room, listening to the distant tinkling of bells and wondered if she was dreaming.

"Where is everyone?" Ailsa whispered.

But then, a soft voice called out. "Hello?"

Ailsa turned, smacking into Maalik's side as she scanned all over for the speaker.

A petite woman leaned out of another huge door to their right. Her dark eyes widened as she took them in and Ailsa wondered what impression they were making. They'd been climbing for days, sweating in their layers and then freezing as soon as they stopped. They hadn't been clean or comfortable since the bathhouse and her body was drained from walking, from using her magic, from fear.

But they'd done it, hadn't they? What they looked like didn't matter.

So instead of worrying, she drank in the sight of the woman before them. Her clothes sparkled, absorbing the light from the chandelier and reflecting it into the hallway, mimicking the stars outside.

Her face was heart shaped, her skin smooth, except over her upper cheeks and forehead, which was covered in splodges. Ailsa narrowed her gaze, trying to make sense of the odd marks. For a moment, Ailsa thought the woman had a cluster of birthmarks, just like her own. But then she blinked and realised a swirling galaxy was painted across her skin, blending into her dark purple hair.

The woman stepped out of the door, her gaze never leaving Ailsa, and then she smiled. "You're late," she said, emotion choking her voice.

Then she beckoned them closer, through the portal.

Without hesitation, Ailsa's feet carried her across the marble, and she wondered if she was under some sort of spell. Somehow, she thought not. Whatever was behind the colossal, ornate door, she wanted to see.

This is what you've been waiting for.

The woman bit her lip as they approached, and then slipped inside. Ailsa looked back at Maalik, at his unreadable eyes, before following the stranger.

Ailsa's gaze was dragged up, up, up to the high ceiling, darkened in a mirror image of the sky outside. From it hung more chandeliers, glittering with diamonds. She followed their light as it spilled down to take in the grand space; larger than Dunrigh's ballroom.

The walls were covered in cascades of beautiful flowers, releasing the scents of jasmine and lilac into the warm air. But it was the inhabitants of the room that took her breath away. The place was filled with hundreds of people, all frozen as if they'd been milling about and talking, before being interrupted. Many of them sat in chairs and low couches, but as Ailsa and Maalik entered, they stood as one. Some were smiling and others looked as dazed as she felt.

What is this place? She wondered distantly.

As she stared around the room at the sea of faces, more light lit the marble floor surrounding her. She looked down to find the source and found her skin glowing.

She turned to Maalik in awe. "What—"

Then a wave of power crashed into her body.

And Ailsa began to change.

About the Author

Caroline Logan is a writer of Young Adult Fantasy. The Sword of Light is the third in The Four Treasures series.

Caroline is a high school biology teacher who lives in the Cairngorms National Park in Scotland, with her husband and dogs, Ranger and Scout. Before moving there, she lived and worked in Spain, Tenerife, Sri Lanka and other places in Scotland.

She graduated from The University of Glasgow with a bachelor's degree in Marine and Freshwater Biology.

In her spare time she plays Dungeons and Dragons, watches Disneyworld videos, and tries to make a dent in her To Be Read book pile.

Instagram: @CaroLoganBooks
Twitter: @CaroLoganBooks
Web: carolinelogan.co.uk

Acknowledgements

Whenever I finish writing a book, I try to remember all the hours spent on it but it usually feels like a fuzzy sort of dream. I do remember that this one was hard. It was written entirely in a global pandemic, in a year where expectation and reality were constantly shifting. But it's here, it's real, it's done. As always, there are many people to thank for this.

First, to Anne Glennie at Cranachan Publishing; thank you so much for taking a chance and then sticking with me throughout this series. I can't imagine the time, the energy and the heart you've put into all of the books this year but I really appreciate it.

Thank you so much to my family. I know we haven't been able to see each other this year and I miss you so much.

To all my fellow Clan Cranachan authors: thank you for lending a digital ear, for attending events and hyping up my books. To have a support system like you is very rare.

Thank you to my friends, who've got me through these lockdowns and who I know are always there for me. We may not speak often, but I know you've got my back.

Special thanks to all of my online friends and book reviewers that have supported me. I'm your biggest fan! Caitlyn, Jacky, Abi, Connor and Eleanor: you are absolute gems.

To my students: if I ever had the pleasure to have you in my class, know that my greatest joy in life is seeing you grow up and become the incredible people you are.

Thank you to my Dungeons and Dragons crew: Hannah, Talia, Jon and Lisa. You are all Nat 20s to me. And thanks for letting me steal your character names. Hellfyre Club 4 lyf.

Finally, thank you to my three loves: Vince, Ranger-Danger and Scoots.

A Four
Treasures Novel

The Spear of Truth

Book 4

October 2022